Summer at the French Olive Grove

About the author

Sophie Claire writes emotional stories set in England and in sunny Provence, where she spent her summers as a child. She has a French mother and a Scottish father, but was born in Africa and grew up in Manchester, England, where she still lives with her husband and two sons.

Previously, she worked in marketing and proofreading academic papers, but writing is what she always considered her 'real job' and now she's delighted to spend her days dreaming up heartwarming contemporary romance stories set in beautiful places.

You can find out more at www.sophieclaire.co.uk and on Twitter @sclairewriter.

Also by Sophie Claire

The Christmas Holiday
A Forget-Me-Not Summer
A Winter's Dream

Sophie Claire

Summer at the French Olive Grove

HODDER

First published in Great Britain in 2021 by Hodder & Stoughton
An Hachette UK company

1

A CIP catalogue record for this title is available from the British Library

Paperback ISBN 978 1 529 34995 5
eBook ISBN 978 1 529 34996 2
Audio ISBN 978 1 529 34997 9

Typeset in Plantin Light by Palimpsest Book Production Limited,
Falkirk, Stirlingshire

Printed and bound in Great Britain by Clays Ltd, Elcograf S.p.A.

Hodder & Stoughton policy is to use papers that are natural, renewable and recyclable products and made from wood grown in sustainable forests. The logging and manufacturing processes are expected to conform to the environmental regulations of the country of origin.

Hodder & Stoughton Ltd
Carmelite House
50 Victoria Embankment
London EC4Y 0DZ

www.hodder.co.uk

Chapter One

The sun had almost completely sunk behind the forested hill to her right, but the blue-tinged fading light wasn't the only reason why Lily didn't see the men coming. She was intent on her task of filming Yolanda as they walked home from the coffee farm, using her tiny, hand-held camera to capture the words as they spilled from the other woman's lips. Yolanda's dark eyes were glazed with tears as she spoke slowly, allowing Maria, the young interpreter, time to repeat her words in English. Lily did her best to keep the camera level and listened, spellbound.

'I came here with nothing,' Maria translated. 'No experience, no skills, no tools. Nothing but my children and the clothes on our backs . . .'

Lily's breath caught, and excitement gathered in her stomach. She knew this feeling: on the cusp of a revelation. The turning point when her work came to life, when a potentially dull documentary about a women's cooperative producing coffee in Colombia became a personal story, a heroic account of adversity overcome. Her heart thumped in anticipation and she hoped the light would be strong enough for her camera to catch the haunted look in Yolanda's eyes.

But those same eyes glanced ahead, looked twice, then widened with fear.

Yolanda stopped in her tracks. Next to her, Maria gasped. Still holding up the camera, Lily frowned and turned to follow their frightened stares.

Three men stood in the middle of the road, blocking their path. She took in the shadow of a knife, the barrel of a shotgun and dusty scuffed boots, and though she didn't follow every word of the rapid-fire Spanish that their leader spoke, she got the gist. The man was the eldest of the three, his skin like worn leather, and something in his eyes made Lily shiver. She lowered her camera.

'Th-they want our money,' Maria whispered.

Lily nodded but didn't take her eyes off the men. Their narrowed gazes flickered as they registered her scars, then hardened. The leader sneered.

'We don't have any money,' Maria told them in clear, careful Spanish. 'We've been at work. All we have is our tools, see?' She nudged Yolanda who held open her bag.

Her words seemed to anger him. His lip curled as he spat out more words even faster. Lily strained to understand what he said and simultaneously she scanned her surroundings, looking for help. The bus which had dropped them had long since gone, and they were still half a mile or so from the village; there was no one around on this lonely road. Here in Colombia roadside robberies were notoriously common. And violent.

Her skin tightened and memories of terror crashed back. This wasn't the first time she'd feared for her life. She pushed the flashbacks aside and looked at the women next to her. Maria was barely eighteen, and Yolanda had four beautiful children waiting at home who were dependent on her. Whereas Lily had no one.

No, she didn't have no one. Mamie's face sprang up in her mind, and Lily's heart kicked as she thought of her grandmother. But she couldn't stand back and do nothing. If anything happened to Yolanda, Lily would never forgive herself. So she sucked in air and stepped forward, placing herself in front of the women. She kept her spine straight as she met the angry man's gaze and said in his language; 'These women have nothing. Here, take this.'

She held out her small camera and it was snatched from her hand. Over her shoulder was the case containing her large camera and tripod. She prayed they wouldn't want it. Other people treasured their wedding ring or a favourite watch or trinket – but her most valuable possession would always be her camera.

'I have cash too,' she said, opening her bag and willing them to take the money and leave.

The older man glared up at her. He was a foot smaller than her, but that didn't give her much of an advantage when he was armed with a shotgun.

He took the cash, and nodded at her shoulder. 'The bag,' he commanded.

She glanced at the strap. 'It's just a camera. It's old, not worth anything.' It might fetch a little cash, but to her it was invaluable. She had insurance of course, but there were hours of great footage on there, crucial scenes which she hadn't yet uploaded to her laptop and which she'd never be able to recover.

'Give it to me,' he said.

There was a cold glint in his eye which turned her skin to ice, but she held his gaze. 'Here, take my watch,' she offered instead.

He took it. 'And the bag,' he insisted.

The men flanking him watched impassively.

'Give it to him,' Yolanda whispered from behind.

Lily's hand squeezed the strap. Her camera meant a lot to her but it wasn't worth endangering lives for. Only a fool would do that. And she couldn't risk Yolanda or Maria getting hurt. She went to lift the strap from her shoulder, but she had hesitated a moment too long and the man lost patience.

He lifted a hand and the two others stepped forward. The butt of a rifle connected with her shoulder, and the blow was hard and swift. Lily staggered back, stunned. As she clutched her shoulder, they hit her again and she landed faced down in the dust. She saw the glint of a knife. Yolanda screamed. Arms and faces blurred as she tried to shield her head. She felt more thumps and she heard the women's cries, but pain was making Lily gasp and her eyes screwed shut as she battled to control it.

The men's footsteps pounded the road and quickly vanished.

Yolanda's face appeared over her. 'Lily! Lily, are you alright?'

'Yes,' she managed through gritted teeth. It was a lie. Her shoulder and arm were screaming with pain. 'Did they hurt you? Where's Maria?'

Yolanda shook her head. 'They didn't touch me. Maria's gone to get help.'

Lily looked around. 'My camera?'

Yolanda hesitated before answering. 'They took it.' She picked something up from the ground. Lily recognised the strap of her case. It had been sliced with a knife. 'They took your purse too. I'm sorry.'

'The purse doesn't matter,' said Lily. Unlike her camera, she thought heavily. But at least she was alive, and the women – as far as she could tell – were unharmed.

Yolanda bent over her again and said something. It was becoming an effort to understand, even to think. Lily caught the words: 'Doctor . . . Don't move.' Yolanda's face, her words – everything was becoming pixelated and breaking up.

She let her head fall back. The charcoal sky and the faint line of the moon swam above her like reflections in a pool of water, then sank into darkness.

Chapter Two

People pushed past Lily as she bent to pick up her small suitcase and cross the road to the taxi rank. It was tricky juggling two cases with one arm bandaged in a sling, and her laptop case slipped off her shoulder. She reached down to pick it up, but a large hand swiped it away.

'Hey!' She gripped the strap, the robbery all too fresh in her mind.

'Let me help you with your case,' said a deep voice.

As she looked up, her eyes widened. 'Olivier!'

She stared at him, seeing both the boy he'd once been and the man he had become: tall and well built, his muscular frame filling his white t-shirt and black jeans. Memories flashed up like film clips. The two of them as children chasing through the olive grove, dangling from tree branches, dreaming up dares – and then that fateful kiss in the midday sun.

Even now, thirteen years on, her skin heated at the thought.

'Who did you think it was?' he grinned and looked at her hand, still holding on tight to the strap.

Embarrassed, she let it fall to her side. 'I thought – I don't know . . .'

'Hello, Skinny,' he grinned, and bent to kiss her on both cheeks. His scent was woody and enticing, and Lily tried to feign indifference as he drew back, but heat stole through her.

Until his gaze lingered a fraction of a second too long on the left side of her face. Quickly, she dipped her head, letting her long brown hair fall forward over her cheek.

'We'd better move,' she said, nodding at the busy road she'd been about to cross. Cars and taxis juddered past, hooting impatiently and weaving in and out of pick-up zones. 'We're getting in everyone's way here.'

'My car's just there,' he said and pointed. He had slung her laptop case over his shoulder and was wheeling her suitcase away towards the car park. She had to walk fast to keep up.

'I wasn't expecting to be collected,' she said.

'Mamie sent me.' Something stirred in her chest when he called her gran by the same name she used. He'd always done it, claiming she was like a grandmother to him, even if they weren't related. 'She was worried you wouldn't be able to carry all your luggage with a broken arm, but you haven't got much. Where's your camera?' Olivier stopped beside a black car and unlocked it. It was a four by four, she noticed; as solid and sure of itself as its owner.

'It got damaged in the – er, accident.'

'You travel light,' he said, loading her belongings into the boot of his car.

She thought of the huge rucksack which she'd had to leave behind in Colombia because she couldn't lift it with only one arm. 'I left a lot of things behind. I'll collect them when I go back.'

'How is your arm?'

She climbed into the car. 'It's okay,' she said, yanking at the seatbelt with her good hand. Each time she pulled, it sprang back before she could clip it in.

'Here, let me,' he said, and reached across.

She pressed herself back into her seat, but his hand brushed against her hip as he strapped her in and she stilled, caught off guard by the electric charge that shot through her, making her skin spark.

'Did I knock your arm?' he asked, seeing her rigid frame.

'No,' she said quickly, 'I . . . I'm fine.'

She looked away, mortified that she was so sensitive to him. Nothing had changed, then. She still responded to him like a hormonal teenager, and he was still completely indifferent.

He put the car into gear and navigated his way out of the car park.

'You seem to know the airport well,' she said, amazed at how confidently he steered his way through the complicated maze of lanes and signs. The roundabout ahead was planted with palm trees that shimmered in the heat, and she was glad that the car's air-con had already kicked in.

'I suppose I do. I often fly down to see my parents.'

She nodded, and tried to picture him in Paris, master baker with his own chain of bakeries and a training school, but it wasn't easy. In her mind he would always be a young boy with a gleam in his eye as he set her yet another challenge.

'I hope you're not too tired after the journey,' he said,

'I'd better warn you, Mamie has prepared a feast for you tonight. Everybody's coming.'

They pulled on to the motorway and the car picked up speed.

'Really?' Her brow creased. 'I didn't want her to go to any trouble . . .' Though she had to admit that her heart lifted at the thought of seeing his parents and brothers. As a girl she had loved spending time with his family. Perhaps it was because her own parents were divorced, so most of the time it had been just her and her dad, that she used to love the noise and chaos at the Lacostes' home.

'You know what she's like. Besides, she's thrilled that you'll be staying so long for once. Is it a record?'

'Is what a record?'

'You staying here more than five days.' Was it her imagination or did she hear an edge of criticism in his voice?

'I try and get here as often as I can, but between filming and editing, I don't get much time off.' She could have gone to her flat in London to recuperate but, much as she hated to admit it, even to herself, her injury meant that she needed help.

'Not even to see your grandmother?'

Lily looked at him. Was he judging her? There had been a time when she would have known him well enough to tell, but now she wasn't sure. They hadn't spent any real length of time together for years.

'How often do you come home?' she countered, although she knew the answer because Mamie always told her about his visits. She and his mother, Béatrice, were close. Neighbours, they saw each other practically every day.

'Every month,' he said with a shrug. 'And all the holidays of course.'

'Is that why you're here – for the summer?'

He nodded and she felt a sinking in her stomach. It would be impossible to avoid him if they were both here all summer. She read the signs at the side of the road and calculated that they were still over an hour away from the seaside village of St Pierre. Perhaps it was because she hadn't slept much on the plane, but she couldn't relax, her body was too tense, too aware of the man sitting beside her. Why had Mamie sent him and not his dad, Raymond, or one of his brothers? Anyone but Olivier.

She surreptitiously eyed his long fingers that made the steering wheel look small, and the knotted muscles in his forearms, the bronzed skin dusted with rough hair. Why was she so bothered by him? Because of that kiss? Surely not.

And yet it was still fresh in her memory; the pitying look in his eyes as he'd prised her off him and crushed her with his gentle words of rejection. Her cheeks had burned with humiliation.

She tried to push it out of her mind and focus on the here and now.

'Actually,' he said, 'it might be a more long-term arrangement if things go according to plan. I want to move back home.'

'Really? You'd leave Paris? That's a big move.'

He nodded. 'I'm house-hunting at the moment.'

'Seen anything you like?'

'No. I've visited a few but none of them were right so far.' His dark brows pulled together in a deep frown and she wondered why he was so worried about it.

'Won't it make things difficult for you professionally to base yourself so far from your headquarters?'

He shrugged again. 'It shouldn't make much difference. I spend most of my time overseeing the business and sitting in meetings rather than working in the bakeries. I can travel to Paris or work from here just as well.'

She supposed that having reached the height of his profession he could afford to take a backseat if he wanted to. But she couldn't picture him as the type to sit back and do nothing.

'So how did you break your arm?' he asked. 'Mamie said the phone line was really bad when you called. She didn't catch what you said.'

Lily stiffened at the memory of the assault. She'd been deliberately vague on the phone to her grandmother. If Mamie knew about the robbery she'd be worried sick when Lily went back to finish the film. 'It was a silly accident. I was in the wrong place at the wrong time . . .'

'Don't tell me – you fell out of a tree?' He winked, and the laughter in his eyes made her stomach tighten.

'That was *your* speciality, not mine!' Why did remembering their childhood days fill her with the warmest of sensations?

'So what happened?'

She didn't want to lie, but she had to protect Mamie

from the truth. 'I was filming and – er – next thing I knew I was on the ground.'

'So you did fall out of a tree. That's not like you, Skinny. You must have been totally caught up in the filming.'

'I was.' If she and Yolanda hadn't been so engrossed in conversation, they might have seen the men coming.

'Have you finished the film?'

She shook her head. 'I had only just started. It's so frustrating that I had to leave, but I couldn't film with this,' she nodded at her sling, 'and I was staying with a family of five who didn't have much room. I didn't want to get in their way while this heals. It's going to be weeks before I can use it again.'

She pictured Yolanda's home where she'd been staying: a rough shack made of wood and corrugated metal, the roof held down with bricks, and four children squeezed into one bed so that Lily could have the other. Though she'd been reluctant to leave, she'd had no choice. With her right arm in a sling she couldn't even pick up a camera, never mind use one. She'd needed help from the nurses just to get dressed to leave hospital.

But frustrating as it was, she had to focus on getting better and then she would return to finish the documentary.

'You're already thinking about going back?' he laughed. 'Why not look on the bright side? It's July – summer is the best time to take a break and spend some time at home with your family.'

'Actually, the timing is terrible. I can't wait to get back. The film is due in October and it's really important. My first real commission – if I let them down, I may as well kiss goodbye to my career.' It would be a huge black mark against her name. And then, of course, there was the prestigious film prize she hoped to enter. This film would meet the criteria perfectly.

'Can't you speak to them and ask for the deadline to be extended?'

'No. They said from the start that the deadline was fixed and I agreed to it. I'll look totally unprofessional if I don't deliver on time.'

He glanced at her, one brow raised. 'Even though you broke your arm?'

'Yes.' He didn't understand. This was her first real opening, and opportunities like it were so rare. She simply couldn't afford to fail because there might never be another.

'So what's your film about?' he asked.

'A women's farming cooperative,' she said, her voice instantly brightening. 'They grow coffee. Women running their own business is pretty revolutionary in such a macho culture. They're inspirational. Determined to make a success of it and to be financially independent and self-reliant. They have fascinating stories to tell.'

It was all the more frustrating that she'd just started to earn their trust and get them to open up when the robbery had interrupted everything.

'I've done the maths, though. If my arm heals fast, I should be able to get back by the beginning of September and that will give me just enough time to finish it.' It would be tight. Really tight. But she'd work all hours, editing through the night if necessary to get it done.

'You're passionate about your work,' he said, casting her an assessing look. Why did he sound so disapproving?

'Of course. If I let them down, my reputation will be ruined.'

'Your reputation,' he said flatly.

'Why the black look? Or have you climbed so high you've forgotten what it's like to be at the bottom of the ladder trying to work your way up?'

'I haven't forgotten. But I have learned that reputation and status are not the be all and end all.'

She glared at him, wondering why he sounded so bitter. 'That's easy to say when you're a celebrity with ten bakeries to your name.'

'I'm not a celebrity,' he muttered and indicated right to leave the motorway. 'I don't do anything to court attention.'

'You're still a celebrity.' The papers and gossip magazines adored him. Handsome and successful at such a young age, he was bound to attract attention, whether he welcomed it or not.

He slowed the car as they approached the exit and the tollbooths marked *péage*.

Olivier slotted his card in the machine and waited impatiently to retrieve it. He'd jumped at Mamie's request to meet Lily, seeing this as a chance to spend quality time together – something they hadn't done for years. But hearing her talk about her work like this made him tense. She sounded just like his ex, Nathalie. Ambitious. Self-centred. Mercenary.

And yet that wasn't how he remembered Lily. As a child she'd been endlessly curious, adventurous, concerned for others. But a lot had changed during the intervening years. His mouth flattened. What about spending time with her grandmother? Was that not important to her?

He plucked his credit card out of the machine and went to slot it in his wallet but missed.

'I'll do it,' said Lily, holding out her hand. Her stunning Audrey Hepburn eyes met with his.

'Thanks,' he said and his gaze dipped to her scarred cheek as he handed her the wallet and card. He drove on, trying to concentrate on the road, the roundabout, anything but Lily and her damaged face.

Her scars always disturbed him. They had faded now, but when he'd visited her in hospital her injuries had been livid and looked intensely painful. Lily never mentioned the pain, though. Then again, her burned and blistered skin must have been nothing next to losing her father. They'd been so close, father and daughter.

Olivier's chest tightened in sympathy for the grief she must have felt. And he wondered, as he'd wondered so many times before, if the fire was the reason why she didn't come back here as often? Certainly it had changed her, but why hide from those closest to her? It didn't make any sense.

Yet the facts were, she kept herself to herself, she only saw his family for the odd meal, and every time he came home she found a reason to suddenly leave. Let's face it, most of her visits didn't coincide with his at all. How many times had he been disappointed to learn that she'd left the week before he arrived? It couldn't be coincidence: she was as elusive as a bird. The last time they'd spoken properly had been before the fire, when he was seventeen and she'd tried to kiss him – and he'd so clumsily rejected her.

His hands gripped the steering wheel tighter. He hadn't handled that well and he'd felt guilty for a long time afterwards. But it had been years now, and Lily was a tough cookie. She'd probably forgotten all about it.

'You still have an English accent, you know,' he said. Although she'd grown up in London, her French was almost perfect, but as a boy he'd teased her mercilessly for every vowel sound that was even slightly off the mark.

'Oh yeah? And how's your English?' she retaliated with a smile.

'I'm just a baker. I don't need to speak English.'

She casually stretched out her long legs in front of her. Although she'd been skinny as a child, the nickname wasn't really appropriate any more. She'd grown up from the awkward, gangly teenager to be tall and slim, with an athletic figure other women must envy.

'Just as well. No one would understand you, Chicken.'

His lips curved as she used her old nickname for him. He hadn't thought of it for years. 'That name was never justified. I never chickened out of any challenge. Not one dare.'

'But you wanted to.' She flicked her hair back over her shoulder. It was smooth and glossy like caramel.

'Yes I wanted to, I admit it. It's perfectly normal not to want to throw yourself off a cliff or break an arm swinging from the trees. I don't have a death wish.'

'You were as competitive as I was. It worked both ways, Lacoste.'

True, he acknowledged with a nod.

'Have you seen your mother lately?' he asked as they turned off the main road and headed toward the fishing village of St Pierre.

Instantly, he sensed her withdrawal.

'No.'

He glanced sideways and saw her chin lift as she turned away and studied the plane trees at the side of the road, her expression giving nothing away.

'She's busy touring?'

'How would I know?'

'You don't talk?'

'She emails from time to time. I don't reply.'

He didn't blame her, yet he didn't know how she could talk about it so calmly. It had made him seethe that when Lily's father had died and Lily was in hospital, Darcy Green, the accomplished English pianist, hadn't allowed the news to interrupt her international concert tour. Most mothers would have rushed to be with their child. Not her. It was Mamie who had flown to London and stayed at Lily's bedside during the long months it took for her to recover.

Darcy had only turned up once her daughter was ready to be discharged from hospital. It had broken Mamie's heart to see Lily go with her, but they'd all hoped that the woman who'd been so absent from her daughter's life might now change and step up to the mark.

They were disappointed. Within a year, Lily was in boarding school and Darcy was on the road again.

'You cut her off?' he asked, casting her a wary glance.

She sat tall, rigid in her seat, eyes narrowed. 'I don't want to have anything to do with her.'

'She's your mother,' he suggested quietly.

Lily barked a laugh. 'Only in name. She didn't do much to live up to the title.'

'I shouldn't have brought it up. I'm sorry—'

'Don't be.' She turned to look at him and her sage-green eyes held his gaze. 'I'm not.'

He slowed down as they approached Mamie's house and turned left off the road before the steep slope down to the village. Outside the green metal gates, he unfastened his seatbelt.

'You can drop me here,' Lily said as he went to open his door.

'I'll help you with your bags.'

The rusty gate squeaked as she pushed it open, and they ducked under the waterfall of magenta-coloured bougainvillea flowers. The gravel crunched underfoot as they approached the old farmhouse. It was very different from his parents' next door. Where theirs was modern and had repeatedly been extended or improved over the years, Mamie's house was exactly as it had always been: built from uneven stones, sandy and pink in places, with undulating terracotta roof tiles and a square turret. Olivier glanced up at the grapevines, already heavy with fruit, which hung from the pergola. The kitchen doors stood open and he stepped inside. The oven was on so he knew Mamie must be nearby somewhere.

'Want me to carry these up for you?' he asked, holding up Lily's small cases.

She rolled her eyes. 'I can manage,' she said, and the flash of her smile transported him back to when they were eight and she used to laugh off his challenges, then turn them back on him. 'I have a broken arm. I'm not completely helpless.'

'Never said you were,' he smiled. 'See you this evening, then.'

'Yes. See you later.' She looked around her, and her eyes brightened visibly as she took in the rustic wooden table and the old dresser against the wall.

He hesitated a moment before saying, 'It's good to have you back, Skinny.'

And he meant it. Selfish as it might sound, he was glad she'd broken her arm because Mamie needed her here. This was where she belonged, it was her home, and he'd seen the way her eyes lit up when they'd rolled up outside Mamie's rusty gates.

Having Lily back was like September rain after the long, dry summer. She'd breathe new life into the place. He'd missed their sparring, their teasing, he'd even missed their arguing. He might be a responsible adult with commitments, but Lily reminded him of the kid he'd once been and she'd always have a special place in his life.

She looked surprised, and her cheeks flushed.

He strode off, and as he ducked through the doorway he heard her call after him, 'Thanks for the ride, Chicken!'

He shook his head and grinned as he made his way back to his car.

Lily paused, hit by the rush of familiar scents of the old farmhouse: the sweetness of garlic cooking, the faint drift of Mamie's perfume, and the woody smell that simply belonged to this place. It was all exactly as she remembered it, from the centuries-old fireplace to the mismatched chairs around the table, and the chunky blue and green Moustier plates displayed on the dresser.

Her pulse picked up speed as her grandmother appeared in the doorway. She seemed even smaller than before, but she wore her usual peacock-coloured kaftan, and the sight of her made Lily's heart sing.

'Lily!' said Mamie, holding her arms open. Lily scooted across the room and hugged her as tight as was possible with one arm in a sling. She breathed in her grandmother's familiar perfume, and it transported her back to her childhood. Cuddles, kisses, love. She'd always adored her grandmother and knew she was loved unconditionally in return. 'Did Olivier find you alright? How are you, little one? Let me look at you. How is your arm?'

'It's fine,' she said, and glanced down.

'I was so worried when you called me from the hospital!'

'It's only a fracture.' Lily did her best to hide her shock as she hugged her grandmother. Why did she look so tired and frail? She'd always been a bundle of strength and energy.

'Well, I'll take care of you until you're better,' Mamie said with relish, causing Lily to feel a spike of guilt because she should be the one taking care of her gran, not the other way round.

'Olivier said you've invited everyone for dinner tonight.'

'Yes, a welcome home meal. I thought you might like to see them.'

'I hope you haven't tired yourself out.'

Mamie dismissed this with a wave of her hand. 'Cooking is a pleasure, not a chore,' she said, but she looked tired. She nodded at the oven. 'I've made your favourite; *Daube de Boeuf*.'

A memory flashed up in Lily's mind of sitting at this kitchen table when she was tiny, eating the beef stew with mashed potatoes from a plastic orange bowl.

'Thanks, Mamie.' She squeezed her again. 'I've missed you so much, you know.'

'And I've missed you too, but you're here now. That's the important thing.' She looked at Lily's tiny suitcase. 'Shall we get you settled into your room?'

A couple of hours later, Lily was showered and had changed into shorts, a brown linen top and sandals, which were refreshingly cool on this warm evening. She was glad she had a wardrobe of clothes here because she'd only brought a couple of outfits back from Colombia, and the long trousers she wore for filming were too warm for this dry heat.

Olivier's family arrived with a flurry of noise and kisses and bottles of wine, then they all took their seats around the circular table beneath the pergola.

'Lily, come and sit here with me,' said Mamie.

The smell of cooked food mingled with the scent of lavender and rosemary which grew in pots around the edge of the terrace. Lily sat down, trying to hide her discomfort at finding herself next to Olivier again.

'Help yourselves,' Mamie told them, and gestured to the dishes she'd laid out.

Olivier's mother, Béatrice, lifted the lid off the terracotta pot and began to spoon out the beef stew with its rich sauce. She handed each plate to her son, Mathieu, who passed them round, and everyone helped themselves to fresh bread.

'It's very dark out here,' said Claude, the youngest of the three brothers, as he lit the well-used candles in the middle of the table.

Lily's eyes widened. She pulled back, rigid in her chair. The flames leapt and danced wildly before her and in her mind they were only a whisper away from reaching the tablecloth or the wooden pergola. She blew them out quickly.

'What the—?' said Claude.

'I'll put the lights on,' said Mamie, and glanced at Lily as she got up.

'Sorry,' Lily said to Claude. Her heart was still beating fast, like frenzied wings against her ribcage. 'I just can't,' she swallowed, 'can't—'

'It's alright, Lily,' said Béa. She scolded her son. 'Claude, what were you thinking?'

Realisation dawned. 'I forgot. Sorry, Lil.'

Her cheeks heated with guilt for causing such a fuss. Although it had been thirteen years since the fire, her fear of naked flames hadn't diminished. Candles, an open fire; they all put her on edge.

The electric light came on overhead, bathing the table in a golden light which was reflected in all the wine glasses.

'So how is business at the *boulangerie*?' Lily asked Olivier's father.

'Busy,' grumbled Raymond. 'The tourists have arrived and they all need feeding.'

'What he means, in his dour old way,' said Béa, shaking her head and smiling, 'is that business is doing very well.'

He shrugged. 'But we can't get the staff. Nobody wants to be a baker any more. They're all happy to eat the manufactured factory rubbish that tries to pass itself off as bread!'

'You might have been away a while, Skinny,' said Olivier, turning to her with a wink, 'but you see nothing changes. My father is just as grumpy as ever. Green beans?' he asked Lily, and held the dish for her to help herself.

'Not grumpy,' Raymond corrected, 'I'm jaded. Life has made me so.'

'You should be more grateful, Raymond,' said Mamie, sitting down again. 'You have a thriving business and a wonderful family. You and I are very lucky.' She turned, beaming, to look at Lily, and patted her hand.

Lily felt a lump in her throat because Mamie considered herself lucky, but Lily was her only family and she spent so little time here.

Yet coming back here was so hard for her. She adored Mamie, she treasured any time she could spend with her, but this place . . . It held so many reminders of all the things she'd lost. Her childhood. Her face. Her dad. She glanced at Olivier beside her.

And him. Don't forget him.

Raymond tore off a piece of bread, inspecting it before he put it in his mouth and chewed. 'So how did you break your arm?' he asked Lily.

'She fell out of a tree while filming,' Olivier answered for her. His lips curved in a mocking smile.

Lily's cheeks heated, but having seen how frail Mamie looked, she knew she'd done the right thing concealing the truth.

'Do you often film from treetops?' asked Raymond, deadpan.

'Yes I do,' Lily laughed, relieved that this, at least, was true. 'If it gives me the best angle, I do it. I've filmed from hilltops, rooftops, ladders – whatever it takes.'

'Nothing changes,' said Mamie. 'You were always climbing, from the moment you could walk.'

Béa looked at Lily and Olivier and shook her head. 'The number of times I had to drive you two to hospital because you'd hurt yourself with one of your silly pranks. You were always up to no good.'

'They weren't pranks, they were dares,' Olivier corrected.

Lily's mouth twitched at his serious tone. He met her gaze with a look of challenge and the old rivalry between them surged again. She remembered when it had always been like this. His little brothers had tagged along, taking part in their games, but the real competition – the only one which mattered – had been between her and Olivier.

'Do you remember when we had a contest to see who could eat the most raw chillies?' asked Mathieu. He looked at Olivier. 'You managed six and I was in awe!'

Claude laughed. 'And you went red in the face but refused to drink any water.'

Olivier smiled. 'Water wasn't allowed – that was the rule. And I had to beat Lily's record. She'd eaten five.'

'You didn't *have* to do anything,' said Béa. 'They were stupid games. I don't know why you two always had to be so competitive.'

'The best one,' said Claude, 'was when you stole the priest's underpants from his washing line. Remember that?'

His brother, Mathieu, laughed. 'Yes, that was hard to beat.'

Mamie crossed herself and muttered a quick prayer.

'No,' said Olivier, looking at Lily, 'the best one was when you blocked the fountain and put red food colouring in the water to make it look like blood. Remember how we hid behind a tree and listened to the screams?'

The admiration in his voice made Lily blush. 'That *was* the best one,' she agreed, and dipped her head, trying to conceal her smile. She had forgotten about the fun they'd had together, and warmth flowed through her. She hadn't experienced that closeness with anyone since.

Raymond scowled. 'That was nothing to be proud of, Lily Martin! That earned me a visit from the *gendarmes*.' Nevertheless, the corner of his mouth twitched.

'The police?' Mamie gasped and looked genuinely shocked. 'You never told me.'

'Olivier took the rap for it,' said Raymond. 'He confessed to it all.'

'To protect Lily?' Mamie beamed at Olivier.

'Don't look at him like that, Simone. He put her up to it in the first place. It was only right that he should take the blame. Besides, they let him off with a warning. He deserved far worse in my opinion.'

Mamie tutted. 'How I used to worry about the pair of you. I always thought you would get into trouble one day.'

Olivier and Lily shared a brief glance and a smile.

'Such a bad example you both set,' teased Mathieu.

'Well they turned out alright in the end, thank goodness,' said his mother.

Embarrassed, Lily reached for her water.

Claude continued; 'To think that Oli will soon be married with kids of his own, eh? I wonder if they'll be as bad as you, big bro.'

Lily froze, the glass at her lips. She blinked and stared at Olivier. He was playfully teasing Claude in return but she didn't hear what he said.

'You're getting married?' she asked.

Her stunned tone quickly silenced the noisy table.

Olivier turned to look at her and the faintest strip of

colour touched his cheekbones. 'Yes,' he said. 'You didn't know?'

'No,' she said.

She'd had no idea. She looked at Mamie, then at Béa. Why hadn't anyone told her? Why hadn't he mentioned it during the journey from the airport earlier?

'Well, with your accident and everything maybe your grandmother didn't get the chance to tell you,' Béa suggested diplomatically. 'Oli only announced it a couple of weeks ago. The wedding will be early next year.' Her eyes shone with excitement.

Early next year was only six months away. Lily tried to take it in: Olivier was getting married? Who to? Somehow she couldn't bring herself to ask. It took all her energy to turn to him and force her lips into a smile. 'Congratulations,' she said. 'That's . . . wonderful.'

The conversation moved on and Lily let her long hair fall forward as she pretended to concentrate on her food. She was annoyed with herself for being so shaken up by the news. It shouldn't have come as a shock. Of course Olivier was getting married. He was a good man, intelligent, successful and good-looking to boot – it was a miracle he hadn't already been snatched up. She took a sip of her wine and tried to identify the jittery sensation in her chest.

She was just tired. She hadn't slept much on the plane because the painkillers had worn off and, added to that, she was frustrated about her film, worried about meeting the deadline. Yes, she decided as the conversation around her moved on, she was simply exhausted. Not upset at all.

Chapter Three

Mamie knocked on her bedroom door. 'Lily? I brought you a glass of water.'

'I'm just . . .' Lily's words were muffled as she tried to wriggle free. Getting ready for bed, she'd somehow tangled her top around her head and couldn't get it off without pulling on her injured arm, 'I'm a bit stuck!'

She heard footsteps approach. 'Here, let me help you,' said Mamie, and released her from the tangle of linen fabric, making her feel like a child again.

'Thanks,' said Lily, and took a deep breath of the cool night air that drifted in through the open window.

Her bedroom was decorated in cream and pale blue, colours which she'd chosen as a child mainly because she hated pink. Now she found them restful and calming.

'You know, you should ask for help when you need it,' said Mamie. 'Being independent is one thing, but we all need help from time to time.'

'I know.'

Mamie picked up the nightie on Lily's bed and helped her put it on. 'You were very quiet tonight. Are you upset?'

'No, of course not. Why would I be?'

Mamie studied her closely. 'Because Olivier is engaged?'

'Oh that. I was just – just surprised.' She tried to feign indifference. What Olivier did, who he married was of no importance to her. And yet she felt a hard knot in her chest at the thought of his impending wedding. She turned to her grandmother and asked, 'Why didn't you tell me?'

Mamie sighed. 'I suppose I hoped he would change his mind.'

Lily frowned. 'Why? You don't approve of his fiancée?'

She picked up the glass of water which Mamie had put by her bedside and took a sip.

'I've only met her once or twice. He hasn't known her very long, and—' Mamie paused, then confessed; 'I always hoped the two of you would get together.'

Lily spluttered. 'Olivier and me?' She wiped the water from her chin whilst watching her gran with wide eyes.

Mamie nodded. 'You were so close when you were young. Inseparable.'

'Oh Mamie,' she put the glass down next to her dog-eared passport stuffed full of stickers and stamps from all over the world. 'That's never going to happen. Not me and Olivier!'

Yet even as she said the words, her cheeks heated and she remembered the slam of excitement she'd felt when she'd seen him at the airport, the hum in her veins during the car journey here.

But she hadn't known then that he was engaged to be married.

'You don't know that,' said Mamie. 'Admit it – you're both very fond of each other still.'

'Well, yes . . . but—'

'There you are, then.'

'Mamie, he's engaged!'

'Pff!' Her grandmother waved a hand through the air to show what she thought of that.

'And – and we're not . . . It was never like that. We were only ever good friends.' Perhaps that wasn't strictly true. She had hoped for more, but when she'd tried to kiss him and he had pushed her away, he had killed those hopes.

Mamie didn't say anything. Instead, she arched a brow.

Lily laughed. 'We were!' she insisted. 'Nothing more is ever going to come of our friendship.'

'We'll see,' said Mamie. 'Time will tell.'

Mamie kissed her on the cheek, and went to leave. Her steps were small and slow, and Lily's chest squeezed with anxiety. 'Mamie?'

Her gran stopped and looked over her shoulder at her with sharp green eyes. 'Yes?'

She swallowed, afraid to ask the question. 'Are you – are you alright?'

'Yes. Why?'

'You look tired.'

'Pff!' She shrugged off the suggestion. 'I'm slowing down, that's all. Perfectly normal at my age.'

Lily's eyes filled with sudden tears and she blinked hard. 'I feel bad that I can't do more to help.' For the hundredth time she cursed her bandaged arm.

'I have plenty of help from Béa and her boys.' Mamie's eyes lit up and her smile made the lines in her face fade as she added, 'And you know there's nothing I like more than having you here with me.'

Lily nodded but she didn't feel reassured. Mamie went to leave, then stopped again.

'Actually, there *is* something I'd like you to help me with.'

'Oh yes? What is it?' She brightened at the thought of being able to do something for her gran.

'It can wait until tomorrow. I'll talk to you about it then. You need a good night's sleep after all that travelling. Goodnight, little one.'

Lily woke to the sound of doves calling in the turret above her room. A beautiful musical sound that she always associated with this place and, for a split-second before fully waking, she was transported back to her childhood: she was eight years old and her dad was asleep in the next room.

Then she blinked and reality re-asserted itself with a solid thump. She wasn't eight but twenty-eight, with a broken arm and several weeks to fill before she could return to Colombia and finish her film. And while she was grateful for this time with Mamie, she couldn't shake off her worry about how tired and frail her grandmother had become.

Lily got up and opened the shutters a crack to let the light in. Her room was at the back and overlooked the Lacostes' house, and age-old habit made her pause to check if the shutters of Olivier's room were open.

They were, and a dark-haired figure was powering through the swimming pool, completing length after length in quick, confident strokes. He paused for breath at one end, his shoulders rising and falling quickly and Lily instantly knew it was him. Whereas both his brothers had brown hair, Olivier's was black, and she recognised the way he impatiently swept his wet hair back from his face and focused straight ahead before pushing off into the water again. Neither of his brothers had the same energy or determination.

She showered quickly, being careful with her arm and savouring the luxury of warm running water after the buckets that Yolanda's family had used to wash, then got dressed as best she could in her favourite denim shorts and a t-shirt. Buttons were impossible to fasten one-handed, however, so she zipped up her shorts and left the button undone but hidden beneath her top. Downstairs the house was quiet and still, and her gran's big straw shopping basket wasn't in its usual spot beside the French doors. Mamie must have gone down to the village as she liked to do each morning to buy fresh groceries, and Lily cursed herself for having slept so late. She could have gone with her and helped to carry the shopping, albeit only with one hand, and she would have made sure Mamie was alright stepping on and off the bus.

Frowning, she opened the back doors and began to prepare breakfast. She needed some caffeine to clear the fuzziness in her head. But the packet of coffee was new and she couldn't open it one-handed. She tugged and pulled, and tried holding it in her teeth and pulling with her free hand, but it remained stubbornly sealed without even the slightest tear. Lily banged it down in frustration.

She couldn't work, she couldn't dress herself properly, she couldn't even make a cup of coffee! Frustration boiled through her at her cursed injury. She was used to independence, action and adventure – not this stifling helplessness. Her gaze was drawn to the garden and the early morning light that filtered through, lighting up the hollyhocks, making the morning dew sparkle and shimmer. How would she get through six weeks stuck in one place unable to do anything for herself?

Giving up on the coffee, she escaped outside into the fresh air. At least her broken arm couldn't stop her from walking, and perhaps that would help work off some of her frustrations. She marched through Mamie's garden, past the delicate mimosa tree and the oleander bushes with their exuberant pink and red flowers, through the gate and into her favourite place: the olive grove. She hadn't visited it for a long time and talking about their childhood pranks last night had made her curious to know if it had changed. Of course it hadn't. Time had stood still for centuries here, and she wondered what stories the trees would tell if they could recount all that they'd witnessed. Warm sunlight touched her shoulders and she breathed in the familiar scents, including the faintest tang of sea air carried on the breeze. Dry grass crunched under her flat sandals as she stomped through the trees, reassured that Olivier was in the pool.

Olivier who was soon getting married, she thought,

and was surprised that even today she still felt a sharp squeeze of emotion.

Get used to it, Lil. She had to stay focused on her life and her own plans. She began to make lists in her mind: she would keep in contact with the women in Colombia, making sure they knew when she was planning to return; and she would email the television company to let them know about her accident – but also to assure them that she'd still deliver the film on time.

She turned right, weaving through the oldest, largest trees with their gnarled and crooked trunks, and realised her pace had slowed a little, her thoughts had become less frenetic, and she knew it was the olive grove working its special magic. It was so still and peaceful, and when she was here she remembered how it felt to be a child again: carefree, happy, living in the moment. She craned her neck, searching through the branches and silvery leaves for the rope swing they used to hang from.

'What are you looking for?'

Her skin prickled at the sound of his gravelly deep voice and she span round. Olivier stood, hands in pockets, his wet hair gleaming like a dark halo in the sunlight. 'Olivier!' she said, heart racing. 'I thought you were in the pool.'

'Ah. So you still spy on me from your window,' he said, one brow raised in a knowing look.

Her cheeks heated as she realised she'd given too much away. 'Of course not! I just – I noticed when I opened the shutters, that's all. Why would I spy on you? We're not children any more.'

She turned to carry on and he fell into step with her. He wore long, sandy-coloured shorts that looked pale against his dark bronze legs. 'Well, old habits die hard: I confess I saw you from my window.'

His conspiratorial look made her twist inside. It was like they were best buddies again.

Except they weren't. Because they used to tell each other everything back then.

He nodded at the branches above their heads. 'You were looking for the rope swing, weren't you? It went years ago.'

'That's a shame.' She bent to snap off a sprig of lavender and held it up to her nose. The sweet dry scent transported her back in time. She quickly let her hand drop and twisted the lavender between her finger and thumb. 'This place is so special.'

'Papa's had so many offers for this land, but he won't sell. He's very superstitious about it. He and Maman have always believed that olive groves are sacred places, but this one they're convinced is particularly special.'

Sunlight trickled through the leaves, its warmth whispering against her bare arms, and she remembered Raymond telling her that some of these trees were over a thousand years old. 'I don't know about that, but I have a lot of good memories here.'

When they were kids there had been fields all around which had now been replaced with houses, but the olive grove was unchanged, and it had always been their favourite meeting place; midway between both houses, and full of hiding places and trees to climb.

She threw him a sidelong glance and asked; 'Do you remember the time you were grounded, so you climbed out of your bedroom window using a piece of rope?'

He grinned and it made her insides melt to see his eyes spark with laughter. 'I remember. It didn't end well, and I still blame you for daring me in the first place.'

'Me? You should have tied it to something solid – not a chair!' She laughed, remembering his look of horror when the chair had appeared in the window, followed by the snap of wood before he and the length of rope had both tumbled to the ground.

How easy it was to let the years slip away and imagine she and Olivier were close again.

She stopped and turned to face him. 'Why didn't you tell me you're engaged? We spent two hours together in the car from the airport. You didn't even mention it.'

A look of surprise flickered through his eyes, then he frowned. 'You're upset?'

'No!' Heat seared her cheeks, betraying her. Of course she was. Any good friend would be. 'I don't understand why you made a secret of it.'

He raised his hands in the air in a gesture of surrender. 'It's not a secret. Everyone knew.'

'Everyone except me. Most people, when they get engaged, are brimming with excitement. They talk about nothing else, they can't contain themselves. You didn't say a word.'

His broad shoulders lifted in a shrug. 'Corinne and me – we're not like that. We don't see the engagement or the wedding as an excuse to spend lots of money on lavish parties and superficial festivities. It's all been low key and we intend to keep it that way. We're pragmatic about our relationship.'

Corinne and me. Her chest tightened at the affection in his voice, at the way he made them sound like a solid unit. 'Pragmatic?'

'Yes. We're simply looking forward to settling down and starting a family together.'

Starting a family? It was still a shock to have learned he was engaged. 'Corinne – that's her name?'

He nodded.

'You didn't have an engagement party?'

'We had a small celebration in Paris with close friends,' he conceded. 'But nothing fancy. Corinne isn't silly about these things like some women.'

She tried to ignore the stab she felt when he said *close friends*. She felt excluded in every possible way. But then, she hadn't been close to Olivier for years now, and that was her doing. It was definitely better that way.

'So what's she like?'

He shrugged again, as if she'd asked an impossible question. 'Thirty years old. Blonde. Female.'

'Very funny, Mr Comedy.' It was like trying to have a conversation with a brick wall and she wanted to wring his neck for being so unforthcoming. Why was he so reluctant to talk about his fiancée? Wasn't that a bad sign?

Why did he feel so uncomfortable answering Lily's questions? Olivier was unsure. Perhaps it was because she had distanced herself over the years, putting so much space between them that he felt he didn't know her any more. And his impending marriage was close to his heart. You didn't open your heart to a stranger, did you?

Yet at the same time, when she was teasing and mocking him for things he'd done when he was ten, the years fell away and the old bond was still there. Like a solid length of rope in his hands. Friendships like that were rare – he knew that now. He'd never had a friendship like it since Lily. He intended to treat it carefully, nurture it. He wouldn't let it slip away a second time.

'What do you want to know?' he asked. They wove a winding path through the trees. He slowed his pace and they fell into step.

'More than what's written on her passport! What does she do? What kind of person is she? What do you love about her?'

'Okay. She's a nurse. And she's pretty and clever and caring – that's what I love about her.' Warmth flowed through him at the thought of their relationship. 'And we have a lot in common – we both want the same things from life, share the same dreams, the same values . . .' They were the perfect match. He glanced at Lily. 'You would like her.'

Her brows lifted. 'So when is the wedding exactly?' she asked.

'We haven't set a date yet – I want to find a house first. But once I've found one then February hopefully.'

'So soon?'

'Why waste time?'

'How long have you known her?'

'Four months.'

She bit her lip. 'That's not very long.'

'Long enough.' He had known from their first meeting that they were right for each other. They'd been in line at the supermarket when a young man had fainted. Whereas others had panicked, gasping, stepping back, Corinne had calmly taken charge. She'd crouched down to examine the man, then instructed Olivier to help her move him into the recovery position.

He'd admired how calm she was in a crisis, he'd been drawn to her caring nature. She was pragmatic, uncomplicated, open. It was the cornerstone of their relationship that they could discuss things without drama, without exaggerated emotions. He found this refreshing. Unlike his past relationships, his relationship with Corinne was straightforward, and he knew that was what made it so special.

'You always were impatient.'

He frowned. 'What do you mean?'

'When you had made up your mind to do something, you never waited. You wouldn't let anyone or anything stop you or stand in your way.'

He didn't know why she said that as if it was a flaw. 'It's a useful skill in life, to know what you want and go after it. I don't mess around hesitating or delaying when there's a decision to be made.'

She nodded. 'You have focus, that's for sure.'

'So does Corinne. She's the most rational woman I've ever met. She isn't ruled by emotion like some women

I've met. With her I know we can always talk through a problem or an idea logically. That was how we came to the conclusion that we should get married.'

'How romantic,' she said drily.

He didn't answer. She didn't understand how relieved he was to be in a relationship that was solid and grounded. Based on reason rather than uncontrollable impulses. His relationship with Corinne was certain to be more reliable in the long term.

'So she's a nurse? Where does she live? Where is she now?'

'She's working in Paris. But she's applied for a transfer. It shouldn't be too long before she gets a job down here in the south.'

'Ah, that's why you're house-hunting,' she said, as if the facts were all falling into place.

'I want my children to grow up here. It's the perfect environment in which to raise a child: part of a village community with the sea, the hills, the sun. I had a great childhood here. I want the same for my own family.'

Eyes wide, she asked, 'You're already thinking about children?'

'Yes.'

'Wow. You've got it all planned out.'

Olivier's mouth flattened. Why did she make that sound like a negative thing? He wouldn't be where he was in life without focus and planning. 'I'm thirty-one. It's natural for me to be thinking about settling down.'

Lily nodded. 'Well, I'm glad for you. Corinne sounds lovely.'

'Thanks, Skinny. You'll be able to meet her soon. She's coming to stay in—'

Lily tripped on a tree root.

She gasped and he lunged forward, catching her by the waist. His hands closed around her slim figure and he felt a jolt. The feeling caught him by surprise as he stared into her beautiful green eyes.

'Christ!' he said, ruffled, though he didn't know why. His feelings for Lily were purely platonic. Once he might have fleetingly wondered about taking their relationship further, but that was a long time ago. He was a different man now. And he'd been lucky enough to have found the most perfect woman with whom to share his future. 'You almost broke your other arm!'

She shook his hands off. He frowned as she smoothed out her t-shirt and shorts. Her long brown hair spilled forward over her face but he could see that instead of being relieved or grateful, she was annoyed.

'You alright?' he asked.

'I'm fine.' She had always been like this: tough, independent.

So why did he feel a rip of irritation? Why did he feel like she'd just pushed him away? Again.

'Your button's undone.' He nodded to her shorts.

Her cheeks coloured up. 'I know.'

She tugged her t-shirt down to hide it.

'Aren't you going to fasten it?'

She looked away. 'I can't,' she muttered.

He frowned, then realised what the problem was and smiled. 'Ah. Your arm. You should have said. I can help you—'

'It's okay,' she said quickly as he stepped forward.

'Come here–'

'No!'

She held him off with the palm of her hand against his chest. He stared at it and at her fierce expression that warned him not to get any closer, and something snapped in him. 'For goodness' sake, Lily! Would it be that bad to accept help from me?'

'It – it's only a button,' she said, dropping her hand away. 'It's not important.'

His gaze lingered over the distorted skin on her cheek and jaw. She was so determined to take care of herself, yet so vulnerable at the same time. He wasn't sure how to behave around her. One minute they were back to their familiar teasing, the next they were arguing. And in the blink of an eye he switched from being angry to feeling protective. He contrasted this with the calm, rational relationship he and Corinne shared. So what was it about Lily that stirred him up like this?

Because she was his oldest friend. Because they went way back. Because he was frustrated by how awkward and strained their relationship had become when once she'd been like his kid sister. They used to be so comfortable with each other.

But that had changed after her father's death.

He thought back to when he'd visited her in that London hospital. He'd seen her once, but when he went back the next day he was told she didn't want visitors again.

At the time he'd been confused. And hurt. But mostly

he was concerned for her. In the months that followed he worried about what she was going through, and he'd grilled Mamie for every crumb of information she could give him about where Lily was and how she was recovering.

He'd missed her.

And though he'd got over it, he still didn't understand why she'd cut him off. Their friendship might have been put on hold, but thanks to Mamie the bonds hadn't been cut completely. And now he simply wanted them to be good friends again, and for things to go back to how they used to be.

Chapter Four

Lily lifted her head at the familiar squeak of Mamie's gate, and the sound was a welcome diversion from the turmoil she felt. Hearing Olivier speak about his fiancée had made her heart contract. The light in his eyes, the warmth in his voice – they had cut through her. She knew she should feel happy for him, and she did, she was. But she also felt so much more.

Her skin prickled uncomfortably. She tried to quash them, but emotions churned through her which she couldn't untangle and didn't like to acknowledge – even to herself. It didn't help that she'd been wrenched away from her work, her routine, that she suddenly found herself stuck in this place. She glanced around at the quiet olive grove and breathed in the scent of baked earth. This place with all its memories.

She faced Olivier. 'I have to get back,' she said, needing to put some space between them. 'Mamie's home. I'll help her unpack the shopping.'

'I'll come with you,' he said casually. 'I was on my way to see her. She wanted to speak to me about a job she needs help with.'

'Did she? Haven't you got things to do? I thought you were busy house-hunting.'

He studied her a moment before answering, and she

cringed. It sounded like she didn't want to spend more time with him – which she didn't. But if she made it too obvious, she'd have to explain why, and that she would never do. Never.

'I've got a couple of houses to visit later, but I'm on holiday, remember? Then again, you wouldn't understand the meaning of that, Skinny,' he winked, 'being a work-aholic as you are.'

She smiled. She *was* a workaholic, she was the first to admit it. But not many people were lucky enough to have a job they loved and which was as fulfilling as hers. However, her smile turned into a frown as they began to walk back towards the house. She wished she'd visited sooner, because she was really worried about Mamie's health.

'Oli, have you noticed that Mamie's looking a lot older all of a sudden? She wasn't so thin or tired last time I saw her.' Lily wondered if he knew anything; if there was something she didn't know.

'When did you last see her?' he asked.

'In February. I was here for a couple of days between trips. Does she look okay to you?'

He sucked in air and chose his words carefully. 'She's eighty-five, Lily.'

'I know. But she's lost weight, and she gets out of breath just going upstairs . . .' Lily closed her mouth and swallowed. Her eyes were filling with tears, but she blinked them back. She had never cried in front of Olivier Lacoste and she wasn't about to start now.

'If it's any consolation,' he said, 'Maman's been going

round more often, and Mamie often comes to eat with my parents.'

As they approached Mamie's garden, Lily lowered her voice. 'She hardly ate anything last night. Why is that? Is there something wrong? Something she's not telling me?'

'I don't think so,' he said calmly. 'Maman took her to see the doctor a while ago, but the tests all came back clear.'

She felt a jab of guilt that he knew more about it than she did. But then, Mamie was very dismissive about her health, and Lily was certain Béa would have had to push her to visit the doctor. It was a relief to know there wasn't anything seriously wrong, though.

Olivier went on, 'I'm sure it will do her the world of good to have you here for a while. She misses you.'

Lily nodded, feeling the twist of guilt. 'I wish I could do more. I should be the one looking after her, not the other way around.'

'Yes you should.' He held her gaze and for a moment she thought she detected reproach in his coffee-dark eyes.

'Why are you angry with me?'

'What makes you think I'm angry? I just agreed with you.' But the hard glint in his eyes contradicted his words.

She glanced up at the old farmhouse with its simple rustic beauty and quirky square turret, and she had to breathe deeply to try and contain her fear. If anything happened to Mamie . . .

'Look,' she said, 'I know you and your parents do a lot for her and I'm grateful. I really am. I don't know where Mamie would be without you.'

'We're glad to help, she's like family to us, but it's you

she really wants.' He pressed his lips together, and admitted quietly; 'Okay. Maybe I am angry. Why don't you come home more often, Lil?'

The fierce accusation in his eyes startled her. It was typical of him to be so direct but she wasn't prepared for the guilt that rushed through her. 'I visit as often as I can,' she mumbled.

'Really? She's your grandmother, she adores you, and as far as I can see you love her too – so why did it take this,' he pointed to her sling, 'for you to spend any length of time here?'

'I told you, I'm busy. My work takes me all over the world.'

'So does mine.' He paused to hold up a low-hanging branch so she could step under it. He followed.

'You are your own boss, you have people working for you. I'm freelance and still trying to make a name for myself. I can't afford to turn down any opportunity because I never know how long it will be before the next one turns up.'

'So you work constantly? All year round?'

'Pretty much.' He was only intensifying the guilt she felt already, but it was true: financially, she lived hand to mouth. 'I love my work. And . . . and I'm good at it.' She thought of the film prize she was hoping to enter: last year she'd had really positive comments from the judges advising her to submit again. But in order to get her name known she needed to win.

Whereas some of her friends from college had taken jobs in television studios and were filming inane game shows, her work was helping others, even if only in a small way. Her films made a difference to the lives of others, and that was what motivated her.

'You are good at it,' he agreed. 'Your films are exceptional . . .'

Exceptional? Her heart soared at the compliment.

'. . . But family's important, Lily. Nothing more so. You could have visited more, called more often—'

'I do call! I call every week.' No matter where she was in the world, or how difficult the communications, she always called her gran on a Sunday evening. As for visits, well . . . she sometimes dropped by – usually unexpectedly – but she admitted she didn't do so as often as she should. This place held too many reminders. She'd only been here twenty-four hours and already she was being assailed by memories. Lily didn't like to dwell on the past, it was dangerous terrain. She tried to always look forward. The next project, the next adventure.

Olivier didn't look satisfied with her answer. Everything she said seemed to be making him angrier, but she didn't know why. He might think she was lacking as a granddaughter, but Mamie had never reproached her for not visiting more often. Never. She had always been totally supportive of Lily's career and understood that it was the nature of her job that she travelled a lot.

He combed his fingers through his hair and said more softly, 'You could be a successful filmmaker and still come home regularly.'

'One day I hope I will be, but I'm not at that stage in my career yet. Besides, this isn't my home. Not really.'

His frown cut deeper. 'Where is, then? London?'

'No,' she said, thinking of her sparsely furnished bedsit. She'd never bothered to make it more comfortable because she spent so little time there. The memory resurfaced of the burnt-out shell which had once been the house she shared with her dad. 'I don't have one,' she said quietly. Her shoulders went back. 'I'm always on the road so I suppose nowhere and everywhere is home.'

He didn't reply. He didn't need to: she could tell from his face that he disagreed. But what did he know about her life?

Her solitary life.

She shook off that thought. Her career was enough. She was fine by herself.

'Mamie isn't getting any younger,' he ground out.

'I know that.'

'She's starting to feel her years. She would never say anything to you, but I think . . .' He pressed his lips together again.

'You think?' she prompted, and tensed. She adored her gran. Mamie was the only family she had left – well, the only family that counted – and if anything were to happen to her . . .

'I think it's a good thing that you're here to spend some time with her.'

His enigmatic words puzzled her, but there wasn't time to ask any more questions because they'd reached the entrance to Mamie's kitchen. Ever the gentleman, he gestured for Lily to go first, and she stepped inside.

Mamie was sitting at the kitchen table, her shopping trolley beside her, as if she'd come in and immediately sat down. Her face looked pale next to the purple silk of her dress, and her white hair was damp around her forehead.

Lily rushed over. 'Mamie! Are you okay?'

Her grandmother waved away her concern with a weak smile. 'Of course I am. Just getting my breath back. It's uphill, you know, that walk from the bus stop.'

It was uphill, but the bus stop wasn't far from her garden gate; only thirty metres or so.

'Tomorrow I'll get up early and go with you, okay? Promise you won't leave without me.'

'Don't be silly. I do it every day, and you need to rest,' Mamie nodded at her sling. 'You need to get better.'

'I want to go with you. Promise me,' she repeated.

'Well, it would be nice to go together I suppose . . .' Mamie's smile lit up her green eyes and it touched Lily's core.

She turned away and wasn't sure why she had to blink so rapidly to clear her eyes. 'Coffee, Oli?' she asked.

'Yes please.' He was unpacking Mamie's trolley, and from the way he knew where everything went, she had the feeling he'd done it before.

Lily picked up the packet of coffee again. This time she tried using a pair of scissors, but couldn't make them work with her left hand. She kept trying, holding them at different angles, but they stubbornly refused to cut.

Olivier glanced across. 'Why don't you let me make the coffee and you unpack the shopping?' he said, taking the packet and tearing it open in a fraction of a second.

It went against the grain to admit defeat, but she nodded and opened the bag of pastries Mamie had bought. They were from Raymond's *boulangerie* in the village and their buttery warmth rose through the air, filling the kitchen with its mouth-watering scent. Lily opened the fridge and picked out Mamie's homemade fig jam. She put it on the table along with butter, plates and knives.

'So where have you two been this morning?' asked Mamie.

'I was taking a walk around the olive grove when I bumped into Olivier.'

'It was always your favourite place,' Mamie said, smiling. 'Have you had breakfast, Oli?'

'Not yet. I'm starving.' He flicked a switch and the coffee machine began to gurgle quietly.

Lily bit into her croissant. 'I swear these taste more delicious every time,' she said to Olivier as he joined them at the kitchen table.

He shrugged. 'Same recipe. I keep making suggestions but Papa won't hear of changing anything.'

Mamie was spreading jam on a piece of bread. 'I'm glad you're both here,' she said, looking at them each in turn. 'I need your help with something.'

'Oh yes – the job you mentioned?' Olivier's eyes were warm with concern.

Mamie nodded. 'It's my studio. I want to give it a good clear-out.'

Lily stopped chewing. What did she mean, a clear-out?

And why was she including Olivier in this conversation? Last night she'd said she had a job for Lily. She hadn't mentioned that he would be involved too.

'I don't paint any more so I'd like to convert it into something more useful. Perhaps an office where you can work, Lily, if you like.'

'But Mamie, you've always painted!'

'Not for a long time. My hands are too unsteady now.' She looked down at them, resting on the wooden table. Her fingers were twisted, the joints swollen with arthritis and, now that Lily thought about it, it had been over a decade since she'd last seen her paint. She felt a tug of sadness, but Mamie's tone was calm and pragmatic as she continued. 'But I can't clear that room myself. I need your help.'

'Of course,' said Olivier, resting his elbows on the table. 'Tell us what you want us to do.'

Lily glared at him. Didn't he realise what a significant step this was – to box up and say goodbye to the profession, the talent, which Mamie had enjoyed all her life? It wasn't something to rush into.

'Mamie, this is a huge step. What if you miss the studio when it's gone? Even if you can't paint any more, you might enjoy spending time in there. Don't you think you should wait and think about it a bit more before you decide?'

'I've been thinking about it for a while and I've made up my mind,' Mamie assured her. She turned to Olivier. 'I want you to donate my easel and any materials you think are still useable to the local school. They have a wonderful art teacher, Bernard. His mother, Marie, is a good friend of mine.'

Olivier nodded.

'And the rest, the paintings, you can keep for yourselves or sell – it's up to you.'

'You don't want them?' asked Lily.

Mamie pinched her lips together and shook her head firmly.

'But you'll look through them first?'

'I don't need to. I'll give you the name of my agent, though he might not remember who I am any more. It's been years since we were last in touch.' She winked. 'You can tell him I'm – what do they call it nowadays? Decluttering!'

Olivier crossed the room and poured the coffee.

Lily nodded slowly. 'Well, I'll go up and take a look after breakfast.' Despite what Mamie said, she wanted to give her gran as much time as possible in case she changed her mind.

'And will you help, Oli?' asked Mamie.

He put three steaming cups down on the table and sat down again. 'Yes. I have an appointment at two thirty but I'm free until then.'

'I can manage,' said Lily.

'You can do it together,' said Mamie and she had a gleam in her eye that made Lily stiffen. She glanced at Olivier but he was calmly stirring sugar into his coffee, oblivious to her gran's mischievous scheming. 'After all, with your arm in a sling you're not going to be able to lift very much, are you, Lily?'

She cast Olivier another surreptitious look as she picked up her coffee. They would both be on top of each other in that room upstairs. Mamie was wasting her time trying to force them together like this. Her gran hadn't heard him in the olive grove earlier speaking about his fiancée, describing how perfect she was. She hadn't seen the tenderness in his eyes or heard the velvet of his voice, but Lily had.

She's pretty and clever and caring – that's what I love about her . . .

This was just going to make things awkward for Lily who needed her space and wasn't used to being confined to one room with a man who seemed to think he had the right to judge her. But, as Mamie had pointed out, Lily couldn't empty the studio alone. Her gran had always painted on large canvasses and they would be impossible to lift with one hand. However, she couldn't leave Olivier to do it by himself. Even though Mamie said she didn't want to keep anything, there might be paintings in there that had sentimental meaning and he wouldn't recognise those.

'I suppose not,' she said finally.

'Well that's sorted then,' Mamie said happily. 'Why don't you two take your coffees up now and make a start?'

They both got up, and Olivier headed for the door. Lily hung back, however, her fingers curled around the wooden chair she'd been sitting on. 'I'll be there in a minute,' she told him.

She waited until she heard his footsteps on the stairs,

then turned to her gran and asked softly, 'What are you up to, Mamie?'

'I don't know what you mean.'

'You're matchmaking, aren't you? You don't really want to sell all your paintings.'

She half expected her gran to smile and wink as she had done before, but instead Mamie dipped her head and her shoulders sagged. When she looked up again her eyes had greyed over like a misty rainforest. 'I do,' she said.

Lily faltered, shaken by her quiet insistence. 'You . . . you're sure?'

Mamie looked at her. 'I stopped painting when your Papa died, and I haven't been able to go in that studio since. I need . . .' She searched for the words, then gave up and said, 'It's time to let go of the past.'

Lily sank back into her chair and tried to absorb this. She didn't know what to say. She'd had no idea that there was such a clear reason why her gran had stopped painting. She'd just assumed it had been a gradual process, that Mamie had slowed down as the years had crept by. And the fact that Lily hadn't known made her feel terrible for not noticing. But she'd been in hospital at the time. Then she'd moved in with her mother.

It's time to let go of the past . . .

Her dad's face flashed up in her mind and her chest squeezed so hard it was difficult to breathe. She wasn't sure she'd ever feel ready to let go of his memory. But her grandmother's pain was there etched in the lines of her face, and Lily wanted to erase it. She wanted to help in any way she could.

'I see.' Her voice sounded raw and sore.

The fridge hummed quietly in the corner. Upstairs, she could hear Olivier's footsteps as he moved around the studio, the squeak of metal as he opened a window.

'I want you to clear the place out,' Mamie went on, 'and then Olivier will redecorate for me. But first I need you to go through those paintings, Lily. There's no one else who can do this for me; not even Olivier. There might be pieces in there which hold some meaning for you. And it will take time to sort through them. Time you don't usually have when you visit.'

Lily nodded, feeling the pinch of guilt again because her visits were always short.

Mamie reached across the table and cupped Lily's hands in hers. 'You did ask what you could do for me. This would make me very happy. Please.'

She looked up, shaken by the emotion in her gran's voice, and smiled. 'I understand.'

Though it had been closed up for years, the smell of oil paint still hit her as Lily walked into the studio and she paused a moment, transported back to when she was a child and she used to sit cross-legged at Mamie's feet watching her paint. Her gaze zeroed in on the easel. She pictured her gran perched on the stool, brush in hand, leaning into the canvas as she worked. Now it was empty, draped only in a couple of tattered cobwebs.

'Looks like it's been a while since this room was used,'

said Olivier, as he ran his finger along the top of a cupboard.

Lily stepped forward and her presence stirred the air, throwing up dust motes which glowed and spiralled in the shafts of sunlight. 'I know. I didn't realise how painful it was for her to come in here.'

He eyed her carefully. 'Is that what you were talking about just now?'

She nodded.

The studio was at the back of the house, with a square wall of glass which flooded the room with clear morning light. It bounced off the white walls, the ceiling and the whitewashed floor, dazzling her, and she remembered that Mamie always painted early in the morning for this very reason. *The light at that time has a pure quality about it,* she used to tell Lily. *Undistilled. In the afternoon or the evening it's different.*

Olivier began to lift the dust sheets, uncovering piles of canvasses propped against the walls around the edges of the room. She hung back, tense. She couldn't bring herself to touch anything.

'This doesn't feel right,' she said quietly. Although she understood Mamie's reasons for doing it, clearing out all her paintings seemed too – too drastic. Once they were gone, there would be no going back.

Olivier looked at her. 'It's what she wants.'

'But can't you see what a loss it will be to her, to part with this?'

'She doesn't see it that way. And you have to respect her decision.'

Lily nodded. 'I know. But she was so gifted . . .' She wandered over to stand in front of a canvas. It was a still life of aubergines and peppers against a pale background which gave it a modern, fresh feel. Lily tilted the canvas forward to see those behind it: hollyhocks painted in big splashes of colour; a basket of figs; a trellis entwined with climbing roses. She recognised all of these from around the garden.

'I think it's too soon,' she said.

'You want to wait till she's gone?'

His abrupt question startled her. She tried to swallow but her throat felt tight.

'You know what I think?' he said, crossing the room to stand in front of her. 'I think it's harder for you than it is for her.'

'Maybe.' She turned away, fighting tears. How did he always manage to make her feel selfish?

He touched her shoulder. 'You care about her, it's normal to feel the way you do. But you have to respect her wishes. She wants to clear this out and use the room for something else.'

'But she might regret it – when all the paintings are gone.'

He tilted his head to one side as he weighed this up. 'Maybe she's frustrated to have an empty room that she can't use any more, maybe it's worse for her to be reminded of the things she can't do any more.'

And of the people who were no longer here.

Lily nodded. Olivier was right, damn him. Why did he always see everything so calmly and logically – while she was always a fireball of hot and messy emotions around him?

'Do you want to keep them?' he asked.

She looked around at the stacks of canvasses. There were dozens of them. 'I don't know. There are so many and my place in London is only a studio. I don't have the space.'

Mamie's walls were covered with paintings like these, and Béa had several too. But to sell them all off . . . was so final.

'Let's look through them, and you can make that decision later. Come on, Skinny,' he said. 'Let's make a start. I've got a box here for things to give away, and a bag for rubbish. How about I hold the bag and you drop in it whatever you think can go?'

She looked around. 'Okay. We'll start with these oil paints,' she said, walking over to the trestle table. At one end it was covered in splodges of colour and tubes. 'They've dried out so much they're no use to anyone.'

She picked one up and dropped it into the bag he was holding. The tubes were sticky and left smudges of colour on her fingers. A dove called from the loft and she heard the flutter of wings as a bird flew out towards the olive grove.

When all the tubes were gone Olivier plucked a bunch of brushes out of the pot and ran his fingers through the bristles. 'Some of these look like they've never been used. Shall I put them in the box for the school?'

Lily nodded but as she reached for the rest in the pot, he moved too, and their fingers collided. She drew her hand back quickly as if she'd nicked herself, whereas he calmly picked up the pot of brushes and placed it in the box as if nothing had happened. Then he put the box down on the table and began to fill it with palette knives and scalpels, clearing that corner. She scurried away to the other end of the table where paper sketches were strewn all over. As she leafed through them, she snatched a surreptitious look at him and wondered why she was so affected by him? Why did the mere fact of being near him make her feel so on edge?

Any woman would be, she told herself. Anyone with blood in their veins would be aware of how his white t-shirt hugged his broad chest, and that rough beard of stubble emphasised his strong jaw.

Yet once upon a time he'd been just the boy next door. They used to be partners in crime, scuffing their knees together, running in the fields. Why couldn't it have stayed like that – plain and simple friendship? It would be so much easier for her if she could keep her distance, because being around him only nurtured these feelings she had for him. But how was she to keep her distance while they cleared out this studio?

From the loft above came the soft crooning of a dove, then the distant reply from outside. It was a repetitive song of call and answer. Two halves that made a whole, incomplete one without the other. Frowning, Lily tried to concentrate on the sketch in her hand. It was a pencil drawing of boats in the harbour: no colour, just the outlines of hulls lined up in a row. The sketch below it focused on the brow of a boat, the next on a mast, another on a coil of rope. They were rough sketches, pencil-drawn cameos, yet Lily could see how this was the preliminary detail which would make the complete painting so vivid. She wondered if Mamie had ever finished this canvas. Lily gathered a few of the sketches and looked around for a box to put them in, but as she turned, she bumped into Olivier.

She inhaled sharply, hit by another injection of heat from the contact.

'You know, you really don't need to stay,' she told him. 'I can do this by myself.'

'I don't mind.' He carried on picking up Mamie's tools, examining them one by one, and dropping them into the box.

'Really,' she insisted. 'I can manage, even with just one hand. I'm perfectly capable of putting things in boxes myself. And tomorrow we can make a start on sorting through the canvasses.'

He put the palette knife he was holding down on the table.

'You don't want me here, do you?' His voice was deep, loaded with bitten-back anger.

She bit her lip. 'I didn't say that . . .'

'But you were thinking it. Why?'

'Why what?'

'What's the problem, Lily? Tell me.'

'There isn't a problem. I'm just . . . a little emotional, that's all – clearing out Mamie's studio. It's like clearing out a huge part of her life.'

'I didn't mean that. I mean, what's your problem with

me? Because it's not just about clearing this studio, is it?' He folded his arms. 'You weren't happy that I picked you up at the airport, and you were uncomfortable when I sat next to you at dinner last night. In fact, let's be honest, you've avoided me for pretty much the last thirteen years!'

Her heart bumped against her ribs. 'Don't be ridiculous! Why would I avoid you?'

'That's exactly what I want to know.'

She stepped back, trying to put some space between them. The room suddenly felt too small and airless. 'I – I don't know what you're talking about.'

'Whenever I'm home you're either too busy to see me or something takes you away unexpectedly.'

'That's just been bad luck.'

'I don't believe in luck,' he said flatly. Then his tone softened. 'Since the fire you haven't been the same, Lil. Our friendship hasn't been the same.'

The room fell silent. Even the doves couldn't be heard any more. She swallowed and her cheeks heated. She hadn't expected such forthright questioning. But this was typical of Olivier. He'd never hidden from uncomfortable truths or wrapped things up in niceties. He was direct and honest. Blunt. And even now, when he was glowering at her, demanding answers she couldn't voice, she couldn't help but admire him for that.

'Why, Lily?'

Because her feelings for him were more than just friendship.

Of course she couldn't tell him that. He was engaged

to be married. If he knew how she felt, he'd be horrified. And she would be mortified.

'What did I do?' he persisted.

'You didn't do anything, and I haven't avoided you. You're imagining it.'

'I'm not. Whenever I come home they tell me you've just left. And at Christmas you always work it so that we're sitting as far apart as possible, you avoid speaking to me, you don't stay for any length of time.' He paused. 'We used to be friends. What happened, Lil?'

She glanced left and right but in this white room flooded with light there was nowhere to hide.

'Nothing,' she said finally, and looked into his dark eyes. 'We grew up, that's all.'

He dismissed this. 'Other friendships survive that. Why couldn't ours?'

She held his gaze. 'Maybe I changed more than other people.'

His eyes dipped to the scars on her left cheek and she pictured her face as she saw it in the mirror each morning: the raised, twisted cords and ripples of skin.

'I came to see you in hospital,' he said quietly. 'Do you remember?'

She did remember. Despite the heavy cocktail of pain-numbing drugs in her system, her heart had jumped at the sight of him.

Then shrivelled as she saw his expression. She hadn't accepted any more visitors after that.

'When I came back the next day, you wouldn't see me,' he finished.

'I didn't want to see anyone.' But especially not him. 'I didn't need your pity.'

The muscle in his jaw tightened. 'I didn't pity you.'

Heat rose up in her neck. 'You did! You took one look at my face and you – you couldn't speak.'

She remembered the tears which had shimmered in his beautiful brown eyes. He'd looked horrified. And she was horrifying. Back then, when her injuries were still red and raw, everyone had pitied her, even the doctors.

Uncertainty flickered across his face, then he frowned in acknowledgement that she was right.

'I don't know why you brought this up,' she said and turned away. She never talked about that time in her life, and most people were careful to steer away from the subject. They respected her silence.

But not Olivier. No. Maybe that was also part of the reason why she'd avoided him: because she'd been afraid he'd make her confront events and emotions she wasn't ready to face.

'I want to understand what went wrong. It's as if that fire came between us. Why?'

She wrapped her good arm around her sling protectively. 'I'm just not that kid who climbed trees with you any more.' Her voice was low and rough. 'I changed.'

The fire had changed her, and not just physically. Overnight, she had gone from being a carefree child to – to the woman she was now.

'No,' he insisted. 'There's more than that.'

Her chin lifted. 'There really isn't. You're imagining

things.' Her heart was beating so fast it made her veins hum. Sweat pricked the back of her neck.

She felt trapped here in this room, in this place, and she wished she could get away from him. If it weren't for her stupid injury she would snatch up her passport and jump on a plane.

Taking a deep breath, she thought of Mamie downstairs, and her pulse slowed a little, the knot in her brow loosened.

Her gran had asked her to do this one job for her, and Lily wouldn't let her down. This was a tiny ask compared to all that Mamie had done for her, all the years of love and support. She just had to try and keep cool around Olivier until the task was finished. It couldn't be that hard, could it? Avoiding him may have been her strategy for the last thirteen years, but it clearly wasn't going to work any more. He'd sussed her. And he was hurt. She hadn't intended that.

'Maybe it wasn't the fire that changed things between us,' he said softly.

Her head jerked up. There had only been one other landmark event in their friendship and the memory of it made hot, ragged emotions rise up and swamp her.

No. Please don't go there.

'Maybe it started before that,' he went on. 'When we kissed.'

Chapter Five

'Oh for goodness' sake, I was only fifteen!' Lily snapped. Then bit her lip as if she regretted it.

She was pale, her beautiful eyes suddenly too big and dark for her face, but Olivier was relieved that she remembered it. Relieved too to finally be confronting the elephant in the room. It had niggled for years that he'd handled it so badly and he knew they needed to get this out in the open. Only then would things go back to how they used to be between them. He desperately wanted to rekindle the easy friendship they'd once shared. It was still there – he glimpsed flashes of it when they shared a memory or an old joke, but it frustrated him that she was so tense around him. She always looked uncomfortable, as if she'd rather be anywhere but in his company.

'And I was only seventeen,' said Olivier. 'I wasn't mature enough to be able to explain—'

'You didn't need to explain anything.'

'—that I wasn't rejecting you,' he finished.

She gave a dry laugh and shook her head, cheeks blazing, and he knew she didn't believe him. And he could see how it must have seemed to her when he'd pushed her away with the words '*Non, Lily*'.

'You made it quite clear how you felt.'

'That's just it – I didn't!' He'd wanted nothing more than to kiss her. But she was too young, he was too young – he couldn't trust his own feelings. Back then he'd been a swarm of hormones and any attractive girl had caught his eye.

But Lily wasn't any girl. And he hadn't been brave enough to risk spoiling their precious friendship.

So he'd pushed her away, but he'd done it too clumsily and he'd seen the hurt in her eyes, the proud lift of her chin. She hadn't given him the chance to explain.

'You were too young, Lil – a child.'

The roar of a motorbike on the main road rose in a crescendo, then quickly faded. The buttery sunlight was building in intensity as the sun rose higher, and the air in the studio was thick and warm.

She squinted up at him curiously, as if his words surprised her. A silent current charged the air. She held his gaze as she said softly; 'Fifteen isn't *that* young.'

'What I'm trying to say is, I did what I thought was the right thing. Even if it didn't seem that way.'

She stared at him and all the things he hadn't said thirteen years ago burned his lips like an unspoken apology. How much he'd wanted to kiss her, how afraid he'd been of taking it a step further.

Lily cleared her throat. 'Well, that was a long time ago. And a lot has changed. You have Corinne now.'

'Yes. But you – our friendship – means a lot to me. We used to be close, Lil. Growing up, I was closer to you than I was to my brothers. You were like a sister to me.'

A strange look flashed through her eyes, but it was so

quick he didn't have time to identify it. 'Well, I'm here now,' she said quietly.

'Yes.'

'And I haven't avoided you . . .'

He realised with a jolt that he'd been distracted and had wandered from the very subject he'd raised in the first place. But he was relieved to have explained his actions of years ago. Perhaps now they'd cleared the air they could start again. A clean slate.

She flashed a resentful look at her sling. 'If anything, I've avoided being stuck in one place. Feeling trapped like I am here now.'

'Trapped?' He stiffened. In her grandmother's home?

Her eyes narrowed at him. 'You might dream of settling down, but small-town life is my worst nightmare. Being stuck in a village where everyone knows everyone else's business and nothing ever changes – it's stifling. I need variety in my life, adventure, challenge.'

He frowned. 'I see.' It made sense and he admired her adventurous spirit, he understood her need for challenge. But trapped . . .?

It was the same word Nathalie had used when he'd discovered her secret and confronted her: *What did you expect?* she'd said. *I couldn't let myself be trapped. My job means everything to me. I've worked hard for that promotion and I won't let anything stand in its way.*

'Why the dark look?' Lily asked. 'You look like you want to murder somebody.'

Murder. Good choice of word. 'I don't know what you mean.'

'Your fists are clenched and that vein in your neck is about to burst. Is it so hard for you to understand that not everyone wants the same life as you?'

She was right. He might hear echoes of his ex in her words, but Lily was not Nathalie. 'I do understand,' he said tightly, 'but I'm afraid you are "trapped" here, and we've agreed to clear this studio – for Mamie.'

'Yes.' She was still eyeing him watchfully, as if he were a dangerous animal. Then she pulled a strand of gleaming long hair forward and wound it thoughtfully round her fingers, and that tiny nervous gesture sent a stab of regret lancing through him. *Carry on like this, Lacoste, and your friendship will be history.*

He strode over to the window and made himself draw in a long slow breath. His muscles loosened a little as he forced Nathalie out of his thoughts. This was Lily he was dealing with, and surely they could perform this task for Mamie without locking horns? So she reminded him of his ex. So he regretted that she'd been AWOL for the last thirteen years. Wasn't that all in the past? The important thing was, she was here now.

'Do you want me to help?' asked Mamie, and nodded at the tomato salad on Lily's plate.

'I can manage,' said Lily. She was trying to cut the tomato slices with the side of her fork but it was infuriatingly difficult and slow, and she was hungry.

'Here, let me cut them up,' said Mamie, and reached over with her knife and fork.

Lily sat back, reluctantly conceding defeat on this small task.

'So how did you both get on this morning?' Mamie asked as she slid her plate back towards her.

'Oh fine,' Lily said vaguely. 'We made a start.'

'You didn't argue?'

'Why would we argue?'

'I don't know. I thought I heard raised voices.' Mamie chuckled. 'It made me think things were back to normal between you two.'

Lily ducked her head and concentrated hard on spearing a basil leaf. 'I don't know what you mean,' she muttered.

She didn't think things would ever be normal again between her and Olivier. Why had he insisted on talking about that kiss? He said he'd pushed her away because she'd been too young – and he was so honourable, she believed him. At the time she'd regarded herself as grown up, but she was only fifteen. However, none of this changed anything. Her feelings for him then had been unreciprocated, just like they were now.

You were like a sister to me . . . Although it cut through her, she had to accept that was all he'd ever feel.

'I'm going to lie down for twenty minutes,' said Mamie after lunch. 'Have a quick nap.'

Lily tried to hide her surprise. Her gran had never napped before. After meals she used to sit in the shade knitting or reading while she drank a strong espresso. 'Oh – alright.'

'Make sure you stay out of the sun. This is the hottest time of day. I don't want you getting sunstroke.'

Her lips twitched at the corners. 'Mamie, I'm not a child any more.'

Her gran smiled indulgently. 'I won't come down to find you doing cartwheels on the lawn, then?'

'You won't. I promise.'

Lily made herself a coffee and took it outside. A couple of tiny birds trilled as they chased each other in and out of the Mimosa tree, causing a flutter of leaves. From the top of an olive tree a dove called languidly. Lily flicked through a couple of magazines, and looked at her watch. Twenty minutes were up but there was still no sign of Mamie. She closed the magazine, got up and paced restlessly around the garden thinking about her conversation with Olivier earlier and how furious he'd been when she'd said she felt trapped. But she had meant it. How did people live like this? Stuck in a tiny village with neighbours who had no respect for boundaries and wandered into your kitchen, your life, asking difficult questions like *What happened to our friendship?* Refusing to accept her excuses, demanding answers that she didn't want to give.

She blew the fringe out of her eyes. She loved spending time with Mamie but she didn't know how she was going to survive two months of being trapped, so near Olivier. Being drawn into his life. Having to watch as he prepared for his future with the woman he loved. Her heart folded in on itself. That was the hardest part, harder even than not being able to work.

She went inside and returned the magazines to the rack in the lounge. Her eyes settled on the many photos that were scattered around this room: pictures of her grandfather whom she'd never known, of her dad and of her. Mostly of her as a child, though one or two were more recent: her graduation; her professional profile. Mamie was always asking for pictures of her, but there weren't any and that was how she liked it. Her place was behind the camera, not in front of it.

A silver frame caught her eye and she picked it up. How old was she in this one – four, five? She'd been in the olive grove when her dad had taken the photograph. She wore a white dress – she remembered she'd made a fuss because she hated wearing dresses – and she was bending to peer at an insect, though to the camera it looked like she was admiring a chunky white daisy. Beside her was the plastic wheelbarrow in which she'd collected snails. The photograph was romantic. Lily wasn't. She'd always been a tomboy, unable to sit still, chasing after adventure.

Her chest squeezed as she remembered her dad. He was such a great father. He'd doted on her, but never spoiled her. She remembered how she'd been upset once, distraught because her music teacher had written in her school report that she had no musical talent. It had been particularly galling because she'd worked so hard that year in her music lessons. Why wasn't she more like her mother? she'd sobbed.

Her dad had held her by the shoulders and told her that she was a brilliant and clever girl. She didn't need to be musical, he'd said, because she had so many other talents.

Like what? she'd asked, tears still streaking her cheeks.

That's what you need to learn for yourself. Remember, Lil: you can be anything you want.

It became her mantra: You can be anything you want. Her dad had given her the courage to try new things, to embrace new experiences – and in the end, ironically, she found her gift was very similar to his. Behind the lens of a camera.

Which reminded her. She put the picture down and tiptoed upstairs to her room. There she opened up her laptop, and searched online for a replacement camera. She didn't know how long it would be before she could use it, but having it with her would make her feel better. More in control. It might distract her from the storm of emotions that Olivier had whipped up.

Throwing herself into her work always calmed her, it helped her to focus and re-centre. She found the camera she wanted and placed the order. It was expensive but she hoped it wouldn't be too long before the insurance money came through. She bought a small hand-held one too; it might be easier to handle until she got the strength back in her injured arm. Next, she opened her email and scrolled down through her messages, cursing impatiently because it was so difficult to control the cursor with her left hand. But her mood lifted when she spotted a message from Maria in Colombia asking if she'd made it home safely. She replied that she was fine and hoped to return in September to finish filming if that was alright with Yolanda and the other coffee farm workers. Lily sat back in her chair. She'd keep in regular contact with the women in Colombia, and as soon as she was better she'd get back to filming again. Back to her job, the life she knew and loved.

She smiled. Why not begin to plan her return trip? Since she'd left, she'd thought of lots more ideas for her film. Typing as fast as she could with one hand, she began to make notes of scenes to film and questions to ask. She was so absorbed in her work she didn't realise that two hours had passed when Mamie appeared, looking refreshed and smelling of perfume.

'I wish I could help you with that,' said Lily, as Mamie snapped the stalks off green beans and dropped them into a colander. 'It's so frustrating having one arm in a sling!'

The two of them were seated outside beneath the pergola preparing dinner.

'The rest is doing you good,' said Mamie. 'And the more you rest, the quicker you'll heal.'

'I suppose.'

She loved this about Mamie: she was always accepting of what couldn't be changed. Whereas Lily was like her dad. Impatient. Restless. Eager to change things, to make them better, and she supposed that was at the heart of her work and all her films.

'Do you remember how you used to help with shelling the peas?' Mamie chuckled. 'Though when you were "helping" most of the peas disappeared into your mouth.'

'I thought if I did it quickly you wouldn't notice.'

'Oh I noticed alright,' said Mamie. Her eyes creased with quiet laughter, and her gnarled hands continued to snap the stalks.

The breeze ruffled the leaves above them, so that the shade shifted constantly and light flickered across Mamie's face, illuminating her hair with silver threads. Lily felt a rush of love for her, and wished she had a camera with her to capture her serenity and the beauty of this moment.

'Your father had his hands full with you,' Mamie said fondly. 'He used to complain that he couldn't turn his back for one second.'

The shriek of a seagull pierced the quiet afternoon. Lily stilled. How easily Mamie spoke about her dad. As if he'd just popped out to the shops and had only been gone a few moments. Lily couldn't even think about him without feeling a slash of pain.

'Was I a difficult child?'

'Not difficult. Just full of energy. And wilful.'

'That's not a bad thing, is it?'

'No, it's not. But when you were with Olivier you made a terrible pair. I don't know what it was about him, but he brought out the fighter in you. Whatever he did, you had to do better.'

'And vice versa. We were both competitive.'

'Competitive?' Mamie snorted. 'I've never known two people with so much rivalry between them.'

'I guess we rubbed each other up the wrong way.'

'Not at all – you got on so well.' Mamie looked up. 'Or have you forgotten that?'

Lily shook her head. No, she hadn't forgotten. She remembered clearly how in her room in London she used to draw a chart and count the days until her next visit here. She loved this farmhouse, she loved being with Mamie, but most of all she used to love seeing Olivier.

'Your dad always said that Olivier was the only friend who was your intellectual equal.'

Her dad had said that? 'He's all grown up and sensible now. I can't believe he's getting married soon.'

She felt the need to reinforce this, because Mamie still seemed determined to see them paired off together. Her gran tutted, as if to dismiss this fact.

'His fiancée sounds perfect,' Lily went on. 'They're obviously in love.'

'Pff!' said Mamie. 'Anyone can see she's a wet fish. She has no spirit.'

Lily raised her eyebrows, then shook her head and couldn't help but smile. Mamie was so obviously biased.

'His previous girlfriend had more backbone. She was a banker or something like that – an important job in the city.'

'Oh? What happened?'

'I'm not sure.' Mamie snapped the end off another bean, and reached into the bag to collect up the last few. 'We only met her once or twice – she didn't take much time off from her job – then it ended suddenly.'

'Why?'

'He wouldn't say. He wouldn't talk about it at all.'

Lily's curiosity was piqued. But she checked herself.

Whatever had happened, it was in the past and none of her business anyway. She was not going to get drawn into Olivier's life.

'Well, whatever your opinion of Corinne, it's clear that Olivier thinks the world of her.'

'Hmph.' Mamie dropped the last of the green beans into the colander and wiped her hands on the tea towel next to her. 'And what about you, Lily? Is there a man in your life?'

Lily looked away, avoiding her gran's sharp-eyed gaze. 'No. No one special . . .'

She thought of Theo whom she'd met when she'd spent time in the USA last year. It had been nice while it lasted and they still met up from time to time, but she hadn't shed any tears when they'd said goodbye and she'd boarded the plane out of New York.

The same could be said of all her relationships so far. There hadn't been many, but those she'd had had all been short-lived and nothing to write home about. In truth, she couldn't imagine how a relationship would ever be compatible with her nomadic life. Even friendships were difficult to sustain because she rarely stayed in one place long.

But that was a choice she'd made.

'You need someone,' said Mamie.

'Do I? I like my independence.' She hated the thought of having to explain or justify herself each time she wanted to make a trip. Alone, she could just grab her passport and go. Theo understood that. He respected her freedom.

'Still, you need someone in your life. We all do.'

Lily disagreed. Her life was just fine as it was.

The next day, Olivier arrived as Lily and Mamie were finishing breakfast and Lily's heart jumped at the sight of him.

Then she remembered how uncomfortable she'd felt in the studio with him yesterday.

'Ready to do a bit more tidying upstairs?' he asked her.

'I'll just finish my coffee.' Today she would stay calm. She wouldn't get flustered around him, and she wouldn't let the conversation veer into anything emotional. Just keep things neutral and polite, she told herself.

'Ah, so you've been to the market,' he said, spotting Mamie's shopping on the counter. He picked up a peach, and the delicate fruit looked tiny in his large hand. 'How was it?' he asked, before taking a bite.

'Busy as usual. But we got away before it got too hot, didn't we Lily?'

Despite the jetlag, Lily had set her alarm and made sure she was ready in time to accompany her gran. She'd helped by wheeling the trolley which had quickly been filled with jewel-coloured fruit and vegetables from the market. On the way back they'd stopped at the Lacoste bakery to buy a square of cold pizza for breakfast, and Lily was pleased that Mamie had eaten one too. Maybe her appetite was returning.

Lily and Olivier went up to the studio.

'Today we're going through the canvasses, right?' he asked.

She nodded and began to lift the sheets which had been draped over them as protection from the sun. 'I want to have a good look at them all before we decide what to do with them.'

'How about I move them and you tell me if there are any you want to keep?' he said, picking up the painting of aubergines. 'Then I'll group them by size. Small ones over here, large over there.'

'Okay,' said Lily.

The aubergines were soon joined by paintings of holly-hocks and olives in a basket, and Olivier moved around the room, propping them up carefully in tidy piles.

'I've been thinking about what we said yesterday,' he said.

Lily stilled.

'About how selling these paintings feels too final,' he went on. Her shoulders dropped with relief that he wasn't referring to their conversation about the kiss.

'Oh yes?' she said. 'Actually, I had an idea about that too. I've ordered a new camera and I was thinking that I could film the paintings – along with all the pieces which are here in the house and at your parents' house. That way Mamie will have a permanent record of them all.'

'That's a great idea.' His eyes lit up, and his approval sent sparks showering through her. 'The full collection on film.'

'Well, almost – she sold quite a few in the past which we have no hope of ever retrieving.'

'But I thought you couldn't film with your arm in a sling?'

'If you help me set up the tripod we could display each painting on the easel. I'll show you what to do.'

'You mean I'm going to be your gofer?' he asked, with that lopsided smile of his that made her chest squeeze.

She smiled. 'Something like that. It'll do you good, Chicken.'

'What's that supposed to mean?'

'You're the boss of your own company. I'm sure you have dozens of staff at your beck and call. A reality check won't do you or your ego any harm.'

'You're saying I have an ego?' He pretended to look affronted. Then he turned a thoughtful gaze on the canvasses. 'So when you've filmed them all, what will you do with the paintings?'

'Sell them, like Mamie asked.'

'But don't you think it would be nice to celebrate her career in some way? Perhaps we could put on an exhibition and display all her paintings here in St Pierre.'

'That's a fantastic idea! A retrospective.' What a fitting way to end her gran's career.

'If Mamie agrees, of course.'

He uncovered a stack of large canvasses depicting landscapes and Lily looked through them. There was one of a cove just along the coast from St Pierre, and another looking inland with trees in the foreground and hills in the background. The colours were punchy, the brushstrokes robust. Cypress and pine trees were painted with flecks of purple in the bark and blue or yellow in the leaves, the hills were mauve and pink.

'The detail in these is so accurate,' said Olivier. 'Did she use photos?'

'Never,' said Lily. 'She painted from memory or imagination.'

He lifted another sheet, revealing a painting of boats in the harbour.

'Wait!' Lily cried as he went to move it. She stepped forward to take a closer look.

'Wow! This is beautiful,' she said, running her gaze over the glossy finish which shimmered like the water it depicted.

The painting of multi-coloured boats and their reflections in the water was a dazzling spread of colour: egg-yolk yellow, vermilion, blue, white and emerald, shot through with silver reflections. It was so vivid, she could smell the fishy tang of the sea, she could hear the early morning clatter of the fishermen unloading their hauls onto waiting vans. Something stirred inside her. Mamie had captured not only the colours, but the spirit of the port. And although it had been tucked away in here for years, it felt timeless.

'We can't sell that one,' she said.

'Why?'

Couldn't he see? 'It's so . . . vibrant.' She couldn't put into words the emotions it sparked in her.

'You want to keep it?'

She nodded, yet it wasn't so much about wanting to keep it, as not being able to let it go.

'It is beautiful. But then, they all are.' Olivier took another look. 'I know why you love that painting.'

'Why?'

'The boat. Diving. It reminds you of your dad, doesn't it?'

'No!' she said too quickly, then glanced at it again, remembering their trips out to sea. Maybe he was right. 'Actually, yes, I suppose it does. I had forgotten about that.'

'Want to talk about it?'

'No.'

'He was a great guy–'

'I said I don't want to talk about him!' she snapped.

'Okay, okay!' He raised his hands in the air in mock surrender. After a long pause, he added, 'You know it's not good to bottle things up.'

'Stop interfering, Lacoste.'

'I have a small boat like that. I could take you out in it if you like?'

She pointed to her sling. 'I can't go diving. I can't even swim.'

'You can sit in a boat, can't you? We could go to the cove, take a picnic. Sunday maybe, when my brothers are free. It would be fun.'

It was years since she'd been to the cove. She remembered it as an idyllic place, sheltered by tall stone cliffs with a beautiful beach of white sand, and because it was only accessible by boat, they'd often had the place to themselves. The temptation to visit it again was too much.

'That would be nice,' she said, feeling guilty for having snapped his head off when he'd insisted on talking about her dad. 'Thanks.'

⋆

When Mamie called them down for lunch, Lily realised she'd been so absorbed in the task she'd lost track of time. Of course, Mamie invited Olivier to stay and eat with them and he accepted. But when he put the idea of the exhibition to her, and Mamie's reaction was one of delight, Lily felt a burst of joy, and she and Olivier shared a smile.

As they finished their salad, Olivier checked his watch. 'I'd better go,' he said. 'I have an appointment to see another house.'

'How did your visits go yesterday?'

He wrinkled his nose. 'They weren't suitable.'

'Neither of them?'

He shook his head.

'Why not?'

'With the first, the plot was too small, and the other one was too far away, too remote. I want to be near a village with a school and shops. I don't want to have a one hour drive through country roads before I hit civilisation.' His brow creased as he toyed with the glass of water in front of him. 'But I'm worried that perhaps I'm being too critical. I wish Corinne was here too.'

'Why don't you take Lily with you?' Mamie said cheerfully. 'Get a female perspective.'

Lily flattened her lips and frowned at her grandmother. Why did she persist in trying to lever them together? Hadn't she heard him speaking about his fiancée? About wanting to be near a village with a *school*? The thought of dark-haired miniature Oliviers sent a spike of emotion forking through her.

When she realised he was looking at her expectantly,

she laughed off the suggestion. 'Don't be silly. Choosing a house is too personal. I haven't even met Corinne – I haven't got a clue what she would like.'

'It would be good to have a second opinion, though,' he said. 'Someone to bounce ideas off. Sometimes you have to see beyond what's there to the potential of the property.'

'You don't need me to do that. Besides,' she said, giving him a pointed look, 'I want to spend time with Mamie.'

'We can do that later,' said her gran. 'I think you should go, Lily. Olivier is helping us with the studio, and this would help him in return. And what's more it will get you both out of my hair while I take a nap.'

Olivier leaned into Lily and said conspiratorially, 'Did you notice how she said that as if we're still five years old?'

Lily couldn't help but giggle. 'We're not that noisy, are we?' she asked.

'Only when you argue,' said Mamie with a wink.

Her gran did look tired, thought Lily. The lines around her eyes were more pronounced, and her pale cheeks were tinged with grey. Although spending more time with Olivier was the last thing she wanted, they had managed to stay civilised with each other this morning. And it was about time she got over her hyper-awareness of him. Perhaps exposure to him was exactly the remedy she needed.

'Okay then,' she told him. 'But don't blame me if you end up buying a rundown shack in the middle of an empty field.'

⋆

'So you'd live in a rundown shack in an empty field?' he asked as they drove away. They left the coast behind and headed for a forested area inland. The roads here were narrow and twisted sharply as they circled hills and rough woodland. Lily wrapped her hand around her sling to prevent it knocking the car door as another bend in the road made her lean to the right.

'It has been known. I can't afford to stay in hotels, and most of the time there aren't any where I'm filming.'

'So where do you stay?'

'It depends. Usually in the homes of the people I'm filming or working with.' It could feel like an imposition, but it was the best way to get to know them quickly and build trust. 'Or sometimes with someone local who is connected with the filming – an interpreter or a guide.'

'Either way it doesn't sound like five-star luxury.'

'It's not.' But that wasn't the point. Her films were all about understanding the people in them. In order to do that, she had to become immersed in their lives, she had to adapt and blend in and make herself invisible. Her own needs came last and she focused on the people whose story she was telling.

Ten minutes later they turned into a narrow driveway that snaked through spindly pine trees and overgrown shrubs littered with abandoned rubbish. Lily spotted a rusty bicycle, an upturned bathtub, the carcass of an old car.

'What did you say about a rundown shack . . .?' asked Olivier, as he cut the engine and peered up at the house. He cursed under his breath. 'The estate agent said it needed work – she didn't mention that it was a bombsite!'

Lily swept her gaze over the crumbling walls and a boarded window. The roof was jagged with broken roof tiles, and those which weren't missing lay at crooked angles. She told herself to keep an open mind, but it was difficult to block out first impressions of serious neglect.

'On the bright side,' she said, 'you should be able to negotiate a lower price.'

As she got out of the car, she spotted the shell of what had been a swimming pool at the side of the house: the water had been drained and moss and weeds had erupted, turning the blue tiles a murky shade of khaki.

They knocked on the front door and waited.

'I don't want to spend months renovating a house,' Olivier whispered. 'I want to get married and move in as soon as possible.'

She nodded, and tried to ignore the nick of pain his words caused. He was clearly besotted with Corinne, and Lily had to wonder what kind of woman his fiancée was to have cast such a spell over him.

'You have to do it in that order?' she asked.

'Yes.'

'Who'd have thought you were so traditional,' she teased.

He shrugged but she could see he was deadly serious about it.

Footsteps approached from the side of the house and

Lily tried to hide her horror as the owner greeted them, wearing nothing but flip-flops and a bathrobe which barely covered his generous rolls of hairy white flesh.

'*Bienvenue!*' he said, and waved a hand through the air in a theatrical gesture that implied this was a grand estate. He transferred his cigarette to his left hand before extending his right to shake Olivier's.

'The estate agent did warn you that we were coming, didn't she?' asked Olivier.

It was three-thirty in the afternoon, and the man's hair was uncombed, his eyes were bloodshot and bulged from his sweaty cheeks.

'Yes, I've been expecting you, Monsieur Lacoste.' He turned to Lily, flashing her a lustful smile. 'And you must be Madame Lacoste.'

Lily forced a polite smile to her lips as he took her hand. 'No,' she said. 'I'm just a friend.'

The man kept hold of her hand longer than necessary and shot her an appraising look which made her stomach turn, then he smiled. 'I expect you'd like the tour. Come!'

'We'll start with the kitchen,' he said, as he led them around the house and in through an open door. 'It needs updating, but it's a very good size,' he said proudly.

Lily's stomach turned at the dirty crockery which littered the surfaces, and dark stains splashed across the walls. A feral-looking cat jumped up onto the small table and sniffed a plate of half-eaten fish before stalking away, leaving it untouched. She contrasted this room with Mamie's traditional yet cosy kitchen which was well-scrubbed and always smelled of delicious food.

'As you can see, it has a lot of potential,' the owner went on, and led them through the dining room to a lounge.

There, Lily and Olivier looked around while the owner droned on, gushing about the property's age and perfect location. 'So what do you think?' he asked.

Lily couldn't find anything polite to say. It was impossible to see past the filth and clutter and the smell. She had stayed in mud huts, in makeshift cabins, in tents – but all those places had been swept and clean and carefully maintained. This, in contrast, was squalid. The whole place would have to be stripped and fumigated before new occupants could move in here.

'Can we see upstairs?' Olivier asked impatiently.

Lily glanced at him. His eyes were narrowed and his mouth was a flat line. He definitely wasn't impressed.

'Of course, but let me point out the original stone fireplace here,' said the owner, 'and note the quality parquet flooring—'

'Noted,' Olivier said impatiently. 'I'd like to see the bedrooms.'

The man's proud smile was wiped away. He turned hopefully to Lily. 'Perhaps Madame Lacoste would like to look around a bit longer?'

She shook her head. 'And that's not my name. We're not married,' she repeated, darting Olivier an embarrassed glance.

'Is that so? Well, people are more relaxed these days. I bet you can picture yourself living here. There's plenty of room for a family too. Come. Let me show you upstairs!'

'Can't wait,' Olivier muttered under his breath, as they followed him into the dark hall.

'You'll see that this house is a potential goldmine,' boasted the owner, breathless, as he climbed the stairs.

Olivier hung back and whispered to Lily. 'I've seen pigsties that were cleaner.'

She suppressed a giggle, then had to avert her eyes against the flashes of naked flesh the man exposed as he wheezed his way up ahead of them.

The owner patted the bannister. 'See this staircase? Solid oak.'

'It's definitely not solid,' Lily whispered, 'I can hear the woodworm munching.'

'And the woodlice,' Olivier added, and ran his fingertips up the back of her neck like a crawling insect. She giggled and batted his hand away. It was like they were kids again.

In the master bedroom the owner turned to Lily. 'What do you think, Madame? Can you see yourself living here? The views are incredible . . .'

She eyed the unmade bed with its stained sheets and had to swallow down her revulsion. 'The view is lovely,' she said politely. It was just a shame about the rest.

Olivier strode across the room and inspected the wall more closely. 'I see you have a problem with damp,' he said, nodding at a large patch of grey mould which had spread down from the ceiling into the wall behind the bed.

'Oh that. It just needs a lick of paint, that's all.'

'Or a new roof perhaps?' Olivier suggested. 'That might be where the water's getting in.'

The owner waved his hand through the air dismissively. 'There are a few tiles loose, that's all. It's not a big job to fix.'

'No. Of course it isn't. I could probably do that myself.' Olivier winked at Lily and she had to turn away to hide her smile.

Chapter Six

Ten minutes later they drove away laughing.

'That house was hideous!' said Lily. 'Tell me you're not thinking of buying it?'

'It's out of the question. I'm not sure I could ever get rid of the smell.'

'Or the memory of him wearing nothing but that dressing gown.' She shuddered.

Olivier felt a ripple of disgust remembering the lascivious look the man had shot her. He'd wanted to punch the guy. No one should look at a woman like that – especially not Lily.

'You mean you didn't find him attractive?' he teased.

She grimaced, and Olivier smiled. He should be furious with the estate agent for even suggesting they visit that house, but he was buoyed up by the fun he and Lily had had. It was as if they'd gone back in time, back to the closeness they used to share and he was surprised by what Lily brought out in him. He ran a successful business and carried the weight of all the pressures and responsibilities that involved, but it seemed that beneath it all the mischievous child in him still lurked, and he was thrilled by that discovery. There was nothing like an old friend to remind you who you were.

'He wants a ridiculously high price for it. Even the estate agent said it was overpriced.'

'Dare you to show Corinne that house. Dare you to tell her that's the one and that you love it for its potential and beautiful views.'

'I don't think so.'

Her smile vanished and a tiny frown flickered across her forehead. 'You never turned down a dare in the past. What's wrong? You're too old for a prank now?'

'It's just not the kind of relationship we have, Corinne and me.'

'What kind of relationship do you have?'

'Mature. Sensible. Steady.' Okay, saying it like that, it sounded a bit dull. But those virtues were what made it a solid relationship. The kind that would last.

'She wouldn't see the funny side?'

He pictured Corinne's reaction. She'd be horrified. He wasn't even sure she would have agreed to step inside a place so unhygienic. Unlike Lily who was game for anything. 'No.'

'Have you got any others lined up?'

'A few. To be honest, though, it's becoming a worry that I can't find anything suitable. I'm beginning to wonder, am I being too fussy? It's not as if money is a problem.'

In his work he demanded perfection of his staff. Perhaps he was expecting too much. Yet he couldn't let go of the dream house in his head, the perfect place where he'd raise his family and his kids would know the happy childhood he'd enjoyed. Was that too much to ask?

'So what is it like, your dream house?'

'Big enough to house a family but not so big it feels like a museum.'

'With a state-of-the-art kitchen, I expect.'

'Not necessarily. I can modify what's there to suit me.'

'Town or country?'

'Near a village or town but with lots of privacy and space around it for a garden or an orchard – or an olive grove,' he added wryly.

Her eyes widened with curiosity. 'You're looking for something like your parents' house, aren't you?'

He considered this. He simply wanted his children to have the same freedom he'd had growing up. 'I suppose I am, yes. Is that asking the impossible?'

'Not necessarily. If you're patient, the right one will come along and you'll just know when you find it that it's The One.'

'I'll just know?' he said dryly. She might believe that, but in his mind choosing a house had to be a rational decision, not one made on nebulous notions of gut feeling.

'Definitely.' She nodded. 'It will just feel . . . perfect.'

He shook his head and laughed affectionately. 'I prefer to use logic. I have a list of criteria and it needs to match them all. Or nearly all of them.' Trouble was, nothing so far had come even close.

'Whatever. But something will come along, I'm sure of it.'

His hands gripped the wheel. 'I don't want to waste any more time. Corinne and me – we want to start a family.'

'So you said, but what's the hurry?'

'Why waste time when we both know what we want?' He'd already wasted two years of his life with Nathalie. But that experience had made him realise what was important to him.

'Oli,' Lily said carefully, 'don't you think you're rushing into this?'

'Into what?'

'Marriage, children. You only met Corinne four months ago.'

'So? It works. We're right for each other.'

'But it's so soon–' She turned to look at him as if a thought had suddenly occurred. 'She's not pregnant, is she?'

'No.'

'In that case, why not take your time? Maybe move in together and see how it goes?'

'Because this is what I want – what we both want. Family is important to me.'

It might be hard for Lily to understand when she didn't value family in the same way – she never came home, she'd said she didn't even think of this as her home – but with Corinne his future was clearly mapped out, and that thrilled him. And perhaps it was because he could see his own future so clearly that he worried about Lily. He worried that she was so alone, that she'd chosen such a solitary path, focusing only on her career. A career wouldn't keep her warm at night, it wouldn't take care of her in difficult times, it wouldn't give her the love she deserved.

'We've given it a lot of thought and we both agree that marriage is the next logical step in our relationship.'

'The next logical step? You're talking about it as if it were a project or – or a business decision. You can't apply logic to relationships!'

'Of course you can. It's about compatibility.'

'Matters of the heart are about love, not logic.'

'I love her.'

There was a long pause. Then, 'Still, you hardly know her. You can't after four months.'

'Well I do,' he said impatiently.

'Really?'

'Yes really.'

'What's her favourite food, then?'

'Apples.'

'Apples? Seriously?'

'Why the incredulous look?'

'Because most people love chocolate or donuts – something wicked and indulgent!'

'She's a nurse, remember? She tries to stay healthy.'

'So what does she make of your baking? Your éclairs? They're to die for!'

'She's never tasted them. She doesn't eat refined sugar.'

Lily gasped. 'You're jok–' She cut herself short. 'You're not joking, are you? Wow, that's one hell of a strict diet. Is she diabetic? Does she have a heart condition?'

'No and no. She's just health conscious.'

She studied him a moment longer. 'Fine. Moving on, what are her favourite flowers?'

'Roses – I think.' He racked his brain. 'Or maybe tulips. Yes, tulips.'

'Star sign?'

'You know I don't believe in that nonsense.'

'Okay, then. What does she dream of, what does she want more than anything in the world?'

'Er – me? To be a mother?' He wasn't sure. Lily's questions were causing an uneasy chill to creep up the back of his neck.

'As a five-year-old, what did she want to be when she grew up?'

'That's not fair! How would I know that? And why does it matter what she wanted when she was five?'

'Because these are the little details that make a person. Their hopes and dreams, their achievements, all the things that have shaped them and are important to them.'

He frowned, but told himself there was no reason to worry. He and Corinne wanted exactly the same things. Their future together was all mapped out. He just needed to find a house.

'So what do you wish for more than anything in the world, Skinny?'

'To win the One World Film Prize,' she said without hesitation.

'And when you've done that?'

'To make more films – films that will make a difference.'

There was no doubt in his mind that she'd succeed in this. He knew how talented she was, how moving her films were. 'Is it all about work? You don't want to have a family somewhere along the line?'

'I've no plans to.'

'You say that now, but when the time is right, when you meet the right man . . .'

She raised a brow. 'Are you assuming because I'm a woman that's what I'll want – to marry and settle down?'

'That's not what I assumed at all,' he said grimly, and thought of his ex, Nathalie, who hadn't wanted a family because it would have jeopardised her career and her ambitions. Who'd been more selfish and mercenary than he could ever have imagined.

'I love the life I have. Being able to up and go whenever I feel like it, wherever the job takes me. Seeing the world, learning about the different ways people live. It's endlessly fascinating. It teaches us new perspectives. You should try it some time.'

His jaw hardened. 'When I travel with work the best part is coming home. I like to feel grounded – like I do when I come home to St Pierre. Where everyone looks out for each other.'

'Haven't you ever felt the thrill of boarding a flight to an unknown country, of disembarking in a foreign culture with its own traditions and codes of etiquette and ways of doing things which are completely alien and new? Can't you imagine the sense of wonder it inspires?'

He shook his head, but she hardly noticed. Her eyes had taken on a dreamy expression and they glinted like mossy jewels. He could hear the passion in her voice as she went on. 'My job is an endless adventure. Each day I wake up wondering what the day will bring, which new insights the people around me will reveal, which beautiful scenes I'll capture on camera.'

'You feel that way now but will you feel the same way in ten years' time?' he asked, casting his mind back over his own career, and the passion he'd once felt for baking. It was what had driven him to push himself, to learn from the best, to be the best. He was competitive by nature, but having established himself, what was he supposed to aim for now he'd achieved his goals and made his name? He thought of Raymond who was content to own just one bakery and stubbornly refused to retire. How was he still so committed after all this time?

Olivier didn't have any answers. All he knew was that the most important goal for him now was to marry and start a family.

'I'll never tire of it,' said Lily. 'There are endless more places to visit, infinite stories to tell. To be restricted to one place, one life would be like being chained to a post.' She gave a little shudder and turned to him. 'You know, people around the world look and live so differently, and yet they're so similar. That's what intrigues me the most in my work. They all want the same thing.'

'What's that?'

'To be safe, and to be with their loved ones.'

He thought of her rare visits here and arched a brow. 'Except you.'

She stiffened, and a pained expression flickered in her eyes before it vanished. 'I suppose I'm married to my job and making films,' she conceded quietly.

'But when you're travelling don't you miss home? Miss

the people who matter in your life? I know I do when my work takes me away.'

She didn't quite meet his gaze. 'Just as you want a house and a family, so I want to travel and make films. We simply want different things. When I stay in one place I get itchy feet.'

Olivier kept his eyes on the road but his jaw pulsed with bitten-back anger. He didn't like this side of her, but not because he expected women to be tethered to the kitchen sink. Because family was precious, it was to be treasured, and it made his blood boil that she didn't appreciate that. Just like Nathalie, she put her career before everything and everyone else.

They'd had fun together this afternoon visiting that house of horrors, but hearing her speak about her work highlighted how much they'd grown apart. The more time he spent with her, the more it drove home their differences.

But that didn't matter. He focused his thoughts on Corinne and felt the familiar rush of affection, the welcome sense of being grounded again. He and Lily might disagree about this but thankfully he and Corinne shared the same priorities.

As he dropped Lily outside her home he said, 'Mamie looks a lot better, don't you think?'

Her brows knotted and her eyes misted with concern. 'She's still very tired.'

'But she's brighter since you came home.'

'Is she?'

'Definitely.'

'What are you saying, Lacoste? Is this leading to another lecture about how I should stay home more?'

'There was no hidden message, Skinny. I'm just saying that she looks well.'

'I can't talk long,' said Corinne down a crackly phone line. 'I have to leave for work soon. But I've seen a great venue for the wedding reception.'

Olivier looked out over the olive grove. The leaves glinted silver in the sun as the breeze caressed them, and olives dripped from the trees like precious gemstones waiting for summer to tip into autumn. This year's harvest would be bountiful – providing Mother Nature didn't spring any nasty surprises between now and then. 'I thought you liked the chateau we visited?' It was an hour's journey from the city but they had agreed it was really special.

'I do, but this hotel is only a ten-minute walk from the church, so although it's not as romantic as the chateau it will be much easier for our guests to get to. And cheaper too.'

He smiled, loving how practical she was. She wasn't making ridiculously lavish demands like some people would. 'That's good. Hopefully by the end of this summer we'll have found a house and then we can get a date in the diary and book all these things.'

'Yes,' she said fondly. 'How are you getting on with house-hunting?'

He decided there was no point in telling her about the house he and Lily had visited today; it had been so terrible it was best forgotten. And perhaps, if he was honest, he was also a little embarrassed about the childish fun they'd had.

'I've got a couple of appointments to visit houses tomorrow,' he told her instead. 'One of them comes with a large plot of land. It means we could extend it and still have space for a nice garden.' He pictured a swing and a pool, maybe a treehouse too.

'Sounds great. Have you seen Lily? Did you manage to spend some time together like you hoped?'

'Yes. Mamie's asked us to clear out her studio, so we've made a start on that.'

'Was it good to see her again?'

He hesitated, thinking of how Lily's career focus grated on him, how her scars unsettled him, how her teasing smile woke something in him, a lightness and a sense of fun he'd forgotten existed. Yet at the same time he was unnerved by the chaotic jumble of emotions that she sparked in him. Thank goodness that with Corinne his feelings were clear and uncomplicated.

'Yes,' he said finally. His voice softened. 'But I'm looking forward to seeing you.'

'So am I. Not long now,' she said, and he heard the smile in her voice, but he also heard the buzzing of her pager. 'Sorry – better go!'

'Oh, I nearly forgot to tell you,' Mamie paused from putting on lipstick in preparation to go out and meet friends, 'Olivier called earlier.'

Lily was trying to eat cereal but finding that her left hand couldn't keep the spoon straight enough to prevent the milk and cornflakes slipping off before they reached her mouth. 'Oh yes?' At the mention of his name she felt a shot of heat, as if she'd walked outside into the dazzling morning sun.

'He said he'll be a bit late this morning because he's helping in the bakery. One of Raymond's staff called in sick.'

Lily pushed away her bowl, giving up on the cereal. 'I expect Saturday is their busiest day.'

A bubble of joy rose in her as she remembered how much fun they'd had visiting that awful house yesterday – but it hadn't taken much for them to fall back into arguing again. Perhaps she shouldn't have commented on how new his relationship with Corinne was. But then, he didn't hold back from criticising her about how career-focused she was or how little she came home. Came *here*, she corrected herself.

'It is,' said Mamie, and dropped her lipstick in her handbag. 'I doubt whether he'll have time to help with the studio today. By the way,' she said, stopping suddenly as if she'd just remembered, 'when I went past the studio yesterday I noticed you've put two paintings apart from the others.'

'Yes. I really like them. I thought I might keep them – is that alright?'

'Of course! I told you, you must do whatever you like with them. I don't need the money. What interested me,' her gran continued, 'was which paintings you picked out. The olive grove – why that one?'

'It reminds me of all the times I played there as a child.'

'And the fishing boats in the harbour?'

'I don't know, but I really love that painting. I just couldn't bear to part with it.'

Mamie's eyes lit up as she smiled. 'I painted that when you were born and I'd been to see you for the first time.'

'Really?'

'Yes. I knew you were going to be a little adventurer.'

Lily laughed. 'How could you know?'

'Gut feeling,' Mamie shrugged. 'Can't be explained, but I'm rarely wrong about these things.'

'So – what is the significance of the boats? The harbour?' Why did that painting speak to her? What had Mamie been thinking of when she painted it? Was Lily like those boats? Dropping anchor here in the little port, but restless in the water, never static, always ready to sail off on a new dawn and start a new adventure.

'Oh, a painting doesn't need to have an explanation. We each interpret them in our own way, and sometimes we respond on a visceral level. They provoke an emotional reaction. We don't need to analyse it, but simply enjoy it. And accept it.'

Lily nodded her understanding. When she was editing her films she didn't follow a plan but let her instinct guide her. She put clips together because it felt right, and usually some kind of order or story emerged of its own volition.

The loud hoot of a car horn made them both look up.

'That's my lift,' said Mamie.

'Who are you meeting?'

'Oh. Just a friend.' Did she sound a little cagey? Lily

peered more closely at her gran. Was it her imagination or were her cheeks flushed?

'Are you sure you don't mind collecting my prescription from the pharmacy? It'll be ready after nine-thirty.'

'Of course I don't mind,' said Lily. It was the least she could do to help.

'Right – well, I'll be back for lunch.'

'Have fun!' she called as her gran hurried away and the gate creaked shut.

She trudged upstairs and pushed open the door to the studio. The blinds were down, casting shadows across the room and over the box containing the new cameras which had arrived the previous day. She wondered how long it would be until Olivier finished at the bakery. He might be tired, he might decide not to stop by today. Her stomach sank at the prospect. The house was quiet without him around.

That thought made her stop, horrified at herself. Was she missing him?

She glanced at the delivery boxes again, then crouched down and began to prise them open. She wasn't going to sit around waiting for him. Thinking of the women in Colombia, she picked up the small hand-held camera, switched it on, and fiddled with the settings. Then she held it up with her left hand. If she practised, who knew – perhaps she could get used to working left-handed. She craved the pleasure of filming, of doing what she was good at. So she wound her way through the house filming the lounge with its large, empty fireplace which Mamie must have cleared for Lily's benefit, the kitchen with its cosy clutter of day-to-day living, the garden and the sound of seagulls calling and the wind rustling the olive trees.

But when she sat down in the shade and replayed it the picture was unsteady, the camera pitched and rolled, and the effect was worse than amateur. And that was with the small, lightweight hand-held camera; there was no hope of her being able to use the full size one.

She bit her lip against the frustration and glared at the trio of seagulls circling high above the palm tree, three lofty white arcs in the indigo sky. She knew she was wishing for the impossible, but if only her arm would heal quicker. She felt like a caged animal, trapped and tetchy.

And why hadn't Maria answered her email confirming that it was okay for her to come back in September?

It had only been two days, she told herself. Maria was probably just busy working on a new job, or maybe she hadn't seen Yolanda to check with her.

Glancing at her watch, Lily remembered her promise to collect Mamie's prescription. She grabbed her purse and made her way down to the village. As she passed the ice cream kiosk, the stallholder waved and beckoned her over. 'Lily Martin,' he grinned affectionately.

'Monsieur Arnaud!' she smiled. 'You remember my name?'

'How could I not? You and the Lacoste boys used to be my best customers.'

'Well your ice cream was delicious.'

'Still is.' His smile faded to a look of concern. 'I heard you had a bad accident. How are you?'

She instinctively lifted a hand to her cheek, but he nodded at her arm.

'Is it healing well?'

'Oh. Yes, it's getting better – slowly.' Too slowly for her liking, but as she spoke she realised that the pain had subsided considerably and she hadn't needed any pain-killers for the last couple of days.

'I'm glad. Your grandmother worries about you.'

'Well I'm home now, and she's taking good care of me. If she carries on feeding me so well, I'll be the size of a house.'

'She's a talented cook, is Simone. Her plum tart is the best I've ever tasted–' he shook his head sadly, 'but she won't give me the recipe, you know.'

Lily smiled. 'She's always been secretive about her recipes. How are your children?' She remembered he had a boy and a girl, a little younger than her.

'Oh they're all grown up now and I'm going to become a grandfather soon. You might have bumped into Anne-Marie already?'

'No,' said Lily. 'I haven't been back long.'

'Well she and her husband run the new *crêperie* on the port – pop in and say hello if you have time. I recommend their chocolate and hazelnut pancake,' he winked and leaned forward across the counter glancing left and right before adding, 'It's even nicer than my ice cream – but don't tell her I said that!'

'I'll look out for it.'

'It's lovely to see you, Lily. And say hello to Olivier!'

The smile vanished from her lips. Just because they'd

run around together as children, why did people assume they were still a pair? 'I will – if I see him.'

'Of course you'll see him. Aren't you clearing out Simone's studio together?'

Lily blinked. He knew about that? Was there no privacy at all round here?

Olivier parked his car at home, scooped up the white cardboard box from the passenger seat, and walked through the olive grove to Mamie's garden. Lily was standing near the gate, looking up at the dovecote, a tiny camera in her hand. She was wearing the same scruffy denim shorts as yesterday and flat sandals, and he remembered how, as a girl, she'd hated wearing skirts or dresses. She'd only been back a few days but her long legs were already the colour of honey. At the sound of his feet crunching on the gravel path, she whirled round, eyes wide with fear.

'Oh – it's you!' she said, shoulders sagging with relief. 'You startled me.'

'Hello Skinny. Why are you so jumpy?'

'I – I don't know. You have a habit of creeping up on me, that's all.' Her gaze slid away from his and she glanced at her bandaged arm.

There was something vulnerable about the look in her eyes and he felt a tug of concern. 'Maybe I should wear a bell round my neck like next door's cat – that way you'll hear me coming.' He was pleased that his words made her smile and chased away the grey in her eyes. 'What were you filming? The roof of the house? I hate to break it to you, Lil, but I wouldn't pay to watch that movie.'

She rolled her eyes. 'I was filming the doves. I'm practising using my left hand, but it's no good. I don't have anywhere near as much control as with my right.' She put the camera down on the table and flexed her arm and fingers.

'That's perfectly normal,' he said. 'Is it so compulsive – the need to film?' Couldn't she just let it go and enjoy having a couple of weeks off?

Her green eyes flashed. 'It's what I enjoy. And you never know, it might come in useful some time, to be able to use my left hand. So how did you get on at the bakery? Were you up at the crack of dawn?'

'Yep. Three am. You hungry?' He nodded at the box in his hands.

'Starving. I didn't have much breakfast.'

'Good. I brought cake.' He opened the box to show her. '*Religieuses*.'

She peered at the choux pastry cakes glazed with a coffee-flavoured ganache and filled with *crème pâtissière*. 'Delicious! I'll get plates.'

He followed her inside and put the box down on the kitchen table. She set out plates and he carefully placed a cake on each one. 'Forks?' he asked.

She went to open the cutlery drawer, but stopped suddenly and turned around.

'Just hands?' she challenged, with a gleam in her eye.

He sighed. 'Do you know how long it takes to make one of these? How much skill and care?'

Her smile only broadened. 'You can't eat a cream cake with a fork – not if you want to get the full experience.'

'Is that right?' He sounded doubtful. 'Or is this because you haven't mastered using cutlery with your left hand?'

Her chin went up. 'What's wrong, Chicken? Worried you'll make a mess? It never bothered you before.'

'You are such a bad influence, Lily Martin.' He pushed a plate towards her, and took the other for himself. 'Fine,' he said, rising to the challenge. 'On the count of three.'

She nodded and they picked up their pastries. Lily licked her lips in anticipation as she eyed the ganache and the golden pastry.

Olivier shot her a crooked grin. 'Three, two – one!' He stuffed it in his mouth and Lily followed suit. The explosion of coffee and cream in his mouth was visceral, and he pushed out of his head thoughts of what Corinne would say if she saw him now.

Across the table, Lily giggled and closed her eyes as she took another greedy mouthful. She was right. This was the way to truly savour a pastry, devouring it, relishing every bite of it – just as they had done as children. Olivier finished his first, but by then they were both laughing so much she had tears in her eyes.

'You see?' she said. 'It tasted so much better without a fork.'

'Infinitely better.'

He took a couple of steps closer. 'You have cream – there' he said, and touched his finger to her cheek.

She froze under his touch, and he suddenly regretted stepping so close. But he was there now, so he wiped the cream away, trying to behave as if he hadn't noticed her reaction. Lily looked up at him, her green eyes large and wary. He stood there a moment, the cream on his finger, his gaze still fixed on her cheek, just above the scarred skin. But he wasn't looking at that: he was distracted by the delicate slope of her cheek, the curve of her lips–

He blinked and thought of Corinne.

'I'll – ah – I'll just wash my hands,' he said, his voice rough around the edges.

Lily nodded. She put the plates in the dishwasher and when he'd finished drying his hands, she said briskly, 'Right then. Shall we get to work?'

'Good idea,' he said, trying to sound enthusiastic, feeling perplexed by the moment of awkwardness.

He'd completely lost the thread of his thoughts for a moment there. What had been the matter with him? And why did Lily freeze every time he came near her? She'd done the same in the studio and when she'd tripped in the olive grove the other day.

She headed off towards the stairs, calling over her shoulder. 'My new camera arrived. You can help me unpack it.'

In the studio he set up the tripod and lifted the camera on to it. It was heavy and he wondered how, even without a broken arm, she managed to carry it for long periods of time. Then again, Lily had always been stronger than she looked.

He propped the first canvas on the easel, but she shook her head. 'The easel needs to go further back. Look,' she said, inviting him to peer through the camera.

He looked and indeed the outlines of the window cast a grid of lines over the oil painting.

'Can you see how the shadows fall across the painting?'

'But if I move it back, it will all be in the shade,' he said.

'That's okay. I can adjust the camera for white balance.'

'White balance?'

'Light,' she explained.

'Right,' he said and moved the easel.

She bent to look through the camera again, pressing buttons and making adjustments, concentrating as she worked. Finally she was satisfied and made the recording. He lifted the canvas down, replaced it, and she repeated the process.

As they worked, he told her about the rude awakening he'd had from Raymond earlier. '. . . So at three o'clock this morning he came in and woke me. "*You must come and help!*"' he said, imitating Raymond's Provençal accent. 'I opened one eye and I said: "*Say please*".'

'You didn't!' Lily's eyes danced with delight.

'I did,' he said. '"*I'm your father,*" he said. "*And I'm your son*" I said, "*You can still be polite.*"'

Lily giggled. 'Left a bit,' she instructed, and he nudged the painting of olive trees along until she nodded her approval and ducked behind the camera again. 'What did he say to that? I can't imagine he was best pleased.'

'His exact words were "*Nom d'une pipe!*" So I said, "*Fine, I'll go back to sleep then,*" and I rolled over. He made a growling noise, then he shouted "*Please!*"'

Lily laughed. 'You're both as stubborn as each other.'

'We're really not,' he said, offended by this. 'He has such a temper. He scowled all morning. It's no wonder his staff don't stay.'

She straightened up and waved her hand to indicate he could replace the painting. He lifted the canvas down and stacked it with the rest. Then he crossed the room and picked up the next one: a painting of the church in the village. The cream stone was painted in vivid orange and yellow brushstrokes that jumped off the canvas.

'He spent all morning cursing his pastry chef because he'd let him down in the first place.'

'So he took it out on you? That doesn't seem fair.'

Olivier laughed. Nothing Raymond did was fair or logical. In this way the two of them were as different as could be. But for determination and dedication, they were equally matched, and Olivier often wondered if Raymond would fight with him as much if Olivier were more pliable, less stubborn. More like his brothers.

He set the painting down on the easel and stepped back. Lily's hair fell around her face as she bent to adjust the focus. 'I couldn't do anything right in his eyes. I got relegated to making croissants because when I filled the éclairs I was too generous with the cream.'

'Does it matter?' she asked from behind the camera. He could hear the smile in her voice.

'It does to him.'

She giggled. 'There aren't many people who would turn down an offer of help in the kitchen from the great Olivier Lacoste. Does Raymond not recognise how skilled you are?'

'He does. But this is his bakery and he's always done things the same way. He's pig-headed.'

'And he doesn't like change,' she sympathised. 'A lot of people don't.'

He nodded and thought of her nomadic life. 'Not like you.'

'I love change. I don't like to stay in one place so long that life becomes predictable.' She looked out the window past the top of the mimosa tree to the blue sky beyond and he could have sworn that the look in her eyes was almost one of fear. Like a canary bird looking through the bars of its cage. He remembered what she'd said about feeling trapped here. The desire to explore and see the world was one thing, but what was she afraid of? He decided not to broach the subject. He didn't want to argue when they were getting on so well.

A quiet pause settled on the room as he replaced the canvas with another of purple grapes tumbling from the vine.

'That one's too small,' said Lily stepping out from behind her camera. She pointed to the top of a white cupboard. 'How about we line up three small ones there and I'll pan across.'

He nodded and set about looking for two more paintings of a similar size. Lily did the same, rooting through another stack with her free hand.

'Do you do much hands-on baking normally or is your life spent in meetings now?' she asked.

'It's difficult. The management side of things keeps me busy.'

Yet it was the physical act of working with pastry and dough that he loved. As a child he'd learned from Raymond in their kitchen at home and then, later, in the *boulangerie*.

He found a small painting of the dovecote turret and propped it up beside the first canvas.

'A lot of successful chefs work on television shows,' said Lily. 'Have you considered doing that?'

'No,' he said brusquely. 'Why would I want to?'

'You'd be really good in front of the camera: you're young and eloquent – plus it's always interesting to watch someone talk knowledgably about their passion.'

He shook his head and frowned. 'It's not for me.'

'Why?'

'Fame, celebrity – I don't want that.'

'The money's good.'

Her words made his eyes narrow. Was that what was important to her? Well, not to him. It had never been what motivated him. Even at the start of his career, he'd been driven to perfect his skills and to be the best in his profession – not to have a fat bank account or celebrity status.

'I have enough money. I don't need any more.'

Lily handed him another small canvas, a close-up of the mimosa tree's powdery yellow flowers, and he set it with the others. She tried to move the tripod closer, but with one hand it was heavy and unstable. He moved swiftly to lift it out of her hand. 'I'm your gofer, remember?' he said, with a wink.

She opened her mouth to argue, but relented. He set

down the tripod where she indicated, and waited while she adjusted the camera again. He watched as she worked with close concentration, and it was difficult not to admire how capable and talented she was, but quietly so. Not like Nathalie who had spoken constantly about her work, speculating on the promotion she was aiming for or the bonuses she expected.

Lily moved the camera from left to right, then frowned and began again.

'What's wrong?' he asked.

She sighed. 'I wanted to pan but I can't get the movement smooth enough.'

'Let me see.'

She stepped back so he could take a look. 'See how the picture judders and slides too fast?'

'Can I try?' asked Olivier. 'I don't have your expertise with a camera, but I have a steady hand.' It was essential in his work.

She nodded and showed him how to hold the camera. 'Start there, and slowly swing to the right. But it has to be done so slowly that the viewer hardly notices.'

He tried a couple of times, then she showed him how to record.

'Do you ever wonder what happens to the people you've filmed after you've gone?' he asked.

Lily turned to look at him with a puzzled look.

'Like the film about the tea plantation workers, for example. Do you keep in touch afterwards or go back?'

She arched a brow. 'You've seen my film?'

'Of course.' He smiled. 'I've seen them all. They're good.'

He admired how sensitively they were made. She never took the obvious clichéd route of demonising or pitying or ridiculing her subjects. She simply entered into their lives and tried to understand their concerns, what was important to them, what they loved or valued or feared. She made sure they were always portrayed as real people, not stereotypes or two-dimensional beings, and there was a sense of quiet wonder and dignity in her films, as if everyone was a hero, even a shabbily dressed woman washing clothes by a stream. It was in the lighting, the angle, the focus. In Lily's films every individual was beautiful in their own unique way. Ironic, given that the person behind the camera was scarred. But not a coincidence, he was certain: she looked beyond the surface.

Her eyes widened and spots of colour blossomed across her cheeks. For a moment she looked flustered, then she said, 'Yes, I do keep in touch where I can. It's not always possible, of course, where people don't have the technology. But for the film about the tea plantation my guide was from a fairly privileged family and she still emails from time to time. Apparently the film resulted in some changes happening: the workers were all given pay rises and the protective clothing they needed for spraying crops. The plantation owners also paid for all the children under fifteen to get free schooling.'

'I'm impressed. Your film really had an impact, then.'

'Yes. The owners were shamed into doing what they should have been doing all along . . .' She blushed and he could see the pride in her eyes that her work had had a positive effect.

Still, he didn't understand why it was more important to her than Mamie.

'It was a small victory,' she went on, 'and that's why I do it.'

'Do what?'

'Make films. You might disapprove of how important my work is to me, but I'm trying to make a positive difference. Exposing injustice or inequality is often the first step towards redressing those imbalances.'

He heard the passion in her voice and saw it in her eyes, and he felt a ripple of admiration. Suddenly he saw that what drove her wasn't selfish ambition; Lily genuinely wanted to help those less fortunate.

'So you're on a crusade to right the wrongs in the world?'

She laughed. 'Even if I only make a very small difference, it's still worthwhile.'

He studied her carefully. 'You have noble intentions.'

'Are you laughing at me, Lacoste?'

'Not at all,' he said, shaking his head. 'I misjudged you. I thought your dedication was about personal gain. Wanting to win the film prize – the money.'

He realised now that he'd been prejudiced, blinded by his ex, Nathalie, seeing reflections of her in Lily, when actually their motives were totally opposite. Whereas Nathalie had been out to achieve status and wealth, Lily was trying to help others, to give the less fortunate and the overlooked a voice. Give them hope. And he admired her for this. Although he still didn't understand how she could prioritise those people over her own family, he saw that her intentions were good.

She shook her head. 'Winning the film prize would raise my profile and make it easier to attract funding for future films – that way I could help more disadvantaged people. The prize itself isn't even a large amount of money.'

He nodded and pointed to the camera. 'I recorded it. Want to take a look and tell me what you think?'

Her hair fell in front of her eye as she watched the playback, and she brushed it away impatiently.

'You're a fast learner, Chicken,' she murmured. 'I'm impressed.'

He laughed at how reluctantly she said that.

'I'll just film these each individually,' she said, and tilted the camera to focus on the painting of mimosa flowers. Her hair fell forward again.

With a sigh of impatience, Olivier took hold of it and held it back. 'I don't know how you can work with this getting in your eyes all the time.'

She stilled. Then gave a small shrug without lifting her head from the camera. 'I'm used to it. It doesn't bother me.'

Still, he held her hair back while she finished filming, noticing how smooth it felt, how it slid through his fingers. He studied the concentration in her face as she worked, aware of the rapid light rhythm of her breathing. His gaze homed in on her scars and he thought about the house fire which had caused them. He knew, because Mamie had told him, that the blaze had started in the kitchen and that her father had taken too long trying to put it out; he'd been overcome by the fumes. He knew that Lily would probably have got out unscathed, but she'd gone back and tried, in vain, to search for her dad.

Her scars were a mark of her courage. And her loss.

'Right. I'm done,' she said, straightening up and stepping away from him. His hand dropped to his side. Her cheeks were flushed and she darted a quick look at the open windows. 'Is it me or is it suffocating in here?' she asked.

He didn't reply but watched as she pulled her hair over her shoulder and smoothed it forward.

'Why do you always wear your hair down?' he asked softly. A sharp splinter of emotion surprised him, but he brushed it away quickly, telling himself it was concern for a friend.

Where was her courage? Her defiance? She might enjoy adventures in wild places, but the woman in front of him hid behind her hair, and that troubled him.

Her hand fluttered to her scars then dropped away, and she stiffened. 'Why do you think?' she said, and her green eyes hardened as they locked with his.

He refused to let her steely tone put him off. 'It's a shame to hide behind it.'

The sound of a dove calling filled the short silence that followed. Lily's chin lifted. 'People stare, Olivier. They turn away, sickened, or tell me I should hide my face. What's the point of inflicting that on them? – Or on me, for that matter?'

His muscles gripped with fury at the thought of people treating her like that. How many times had it happened? And how must she have felt?

Then he pictured her grinning down at him from the highest branches of the tallest tree. 'You're braver than that. You're the bravest person I know, Lil, and you are beautiful. Don't hide it.'

Chapter Seven

Lily stared at him, shaken by his deep voice, by his words and the message they carried. She tried not to let it affect her but it did. Did she hide?

She remembered when they were children and they used to dare each other, how faced with a steep drop or a tall tree she would dig deep inside herself to find the courage to meet his challenge. She swallowed, not knowing what to say. Still feeling the heat of his hand on her nape when he'd held her hair back, the whisper of his fingers. Her pulse tapped wildly, as if it had been locked away and was rattling the cage to escape.

The sound of footsteps on the stairs made her turn.

'Ah, you're both here!' Mamie appeared in the doorway, out of breath from the climb.

'We've just about finished,' said Lily, relief flooding through her at the diversion. 'It's far too hot to do any more.' She blew the hair out of her eyes, thinking she was ruffled again. How did he always have this effect on her? She was too sensitive to him and his opinions.

Mamie looked at her watch. 'Perfect timing. I've made quiche for lunch. Come down when you're ready, and don't forget to wash your hands!'

They both smiled as she pattered away downstairs.

'I don't know how long it's been since anyone told me

to wash my hands!' said Lily. 'I swear she thinks we're still five years old.'

'I know. But we should indulge her, don't you think? Come on, Skinny.'

Mamie was waiting for them on the terrace in the shade, and laid out on the table were a salmon quiche and a colourful assortment of salads.

'Help yourselves,' she said. 'You've been working hard, and it gets hot in that studio at this time. I could never bear to work in there during the afternoon.'

It had been stifling, thought Lily. But not only because of the sun.

When they'd finished the salads and eaten their fill of quiche, Olivier stretched his arms and yawned.

'You should go now,' said Lily, remembering that he'd had an early start this morning and done almost a full day's work at the bakery before coming here. 'Catch up on your beauty sleep.'

'Don't tell me – because I need it?'

She grinned. 'Too right.'

Though if there was one person in the world whose looks couldn't be improved, it was him. Her gaze skimmed over his jaw dark with stubble, and his eyes like molten chocolate.

You are beautiful. Don't hide it . . .

'You're right,' he said, getting up and reaching to kiss them each on the cheek. 'I'll see you lovely ladies tomorrow.'

Lily shook her head. 'Tomorrow is Sunday. We can have a day off and leave the studio until Monday.'

Mamie turned to her. 'Have you forgotten? Béa always invites me for lunch on a Sunday.'

'Oh. Right.' Lily bit her lip. She'd been so disappointed this morning that he couldn't come because he was helping at the bakery. She'd *missed* him. If that had taught her anything, it was that she needed to spend less time with Olivier, not more.

He must have read her mind because he added, 'Unless you're too busy Lily?' And there was a gleam in his eye which challenged her to find an excuse.

She couldn't think of one, and once again she felt like she'd been pushed into a corner. She was beginning to relax around him, their friendship was flowering again, and her intentions of keeping her distance were going out the window.

'I'm not too busy. Lunch will be great. Thank you,' she said, trying to sound as gracious as possible.

When he'd disappeared through the gate back to his parents' house, Mamie and Lily began to clear the table. 'So how did it go today? Are you two getting along better now?'

'We were never not getting along,' said Lily as she put the empty plates down and opened the dishwasher. 'We'd just . . . lost touch.'

'Yes. Well, spending time together is always good – for any relationship. It was good of him to help at the bakery,' said Mamie as she put the quiche in the fridge. 'Raymond has real trouble hanging on to his staff. I think he's a difficult character to work with.'

'Many chefs are. Olivier is the exception.' She couldn't

imagine him being prone to fits of temper or diva-like demands. He was too level-headed and respectful of others – though she was certain he wouldn't suffer fools or lack of commitment in his staff.

Mamie nodded. 'He is. And so talented too. Ironic, isn't it, that he and Raymond share the same talent when they're not even blood relations.'

Lily was slotting the last plate in, but now she stopped. She straightened up, and stared at her gran. 'What do you mean, not blood relations?'

'The adoption,' prompted Mamie.

She blinked. 'What adoption?'

'Béa and Raymond adopted him. They thought they couldn't have children of their own. But then they moved here and Claude and Mathieu came along. Béa has always said it's the olive grove – it's a special place. Sacred ground.'

'Olivier never mentioned it. Does he know?'

Mamie's wavy hair bounced gently as she nodded. 'Of course. They told him when he turned eighteen.'

Lily calculated she'd have been fifteen, so it must have been a few months after the fire – when she'd refused his visits and cut herself off from him. Presumably that was why he hadn't had a chance to tell her.

How had he felt to learn he wasn't their child? Had it been difficult for him – or had he taken it in his stride? Perhaps it made no difference to him and that was why he hadn't mentioned it. The Lacostes were such a tightly-knit family, you'd never guess. And despite his brusque manner, Raymond clearly loved Olivier like his own flesh and blood.

Lily felt a twist of guilt knowing that she'd pushed Olivier away just before he'd learned about it. What if he'd needed a friend at that time?

The sun had gone down, and Lily and Mamie were cosy in the lounge watching television. Mamie was engrossed, her eyes glued to the screen while her fingers worked and the knitting needles clicked busily. She cursed when she dropped a stitch and had to tear her eyes away from the programme to fix the problem. Lily sneaked a smile and glanced out the window at the house next door, illuminated with golden lights from inside. Idly, she wondered what Olivier was doing right now.

You're the bravest person I know, and you are beautiful. Don't hide it.

Had he meant it? Olivier never spoke anything but the truth as he saw it. Yet she knew her face was far from beautiful.

She remembered her mother's barely concealed disgust whenever she'd looked at Lily's face. *You can't go out in public like that,* she had told Lily, and brought home leaflets about skin camouflage and make-up. But it was difficult to apply, it required time and patience, and Lily, who'd never worn make-up before, soon gave up. Her scars were impossible to hide completely, so why bother? With time she'd developed the attitude that if people couldn't accept her as she was, then hard luck.

Was that why she refused to see her mother any more?

Partly. Her mother had had nothing to do with Lily

for most of her life. She'd taken her in reluctantly when Lily's dad died, concerned about her public image if she wasn't seen to do the right thing. But she wasn't a loving person, she didn't have the slightest maternal instinct. Her opulent home had been cold and unwelcoming. So cold that Lily had preferred to leave and board at school.

She touched her cheek, and pulled her hair back, as Olivier had done earlier. She could still see the tender look in his eyes.

He was engaged to be married, she reminded herself. However his look and his touch had felt, the gesture had been made out of friendly affection, nothing else.

She knew all this, her head understood it, yet the wild clatter of her pulse suggested that her heart wasn't listening.

Lily crossed the olive grove in quick, long strides, her sandals tapping over the narrow path, her senses alive as she breathed in the fresh morning scent of sunlight on dewy leaves. Her fingers fluttered to the clip at the nape of her neck holding her hair back, and a secret smile touched the corners of her lips.

In the Lacostes' kitchen Béa was standing at the stove stirring what smelled like soup.

'Hi Béa. Do you know where Oli–' Lily began. She stopped in her tracks. 'Oh.'

Olivier was sitting at the table, deep in conversation with a young woman, and seeing their bent heads and tender smiles, Lily knew she'd just interrupted a private conversation. Her chest tightened.

Olivier pushed his chair back and stood up. 'Lily!' he beamed. 'What are you doing here so early? I'd like you to meet Corinne.'

The young woman rose to greet Lily. She was petite, blonde, and she wore a skirt that nipped in at the waist and coordinated perfectly with her pretty top. When she smiled, a dimple appeared in her left cheek and her blue eyes sparkled with warmth.

'I'm so glad to meet you,' she said, reaching up to kiss her on both cheeks. Her fresh, citrus scent lingered in the air even after she drew back. 'Olivier's told me so much about you – and your broken arm. You poor thing!'

'Oh, it's nothing.'

Corinne's gaze flickered briefly over her face. Still smiling, she was evidently trying hard not to stare but, like most people, she found it impossible to tear her gaze away. Lily silently cursed herself for having tied her hair back.

'It's lovely to meet you too, Corinne,' she said, trying to remember her manners. She forced a smile to her lips but it was fleeting. 'And congratulations on your engagement.'

'Thank you.'

Corinne rubbed the ring on her left hand and they both looked down at the blue sapphires and diamonds set in a platinum band. It was a stunning engagement ring.

'I still can't believe it,' said Corinne, and flashed Olivier a radiant smile that lit her eyes. 'It's all happened so fast.'

'Not too fast, I hope,' said Lily, and immediately wanted to bite back her words. She sounded disapproving. Jealous.

But Corinne didn't seem to notice. 'No, not at all. I can't wait to start a new life together. It's felt like it was meant to be right from the start.'

Olivier stepped forward and wrapped an arm around his fiancée. Lily hated to admit it, but they made a beautiful couple. A study in contrasts: he was dark-haired, she was blonde; he was tall and athletic, she was petite and feminine.

Corinne was everything Lily wasn't. And, standing beside her, Lily felt gangly and awkward in comparison. *Skinny*.

But nobody's comparing you, she told herself sharply, and tried to release the ugly emotions which clawed at her.

'Sorry to interrupt,' she said. 'I didn't know you were coming to stay so soon, Corinne.' She glanced at Olivier, wondering why he hadn't mentioned it.

'Corinne only arrived half an hour ago. She got the sleeper train down after her shift finished.'

'It was a spur of the moment thing,' Corinne added. 'I just got my new rota and saw I have two days free and rather than sitting around on my own in Paris, I thought why not travel down here and see everyone?'

Lily glanced at Béa whose broad smile made Lily shrink back, suddenly feeling like an imposter in this house which had once felt as much like her own as Mamie's. She and Olivier used to run in and out of this kitchen, usually chasing one another or his brothers, helping themselves to bread and chocolate as they passed through.

'Everyone?' Olivier teased Corinne. 'You mean me.'

Her dimple flashed. 'Well, you were a small part of it . . .'

He kissed the top of her head and that intimate gesture hit Lily in the chest.

'I'm glad you did. It's still a long wait until your annual leave begins.' A deep frown cut through his brow, and Corinne's smile faded. She looked at her feet.

'Well, I won't stay,' said Lily, sensing tension between them. 'You probably want to unpack and settle in.'

Her words conjured the picture of Corinne unpacking in Olivier's bedroom and Lily's cheeks coloured furiously. She turned to Olivier. 'I just wondered where's the painting of the boats? The one I want to keep. I can't find it.'

'I covered it and put it behind the table, away from the rest.'

'Right. Okay.' She felt foolish now. It had been a trivial thing to call round for. It could have waited. 'Well – er enjoy the rest of your morning.'

'We'll see you later for lunch,' Béa reminded her. And was that a look of sympathy in her eyes?

Lily nodded. 'Yes, of course. See you later.'

She rushed out, her heart beating faster than when she'd come face to face with a grizzly bear in Canada. Yet Corinne was nothing like a grizzly. She was pretty and friendly and very obviously in love.

Back in Mamie's studio, Lily found the painting. She removed the protective cover and carried it carefully into her bedroom. As she leaned it against the wall, she noticed her hand was trembling. Why was she so shaken up? She pulled the clip from her hair and flung it onto her bed, then she paced the wooden floorboards, mortified as she remembered how eagerly she'd raced over to Olivier's this morning. The painting had been a weak excuse to see him. She'd been buoyed up by his words yesterday when he'd told her she shouldn't hide behind her hair. She'd misinterpreted them. Read too much into them. She had to remember that he was planning his wedding with Corinne.

For the millionth time she cursed her broken arm. If it weren't for her stupid injury, she wouldn't be stuck here in this melting pot of emotions and memories that made her feel unsettled and so unlike her usual competent self. Behind the lens of her camera she was in control.

From above, came the quiet crooning of a dove. Lily picked up her passport from beside her bed and absently ran her fingers over the dog-eared pages. Right now, she would give anything to escape back to filming and documenting other people's lives because her own was following a script she didn't like one bit.

She put the passport down, telling herself she had to keep busy. Her gaze settled on her laptop and she quickly crossed the room. With the jab of a button it powered up and she checked her emails, hoping for something from Colombia. Still nothing, but there was a message from Mamie's former agent. In fact, it was from his nephew, Monsieur Masson, who had taken over the business when his uncle had retired. Monsieur Masson was holidaying in the area, a couple of hours from

St Pierre, but he was keen to see the paintings and offered to pay them a visit.

Lily responded, then sat back in her chair. Once she was back at work she'd forget about Olivier. That day couldn't come fast enough. She closed her eyes, thinking of the women's coffee farm and the film prize, and all her goals and ambitions which were temporarily on hold. She couldn't wait to get back to them.

Chapter Eight

Sunday lunch at the Lacostes' place was eaten outside at their long rectangular table under the plane tree and next to Béa's outdoor kitchen.

'Come and sit down,' Béa called when she spotted Lily and Mamie approaching through the olive grove.

'We brought a *vacherin* for dessert,' said Mamie, and handed the box containing an ice cream cake to Claude.

Lily gave Béa a bunch of flowers, then deliberately walked past the empty seat next to Olivier, leaving it for Corinne. However, she wished she hadn't when Béa directed her to the seat opposite him because there it was difficult not to look at him or to notice how attentively he listened to Mamie on his left. Why did he have to be so caring with her grandmother? So devoted? He laughed at something Mamie said and flashed her his charming smile, the one that made his eyes crease, and Lily's heart folded. Claude sat beside her; he was closer to her in age, and his brother Mathieu was opening the wine, but Lily was barely aware of them. It had always been Olivier who captivated her.

Now she knew about the adoption, she wondered why she'd never seen it before; how different he looked from his family. His brothers both had Béa's brown hair, Claude had Raymond's eyes, Mathieu his short build.

But Olivier was unique. He was taller, darker, his jaw was more solid. The only thing he had in common with any of them was his talent for baking, but if he hadn't inherited it from Raymond, then where had it come from? Was it simply the result of having spent hours in his father's kitchen practising his skills? She glanced at Olivier, but she'd have to wait until they were alone to ask him about such a sensitive subject.

'Where's Corinne?' asked Mathieu. 'Does she know lunch is ready?'

'She's unpacking,' Olivier told his brother. 'I'll go and get her.'

'No,' said Mathieu, 'I'd better do it – for chastity's sake!' He winked and disappeared into the house.

'Papa's decreed that Olivier and Corinne must sleep in separate rooms,' Claude explained to Lily. She raised a brow in surprise. At the head of the table, Raymond shrugged his shoulders and scowled.

'He's old-fashioned,' Olivier smiled good-naturedly. 'One day he'll catch up with the twenty-first century.'

'When you're married,' his father told him, 'then you can share a room. Not before.'

Mathieu returned with Corinne. 'Were you talking about me?' she smiled.

'He was explaining the sleeping arrangements,' said Olivier.

Mathieu went to sit next to Lily, but Corinne stopped him. 'Can I sit next to Lily?' she asked. Lily looked up in surprise as Corinne beamed at her. 'I'd love to get to know you better.'

Lily forced a smile. 'Me too.'

'Papa,' said Claude, continuing their conversation, 'you know that in Paris Oli and Corinne live together, don't you?'

'Actually, I have my own place in the hospital,' Corinne corrected him.

'Yeah, but when you're not working you stay at Oli's, right?'

'Right.' Now it was Corinne's turn to colour up, and her cheeks flushed as dark as peaches.

Raymond waved a hand through the air to dismiss all their talk. 'This is my house, my rules.' He got up and went to help Béa with a large platter of roast beef.

Corinne smiled and told Lily, 'It's really not a problem. My room here has an amazing view. I can see right down to the port.'

'It's beautiful at night, isn't it?' said Lily. 'With all the lights reflecting in the water, and the colours from the night market.'

'It's the village festival this week,' said Mathieu. 'The travelling fair is arriving on Saturday. We should go down. Do you fancy that, Lil?'

Lily glanced at Mamie. How would she feel if Lily left her alone for the evening?

'You should go', said Mamie, as if she'd read her mind. 'Have some fun. Don't worry about me.'

Lily's gaze slid to Olivier. The trouble was, she was in danger of having too much fun. Thankfully, she was spared from answering because Raymond and Béa arrived with the rest of the food.

'Help yourselves,' said Béa, and set down bowls of roasted shallots and carrots next to the platter of roast beef.

As everyone grabbed food and ladled it out, the conversation fragmented into the usual chaotic and noisy chatter. Lily took some vegetables and passed the dish to Corinne.

'Olivier said you're looking for a job down here?'

Her dimples flashed and she nodded. 'I'm sure it won't be difficult. And I'm looking forward to moving – this is a great place to live.'

'Yes, Oli mentioned that you're house-hunting.'

'I hope we find something soon. I can't wait to find a place and get married, have kids,' Corinne confided with a wide smile.

Her frank admission caught Lily on the back foot and she tried to hide her discomfort. Strange, because when she was filming she encouraged people to discuss intimate topics; openness and emotional honesty made for great viewing. Yet hearing Corinne speak about having Olivier's children made her wish she was anywhere but here. It triggered prickly, ugly emotions that she was ashamed of but couldn't prevent. 'Oli mentioned something about that,' she murmured politely.

The dishes of food finished circulating and everyone tucked in hungrily.

'We're hoping to have a big family. I'm one of seven children.'

'Seven? Wow.' Lily pierced a shallot with her fork. 'I can't imagine being one of seven. I was an only child.'

Her dad had told her she was a precious gift, a miracle. Her mother, in contrast, didn't want children at all but had been too far into her pregnancy to prevent it when she learned she was expecting Lily.

Corinne smiled and nodded. 'Olivier and me are hoping to have four, but we'll see. We might have more.'

'No wonder he's looking for a big house!' Lily glanced up at him but he was engrossed in conversation with Mamie.

'Yes.' Corinne smiled fondly at her fiancé.

Lily pulled her hair forward with her left hand. Sitting on her left, Corinne had full view of her scar, and she was so petite and feminine it made Lily feel even more self-conscious than normal.

She bit her lip, then asked, 'Do you worry about how it might affect your career if you were to have children?'

'Oh it shouldn't be a problem at all! I can work part-time and Olivier's parents are keen to babysit.'

Lily looked at Raymond and Béa. They would make wonderful grandparents. Corinne and Olivier had their future all planned out.

'Why aren't you eating, Lil?' asked Olivier. 'Do you need someone to cut up your food for you?'

Everyone laughed and Lily blushed.

'It's impossible to cut meat one-handed,' said Béa and shot her a look of sympathy. 'Claude, will you help Lily?'

She leaned back while he cut her beef into bitesize pieces. Olivier chuckled, so she shot him a look of mock anger.

'I'm the second eldest,' Corinne went on, 'so I helped

a lot with looking after my little brothers and sisters. It was like playing dolls, but for real. I loved it.'

Lily nodded. She had to give it to Corinne; it was clear that she'd make the perfect mother for Olivier's children.

'Lily doesn't know what you're talking about,' said Olivier. 'She never played with dolls.'

She darted him a quick glance.

'Not at all?' asked Corinne, brown eyes wide with incredulity.

'No,' admitted Lily. 'I preferred being outside, running around getting mucky and having adventures.'

'Which usually involved tearing holes in the knees of her jeans,' said Mamie.

'Nothing much has changed,' Olivier said with a nod at her bandaged arm.

'No. Well, that's just the way I am,' she said stiffly.

'Talking of adventures,' said Olivier, addressing Corinne and his brothers, 'I thought we might take the boat out to the cove this afternoon. What do you think?'

Lily's spirits lifted at the prospect of a trip out to sea. But the thought of spending more time with Corinne immediately made them sink again.

'Sounds good,' said Mathieu. 'It's ages since I went there.'

Claude nodded. 'We could go snorkelling. Are you coming, Lil?'

Lily nodded, torn between excitement at the thought of revisiting the cove again, and hesitation at spending more time with Corinne and Olivier. *Get used to it, Lil.*

'Great,' said Claude. 'Have you been there already, Corinne?'

They all turned to Corinne whose cheerful smile had vanished. 'No. I haven't.' She bit her lip. 'I – er – I'd rather stay here if you don't mind.'

Raymond and Béa had been engrossed in conversation, but Béa stopped talking and turned.

Olivier's brow furrowed. 'You don't want to come?'

Corinne shook her head. 'You go ahead. I'll be fine.'

'Why don't you fancy it?'

Corinne glanced left and right. Everyone had fallen silent and they were all looking at her. 'I – I'm afraid of water,' she said quietly.

Olivier looked perplexed. 'I didn't know that.'

'I had an accident when I was very small. I nearly drowned.'

'What happened?' asked Bea.

'We were on holiday, I jumped into the pool, my rubber ring stayed on the surface while I went under . . .' She shrugged.

'Was no one watching you? Your parents?'

'I don't remember. I think my mum had gone to the bathroom with my little brother.'

'Can you swim?' Béa asked gently.

Corinne shook her head. 'No. After that, I screamed blue murder if my parents tried to take me anywhere near water. I've never been able to overcome my fear.'

'That's a shame,' murmured Mamie.

Lily glanced at her, but her gran blinked innocently.

'We'll do the boat trip another time,' Olivier told Lily.

'Of course,' she said quickly. 'It's not important.'

'How about we have a table football competition

instead?' grinned Claude. Mathieu smiled and nodded. 'Lil?'

She lifted her sling. 'I'm at a disadvantage with only one hand.'

'No problem,' said Claude. 'I'll fetch some bandages and we can all play left-handed!'

Olivier laughed. 'The worst is, I think he's serious.'

The tiny white ball shot through the goal, provoking a cheer from Claude, who held up his hand. Olivier high-fived him, grinning.

'Eight–four,' declared Mathieu, and slid a counter along. 'You're still behind, you two. We haven't lost our touch, have we, Lil?'

'Hey, wait a minute!' cried Claude. 'You haven't scored eight!'

'We have!' laughed Lily.

While the three of them argued over the score, Olivier shot a glance at Corinne. She was sitting sedately with his parents, sipping coffee and chatting quietly with Béa in the shade of the two parasol pines that leaned towards each other like doting lovers. Raymond had fallen asleep beside his wife, and Mamie had gone home for a nap.

You hardly know her. Lily's words came back to haunt him. Was she right? Maybe he and Corinne didn't know each other well enough. Her fear of water, for example – why hadn't she mentioned it before? Judging by the way her cheeks had coloured, she was clearly embarrassed, but there was no shame in it and he had to admit, he was disappointed that she hadn't confided in him. There was nothing she didn't know about him.

His mind homed in on Nathalie and their break-up. Well, almost nothing.

And that was different: not so much about him but Nathalie and what she'd done. He hadn't discussed it with anyone, and he didn't intend to.

These are the little details that make a person . . . all the things that have shaped them and are important to them.

His brothers roared as Lily scored another goal. 'Come on, Oli. Concentrate!' said Claude, digging his elbow into his ribs. 'That's Lil's third goal in less than two minutes.'

Olivier smiled and tried to return his attention to the game.

It was only a small thing, he reassured himself. His feelings for Corinne were as solid as the ground beneath his feet.

'Are you cold?' asked Mamie. 'You're shivering.'

Lily glanced down at her arms which were covered in tiny goose bumps. She'd been trying to concentrate on the film but her mind kept wandering and she'd been so lost in thought she hadn't noticed. 'A little, I suppose.'

Mamie glanced briefly at the fireplace, then said, 'There's a lap blanket in there.' She pointed a twisted finger at the heavy wooden chest in front of them which doubled as a coffee table.

Lily lifted the lid and peered inside. There was a neatly folded quilt made from patterned red and white Toile de

Jouy. Beneath it were a couple of larger, more heavy-duty woollen throws. With one hand she shook out the small quilt and laid it over her legs.

'Tuck it in around you,' said Mamie, and put her knitting down to help. 'Like this. There, is that warmer?'

Lily smiled. 'Sometimes I wonder if you notice that I'm a grown woman – tucking me in like a six-year-old! I can look after myself, you know.'

Mamie stopped and her hair gleamed pearl-white in the soft lamplight. 'In my eyes,' she said softly, 'you will always be a little girl who needs looking after.'

Lily's chest squeezed. She swallowed and picked up the remote control. 'Shall we carry on with the film?'

Mamie nodded.

But Lily just couldn't stay focused on the film. Her mind was still next door, stuck on replay, going over the meal they'd shared with Olivier's family. She hadn't expected to like Corinne, but who wouldn't? She was friendly and warm and caring. The perfect match for Olivier, Lily acknowledged, and gazed thoughtfully at her lap. She touched the quilt and ran her fingers over the hills and dips of the diamond-shaped quilting and the delicate design of windmills and trees and people working the land. Lily had been worried – as any friend would be – that he was rushing into marriage, but now she'd met Corinne for herself she saw that she'd be exactly the wife Olivier was looking for. Lily was happy for him.

Yet that wasn't all she felt, was it?

Sitting next to Corinne, a part of Lily had curled up

on itself, it had shrunk back. A frown touched her brow. She felt inferior. Pretty women had that effect on her, and what marked out Corinne was that her beauty wasn't only skin deep.

Lily tried to push these uncomfortable thoughts away and to concentrate on the film. She wouldn't let her own insecurities cloud her mind, she vowed. Olivier was happy, and that was all that mattered.

Lily perched on the stool and stretched to retrieve the small canvas hidden at the back of a pile on top of the large white cupboard. Those in front were tilted forward and balanced against her bandaged shoulder. Their weight pressed painfully against her, but she almost had hold of the canvas now, she just needed to pull it free. She grasped it with the tips of her fingers, leaning forward a fraction more—

The stool toppled sideways and she fell, clattering to the floor along with the canvasses.

'Lily?' Mamie's voice travelled up from downstairs.

She surveyed the scattered paintings in dismay. Oh no, what had she done?

'I–I'm okay!' she called, and shakily got to her feet.

One by one, she picked up the canvasses. The one which had been at the front was damaged: lavender pots painted in oils, the corner of it crumpled and squashed where it had hit the floor. Mamie's work ruined. Tears burned the backs of her eyes.

Why had she been so confident she could reach? Why

so impatient to get on with the task? She should have moved them all aside individually, or waited until Corinne had gone and Olivier was here. Or even better – found something else to do. But she'd been desperate to get back to filming, so she'd gone into the studio and tried to continue where she and Olivier had left off the other day. She'd filmed a couple of the smaller canvasses – the large ones were too awkward to lift one-handed – then she'd searched for more and spotted this one right at the back of the pile.

'Lily, are you alright?' Mamie appeared, breathless, in the doorway.

'Oh Mamie,' she said, and held up the damaged painting for her to see. 'I'm so sorry.'

Her throat squeezed. Mamie had trusted her with this job and she'd let her down because of her foolish impatience. Because she'd been so desperate not to think about Olivier with Corinne and what they might be doing.

Two days ago she'd been doing everything in her power to avoid him, but this morning she'd woken with a leaden feeling in her stomach, disappointed because she wouldn't see him. Lily's heart had fluttered with panic. She'd only been here a few days and she was already craving his company? She couldn't allow herself to feel this way, she mustn't get attached.

She didn't know when Corinne was leaving, and she didn't want to ask. If she did, she knew her voice would betray her and Mamie would know how much it bothered her.

Her gran stepped forward, squinting to see. When she

saw the damaged painting, she waved a hand through the air. 'Pff! That doesn't matter,' she said, and cupped Lily's chin in her gnarled hands. 'Are you hurt?'

'I'm fine. But this is ruined.' Lily put the painting down, feeling sick. She was so angry with herself.

'I never liked that painting,' said Mamie. 'The colours are flat, there's too much grey, and look – the perspective here isn't right.'

'You're only saying that to make me feel better.'

'Not at all. I told you, I just want to be rid of these paintings. None of them are of any importance to me any more.'

'They're beautiful. And I should have taken more care. I should have waited until Olivier was around, but I hate doing nothing. This,' she glared at her bandaged arm, 'is so frustrating!'

Mamie pursed her lips and studied her closely. 'Why don't you come out with me for lunch?'

'You said you were meeting a friend. I don't want to interfere with your plans. I'll find something else to do. Don't worry about me.'

'I want you to come. There's someone I'd like you to meet.'

Lily regarded her grandmother warily. 'Who?'

'His name is Alain.'

'Mamie, I told you, I don't need fixing up with men.'

Mamie chuckled and shook her head. 'Alain is *my* friend. He's 82. Too old for you.'

'Oh.' Lily didn't know what to say. Mamie had a male friend? Was that who she'd been so cagey about going out with the other day? 'Well,' she said, intrigued, 'if you're sure . . .'

'Good,' smiled Mamie. 'That's decided, then!'

They met Alain for lunch in one of St Pierre's most upmarket restaurants, where the dishes were of Michelin star quality and served on square plates like framed pieces of art. Alain insisted that it was his treat, and it became rapidly evident to Lily that his feelings for Mamie ran deep.

She watched, fascinated, as he joked with her grandmother and teased her good-humouredly. The pair of them knew each other well, Lily could tell. He was charming, he treated Mamie with respect, and the look in his eyes was one of . . . – it took her a moment to identify it – reverence. The kind of look she would have been thrilled to catch on film because it was so revealing.

'He's a true gentleman,' said Lily, after he'd insisted on driving them back to the farmhouse.

'He is,' said Mamie, as she put her bag down on the kitchen table and began to sift through her mail. The beads on her turquoise dress caught the light as she moved. She'd dressed up for lunch and worn her brightest lipstick.

Lily knew her gran would soon disappear upstairs for a nap, but there were hundreds of questions spilling through her mind. Why hadn't she mentioned him before today? Because she didn't want to upset Lily? It didn't upset her, and this wasn't about her, anyway. If Alain made Mamie happy, then that was the only thing that mattered.

'So, about you and Alain – is this a romantic relationship?'

Mamie paused from opening a letter. 'Oh, he asks me regularly if we couldn't make something more of our relationship, but companionship is enough for me.'

Lily hesitated a moment before asking, 'Why not have more?'

'More?'

'You could live together.'

Mamie shook her head and tutted. 'No,' she said. Then added quietly, 'I will always love Maurice – your grandfather.'

Lily blinked. 'But he's been gone thirty-five years!'

'Yes.' Mamie pulled out a bill, and put it down on the table, discarding the envelope.

Lily watched as she picked up another letter and sliced it open with a knife. She said carefully, 'You could still love Maurice but have another relationship.'

'No,' she said firmly. 'Besides, I like my independence too much. Can you imagine it? A man coming here with all his belongings? I'd have to make room for his pictures on my walls and his clothes in my wardrobe!'

Lily followed her gaze through the open door and the lounge beyond which was filled with photographs and Mamie's paintings.

'I see what you mean,' she said quietly. 'But you're the one who told me that we all need someone.'

'I'm eighty-five. I have loved and my heart will always be with Maurice. Alain is a good friend and I enjoy his company; he makes me laugh, he pays me compliments. But that's enough for me. I'm stubborn and set in my ways. The only person I will share my home with is you.'

Mamie scanned the last of the letters and put it down with the others. She pushed them together to make a neat pile.

Lily smiled and said softly, 'Thank you, Mamie.'

Sharp green eyes looked up at her. 'Whatever for?'

'For looking after me.'

'Pff, it's nothing. I wish I could always have looked after you. I wish that mother of yours had let me bring you here after your accident.' She pulled out a chair and sat down, suddenly looking weary.

Lily dipped her gaze. She didn't like to talk about that time in her life. It was history, it didn't matter any more.

'Do you ever hear from her?' asked Mamie.

'Occasionally.' The house was silent. Outside, the main road was quiet and the world seemed to have gone to sleep in the early afternoon heat. 'I don't reply.'

She picked up the empty envelopes and put them in the bin, but she could feel Mamie watching her as she did so.

'I shouldn't have let you go to that boarding school,' she said eventually. Lily looked up in surprise. 'That's when you began to withdraw into yourself.'

What did she mean, withdraw into herself? 'I wanted to go there. I needed to be with people who already knew me. I didn't want to have to start again in a new place where people would stare.'

'Didn't they stare anyway?'

'Well . . .'

'I should have insisted that you came back here with me. You needed me.' Regret cut through Mamie's voice, and it shocked Lily, because Mamie was never one to look back. Always optimistic, she was accepting of life and happy with her lot.

'I was fine. And I came ho—' she hesitated, 'I came here every holiday.'

'But you were so quiet. It wasn't the same.'

'Mamie, please don't regret the past.'

'I do, though, Lily. I regret that I didn't fight for you. Your mother was your legal guardian, but I should have challenged her.'

'In court, you mean?'

Mamie nodded.

'Those things take so long. I would have been eighteen before the case was heard.'

Her gran went on as if she hadn't spoken. 'The only reason I didn't was because I thought you wanted to spend some time with her.'

'I did. At the start, anyway. I wanted to get to know her.' She gave a bitter laugh. 'I hoped that after all those years of silence, she would step in and become the person I'd secretly hoped she would be. Loving. Warm.'

But within a few weeks Lily realised that whereas before the fire she'd been a nuisance, now she'd always be an object of disgust to her mother.

'Oh Lily . . .'

Her spine straightened. The air was thick and heavy. She crossed the room and stood by the open doors and stared out at the lawn that struggled to remain green in the arid heat, and the palm tree with its rough, criss-crossed trunk.

'Living with her made me stronger. It made me realise I don't need others to be happy. I can manage perfectly well by myself.'

'You can. But do you want to be alone?'

Lily faltered. 'I . . .' She'd never seen it as a choice. Rather, as the status quo.

And she was proud of her achievements. She was a survivor. The fire and her scars and her lousy mother hadn't held her back. If anything, they'd propelled her into a career she loved and found fulfilling.

Although, admittedly, it did feel lonely sometimes.

But usually, she fixed this by getting her laptop out and losing herself in her work.

'You don't need to be alone, Lily. You have a family here. We all love you.'

Lily's heart pinched. Mamie was fixated with pairing her off with Olivier, but couldn't she see? He didn't love her in that way. And she couldn't be part of his life, watching from the sidelines while he married Corinne. That would be excruciating.

'I don't regret what happened. I'm happy as I am. I love my job.'

There was a long pause. 'But life is not just about work, is it?

She looked at her gran. 'It can be. Times have changed.'

'I know. And I understand. I had a successful career too.' Mamie pressed her thin lips together. From the direction of the olive grove a cicada started its grating song.

'Still, I would dearly like to see you settled and happy. It's time, Lily.'

Lily bit her lip and didn't answer.

Mamie was wrong: it wasn't time. Her career was just beginning to take off, she'd got her first commission, and then there was the film prize. Only when her name became known could she begin to make a real difference, attracting funding to make more films which would help more people.

And settling down wouldn't make her happy, anyway. She needed to travel like she needed to breathe.

Chapter Nine

The hairdresser, Monsieur Canolle, greeted her as if she were a long-lost daughter. 'Let me look at you, my darling little Liliane!'

Lily's cheeks heated as heads turned around the salon, and she was glad she wasn't wearing her usual scruffy denim shorts, but a fresh white pair and a navy blue halter neck top which looked stylish and wasn't too difficult to put on with a bandaged arm.

The salon owner slid his fingers through her long hair, drawing it forward in a habit she recognised of old, and smiled. 'You look so well, and all grown up!'

'Well, yes, Monsieur Canolle.' Her lips curved mischievously. 'I've been grown up for a while now.'

'I know, I know, but we lose track of time. And your grandmother keeps me up to date with everything you get up to, you know, so it feels as if you never left.'

She smiled.

'Are we cutting your hair today?'

'No. Just Mamie's,' she said, and examined a few strands of her own hair to check – there were no split ends and it looked fine to her.

Whereas others might regard a couple of hours in the salon as pampering, Lily only had her hair cut when absolutely necessary.

'You never could sit still, could you?' Monsieur Canolle grinned. 'Some things don't change.'

A young man ushered her gran away into a chair and a black gown, and Lily called to her. 'I'll come back in a couple of hours, then?'

'You don't have to,' said Mamie. 'I can get the bus home by myself.'

'I want to. See you later!'

Lily stepped out into the morning sunshine and wandered around the village for a little while. The church bells chimed the hour. How was she going to keep busy for two hours? She wandered up and down the nearest street, glancing at the cobbled alleyways lined with shops, but they were crowded with tourists and she wasn't in the mood for shopping. She had time to go home and come back but she was feeling restless again. Anxious to get back on the move, back to work.

It worried her that Maria still hadn't replied to her email. She would have liked to fix a date for her return to Colombia, to book the flight and start firming up her travel plans. But until Maria replied, she couldn't do anything but wait. Her mind flitted to Olivier and she wondered fleetingly what he was doing.

Instantly, she crushed that thought. He was with Corinne, of course.

She made her way down to the harbour and her eye was caught by the boats swaying in the breeze, their colourful reflections dancing in the water, metal bars gleaming, throwing knives of light that were temporarily blinding. Mamie's painting in her room back at the farmhouse was of three rudimentary fishing boats. These were bigger, but they sparked the same excitement in her, making her pulse quicken.

Lily looked around. Nearby was a quiet café which was more popular with the locals than the tourists. She chose a seat at the front, beneath the shade of a palm tree and near the tethered boats. Once she'd ordered coffee and breakfast she returned her attention to the boats, watching the gentle breeze nudge them from side to side so their masts danced and the ropes chinked like bells as water slapped against the wooden hulls. Olivier had been right: they did remind her of when her dad used to take them out diving. She looked out beyond the harbour where the water was indigo deep, and she leaned back in her chair.

She couldn't explain it, this wanderlust she felt; the strongest sense that the world out there held a trove of possibilities waiting for her to explore. Why was it that while other people craved routine and family life, she was so different? Perhaps it was because, as a girl, she and her dad had shuttled between England and France, slipping into local life so easily that it had become second nature to her. She ate a slice of brioche and sipped her coffee and savoured the whisper of warm air against her bare legs and sandalled feet. How she used to miss the heat and the vivid colours of this place when she was at school in England. On a damp winter's day she would sit by the classroom window and try to conjure in her mind the startling blue of the sky, the sweet scent of pine trees and the strong flavours of Mamie's delicious cooking, but it felt so far away. And yet when she was here, it was as if she'd never been away. Her dad used to miss St Pierre too, and they came here at every opportunity: Christmas, summer, Easter too if his budget allowed. He'd always intended to retire here: his photography business meant he had to live in London but, he'd told her, one day when he'd saved enough he would return to his roots.

As she ate breakfast, locals hurried past carrying baskets of shopping, and tourists strolled at a more leisurely pace, admiring the pretty harbour lined with brightly-coloured buildings and elegant palm trees. She almost didn't notice the tall figure which scooted past, but he glanced up and, seeing her, did a double take. He turned around and came back. Lily's heart jumped at the sight of him.

'Brioche – just what I need,' said Olivier and leaned over to help himself to a huge chunk.

'Hey!' Lily tried to bat his hand away but she was too late. Her body flickered like a live electric wire, but the thought of his kind, caring fiancée snuffed out the sparks. She looked around for Corinne but couldn't see her.

He tasted the sugar-crusted bread and frowned. 'This isn't from Lacoste.' The waiter approached and Olivier shook his head and held up the brioche. 'Pierre, you'll lose customers selling them inferior quality products like this,' he joked.

'Olivier. Good to see you.' The two men shook hands energetically. 'I heard you're engaged. Congratulations.'

Lily listened, marvelling at how fast news travelled in a small village like this – even at the height of the tourist season when she'd have thought the locals would be too busy to have time for gossip.

When he and Olivier had finished catching up, the waiter asked, 'Shall I get you a coffee?'

'Thanks,' said Olivier and lowered himself into the chair next to Lily. 'I can't stay long, though,' he said, looking at his watch. 'I promised Papa that I'd look over the books for the bakery. I was heading over there to pick them up.'

Lily tried to make herself relax, but she was aware of his large frame filling the chair, of his long legs that he stretched out in front of him.

'And here was I, enjoying some time to myself,' she said dryly.

'No you weren't. You were getting bored waiting for Mamie who's in the hairdresser's.'

She laughed. 'How did you know?'

'She always has her hair done on a Tuesday morning. And you don't like her getting the bus back by herself.'

'She gets so tired coming up the hill, even in the morning when it's still relatively cool. I worry about her.'

'I know,' he said softly.

'Do you think I'm cramping her style? She likes her independence.'

'Not at all. She's thrilled that you're here, and that she's spending so much time with you.'

Lily nodded, relieved. Though she had to ask herself, why did it matter so much to her what he thought?

She looked around the busy port. 'So where's Corinne?'

'She got the train back to Paris last night.'

The wistful look in his eyes made Lily's chest pinch,

but she made herself ignore it. She was happy for him, happy that he'd found the perfect woman to spend the rest of his life with. Although marriage wasn't for her, she appreciated that it must be a very special feeling to find that kind of relationship.

'I enjoyed meeting her. She's lovely.'

'You think so?'

'Yes. She's sweet. Kind. Perfect for you.'

'You've changed your tune. I thought we were rushing into it and I don't know her well enough.'

'That was before I met her.'

She picked up the small burgundy napkin and twisted it between her fingers.

There was a pause before Olivier asked, 'You don't think it's too soon to get married, then?'

Lily glanced at him. It wasn't like Olivier to ask a question like that. He was always sure of himself and determined. Once he'd made a decision there was no changing his mind. 'No. I don't.'

He grinned and relaxed. 'She's something special, isn't she?'

'She is.' Her heart folded up a little tighter.

'How long until her annual leave begins?' she asked.

He made a mental calculation. 'Two weeks.'

'Was it nice to see her? You must miss each other.' She tried to keep her voice flat and devoid of the emotions that were bubbling beneath the surface, but no matter how hard she tried, it was impossible for her to feel only platonic concern.

He nodded. 'It was great. We went to visit a few houses

together so I have a better idea of what she wants – and what I want too.'

'Right. You didn't find any that you liked?'

His lips pressed flat and he tilted his head to one side. 'We saw one that Corinne likes, but I'm not sure about it.'

'Ah. Tricky.' She looked away. A trio of seagulls were spinning circles in the sky above the boats and calling noisily to each other.

'Yes. I'm going to visit it again tomorrow.' He threw her a sideways glance. 'Would you come with me?'

She felt a shot of joy that he wanted her help, but immediately she put the brakes on that. 'I don't think that would help. This is between you and Corinne . . .'

'I know. But it *would* help. It'd help me a lot to know what you think.'

'Me? Why? I'm really the wrong person. Buying a house, settling down – that stuff doesn't interest me.'

'That's exactly why you're the perfect person to help. Don't you see? You can be one hundred percent objective.'

She didn't know what to say to that.

'Come on, Lil. It's not asking much, is it? An hour of your time, at most.'

He was right, it wasn't asking much, and now she'd met Corinne it was as if an invisible wall had sprung up between her and Olivier. If Lily could help in any way, she would. She'd be the friend he wanted her to be. Only a friend. She'd ignore the attraction, pretend it wasn't there. 'Well if you're sure . . .'

'Great!'

She picked up what was left of her brioche and ate it.

'So will you still do anything for a brioche, Skinny?' he asked and nodded at the boats in front of them.

Smiling, she followed his gaze. He'd once dared her to cross the length of the harbour, hopping from boat to boat, in return for a brioche. She'd done it, but she'd also received a scolding from one of the boats' owners who'd caught her.

'These days I can pay for them myself. How about you? Is ice cream still your weakness?'

'Actually, now it's red wine and a ripe camembert,' he admitted ruefully.

The image sprang up in her mind of him and Corinne spending a cosy night in, sharing a plate of food and kicking back with a bottle of wine. She hastily chased the image out of her head.

'You'll get fat, Chicken,' she teased, though the idea of him becoming overweight was difficult to imagine when he was as toned as any athlete, 'and then how will you climb trees? Perhaps now you'll admit that I was always a better climber than you?'

'I climbed every tree you did!' he said, pretending to look affronted.

'But I was quicker and more agile.'

'I'm not going to admit defeat. I could beat you to the top of that plane tree right now!'

She followed his gaze and eyed up the tree. It was huge, but there was a newspaper stand beside it which would get her up to the bottom branch, then–

Olivier chuckled. She turned to look at him, and only then did she remember her arm was in a sling.

'You were considering it, too!' he laughed. 'Well, in one way at least you haven't changed.'

'What does that mean? How have I changed?'

His smile faded and he suddenly became serious. 'You keep us at arm's length.'

Us? Who did he mean by that? 'You make that sound like a bad thing.'

'I preferred it when you said what was on your mind,' he said, and his eyes gleamed, 'even if it meant I got a kick in the shin when you weren't happy.'

She considered this a moment then said quietly, 'I grew up, that's all.'

The waiter brought his coffee and Olivier handed him a note.

'I'll get this!' said Lily, reaching for her purse.

He waved away her words and winked. 'You're a free-lance filmmaker living on the breadline.'

'I never said that!'

The waiter vanished inside with his money and she knew her protests were in vain. 'It's a coffee, Lil. Let me treat you.'

'Coffee and a brioche,' she corrected.

'An inferior quality brioche best forgotten,' he said, downing his espresso in one go.

'Well I enjoyed it – at least, I enjoyed what was left after you'd stolen half.' As if on cue, her tummy rumbled loudly.

Olivier laughed. 'Tell you what, come with me and I'll

get you a proper one from Papa's bakery.' He placed both hands on the arms of his chair, poised to get up. 'You ready?'

She hesitated and glanced in the direction of the hairdresser's.

'You've still got an hour until Mamie's ready,' he said, reading her mind.

'I did promise that I'd get the bread . . .'

'That's settled then,' he said, and stood up. 'Come on.'

Waving goodbye to the waiter, he darted off. Lily hurried to keep up with him, glad as she'd always been, that her long legs made it easier to do so. However, having her arm in a sling didn't. It affected her balance, and it was difficult to protect her injured arm in the tourist-filled streets. If she knocked it and did more damage, she risked prolonging the healing process, and she didn't want that, least of all because it would delay her return to Colombia.

'Oli, slow down,' she panted when she finally caught up with him. 'It's not easy to navigate a crowded street with one arm in a sling.' She nodded at the narrow street ahead, crammed with people and colourful displays of baskets, perfumed lavender bags and all the other souvenirs laid out to tempt the tourists.

'Ah yes – sorry,' he said. 'I forgot.' He moved to stand on her injured side and slipped his arm around her waist, positioning himself as a shield against the crowd.

The touch of his hand on her side made her skin tighten. She glanced sideways at Olivier and reminded herself that he was Corinne's, that this small gesture, chivalrous though it might be, meant nothing to him. Yet that didn't prevent the quiet tug in her chest when, later, as the crowd thinned, he withdrew his arm.

'Let's go this way,' he said when they were halfway up the hill. 'It'll be quieter.' And he led her off into a quiet side road, even narrower than the last, but with no shops to lure the tourists.

They passed René the postman whistling a children's rhyme as he made his morning deliveries. 'Liliane Martin!' he said, looking up. His face broke into a smile. 'Good to see you.'

Lily grinned. 'I can't believe you remember me after all these years.'

'How could I forget?' he said. 'I deliver your letters to Simone every week, and every time she invites me in for a coffee. I always take her up on it. That hill is quite a climb.' He looked from her to Olivier and back again, then shook his head. 'You two! It's like going back in time, seeing you together. I hope you're not up to your old tricks again. How many times did I catch you playing knock and run down here?'

She looked at Olivier and they shared a smile.

'We're grown up and sensible now,' said Olivier. 'Anyway, I don't have the legs to run away fast enough any more.'

'That will be a relief to the good people of this village,' said the postman. 'Better go – I have a full bag today.' He doffed his cap and moved on, whistling cheerfully.

Olivier and Lily turned the corner and her sandals tapped along the cobbles.

'You write home every week?' he asked.

She shrugged. 'Mamie struggles with email. And I phone her regularly, but she likes letters most of all because she can read them over and over again.' They had always written to each other, ever since Lily could remember. 'I try to send her postcards so she can picture where I am.'

They reached the Lacoste bakery and stopped outside. It was so crowded that people were queueing out of the door.

'Is it a baguette you want?' Olivier asked.

Lily nodded.

'Wait here,' he said and disappeared round to the back door.

She stood to one side where she wouldn't be jolted by the crowd, and waited. The narrow street was shaded from the sun but, although it wasn't yet midday, the air was already uncomfortably heavy and warm. Lily reached into her bag and pulled out a leaflet she'd picked up earlier; she used it to fan her face. There was talk that a heatwave was coming and she could believe it. The nape of her neck was hot and sticky as she swept her hair back from her face.

A family emerged from the bakery, a boy and a girl both holding *chaussons aux pommes* and grinning excitedly, their eyes wide with greedy anticipation. Lily smiled at them as they passed. The little boy looked up and, seeing her scars, stopped dead and gasped.

'Maman!' he said and pointed. 'What's wrong with her face?'

His mother glanced at Lily and apologised. She tried

to hurry her son away, but he didn't move and clutched her skirt, staring.

Hot colour rose from Lily's neck as heads turned and passers-by peered curiously. Her heart hammered and she fought the instinct to retreat and hide. All the past incidents when people had reacted to her scars with disgust – or worse – rose to the front of her mind, and her skin prickled. But this boy was only young. His shock was innocent, not malicious.

'I was burned in a fire,' she told the boy gently and crouched down so she was on his level. He took a step back but at the same time his eyes widened with fascination. 'These are just scars. They don't hurt now.' Her fingers touched the smooth ridges on her left cheek and jaw.

His expression changed to one of curiosity. 'They don't hurt at all?' he asked. 'What about when–?'

'Come on now!' his mother said sharply. Then to Lily, 'I'm really sorry.' She nudged the boy again and this time he responded. 'Lucas, you mustn't point like that . . .' she scolded as they hurried away up the hill.

Olivier dodged through the busy kitchen, the ring binder under his arm. Despite years of trying to persuade him, Raymond refused to file his accounts on a computer. Even though his accountant had pleaded with him, even though the tax system required it of him. Olivier shook his head at his father's stubborn refusal to accept any form of change, and grabbed a baguette and a brioche from the shelves. He exchanged a couple of words with the staff, then emerged into the sunshine and looked for Lily.

He spotted a small crowd, strangely hushed, and it was only as he drew closer that he saw she was at the centre of it, crouching to speak to a boy who had his arms wrapped around his mother's legs. Muscles tensing, Olivier hurried forward.

'These are just scars. They don't hurt,' he heard Lily say, before the mother ushered the boy away.

Lily straightened up and watched them disappear into the crowd, a haunted look clouding her sage eyes. Passers-by lingered curiously before they too continued on their way.

He put his arm around her protectively, and asked, 'Are you alright?'

'I'm fine,' she said but didn't look at him.

He scowled, feeling like an ineffective guard dog. He'd arrived too late. 'He was just a child. He didn't know any better–'

'I know,' she said quickly.

The tension leaked from him as he realised she wasn't upset. But this didn't stop the wave of anger that followed. 'His mother should have let you speak. She shouldn't have rushed him away like that.'

'She meant well,' she said flatly. 'I've had much worse.'

'Worse?'

She kept her gaze fixed straight ahead and her eyes were glazed with memory as she nodded.

'Tell me.'

'It's not important.'

'Tell me,' he insisted.

She shrugged. 'People who've screamed when they saw my scars; shopkeepers who've ordered me to leave their premises; men who've met me in badly lit bars and asked me out on dates only to be horrified when they saw my face in daylight. One guy escaped through the kitchen of a restaurant, he was so desperate to get away from me.' She gave a dry laugh. 'I wouldn't have minded, but he'd ordered a really expensive bottle of wine and I was left to foot the bill.'

Olivier's jaw clenched. She was brave to laugh it off, but being left with a big bill couldn't have been half as bad as the humiliation of being abandoned by your date. His fingers curled around the file under his arm, gripping it tight. Anger rolled through him at these men he'd never met, men who didn't deserve to even breathe the same air as her. How could people behave like that? How could they have so little thought or feeling for the person behind the scars? How could they not see the beautiful and talented woman in front of them? Wasn't it bad enough that she'd suffered the burns in the first place?

But what dismayed him most was Lily's flat acceptance. What had those people done to her?

Lily ran her fingers through her hair and stared thoughtfully at the spot where the boy and his family had disappeared into the crowd. Her chin was up and he couldn't prevent the wave of admiration that rushed at him. She was composed and serene, and when she'd spoken to the boy, she'd done so patiently and with understanding, her only concern to reassure the child. Olivier's eyes followed the slope of her cheek to the outline of her mouth, and he felt a quiet tug.

'Did you get what you needed?' she asked.

He inhaled sharply, aware of her soapy scent. Aware of her. The busy street became a blur around him as he tried to make sense of the fiery emotions that scattered through his brain, confusing him, making his head spin.

'Oli? Did you get what you needed?'

He blinked, then glanced at the ring binder tucked under his arm and nodded. He held out the bread and brioche. 'For you,' he said, and his voice sounded unusually gruff.

'Thanks,' said Lily and peered at him. A frown knotted her brows.

He attempted to marshal his thoughts. What was the matter with him? It must be the heat. He'd never felt awkward like this around Lily.

Actually that wasn't true. He had once. When she'd kissed him.

'Mamie will be ready soon,' she said, looking at her watch. 'I'll go down and meet her.'

'I've got the car. I'll drive you both home.'

She opened her mouth to refuse, but thought better of it. 'Thank you. That's very kind. Mamie will be glad not to have to wait for the bus in this heat,' she conceded.

He nodded and they set off down the hill towards the hairdresser's. He settled his arm around her waist, shielding her injured arm from the rough jostles of the crowd.

They collected Mamie, admired her freshly tinted and coiffured hair, and he drove them all home. His eyes kept flickering to Lily in his rear-view mirror. She was quiet in the backseat as she stared out of the window, the brioche he'd given her untouched in its paper bag. He tried not to think about what he'd felt back there in the street outside his dad's bakery, about the bullet of heat which had fired through him or the ferocious need he'd felt to protect her.

It had simply been a moment of confusion, he told himself. His brain had mixed up brotherly protectiveness with – with something else. Perhaps he was missing Corinne.

He pictured his fiancée and his pulse slowed down and calm was restored. He focused his thoughts on how much he'd enjoyed her unexpected visit and how sorry he'd been to say goodbye to her at the station. Everyone could see how perfectly matched they were, how logical their pairing was and how successful their marriage would be. Now he was more determined than ever to begin planning the wedding in earnest. He wanted to set a firm date and pin down the details: book the church, the reception venue, the guest list. But first he had to find a house, he thought with a sharp frown. One they both liked.

He pulled up in front of Mamie's metal gates. 'I'll carry your shopping in,' he said automatically.

'It's only a baguette. Lily can manage!'

'Oh yes,' he said quickly. 'I wasn't thinking. My mind was elsewhere.'

Mamie cast him a curious look. 'Yes, I can see that.'

He jumped out and opened Mamie's door, helping her out of the car. As he did so he kept one eye on Lily as she got out the other side and the sunshine picked out threads of honey in her long hair. She'd pulled it forward around her face again, he noticed with a stab of disappointment.

'Shall I drop by this afternoon? To do a bit more work on the studio?' he asked, as Mamie shuffled away towards the gate.

Lily hugged the baguette to her and squinted as she looked up at him. 'I thought you were helping your dad with the books?'

'Oh yes.' He wasn't sure where his head was. Maybe he had a touch of sunstroke. 'Well, I'll see you tomorrow then. I'm going to visit the house in the morning. I'll pick you up at nine?'

'If you're sure you want me to come.'

'Of course I'm sure.'

'Corinne won't mind?'

Corinne didn't know, but he was certain she would be fine with it. 'Why would she mind?'

'Because it's a personal thing, finding a house you both like.'

'She knows you're like a sister to me, and that you're rarely here. I want to spend as much time with you as possible.'

It was perfectly normal. All good friends felt this way: a fiery sense of wanting to spend time together, a kick of pleasure at being in each other's company.

*

'So tell me about this house we're going to see,' said Lily.

Olivier kept his eyes on the road, carefully navigating the tight bends as they wove their way higher and higher up the inland peninsula. The terrain here was more rugged than the neat hill on which his parents' house was perched, the soil was redder, more parched, the vegetation less lush and hardier.

'On paper it's perfect. It's big, it has a good size garden, it's not too far from the nearest village, and Corinne likes it – but . . .'

It had been troubling him for the last two days, but he still couldn't explain why he couldn't share Corinne's enthusiasm for the property. Was he being too difficult? If Corinne loved the house, wasn't that reason enough to buy it and make their home there? Should he stand his ground and hold out until they found a place they were both equally happy with?

'But?' Lily prompted.

He gripped the steering wheel and sighed. 'I don't know. I can't bring myself to make an offer. It doesn't feel . . . right.'

He slowed down as the road narrowed, aware of Lily's gaze fixed on him as she studied him for a moment.

'Can you picture yourself living there?' she asked.

The village in which it was situated was smaller than St Pierre and didn't attract the same volume of tourists, which made it even more suitable for a family home. Yet there was no doubt in his mind as to the answer. 'No.'

'Then it's not the right house for you.'

'But it should be.' And this was the part he couldn't understand. 'It meets all the criteria we set: it's big enough, the location is perfect for our needs—'

'Whoa, stop!' she cut in. 'You sound like an estate agent. If it doesn't feel right, then it's not. Listen to your instinct. That's what I do when I'm filming and it never lets me down.'

'When you're filming?'

She nodded. 'It tells me who to watch, which questions to ask, when to push, when to back down.'

'That's experience, not instinct.'

She considered this for a moment. 'It's both. Don't you use your instinct in your work? When you're deciding where to open your next bakery? Which new products to develop? Who to hire?'

'No. I base my decisions on facts and hard evidence. Statistics on the location, projected footfall, market research assessing demand for certain flavours or recipes, and so on. I would never use conjecture or emotions to make such crucial decisions.'

He frowned as he steered the car through another tight bend. The last time he'd let himself be carried away and blinded by his feelings it had ended painfully. But he'd learned from that, and now he knew better. He wouldn't fall victim to that loss of control again.

'Nothing is completely scientific,' said Lily, and frustration began to mount in him that she wasn't letting this go. But then, when had Lily ever allowed him to win an argument without putting up a fight first? 'You said yourself that this house seems right on paper but it doesn't *feel* right. Every decision involves some degree of emotion and instinct!'

'Well it shouldn't. Not if you're operating objectively and responsibly.' Perhaps it was different for filmmaking, but in the world of business and retail rational thought and logic were the only dependable methods of decision-making.

She sighed. 'This is your home, we're talking about, Oli. How can you apply logic to the place you're going to live in?' She looked left and right, 'Is this the village?'

'Yes.' He drove carefully through the village square, a line of small shops on the left and a children's play area on the right. Locals sat on benches in the shade of majestically tall plane trees, and it was evident from looking around that the pace of life in a place like this was slower, more intimate.

They turned right out of the centre and the road wound up a steep slope. 'Here it is,' he said as they approached a pair of robust metal gates. 'The estate agent is meeting us there.'

They finished the tour of the house, then the estate agent left them to wander through the garden while she dashed off to another appointment. Lily stood on the terrace and drank in the view of clay-coloured hills stretching away left and right, with ink-blue sky above her.

She could see immediately why the house wasn't right for Olivier. Perched high on the arid back hills, it might be an expensive architect-designed property, but it had no soul, no character. In fact, there was an air of sadness about the place, and when the estate agent had told her the owners were going through a divorce, it hadn't come as a surprise. The only thing she didn't understand was why Corinne liked it so much. Although it was on the outskirts of a village with a school, shops and all the necessary amenities, it felt isolated on its own generous plot of land, and its harsh square lines were out of place with the rugged landscape.

The garden was a modern design with spiky architectural plants and a lawn riddled with irrigation hoses to keep it green despite the withering heat. It felt plastic and artificially perfect; like a show home with no heart.

'Tell me what you think,' said Olivier.

She bit her tongue. 'It's not about what I think. It would be yours and Corinne's home. You have to decide how you feel.'

If Corinne liked it, then it wasn't Lily's place to criticise or interfere in any way. She picked her way through the thick, prickly grass, treading carefully to avoid the white snails. Yet she couldn't imagine Olivier agreeing to anything he wasn't one hundred percent happy with. He'd always been single-minded – obstinate even – and that was partly why they used to clash as kids: Lily stood up to him. But his relationship with Corinne was completely different, and much more harmonious than their tempestuous friendship.

'I didn't bring you here for you to be so diplomatic, Skinny. I thought I could count on you to give me your honest opinion.'

A deep frown cut through his brow, and disappointment was etched into his face. It tugged at her. She might not want to interfere, but surely she could give him her opinion – as a friend.

'Honestly?'

He stopped walking, and his dark gaze met hers square on. 'Honestly.'

She stopped too, and glanced up at the white cube-shaped building that loomed over them, the sun hammering down on its flat roof. 'I just can't picture you here. I don't think you'd be happy.'

'Why not?'

'I see you somewhere more traditional, with more character.' He had taste, and he wasn't one to slavishly follow fashion. 'The fact that you're asking my opinion when normally you're so sure of yourself speaks volumes. This place just feels wrong for you.'

'It feels wrong . . .' he repeated, and shook his head. The corner of his mouth lifted. 'That's your scientific analysis?'

She laughed. 'Yes.'

'It's maddening that I can't find a house I like,' he said quietly. 'The estate agent suggested I look further afield but I really wanted to be near my parents.'

Lily thought about his adoption and bit her lip wondering how he felt about it. He never mentioned it and always referred to Béa and Raymond as his parents.

'Wouldn't it be stifling living so near them?'

'Not at all. They want to be a part of their grand-children's lives – providing we're lucky enough to be able to have children, of course. I want my kids to enjoy the same freedom you and I had as children.'

She nodded politely.

'Course, I'll make sure that they don't mix with any tree-climbing tomboy neighbours,' he grinned. 'We both know they're a bad influence.'

She thumped him playfully on the arm, and they began to walk back towards the front of the house where he'd parked his car.

'It's not an interesting garden, is it?'

'No. It's very impressive, but a little man-made,' she said, thinking of Mamie's which was a quarter of the size but as colourful as an artist's palette. The fuchsia-coloured bougainvillea spilled over her gate and scattered petals like confetti, scarlet geraniums lined her windowsills, and hollyhocks burst up like fountains against the stone walls of the farmhouse.

'A little?' he said dryly.

She bit her lip. 'Oli?'

'Mm?'

'Mamie mentioned something the other day . . .'

'Oh yes?' The sweet scent of conifer teased her senses as they passed the perimeter hedge, and their feet crunched over the white gravel drive.

'She said you were adopted. It came as a bit of a shock.'

He glanced at her but didn't break stride. 'I thought you knew. They told me years ago – when I turned eighteen.'

'About the time I was in hospital?'

'A few months after, yes.'

She paused, choosing her words carefully. 'It must have been difficult for you.'

He shrugged off her question. 'Why? I had a happy childhood. The best. As you know. You were there.' He sounded casually accepting of it, yet she sensed there were stronger feelings lurking beneath the surface.

'Still, it must have been a shock to learn that Béa and Raymond weren't your biological parents . . .' She watched him and saw the mask of indifference fall away. His mouth pressed flat.

'It was at the time,' he conceded. 'I took it very badly at first. I went out in a rage, got very drunk. I was confused and upset, I suppose, and didn't know how to express that.

'The next day I was ill with a hangover. But they didn't say anything. Normally Raymond would have shouted; instead, he was concerned.' Olivier gave a rueful laugh. 'And that made me feel even more ashamed. They both loved me – that much was obvious.'

'It is obvious,' she said softly. 'And they *chose* to adopt you.'

'They thought they couldn't have children of their own so they adopted, then miraculously' – he clicked his fingers like a magician producing a coin or a dove – 'they conceived, and before they knew it, they had two more boys and the family they'd always wished for!'

She smiled at his expressive gestures and they carried on walking in companionable silence until they reached his car. 'Did you ever think about tracing your real parents?'

'Yes, I did it. I looked for my mother – my father was never named on my birth certificate – but she had died a year before. A drug overdose.'

'I'm sorry,' she said quietly. 'Though if she was anything like my mother, you were probably better off without her.'

'You never talk about your mother. What *is* she like?'

Lily pressed her lips together, wishing she hadn't mentioned her.

'What happened when you went to live with her?' he persisted. 'Did she hurt you?'

No. Yes.

She inhaled a long deep breath trying to put into rational language what felt so monstrously irrational and raw. Even after all these years.

'She didn't want me there. She only took me in because she was afraid of what people would say if she didn't. Her reputation was what mattered to her – not me.'

Olivier said nothing. He waited for her to go on.

'I was very unhappy living with her, that's all. So I chose to go back to school and board there. I wanted to be with my friends, with teachers who knew me, safe in the school grounds.'

'Why didn't you come here?' he asked quietly. 'You could have lived with Mamie and gone to school with me and my brothers.'

'That would have meant starting again and facing a classroom full of strangers. I didn't want to be pitied, or for my scars to define me. At my old school everyone knew me already. I could still be me – Lily – and not just a girl with a burned face.'

He took a moment to absorb this. Then asked, 'How did your mother react when you decided to leave?'

'She was indifferent.' And how that indifference had hurt.

Lily had tried to mirror it and hardened her heart. Yet the sense of betrayal had cut deep. Wasn't a mother's love supposed to be instinctive?

'Secretly, she was probably relieved.'

'So you haven't seen her since?'

'No. I don't want anything to do with her. When I needed her most she let me down. I needed to be accepted and loved for who I was, but she looked at me as if I was a monster. She told me to hide my face and plaster it with make-up. She made me feel . . .' She broke off and turned away, blinking hard.

Ugly. Unwanted. But that was only scratching the surface. Words couldn't fully describe how her mother had made her feel.

'Lil?' Olivier said quietly. His hand touched her shoulder, and she turned back to face him.

The concern in his eyes told her he'd been expecting to see tears running down her face. But she was dry-eyed as she lifted her chin and told him, 'My scars have faded now, but she taught me something important: I don't need people like her in my life.' As she walked round to get in the car, she added quietly, 'I don't need anyone.'

Olivier got into the driving seat. He looked thoughtful. 'I know I'm lucky to have been raised by Béa and Raymond.'

'You are.'

'They've never treated me any differently from Claude or Mathieu. But in here–' he lifted one finger to his temple and smiled, 'I know I am not their son. The four of them share the same hair colour, the same build. But no one looks like me, no one else is my flesh and blood.

'And although I've tried to put it out of my mind, although logically it shouldn't matter when I've always been happy and had the best opportunities in life . . . it does matter.' A muscle flickered in his jaw. 'It matters a great deal.'

Lily looked at him and suddenly it dawned on her. 'That's why you're so keen to have children?'

'It's part of it, yes.' His eyes locked with hers and she saw in them an intense yearning. A deep-rooted vulnerability.

Something inside her squeezed hard. Behind the successful baker, the perfect son and fiancé, was a man who didn't know where he came from, who desperately wanted to belong. His children would be like roots, anchoring him.

'I just want a family of my own. Kids who look like me. Someone else with my genes, my blood.'

'I understand . . .' She did. She saw now why it was so important to him, and she knew Corinne would give him the family life he craved, the children he longed for.

And though her heart contracted at the thought, she wanted him to be happy. That was more important to her than anything else. '. . . And it'll happen soon, I'm sure,' she said, her voice husky.

Chapter Ten

'Is it too late to work on the studio?' asked Olivier as he pulled up outside Mamie's house.

Lily looked at her watch. 'We could do an hour before lunch, I suppose. But the agent is coming this afternoon.'

'Is he? You didn't mention that.'

'You were busy . . .' He noticed that she didn't quite meet his eye, 'with Corinne. Anyway, you don't need to be there.'

'I want to be there,' he said firmly. 'He'll be talking valuations and contracts. I can help with the business side of things.'

'You think I need help? That I can't handle those things myself?'

Too late, he realised he'd phrased that all wrong. 'I didn't say that–'

'This is Mamie's work we're talking about.'

'And?'

'She's my grandmother. I can deal with the agent.'

'Mamie's like a grandmother to me too,' he said, and emotion simmered up inside him as their gazes locked. 'I don't doubt that you can deal with the agent, but I'd still like to be there.'

'Why? You're busy. You have your own affairs to deal with – Raymond's bookkeeping, the house hunting . . .'

Her voice trailed off and he acknowledged she was right, he had plenty in his life to keep him occupied. He glanced up at the old farmhouse and the terracotta turret roof that topped the pigeon loft.

Yet he couldn't extricate himself from Lily and Mamie's lives, and he didn't want to. He meant what he'd said: they *were* like family to him, and he felt a pull, a duty to look out for them and be there when they needed him.

But the fierce look in Lily's eyes was telling him she didn't need him. His mind quickly regrouped.

'I care about Mamie. I'd like to be there,' he said gently.

She sighed as she opened her car door. 'I appreciate your help, driving us home and all the other things you do for Mamie, but . . .' She bit her lip, and got out of the car. He did the same, but didn't take his eyes off her.

'But?' he prompted as they walked round to the front of the car and stopped.

She looked up at him, shielding her eyes from the sun. 'But we're not totally helpless, you know. I manage perfectly well on my own when I don't have this,' she lifted her sling, 'and Mamie has lived independently for the last thirty years.'

She was insulted by his desire to help. Her fiercely independent spirit was trying to assert itself and push him away. The sun beat down on his dark hair. Why did she always resist help? And why did he find it so hard to step back from her life? Was it because the last time she'd shut him out, he'd then spent the next thirteen years regretting that he hadn't fought harder to stay in her life?

'I know, and I respect that,' he said. His respect for her was immense; it always had been.

'So why do you keep treating me like I'm helpless? Incompetent?'

'You're neither of those. But whether you like it or not, I'm involved in Mamie's life. So is all my family, and that's not an insult to Mamie because there have been plenty of times when she's looked after me.' He thought of all the times Mamie had bandaged up his knees or baked his favourite plum tart – not a perfect *patisserie* like Raymond's, but a simple, rustic recipe consisting of nothing but pastry and a jumble of plums sprinkled with sugar. 'So if you're asking me to step away and butt out, it's not going to happen. I'm not going anywhere.' He folded his arms.

She eyed him curiously, and he became aware of the heavy beating of his heart, of intense emotions firing through his veins.

'You're going to get married,' she reminded him quietly. 'You'll have your own family to look after soon.'

'So? I'll still be around.' He couldn't understand why she was looking at him as if he didn't understand. He could be a good husband to Corinne but still be there if Mamie needed him. Or Lily, for that matter. 'Anyway, I don't understand what you're trying to say. We're talking about a meeting with the agent, not my marriage.'

Her brow creased as if she didn't understand either. Somehow this argument had jumped from concrete facts to elusive emotions he couldn't quite grasp.

'Fine,' she said and turned to open the gate. 'Come if you want.'

The rusty green gate protested with a loud creak as he shut it behind him and followed her in. They exchanged a few words with Mamie, poured themselves cold drinks, then went up to the studio and picked up where they'd left off a few days ago.

There were only large canvasses left to film, which meant that Olivier was relegated to lifting and carrying them, while Lily stood behind the camera making adjustments where necessary. He noticed that her hair still fell forward as she worked but he said nothing and wondered if she'd ever find the confidence to tie it back.

'So do you have any hospital appointments for your arm?'

'Next week,' she said.

'How are you getting there?' The nearest hospital was a thirty-minute drive away.

'I'll get a bus – or book a taxi. I haven't really thought about it.'

He wanted to offer to drive her but held back, knowing what she'd say.

'It's hardly more than an ache now. I'm hoping they'll say that it's healing well.'

'Can't wait to get back to work?' he asked. But there was no animosity. He understood her motivation now, he admired her selfless dedication.

Still, Mamie would miss her when she left. And he would too, he realised with a sharp tug.

She looked up from the camera. 'Yes,' she said earnestly. 'I'd like to get everything finalised for my return trip. There's a lot to organise – the flight, a visa, work permit and so on. Although there shouldn't be any problem with that, given what happened–'

She stopped and bit her lip as if something had slipped out which she shouldn't have said.

He frowned. Had he missed something?

'Given what happened?' he prompted.

'Just . . . you know . . . my arm.' She turned away and began to look through a stack of canvasses which they'd already filmed.

Why was she avoiding eye contact? And why did she look so guilty? 'Why would a broken arm guarantee you another visa? It was an accident.'

She shrugged, but still didn't look at him.

He moved to stand in front of her and waited for her to straighten up. 'Lily?'

Panic danced in her eyes and she glanced down at her bandage. It was only a darting glance, but it didn't escape his notice. He remembered what she'd said about falling from a tree, and how unlikely that explanation had sounded. He remembered how she'd jumped the other day because she hadn't heard him coming; how frightened she'd looked.

'You didn't fall from a tree at all, did you?' His voice was deep and low.

Guilt painted her cheeks with streaks of deep purple and confirmed his suspicions.

'You were hurt? Attacked? Who by?'

'You mustn't tell Mamie! You mustn't say anything to anyone!'

'Who hurt you?' he growled, overwhelmed by concern and – and something hot and ferocious.

She considered not telling him – he could see it in her eyes – and he also saw the moment when she capitulated and reluctantly squared up to his gaze. 'I don't know who they were. Three men. Bandits. They wanted our money . . . And my camera.'

Fury tore through him and he stared at her bandaged arm as he processed all this. 'Tell me you gave it to them?'

He imagined she wouldn't have just rolled over, she might have put up a fight – but he hoped to God that she'd had more sense than that.

'They . . . took it.'

'What happened? Tell me.'

'Why? What's the point? You can't do anything about it now.'

'Lil, I want to know.'

'Why?'

Good question.

And one he didn't feel ready to answer. Instead, he glared at her until, finally, she sighed and said, 'They came out of nowhere. They were armed. There was nothing we could do . . .'

'No one intervened? Came to your aid?'

'There was no one else around.'

He nodded at her bandage. 'They broke your arm?'

'It got broken in the scuffle.'

Vicious emotions simmered up. 'Yet you're still planning to go back there?'

'Of course. It was a one off. Bad luck. It could happen anywhere – people get mugged in Paris, New York, London.'

'You can't go back!' he gritted.

Her brows lifted at his fierce tone, and her eyes narrowed to glare at him. 'I can and I will.'

He ground his teeth, his fists curled at his sides. She was too pig-headed to listen to reason. Couldn't she see that no film was worth risking your life for?

Olivier blew out a rough sigh and stepped away, overwhelmed by the emotions rushing through him and rousing a primeval instinct to protect at all cost. He wanted to throttle the people who had dared hurt his Lily. He wanted to throttle her for refusing to listen to sense. She couldn't go back. What if she got hurt again?

He made himself breathe. What was this savage fear for her that gripped him? Its intensity was unsettling. He opened another couple of windows, and noticed his hand was unsteady.

What he felt was simply concern. Nothing unusual about that. He had to stop her going back – for Mamie's sake, if nothing else. Especially as he was the only one who knew her secret, the onus was on him to dissuade her from going back to Colombia.

He was vaguely aware of the sound of a car rolling up outside the gates.

'What do the coffee farmers think about this? Were they injured too?'

A pained expression made her eyes grey over. 'No one else was hurt,' she said quietly. 'Look, Oli, I don't want to argue . . .'

'Neither do I, but you have to see sense–'

'It's fine. I can take care of myself.'

He nodded at her bandaged arm. 'The evidence suggests otherwise.'

'We were mugged in the street. It could happen to you too, and if it did you wouldn't let it stop you from living your life.'

He gave this a moment's consideration, then tipped his head in frustrated and reluctant acknowledgement that she was right.

The main gate squeaked and footsteps crunched on the gravel outside. Lily glanced out the window. A man's deep voice carried up through the open window, and he heard Mamie reply with a welcoming tone.

'Your job is to make films. You can do that anywhere in the world. You don't need to go to the back of beyond and put your life in danger to do it.'

'I'm more streetwise than you give me credit for!'

'Why don't you go and make films with stories – the kind that sell in Hollywood and win prizes at Cannes? Or work in a studio. Film the news, instead of making it!'

'You know why.' Disappointment flashed across her features, and a light went out in her eyes as if he'd just killed her dream.

'You want to help people, but there must be a less dangerous way of doing that.'

'Perhaps, but making films is what I do best.'

His lips pressed flat. Her talent was indisputable. But Christ, it wasn't worth risking her life for.

'Oli, promise me you won't tell Mamie – I don't want her to worry. She's frail enough as it is.'

Snatches of conversation drifted up from downstairs. She was right; Mamie would be beside herself if she knew the truth, and he didn't want to be responsible for causing her distress any more than Lily did. They both cared for her too much.

'Oli?'

Footsteps approached on the wooden staircase.

'I won't say anything,' he promised. But he would do everything in his power to dissuade her from going back to Colombia.

Mamie appeared in the doorway. 'Lily, Olivier – this is Monsieur Masson. He's a little early, but I told him you wouldn't mind.'

They both stepped forward and shook hands. Olivier murmured a polite greeting, but was relieved when the chap turned away and began to examine the paintings. It gave him time to think and space to regroup.

He'd lost it just now, he was aware of that, and perhaps he'd overreacted – but who, knowing what he did, wouldn't have? Lily's injuries could have been far worse, she could have lost her life. And she was planning to go back?

She and the agent were deep in conversation now, and Olivier watched through narrowed eyes as she calmly threaded her way round the room, pointing out canvasses, answering the agent's questions.

He couldn't fathom her. Was she incredibly brave? Or unbelievably stupid? He knew the answer. There was no one braver than Lily. Even when she'd fallen from the top branches of a tree and broken her ankle, aged ten, she'd bitten back the tears. Her face had turned white with pain, but she hadn't cried and had to be persuaded to hook her arm over his shoulder so he could help her home.

His skin prickled with heat and he rubbed a hand over the back of his neck, trying to ease the tension in his muscles. What was this he felt exactly? This vivid, fluorescent, blinding concern for her? Why was he so overwhelmed by it? It had been creeping up on him slowly, stealthily, but now it loomed over him, impossible to ignore any longer.

His world was neatly ordered and predictable, and that was how he liked it. But around Lily things were different. She made him laugh more than anyone else could – but she also enraged him, made him feel confused and out of control. What was it about her that shook up his world like this?

She couldn't go back to Colombia. The thought of her putting herself in danger again made his spine stiffen. She couldn't.

But he knew Lily.

She would.

'Are you sure Madame Martin is ready to sell?' asked Monsieur Masson.

Lily could see that it must seem strange to him that her gran wasn't up here, but she had bustled off to get lunch ready, saying 'I'd much rather you dealt with it, Lily.'

'She finds it . . . emotional to come in here now she

can't paint any more. I suppose it's like a bereavement – she's lost something that was important to her.' Memories of her dad rose in her mind and her throat tightened. Lily lifted her chin. 'But rest assured, she definitely wants us to proceed with the sale.'

Monsieur Masson nodded and crouched to peer more closely at the brushstrokes that made up the painting of the church, St Pierre. He was younger than she'd expected, softly spoken, and clearly very knowledgeable. 'I was told your grandmother had stopped painting years ago.'

'She stopped selling her work, but she continued to paint in private, for her own pleasure until about ten years ago. As you can see.' She gestured with her hand to the stacks of canvasses which filled the room.

He stroked his short beard as he moved from one piece of work to another. Lily remained quiet, letting him take his time. She briefly wondered if she should fetch the painting of the boats from her room, but there was no point in having it valued when she didn't intend to part with it.

Olivier hung back, leaning against the doorframe, his hands in his pockets, a silent and glowering figure. He was still furious about the robbery, and she knew concern was at the heart of his reaction but she couldn't understand why he was so angry with her. If the same thing happened to Corinne in Paris would he tell her never to return there? Perhaps not, but he'd probably insist on escorting her everywhere, she decided. He was overprotective, it was an inbuilt instinct in him, and although it grated on her, she reluctantly acknowledged that it was a noble quality.

But she didn't need protecting. Nor did she need anyone telling her how to live her life. Her film was of huge importance to her. She couldn't wait to get it finished and edited and submitted both to the television company and for the film prize. The robbery had shaken her, but she wouldn't let it stop her from telling the women's story. Yolanda and the rest of the group were sticking their necks out by working independently in a country where men owned most of the land and businesses. And Lily's film would hopefully inspire others to take their lead.

Monsieur Masson straightened up and dusted off his trousers. 'Well, these are certainly of great interest to me. As for selling them, I could have them sent up to an auction house in Paris if you like, but we tend to find that these kinds of landscapes fetch a better price when sold through the art houses in Nice or Monaco. It's something to do with the local setting, the light, the colours and so on.'

'Actually, we were hoping to exhibit them here, in the village first. To give the locals the chance to see my grandmother's work before it's sold.'

He smiled and nodded. 'That's a nice touch – to exhibit them in the locality which they depict. Some of them are paintings of the village, aren't they? The port, the church, the fountain . . . I presume they're all insured?'

'Er – I don't think so. Mamie hasn't mentioned anything . . .'

'You must arrange for them to be insured immediately. They're very valuable.'

'How valuable are we talking?' Olivier asked quietly.

Monsieur Masson pointed to a large canvas. 'This one, for example, I would expect to fetch a high price. This style is very contemporary and in demand . . .'

He named a sum that made Lily's eyes widen. She glanced at Olivier and he looked just as stunned.

His brows pulled together in a deep frown and he said, 'I keep telling Mamie she should take security more seriously. She leaves all the doors unlocked during the day.'

'You're right to be concerned,' said Monsieur Masson. 'You'd also need suitable security for the exhibition.'

'Could you provide that for us?' asked Lily.

'Of course. There's no reason why I couldn't organise the exhibition for you too – it would be a good way of generating interest before the auction. When were you thinking of holding it?'

'Nothing is finalised yet,' said Lily, 'but soon. End of August, beginning of September.'

'That doesn't leave us much time to get the word out. Would the autumn be a better time, perhaps, once everyone's back from their holidays?'

Lily shook her head. 'I'm only here for the summer.'

'You could stay if you wanted to – for this. For Mamie.' She didn't need to look at Olivier to sense his glowering disapproval; it radiated like heat from his corner of the room.

'I can't. You know I can't. I have a deadline to meet.'

Monsieur Masson glanced from Olivier to Lily, no doubt sensing the tension between them, and cleared his throat. 'In that case, I'll see what I can do for early September.'

'Great,' said Lily, deliberately avoiding looking in Olivier's direction, though she could still feel his narrowed eyes on her.

Once she'd shown Monsieur Masson out, she returned to the studio where Olivier was waiting. He was pacing the room, tiger-like and grim-faced. When he saw her in the doorway he stopped.

'You know,' she said with a weak smile, 'it's very admirable that you feel the need to protect me, but it's also rather old-fashioned.'

'Most people learn from their mistakes. They don't repeatedly put themselves in danger's way.' He strode across to the window and buried his hands deep in his pockets.

'I told you, it was bad luck.' She sighed. 'Listen, if it causes so much friction between us, why don't you take a step back?'

His head whipped round. His dark features were twisted with puzzlement.

She explained, 'You have a house to buy and a wedding to organise. I can take care of Mamie and the retrospective by myself.'

His strong jaw looked like it had been cut from rock. 'We'll do it together – for Mamie's sake.'

'Oli, it won't work. We argue too much. You have too many opinions about what I should and shouldn't do. You treat me like a child who needs looking after, rather than a grown woman.'

'You're right! And do you know why?' He sighed and rubbed a hand over his jaw. He looked left then right, before turning his dark eyes on her. 'Because I care. I care about you, Lil, and I care about Mamie.'

She blinked hard, not daring to speak because a sudden rush of emotion hit her square in the chest. She was touched by his words, yet they stung at the same time because he didn't care about her in the same way she cared for him. He had no idea how deep her feelings ran.

He went on. 'I don't understand why you make some of the decisions you do, or why you're willing to risk your safety for the sake of a film, but I want you to be safe and I want you to be happy.'

His black eyes gleamed like polished stones as he held her gaze, and it made her breath catch. She tried to prevent it, but she was aware of layers peeling away inside her, defences crumbling, leaving her heart a little more exposed.

She sucked in air and tried to marshal her emotions. She was strong, she was used to being alone; she didn't need him or his brotherly affection. He should save his concern for Corinne.

'I am happy.' Her words sounded a little strangled.

'Good,' he said quietly, though he looked like he didn't believe her. 'Then we'll work together to organise this exhibition. Agreed?'

'Agreed.'

Chapter Eleven

'Liliane Martin, what will it take for you to wear a dress?' Mamie turned to Olivier and his brothers. 'She has three handsome young men taking her out for the evening, but still she refuses to dress up.'

'I am dressed up!' Lily protested, and smoothed out the black satin of her slim-fitting trousers and a matching patterned top. 'I'm wearing high heels! And lipstick!' Which had been surprisingly tricky to apply with her left hand, but she'd managed in the end.

'You look lovely,' said Olivier.

'Thank you,' said Lily, knowing he was only saying that to humour her gran.

'You do,' Mamie agreed, 'but you would look even lovelier in a dress, that's all.'

'I hate dresses. You know that.'

'I'm not sure a dress would be practical on the fairground rides anyway,' said Claude tactfully. 'Especially the rollercoaster.'

'True,' Lily smiled at him, though she had no intention of going on any rides with a broken arm.

'Ready to go?' asked Olivier.

Lily nodded.

'Oh – I almost forgot!' he said, turning to Mamie. 'Maman asked have you eaten already or would you like to have supper with her? Papa's out this evening.'

'I ate already,' said Mamie, waving away his concern, 'but I'll call her and let her know. Now go and enjoy yourselves, all of you.'

'Goodnight, Mamie!' Claude and Mathieu called from the doorway.

Lily hugged Mamie, then waited while Olivier stooped to kiss her gran on the cheek. 'Make sure you lock the door behind us,' he said. 'Remember what the agent said about the value of your paintings.'

'Pff!' she said, waving away that suggestion. She patted him on the cheek. 'Make sure you take care of my Lily.'

'I don't need taking care of!' Lily groaned. 'Night, Mamie.'

Claude and Mathieu climbed into the back of the car, leaving the front seat free for Lily. She cast Olivier a sideways glance. The hint of expensive aftershave teased her senses and sharpened her awareness of him as they drove down to the village. When he wore shorts she found his bare legs distracting enough, but he looked even more gorgeous tonight in black jeans and a slim-fitting white polo shirt. Despite her protestations, she was glad Mamie had persuaded her not to wear jeans because she would have looked scruffy next to him and his brothers.

In the back seat, Claude and Mathieu were discussing the fair which had been setting up earlier.

'I don't think Mamie will ever acknowledge that I'm a grown woman,' Lily said to Olivier.

He threw her an indulgent smile. 'She loves mothering you. She thrives on it.'

'I don't need looking after.'

'It's just Mamie's way. She mothers me too.'

'You don't mind?'

'Why would I mind? We're not all as fiercely independent as you, Lil. I'm quite happy to be mollycoddled every now and then.' He paused as he slowed for the roundabout that led into St Pierre. 'Admit it – you enjoy it too . . .'

She shrugged.

Claude's phone trilled and he pulled it out of his pocket. 'Hello?'

'. . . Her home-cooking,' Olivier went on, 'having someone there who cares, who will bring you a hot drink in bed if you're ill.'

Or help her fasten her bra because she couldn't do it one-handed, Lily thought with a secret smile.

'Don't you miss all that when you're travelling?' he asked.

'No,' she said quickly. Then conceded, 'Well – maybe a bit.' She felt a pang. *Imagine staying longer. Imagine if this was your home.*

No. Don't get used to it; Mamie won't be around forever.

She shivered and pushed that thought to the back of her mind.

Claude finished his phone call. 'That was Papa,' he said. 'He and his friends are challenging us to a game of *boules* before dinner. Fancy it?'

Mathieu laughed. 'They play so often, they're practically pros. They'll annihilate us.'

'There are three of them, four of us, if Lily's game. What do you say, Lil?'

'I'll have to play left-handed. I'll be terrible.'

Olivier's lip curved. 'You were always terrible anyway. You never know, you might play better left-handed.'

'Thanks a lot!' Lily flashed him a dark look, but couldn't help smiling. She'd never had the patience for *boules*. There was too much standing around waiting. But the temptation was strong, and she couldn't turn down a challenge. 'Yes, I'm game.'

'Claude and Mathieu want to stay for a rematch,' said Olivier an hour and a half later, 'but I'm getting hungry. What do you want to do?'

'I don't fancy another thrashing,' said Lily, her gaze drawn to the harbour with its hive of lights and music. 'Dinner sounds good.'

Olivier spoke to his brothers. 'They'll join us soon,' he said and the two of them headed off towards the village.

Night had fallen, and the port was buzzing with people. The café and restaurant tables were filling up, and crowds of youngsters were streaming towards the fairground.

'What do you want to eat? Pizza? Chinese?'

'How about the pancake place?' Lily suggested. 'I ran into Monsieur Arnaud the other day and he said his daughter runs it.'

'Anne-Marie? Yes. Great idea. Let's go there, then.'

They wove their way through the stalls selling candy floss and waffles and ice cream, past the cafés with rows of tables laid out under the stars, until they reached the lavishly painted sign that read *Crêperie*. They chose the table nearest the harbour and sat down. Lily glanced at the water and the quivering reflections. The hulls of the boats glowed apricot in the gold lighting, and further out one of the large yachts was strung with fairy lights, its deck busy with silhouetted figures drinking and laughing.

She wished she had brought her camera. The neat rows of boats, their graceful curves, the sharp angles and tall masts: it would have made a great shot, perhaps in black and white to emphasise the patterns and lines. There was something about the ever-changing nature of the harbour that fascinated her.

'Hello, you two!' Lily's head whipped round and she smiled as she recognised Anne-Marie. 'I heard you were in town, Lily. How is your arm?'

'It's getting better.' She had the feeling everyone in St Pierre had been talking about her. But she knew their interest was genuine and well-meaning and only derived from Mamie telling everyone what she was up to.

'She's frustrated because she'd rather be at work than here, relaxing in the sunshine,' said Olivier. 'Can you understand that?'

Anne-Marie looked wistful. 'I wish I could have a break – especially in this heat! Unfortunately this is our busiest time. We have to earn enough to see us through the winter months when it's quiet.'

She spotted two groups of customers who had just arrived. 'I'd better go. Have you ordered drinks yet?'

They shook their heads.

'I recommend the cocktails. I hired a new barman, he's Australian and he's designed some interesting new drinks. Take a look . . .'. She handed them menus and scooted away.

'Cocktails it is, then,' said Olivier.

Lily laughed. 'Okay. Why not?'

'But which one? You're not a Cosmopolitan or a Manhattan kind of girl, are you?'

She looked up at him. 'What do you mean?'

'Well you don't go for civilisation so much as remote and exotic places. I'm guessing you're more of a Pina Colada, or maybe a Mai Tai?'

'If you're talking about my work, I go wherever the stories take me,' she said. 'It's the people that are important, not where they live. Though the more varied and interesting the setting, the better.'

'So what do you fancy?'

She scanned the list of names and descriptions, noting the last one on the list which came with the warning: *Very strong, not for the faint-hearted!*

'Dare you to have the Blow-Your-Head-Off-Blitzer,' she said with a mischievous smile.

He raised a brow and the corner of his mouth lifted. 'That wouldn't be very responsible when I'm driving.'

'We can walk home,' she said, and met his eye in a look of challenge.

Was it her imagination or did his dark eyes gleam as he held her gaze? 'Are you having one?' he asked.

'Yes, I am.' She looked at him from beneath her lashes and added quietly, 'What's wrong? Afraid that you might lose your inhibitions and spoil that perfect reputation you have around here?'

He laughed. 'I won't lose my inhibitions after one cocktail.'

'No? Then what's the problem?'

The waitress approached. He smiled. 'Fine.'

When they'd ordered their drinks he turned back to Lily with narrowed eyes and asked, 'What did you mean, "my perfect reputation"?'

'You have it all: successful business, beautiful fiancée. You're the devoted son – and surrogate grandson to Mamie.'

'Perfect?' He shook his head, incredulous. 'I never thought you, of all people, would say that about me.'

Lily rolled her eyes. 'Oh great. As if your ego wasn't big enough already.'

'Am I detecting a hint of jealousy?'

'No! Why would I be jealous of you, Chicken?' She sat back in her seat and smiled. How many arguments had they had like this as kids, perched in the branches of a tree, legs swinging and picking at the scabs on their knees?

The waitress arrived with their drinks: two tall glasses decorated with colourful fruit and umbrellas.

'I'll light the candle for you,' she said, pulling a lighter out of her pocket and leaning over their table.

Lily jerked back in panic, her eyes fixed on the tall yellow flame that leapt up.

Olivier covered the wick with his hand. 'Leave it, please,' he told the waitress.

The lighter went out and the waitress looked from him to Lily, confused.

'I – I don't like candles,' Lily explained. In daylight, her scars would have been obvious, but in the dark and with her hair loose, they were less visible.

'Oh,' said the waitress. 'Right. So what can I get you to eat?' She pulled out a tiny notebook.

They placed their orders for savoury pancakes and the waitress hurried away. When they were alone again, Lily took a sip of her cocktail and regarded Olivier thoughtfully. She hoped his brothers wouldn't be too long. She could relax more when there were other people around. Being out alone with Olivier like this felt . . . wrong.

She might enjoy herself too much.

'Wow, I see where this gets its name,' said Olivier, putting his cocktail down. 'It really does blow your head off.'

Lily coughed. 'I think the back of my throat is on fire.'

'You like it, though?'

'Delicious!'

She pulled the umbrella off her cocktail and ate the strawberry. To their left, the family at the next table had ordered sweet pancakes heaped with ice cream and icing sugar, and the smell of chocolate carried across on the warm evening breeze. The port was getting gradually busier, and people ambled past, filling the air with chatter and the ring of laughter.

'This place is so busy,' she said. 'It's great to see it doing well.'

Olivier nodded. 'Anne-Marie works hard. It's difficult

to run a business like this here. Out of season it's deserted. The resident population is tiny.'

'Won't you find it quiet compared with Paris when you move here?'

'Not at all,' he said. 'I like quiet. I like village life – being surrounded by people you know. People who care about you and have known you all your life.'

Despite having a lot in common and the fun they had together, his words were a reminder that they wanted different things from life.

The warm breeze picked up and the chink of metal made her glance at the boats with their bobbing masts and swaying ropes. The alcohol must be starting to take effect because she felt a little light-headed. Olivier's face was even more handsome cast in shadows that hardened his jaw and turned his eyes a shade darker.

The waitress arrived with their food. 'Any more drinks?' she asked when she'd put the plates down.

'Yes, we'll have the same again,' said Olivier.

Lily raised a brow. They were potent cocktails, but she wasn't going to be the one to refuse and have him tease her for wimping out, so she nodded her assent.

'Did I tell you I've found a plot of land?' he asked.

'A plot?'

He nodded. 'I've given up trying to find the right house, and decided to build one instead.'

'Where is it?'

He pointed towards the next bay. 'On the edge of La Tourelle, high up and quite exposed, but with beautiful views of the sea on one side and mountains on the other.'

Lily glanced in the direction of the next village. 'It sounds wonderful.'

'It is. It's perfect. The only downside is it will take months to design and build a house. We'll have to rent a place until it's ready.'

'But if you design it, it will be exactly as you want it.'

'Yes.'

'Has Corinne seen it?'

'She's seen pictures. We'll go and visit next time she's here. In the meantime, I'm going to see an architect and begin drawing up plans. Want to see the photos?'

Lily nodded, and as he flicked through the pictures, she realised that one day she'd be looking at photos of his children like this. She'd get emails with pictures of a newborn baby and she'd have this same piercing sensation in her chest.

She tore her gaze away from the photos and made herself look up, look into his eyes. 'I'm really pleased for you,' she said. And, although it hurt, she genuinely meant it.

They had finished their meal and drunk a third round of cocktails when Olivier's phone trilled. His lashes dipped as he read the message. 'Claude and Mathieu have met a couple of school friends and gone straight to the fair. They'll grab a snack there.' He looked up. 'So it's just you and me.'

Lily nodded, and felt both disappointment that they weren't coming and relief because she was enjoying being alone with Olivier.

No, not relief, she told herself quickly. Her brain must be getting confused by all the alcohol she'd drunk.

'How about we take a look at the night market?' she suggested. If they joined the throng of tourists, it wouldn't feel so intimate. She wouldn't have these wayward thoughts.

He raised a brow. 'I thought you hated shopping.'

'Just a quick visit. No unnecessary lingering.'

'Okay. I'm game.'

It had seemed like a good idea, but when they reached the line of colourful stalls, Olivier cast a dubious eye over the busy street.

'Will you be alright in the crowd?' he asked. Lily was almost as tall as him in heels, in contrast with Corinne, who only came up to his chest, yet he still felt protective of her. Even more so, which was curious given how fiercely Lily rejected any kind of help. 'What if your arm gets knocked?'

'I'll be fine. I really want to see the stalls. Last time I came here there were only a handful of them selling cheap wristbands. It's changed so much!'

He steered her through the crush of tourists, making sure he positioned himself next to her injured arm. She stopped at a stall selling products carved from olive wood.

'This is all so beautiful,' she said, and gazed in admiration at the bowls and figurines, tealight holders and jewellery.

'You know olive wood was long thought to symbolize fertility,' he said, although for him it would always be a reminder of his childhood and the days he and Lily had spent playing in the olive grove.

'Was it? I didn't know that.' She threw him a cheeky smile. 'You'd better buy some for Corinne then, since you're both keen to start a family quickly.'

She was right. He silently cursed himself. Why did he keep pushing Corinne out of his mind? She should be uppermost in his thoughts. He peered at a necklace of wooden beads and turquoise stones. Lily turned just as he leaned forward to take a closer look and they found themselves face to face, their mouths almost touching. He stilled, his gaze drawn to her lips, and was shocked by the sudden rush of heat he felt. Blood hammered in his temples. He paused, puzzled by the tightening of his muscles, by his inability to tear his eyes away from the soft dark contours of her lips, and the memory flashed up of the time they'd kissed.

He drew back, thinking guiltily of Corinne. It must be the alcohol he'd drunk, he told himself quickly. His fingers squeezed into tight fists by his sides. Lily had turned away, and he prayed she hadn't noticed that momentary flash of – of what? Heat? Lust?

He snatched up the necklace. 'Do you think turquoise will suit Corinne's colouring?' he asked.

'I think it will look lovely on her.'

He nodded. 'Right. I'll get this, then.'

A little further on, Lily stopped to buy napkins for Mamie in a blue and white Provençal fabric. The stallholder wrapped them in tissue paper and waited impatiently while Lily struggled, one-handed, with the catch of her tiny leather purse.

'Here, let me help,' said Olivier, and unfastened it.

She muttered her thanks and pulled out her phone, then rummaged through the notes beneath. Olivier took the phone so she could count her money, and she paid the stallholder.

They turned to move on when her phone buzzed in his hand. A message lit up the screen. Olivier glanced at it, then did a double take.

Hi Gorgeous. Just wondered how the filming's going and if you're still planning to visit next month? Let me know dates so I can get the sheets laundered! T.xxx

He tensed.

'You have a message,' he said stiffly, and handed her the phone.

She shot him a querying look before she read the message. Her cheeks coloured and she hurriedly dropped the phone back in her bag.

'Who was it from?'

If Lily had been in any doubt that Olivier had seen the message, then his disapproving tone confirmed it.

'No one you know.' Her cheeks prickled with heat. She could barely meet his eye.

He raised a brow in a look that was disbelieving.

'Theo. He's . . .' She faltered. How to describe Theo? Somehow she couldn't bring herself to say the word *lover* because that would imply that they were in love. 'He's . . . a friend.'

'A friend?' The look in his eyes told her he didn't believe her. Not for a minute. 'An English friend? Does he live in London?'

'He lives in New York. He doesn't know about my arm or that I'm in France. I was planning to visit him on my way back from Colombia, that's all.'

'That's all?'

Despite the cool night air her cheeks felt hot. 'What does it matter to you anyway?'

A look of hurt flickered through his eyes. She regretted her words instantly, and the impassioned way in which she'd blurted them. Could she have made it any more obvious that she had feelings for him?

'I can tell from the way you're snarling at me that he's not just a friend.'

'I'm not snarling.' She took a deep breath and told herself to stay calm and stick to the facts. 'Theo runs a charity. He and I met at a fundraising event last year. We got on well, and one thing led to another . . .'

'You're lovers,' he said flatly, in that velvety deep voice of his.

'Not really.' That implied commitment.

'Either you are or you aren't!' He took a deep breath, as if he were trying to muster the patience to deal with a petulant child. 'Have you slept with him?'

'Yes,' she said defiantly. 'Though I don't see that it's any business of yours!'

'So he's your boyfriend?'

'Not exactly . . .'

'What then?' He looked genuinely perplexed.

'We meet when our paths cross, and we enjoy each other's company.' Theo demanded nothing of her, and she didn't ask what he got up to either. He was a friend with benefits, though she didn't want to say this to Olivier.

'And you're happy with that . . . arrangement?' he asked incredulously.

'Yes. It suits us both.' It was convenient. It helped to ease the loneliness. A little.

'I see.' He rubbed a hand over his jaw and an angry frown cut through his brow. She didn't need subtitles to understand that he disapproved. But what he thought didn't matter.

He turned back and looked her in the eye. 'You could have so much more, Lily.'

His heartfelt tone sent a ripple of emotion through her like a shockwave, but she told herself to ignore it.

'I don't want more. It meets my needs perfectly.' Oh God, that sounded so cold, so unfeeling. When in fact, Theo was one of the warmest, friendliest people she knew. She liked him a lot. But she didn't love him.

'Does it?' he asked. 'Does it really?'

She didn't know why his question unsettled her so much, or why she couldn't answer.

He sighed. 'I think we should go home now.'

'Why? Because you disapprove?'

'Because you wanted to see the market and we've done it. Let's go.'

'You're angry.'

'I'm not angry!' he said through gritted teeth, and set off at a furious pace up the hill.

'You are!'

Traffic rushed past them on the main road, so she almost didn't hear when he said, 'I'm disappointed.'

'Disappointed?' She was almost running to keep up with him, but she'd be damned if she'd be left behind.

He glared at her.

'Why?' She was breathless, though whether from running or from anger, she couldn't tell.

He stopped and span on his heel to face her. 'Because I think you're selling yourself short. You're a beautiful, talented woman, Lil. You deserve better than a part-time lover in a foreign city! You could have so much more . . .' He raked a hand through his hair as if he couldn't find the words to express what he was trying to say.

She stepped back from him. The ferocity of his words scared her and shook loose memories of all the men who'd walked away on seeing her scars. She had to ask herself, was he right? Had she given up on lasting relationships because of those experiences? Or had she simply learned that she was better off alone?

The thought unsettled her and she couldn't come up with a satisfactory answer.

What was it about Olivier that he asked such uncomfortable questions? It was as if when he looked at her he saw past the surface and directly in to her soul. It was as if he knew her better than she knew herself.

No, she decided, thinking of Corinne and his impending

marriage. She and Olivier might have been close once, but now they were very different and that was why they kept clashing like this.

Cars and scooters sped past, shooting bursts of loud music and rough-sounding engines into the night air. Away from the lights of the port, Olivier's features were cloaked in shadows, but she could see the rigid set of his shoulders and the fierce glint of his eyes.

'I don't want more,' she said finally. 'I've told you before – marriage and relationships aren't for me.'

Yet as she spoke she felt a tug, a yearning. And her words didn't carry the same conviction any more.

Chapter Twelve

'Did you enjoy your evening with Lily?' asked Corinne.

Olivier pressed his lips flat as he remembered their angry exchange in the street. It couldn't have gone more badly really. Even now fury still simmered in his chest and he had to shut his eyes to calm himself. What he felt wasn't rational. It was none of his business what Lily did and with whom. Had he really believed she was single, unattached and untouched? Of course not. She was a beautiful woman – in every sense.

But could she see that? Why did he get the feeling she couldn't? Logically he had no reason not to believe her when she said her life was exactly as she wanted it: she loved her job, she loved to travel. He understood her wanderlust, even if he didn't share it. And as for her scars, he'd seen her response to the little boy outside the bakery: calm and matter-of-fact. Her scars were part of her life, part of the woman she'd become.

Yet he couldn't shake the feeling that something was holding her back. She made herself untouchable and aloof, and her lifestyle meant that no one – not even Mamie – could get too close.

He frowned, and shook his head. *You're talking nonsense, Lacoste.* These roiling emotions were simply protectiveness for an old friend. Perhaps he was more old-fashioned than he realised.

'It was fine,' he said, hoping to brush over it, because he wasn't proud of the way he'd behaved. Why did he always give Lily such a hard time? It was her life. 'How's everything with you?'

'Work is frenetic.'

'More than usual?'

'Yes.' She hesitated. 'Actually, Oli, there's something I need to talk to you about.'

'Oh yes?'

'The hospital asked me if I could delay my holiday for an extra week.'

'But that means you won't get here until mid-August!'

'I know. But they're desperately short-staffed. And there's a new guy in charge. I don't want him to think I'm difficult.'

'So this is about making a good impression with your boss? What about the leave you had booked?'

'He's only asked me to delay it a little. It's not an unreasonable request.'

He bit his lip with frustration. With the exception of her unplanned weekend here, he and Corinne had been apart almost a month now. 'I was really looking forward to spending time together,' he said. 'And talking about the plans for our house, too. I'm getting frustrated at how long it's all taking.'

'I'm sorry,' she said quietly. 'It's only a week, Oli. Then I'll be all yours for the rest of the month.'

'A fortnight,' he said. When it should have been four

weeks. He was riled by this, yet one of the things he loved most about Corinne was that she put others first, she was always ready to do the right thing.

But where was her commitment to their relationship? He'd had her down as the dependable centrepoint in his life, but were her priorities really the same as his? Surely she *wanted* to be here with him? Surely there were other nurses who could provide cover?

Nothing felt certain any more. Last week he'd been surprised to learn about her fear of water, and when they'd visited houses they seemed to be looking for different things.

'Well it's not ideal but I guess it can't be helped,' he said quietly.

'I knew you'd understand,' she said, and he heard the relief in her voice.

'So what's he like, this new boss? Is he making life difficult for you?'

'No, not at all. He's really nice, and new to Paris. In fact, a few of us are taking him out tonight to show him around and–' She paused and he heard a knock at the door. 'That's them now. I'd better go. Speak soon?'

'Yes. Speak soon.'

He put his phone away, and tried to push out of his mind the unwelcome realisation that all his neatly ordered plans had been upended.

'*Bonjour.*'

Olivier's deep voice made Lily stiffen. She looked up

from her laptop. He filled the doorway of Mamie's kitchen; a tall, unsmiling figure.

'Maman asked me to give you this,' he said, handing Mamie a slip of paper. 'It's the number of the computer repair shop you asked for.'

'Ah yes,' she said, putting her rolling pin down and wiping floury hands on her apron. She'd been rolling pastry to make an apricot tart, but now she paused to give Olivier a kiss on each cheek. He looked at Lily but didn't move, and she didn't get up, either.

'Though I might not need it after all,' said Mamie. 'Lily has already fixed my internet, and she's checking the soft drive now.'

'*Hard* drive,' Lily corrected her, and her lip curved despite the black mood which Olivier had caused.

'She's a whizz with computers, you know,' Mamie told Olivier, and turned back to her pastry. She gave it one last press of the rolling pin, then carefully lifted it into the flan dish. 'Will you stay for coffee?'

'No thanks. I have a busy day.'

'Oh yes?' asked Mamie, as she washed her hands. 'Are you helping Raymond again?'

'No. He doesn't need me today.' He threw Lily a dark look as he spoke.

Mamie frowned and looked from one to the other. 'Have you two had an argument?'

'No—' said Lily.

'Yes—' said Olivier simultaneously.

Mamie sighed. 'Nothing changes. What was it about this time?'

'It doesn't matter,' Olivier said quickly.

Lily glared at him. 'He disapproves of my friendship with Theo.'

'Theo?' said Mamie. 'Is he the fireman in New York?'

'Yes,' she said, and stood up. The computer was running a scan and it would be at least half an hour before it had finished.

'Fireman?' Olivier looked surprised. 'You know him, Mamie?'

'Lily's spoken about him. He was badly injured and set up a charity for burns' survivors – is that right, Lily?'

'That's right. He's a lovely guy,' she said pointedly. 'Fun. Caring.'

But she didn't love him.

Was that what Olivier had meant when he'd said she deserved better? *You could have so much more . . .*

She tried to imagine herself in Corinne's place; marrying Olivier, settling down together, having his children. It wasn't the path Lily had chosen, and yet her stomach tightened at the thought, her imagination came alive as she pictured coming home to him, here in St Pierre, near the port, near the sea.

She shook off that thought. What was the matter with her? She was thirsty for adventure, not domestic life. And as for picturing herself with Olivier, she wasn't fifteen any more. She should have long since grown out of such silly adolescent dreamings.

Mamie looked at her watch. 'I'd better bring the washing in before it turns to cardboard in the sun. Am I safe to leave you two alone in the same room? You won't kill each other while I'm gone?' She shook her head and chuckled to herself as she disappeared into the garden.

Lily looked at Olivier and shuffled her feet. Olivier remained exactly where he was, a rigid figure silhouetted in the doorway.

She sighed and said quietly, 'I didn't want us to argue–'

'I'm sorry–' he said at the same time.

They both stopped and smiled awkwardly.

'I'm sorry about last night,' he said. 'But I can't pretend to understand you or the way you live your life.'

'No. Well, we've changed, both of us.'

'Yes.'

A large spider scurried across the floor towards the door.

Olivier watched it scoot past his feet, then looked at Lily. 'I think you've given up hope of having a relationship because you believe your scars will prevent it from happening.'

She shook her head, the anger rising up again, yet at the same time she remembered that moment in the olive grove years ago: the thrill of touching her lips to his, the explosion of desire as the kiss deepened – the gentle pressure of his hands on her shoulders as he pushed her away, and the leaden crush of her heart.

Why did his words make her feel so shaken? Was there some truth in them?

There was no avoiding the fact that the accident had changed her. The scars had changed her. Whether she liked it or not, people treated her differently now. At the time it had been the hardest pill to swallow. The looks, the stares, the fear, the pity in strangers' eyes, disgust in her mother's. She had reacted against it, as any person would, as any teenager would, wanting to bang her fists and go back in time to when she'd been just another girl, not especially pretty but average, and admired for her hard work in the classroom or her success on the sports field. Daddy's girl.

All this she had stewed over while in her mother's care, until the day came when she decided enough was enough. She'd packed her case and gone back to school. Yes, she was scarred, but this was the face she had to live with now. This was who she was.

'I think you say that you don't want it,' he went on, 'but really you believe you can't have it.'

'That's so not true–'

'You can, Lily. One day you will find someone and fall in love. And he'll see past the scars. He'll see how special you are, how loving and caring and perceptive and incredibly talented.'

She blinked rapidly as she stared at him. Her mouth opened, but she couldn't speak. Her throat was clogged with emotion. Olivier thought she was talented? Why did that make her feel giddy with joy? Why did what he thought matter so much to her?

'It *will* happen, Lil.'

His confidence in her was touching. A glow spread from deep within her centre, lifting her and making her blood spark. This, she thought, was the upside of his brotherly concern. He might be overprotective, but he believed in her, he genuinely cared. He was on her side. And realising this made her heart melt.

'Thanks for the vote of confidence,' she said finally, hoping to make light of it and conceal how much his words affected her. 'Why don't we put what happened last night behind us and move on?'

'Good idea.'

The kitchen filled with an awkward silence.

'Do you argue like this with Corinne?' she joked.

'No. We've never argued.'

'Never?' she asked incredulously.

He shook his head. Suddenly all the warmth drained away and she was left feeling like the troublesome little sister.

Change the subject, she told herself. 'So, are you really busy today or do you want to come with me to see the mayor? He phoned earlier. I have an appointment in an hour to discuss the exhibition.'

'I can come with you.'

'We'll have to walk – or get the bus.'

'No need. I jogged down and picked up the car this morning.'

'Okay.' She threw him a sheepish look and added, 'Those cocktails were probably a bad idea, weren't they?'

He smiled, a broad genuine smile that lit his eyes, and it made her stomach turn over. 'You always were a bad influence, Skinny.'

Chapter Thirteen

Lily felt sick. She read the email again to make sure, but it only confirmed what she'd feared during the last few days and weeks of silence.

She snatched up her phone and called Maria in Colombia. The connection was crackly but it began to ring.

'Maria?'

There was a moment's delay. 'Lily! You got my email?'

'Yes. Yes I did.'

'I'm sorry, Lily.' Maria's apology was clearly heartfelt.

'Why, Maria? What happened to make you change your minds? You were so keen to make the film before.'

'Some men have made threats,' Maria said quietly.

'Which men? Why?'

'It doesn't matter. What matters is we don't want to draw attention to ourselves. We just want to live quietly.'

'But don't you see? What you're all doing with the coffee farm is so brave, so unusual. You could be an example to other women. An inspiration.'

'We have to think of our families. They are more important than anything. We're happy with our lives here. We can't risk spoiling that.'

Lily nodded with understanding, but disappointment

roiled through her and she hung up a few minutes later with a heavy heart. She pushed her chair away and hurried out to the olive grove where the morning air was fresh and the faint scent of lavender teased her senses. She paced between the trees, stamping out her frustration. Why hadn't she seen this coming? She understood the women's fears, but to cancel – it was so disappointing. All that work – for nothing. What was she going to do now?

'Something wrong?' asked Olivier. She hadn't noticed him leaning against an olive tree. It was one of the oldest in the grove with a fat trunk which had been hollowed out on one side by a lightning strike.

She stopped. 'How long have you been there?'

'I was on my way over when I saw you. What's up? You seem upset.' His brow was furrowed with concern.

'My film is cancelled. The women in Colombia have pulled out,' she said. 'I'm never going to meet the television company's deadline now. My first commission, and I'm going to let them down.' She pressed a hand against the smooth trunk of the tree. Her reputation would be tarnished and her career over before it had even begun.

'How much have you got? Can't you work with what you have somehow?'

She shook her head. 'There isn't enough.'

'I thought you'd been filming there a week before the robbery?'

'I had. But it takes time to earn people's trust so I always begin by filming them around their home, doing simple tasks like cooking and cleaning and caring for their children. It helps them relax around the camera, it reassures them that I'm not there to judge them, and those small tasks help me understand them better. I had just got to the stage where they were starting to open up to me.'

Yolanda had told her things off camera which had made her certain there was going to be a great story. She just needed to capture it on film. But now she wouldn't get that chance.

She turned away, blinking hard. If she let the television company down and didn't deliver on this commission, she'd have a black mark against her name and all the hard work she'd put in to building her career would be for nothing.

'Show me what you have,' said Olivier.

She peered up at him. The silvery leaves of the tree glinted as they stirred in the breeze. 'Why?'

'Because I'm interested.'

'There's no point.' She hung her head, feeling sick.

'Don't be so defeatist.'

'It's true. You can't help me. No one can.'

'So you're just going to roll over and give up?'

She narrowed her eyes at his teasing, goading tone. He grinned, obviously pleased that he'd got a reaction from her. Her lips tugged.

'I'm interested to see,' he said.

She sighed. 'Fine.'

It would be a waste of time, but she led him inside to her room, opened her laptop, and showed him the scant footage she had collected.

'This is Yolanda's home,' she explained, aware of Olivier's head close to hers as he watched over her shoulder. 'I filmed her sweeping the floor, making bread in the morning, looking after her baby. Here I have a few shots of the women at work, tending to the plants on the farm, and in the factory, sorting the coffee beans and packing them.' It was all mundane stuff; it would be impossible to shape a story out of these clips.

Olivier nodded. 'It gives context. Shows how little they have, what humble conditions they live in.'

'It also shows their personalities.' She skipped forward to the factory owner. 'See her? Marcela. She's efficient and organised, the strong one of the group. And this is Sofia. See how she nurses her baby? She's a really gentle, maternal type.'

The film continued with more clips of Yolanda at home. 'I've got lots of footage of Yolanda because I was living with her. She was incredibly hard-working – she had to be, with four young children to look after. She got up before sunrise to prepare food for their breakfast.'

'Did you say that's bread she's making? It looks like a pancake.'

'It's called *arepas*, it's a type of corn bread cooked on a griddle pan.'

'I like the shots of her cooking. Couldn't you use those to make a new film? A different story – not about the coffee farm, but . . .' He stopped suddenly, as if an idea had suddenly struck.

'But what?' said Lily. These clips had no narrative.

Her films were all based on personal stories and emotion. That, she had learned, was what made a film compelling.

'You could film me,' he said.

Her head whipped up. 'You?'

He nodded. 'Making bread. Working in my bakery in Paris – with the machines and all our state-of-the-art equipment. You could compare and contrast the developed and undeveloped countries, how different the ingredients and the methods are, but also what we have in common – this essential food: bread.'

She considered this. 'It would fit for the film prize too – they want a story with an international flavour and a focus on universal human stories.'

'Have you got any other clips like this – from previous jobs?'

She thought of films she'd made in Ukraine and India and Tibet. There was a lot of domestic material archived which she'd never used. 'Yes,' she said, 'but I'm not sure – what would my story be?'

'What your films are always about – how we're essentially the same. All human with the same hopes and dreams and fears.'

'And the same basic needs of food and water and love . . .' she said, thinking aloud.

'You could call it Bread.'

She smiled. 'I like it.'

She was still worried there might not be enough, but why not try? There was nothing to lose. And the idea of filming Olivier was tempting. Very tempting.

'I thought you were camera-shy?' she said. 'That you didn't want to be filmed?'

'I didn't . . . But this is different.' His gaze met hers. 'I'll do it once – to help you out. And because I trust you. So what do you say? You want to film me?'

'Yes. Yes, I do.'

She still wasn't sure exactly what her story would be, but she couldn't pass up this chance to film Olivier Lacoste, master baker, at work.

'Will you be alright, Mamie?'

'Silly question! Of course I will.'

Lily felt a tug. She'd only been here two weeks, but it seemed like such a long time. She looked around the farmhouse kitchen, disturbed by her hesitance – her reluctance – to leave, even just for a few days. She was getting attached, she realised, and she didn't like it. It made her feel . . . vulnerable.

Perhaps this trip to Paris was good timing. It might help her regain the detached and objective outlook which she was used to.

She hugged Mamie hard. It was a bit easier now she didn't have to wear a sling any more, though her arm was still strapped and bandaged.

'We'll be back in a few days,' she promised her gran.

Mamie's gaze flickered from Lily to Olivier. 'You take as long as you need, both of you.'

Was it Lily's imagination or was there a gleam in her grandmother's eye? Lily shook her head. They were going to Paris: Corinne would be there. Lily suspected that this might be part of the reason why Olivier had suggested the trip in the first place – as an excuse to see his fiancée.

'Drive carefully,' Mamie told Olivier, who smiled and bent to kiss her too.

'I always drive carefully.'

'And look after my Lily.'

He shot Lily a sideways glance and his eyes danced with humour. A syrupy warmth flowed through her. 'You know I will. Anyway, are you sure she needs looking after?'

'Of course she does,' said Mamie, 'despite what she thinks. We all do.'

'I need to film this!' said Lily, eyes wide as she took in the display of *patisseries:* the rainbow-coloured macarons and fruit tarts, the velvet-dark chocolate gateaux and éclairs, all crafted to look like miniature works of art. She bent forward to peer through the glass at the display and saw the impeccable attention to detail of tiny swirls and adornments, all so precise and identical. 'It's beautiful,' she breathed, overawed.

They'd driven all day, but Olivier had insisted on coming straight here to his flagship bakery, *Olivier*, in the heart of the city. His trademark logo of an olive tree was everywhere: on the boxes and bags customers carried away, on the staff aprons, and even on the edible chocolate badges which adorned his cakes.

'I thought you were planning to film me,' Olivier winked. He set down her filming gear which he'd carried in. 'Or are my cakes more alluring?'

Her stomach growled loudly.

'I think I have my answer,' he chuckled. 'You can film the displays tomorrow morning before the place is filled with customers,' he said, and led her through to the back.

Lily wished her arm was strong enough to carry her camera because following him as he threaded his way through the kitchens of his bakery was eye-opening. His staff bombarded him with news and questions, and they all looked genuinely delighted to see him. However, it was clear he was the boss by the respect he commanded, and when he spotted a line of pastries which didn't meet his high standards and reprimanded the chef in charge Lily was reminded of Raymond.

Eventually, they reached a small alcove off the side of the kitchen. Olivier ducked his head under the tiled archway and set the tripod down.

'I can work here,' he said, pointing to the worktop. 'What do you think?'

Lily checked the lighting and assessed the room around her. 'It's great,' she said hesitantly, 'but the kitchens are noisy. It might be nice to have some background bustle, but it could also cause problems for the sound quality.'

'It will quieten down in—' He checked his watch, 'half an hour. And we can film into the evening if necessary,' he said, 'or in my kitchen at home. But this place is better because all the equipment and ingredients are to hand. Shall I set up?'

Once they'd arranged the tripod and camera and lighting, they began with a test run.

'So, Boss, where should we begin?' he asked.

'How about you start with something simple. A basic bread dough, for example.'

'Alright. You want me to talk you through what I'm doing?'

'If you can, yes. Otherwise I could do a sound recording later.'

Lily positioned herself behind the camera and brought it into focus. Excitement bubbled up inside her as it always did when she embarked on a new project in a new place. It was energising, stimulating. This was what she loved, this was when she felt truly at peace and in control; behind her camera. And watching Olivier was mesmerising. His hands, powdery white with flour, worked quickly and deftly, his forearms flexing and knotting, his face a picture of concentration. Her stomach tightened. There was something sensuous about watching his fingers knead the dough and shape it.

His deep voice rumbled through her as he began to explain the recipe and the science behind what he was doing, the importance of accuracy, of precise weights and temperature. Lily was enthralled by his knowledge, his confidence and passion for what he was doing. And by his capable hands. She watched as they smoothed and rolled the dough into long baguette shapes, and she imagined how those same hands would feel on her skin, on her body. Gentle yet confident. Passionate yet controlled. Strong yet tender.

The air stuck in her lungs. The temperature in the tiny alcove seemed to have risen several degrees. She bit down on her lip, and reminded herself that only a few miles away in this city was the woman he was going to marry.

'So what does it take to become a master baker?' she asked, trying to get back into professional work mode.

Olivier had expected to feel self-conscious – uneasy, at the very least – in front of the camera. Normally, when he encountered them, he was caught out by the flashbulb of a paparazzi photographer snapping him in the street, or occasionally by a local news crew desperate for a story where there was none. But right now he felt as relaxed as he always did in the kitchen. It was just him and Lily and the dough he was working.

She intermittently asked him questions in that quietly probing voice of hers, and she seemed to have a knack for drawing information out of him, for getting him to open up.

'So what does it take to become a master baker?' she asked.

He raised a brow and his lip curved in a wry smile. 'Hard work,' he said. 'It's a craft you have to learn like any other. It's about technique, about using the best ingredients to make the best product, but it's also about passion.'

'Passion?'

'For achieving perfection in your product. Every detail

is important: the flavour, the texture, the physical act of mixing and kneading the dough, shaping it, finishing a piece and turning it into a work of art. All this requires total dedication. It's not a profession you can half-heartedly commit to.'

'And what are the rewards for this dedication? What do you love most about your job?'

'I love the creativity of discovering new flavours, of reworking age-old recipes with modern twists or fusing different recipes to make something new. I also love the classics, and the challenge of achieving perfection in something thousands of people have made before you.'

'Do you do much of that now you're head of a chain of bakeries and a training school too?'

He stopped for a moment. 'Not as much as I'd like,' he said, and regret snaked through him.

Now his bakeries were renowned and his name was established, something had gone. Where was his motivation? When had he lost it? He was competitive by nature but, having achieved his goals and made his name, what was he supposed to aim for now?

His mind turned to St Pierre and his father's simple village bakery, a world away from the high-end demands and glamour of his Parisian shops. How was Raymond still so committed after all this time?

What do you love most about your job? They moved on to other subjects but her question ate away at him and wouldn't let him rest.

⋆

'So will Corinne be here tonight?' asked Lily as they drove towards his home. By the time they'd finished filming it had been late, and Olivier had locked up the darkened bakery.

'Not tonight. She's staying at the hospital and working the nightshift.'

'Oh.' Lily tried to ignore her relief. 'What about tomorrow? Will you see her then?'

They drove into an underground car park, and Olivier carried their bags over to the lift. The striplights flickered, casting shadows across his face.

'Maybe. She hasn't got back to me yet.' His mouth flattened, and Lily detected tension in the hard set of his jaw.

She frowned. 'Is everything alright with you two?'

'Yes. It's just this was an unexpected trip so she's trying to rearrange her nightshifts, but it hasn't been easy.'

Lily nodded and followed him out of the lift. She waited while he pushed his key into the lock, then he beckoned her inside. She gazed around at the tasteful eighteenth-century apartment with parquet flooring and large, bright windows that gave onto a small park below. She noticed a vase of greenery over the fireplace and wondered if it was evidence of Corinne's feminine touch. He showed her to her room, and gave her a quick tour of the place. She caught a glimpse of Olivier's large bed on which he dropped his bag, and her gaze stuck, imagining the two of them sleeping there. When he showed her the roof terrace, she couldn't enjoy the view but looked behind her, picturing them both seated at the small table, enjoying a romantic meal for two, far above the bustle of the city streets below.

Her heart pinched. She had to stop doing this. She wished only happiness for him, and he'd found that with Corinne. Why couldn't her heart accept it?

'So what do you fancy doing this evening?' he asked, when they'd eaten a quick snack. 'Cinema? A concert?'

She thought of their night out in St Pierre and how easy it had been, when she was alone with him, to forget that anyone else existed. She also remembered how it had ended in an argument about Theo.

'Actually, I'm quite tired,' she said, her mind springing back to Corinne who was working hard, doing the night-shift at the hospital. 'It's been a long day and we've got an early start tomorrow. I'd like to get an early night.'

'Oh. Okay.'

Did he look disappointed? Only because she was poor company. And he must be longing to see his fiancée. 'I suppose you're right. We'll leave at five am, okay? Then you can see the kitchens in full flow and film the shop while it's empty.'

Lily nodded. 'See you in the morning.'

He bent his head to kiss her goodnight, but her hair was in the way. Carefully, he pushed it back and tucked it behind her ears. She stilled at the surprisingly intimate gesture, and the warmth of his lips as they brushed her cheek. The nerves where her skin was scarred were not as sensitive; nevertheless, his touch sent arrows of heat shooting through her. It took all her self-control not to touch the spot where his mouth had made contact.

Flushed, she mumbled goodnight and scuttled back to her room. As she unpacked her tiny case, she tried to marshal her thoughts back into some kind of order. It had just been a goodnight kiss, nothing more, she told herself, and tried to focus on tomorrow's filming, planning more questions to ask, making mental notes of shots and angles she wanted to capture.

She heard the clunk of metal as Olivier bolted the door of the apartment, and the squeak of wooden shutters being drawn. Footsteps approached in the hall, his bedroom door opened and closed, then everything went quiet. She wondered if he'd call Corinne tonight. Would he lie in bed thinking of her and missing her?

Shaking her head, Lily snatched up her washbag and went to the bathroom. As she brushed her teeth, she noticed there were two toothbrushes by the sink. On the shelf above was a small bottle of perfume and, when Lily sniffed it, she recognised the fresh citrusy scent. She put it back and looked around. A disposable pink shaver on the windowsill, a tube of moisturising lotion: everywhere she looked there were traces of Corinne.

Lily retreated to her room, feeling like an intruder in this beautiful apartment. And it was strange, because her role of filmmaker meant she was accustomed to being the outsider looking in. Yet tonight, for the first time in her life, she felt uneasy in that role.

A sense of longing gripped her, and she couldn't explain it.

*

'You've tied your hair back,' said Olivier.

Lily's free hand left the camera and lifted to touch her sleek, neat ponytail. 'I thought it was more hygienic for working in a kitchen, that's all.'

He couldn't help smiling. 'It suits you.'

'Thanks.' Her cheeks coloured like peaches, and she gestured to the worktop and the wide flat square of pastry in front of him. 'Can we get back to topic? You're supposed to be answering my questions, remember?'

'Yes, Chef,' he winked. 'What was the question again?'

She pressed her lips flat and rolled her eyes. 'Tell me why you became a baker?'

He sliced the thick sheet of dough into squares, then into triangles to make croissants. 'My earliest childhood memories – I'm talking aged two, three – are of eating bread and pastry. The taste, the texture, the pleasure of it. I bake because I want to share that pleasure, I want to make food for others to enjoy.' He put the knife down and looked directly at the camera. 'Ultimately, baking is an act of love.'

The room stayed silent, with only the background noise of the main kitchen next door. He wasn't sure why his words vibrated through him, or why he was strung tight with tension all of a sudden. He was talking about baking, that was all.

Lily straightened up. The air felt thick and heavy, and his gaze flickered briefly over her full lips. 'An act of love?' she probed.

He nodded and looked down at his floured hands, yet he couldn't put into words the satisfaction of counting forty-eight perfect triangles which would roll to make the same number of perfect croissants. Was this what he'd missed? Certainly, there was nothing in the boardroom that gave him the same sense of satisfaction. The sensual act of immersing his hands in cool flour, of creating a dough and kneading it until it relaxed and yielded to his touch and became soft and elastic.

'I . . .' he faltered, but it was impossible to explain. The nearest thing he could think of was desire: when you looked at a woman and knew you had to be with her.

His gaze locked with Lily's and a shock of unwelcome, unsettling emotions powered through him.

'Oli?'

'Sorry – I . . .'

He stared at the slab of raw croissant dough in front of him. His brain had jammed, words dried up on his tongue.

Lily threw him a gentle smile. 'Perhaps this would be a good time to stop for breakfast? I don't know about you, but I'm famished.'

They sat outside in the gentle morning sun, and he watched with amusement as Lily devoured her second *pain au chocolat*. He was still troubled by what he felt earlier. It must be down to their early start, he decided. What else could explain the confusion in his head, the mixed-up sensations he'd felt?

Pushing it aside, he swallowed his coffee and hoped the caffeine would restore order to his thoughts.

She swallowed and flashed him a cheeky smile. 'I

remember before you decided to be a baker, when you wanted to be an Olympic swimmer.'

He grinned. 'I wasn't interested in the swimming. I just wanted a medal.'

'Not true. You wanted to be the best. You always wanted to be the best – in everything.' She held up the last remaining piece of her pastry. 'I suppose you are, but for baking not swimming.'

His smile faded and he looked away at the busy Parisian street, snarled and noisy with early morning traffic, the pavements thick with commuters hurrying to work. 'It's not all it's cracked up to be.'

'You're not happy?' Lily was peering at him, her brow furrowed with concern.

'I'm not unhappy,' he said, balancing in his mind all the reasons he had to be grateful – a loving fiancée and family, financial security, good health – versus this unsettling sensation of having taken a wrong turn somewhere along the line. 'I'm just not as excited about my work as I once was.'

'What changed?' asked Lily.

'I don't know. I guess the job I do has changed over the years as my business has grown. It's less about the baking now and more about the business side. Profitability and so on.' He sipped his coffee, uncomfortable talking about himself. He wasn't the self-pitying kind. He liked order and calm, he liked reliable plans, not the uneasy chaotic sensation that this topic seemed to generate. 'Tell me, when did you stop wanting to be an astronaut?'

She laughed. 'Astronaut. I had forgotten about that.'

'It would have suited you – the ultimate in adventure and travel.' He became serious. 'So what made you decide to become a filmmaker?'

'It was at school,' she said. 'I was sixteen and we were given a camera to use for an art project. We were each allowed to keep it for a week and told to film whatever we wanted.' She sat back in her chair and there was a dreamy look in her eyes. 'I loved the way it made me feel invisible.'

'Invisible?'

She nodded. 'I found that the people I was filming fell into two categories: either they carried on with what they were doing and forgot I was filming them, or the more attention-seeking types performed for the camera. Either way, I didn't matter.'

She'd faded into the background. He could see that for a sixteen-year-old girl with fresh scars that must have been a relief.

'And when I strung together all my pieces of film to make a story I found it really satisfying. So I began to dream of becoming a filmmaker.' She crossed her legs and straightened out the paper napkin on her lap. 'Until then I had despaired that having a visible difference would rule out so many career choices; now I saw a future for myself.'

Olivier nodded and watched a crowded bus shudder past as he absorbed this. The fire had changed the course of her life in so many ways – but in this case, the change had been positive, directing her towards a career she was passionate about. He saw that Lily was a stronger person as a result of her experiences, he appreciated how gifted she was and how her work was making a difference. Yet he still wished she would stay still every now and then. Come home more.

Why? Why did it matter to him what she did and how she lived her life? It wasn't just about concern for Mamie, was it? He frowned, unsettled by that question, and forced it from his mind.

He put his empty cup down. 'Ready to carry on?'

'How do you do that?'

Olivier looked up. He'd been so absorbed in what he was doing that he hadn't noticed Lily had straightened up from behind her camera and was watching him, eyes wide, alight with fascination.

'Do what?'

She pointed to the length of bread dough that he'd rolled to make *ficelles*. 'Can you slow it down for the camera? Your hands move so fast it's like – like magic.'

'Like magic, eh?' he grinned, and did as he was asked, slowing the action right down so she could see how he took the square lump of dough, folded over the edge, and pressed it with the heel of his hand, repeating the process over and over again until he was left with a small tube shape which he then rolled and stretched into a wide length, squeezing both tips into sharp points.

'That's incredible,' she said quietly. 'You're so talented.'

'What's this? A compliment from you, Skinny? That's

a first.' His tone was light, but at the same time his chest swelled. He tried not to let her admiration go to his head, but for some reason it meant a lot to him.

Only because it was so unheard of. He was used to being the butt of her teasing, not of serious compliments.

'Well it's true. You are talented,' she said, and the look in her eyes touched something inside him. It felt like strings vibrating deep in his chest. 'Don't stop. Carry on.'

She disappeared behind the camera and he picked up another square of dough, but now he couldn't concentrate. He dropped the dough cutter, he was heavy-handed with the flour. What was the matter with him? He'd made this bread hundreds of thousands of times. His hands and his fingers were so familiar with the action of pressing and rolling, he could probably do it in his sleep if he'd been the sleepwalking type.

But it had never felt like this.

Alert. Self-conscious. Aware of Lily's eyes following him, intent, dark with admiration as she'd tracked his every move.

Her unabashed admiration had just got to him, he told himself quickly. It had stoked his ego – which was probably why she'd never paid him compliments before.

Yet others had complimented his work and their words hadn't made him swell with pride as Lily's had.

Enough, Lacoste! He turned away, supposedly in search of a metal tray, but really to escape from her camera – and her.

*

'It looks so complicated,' said Lily. 'Can anyone learn the skill of baking, or do some people have a natural propensity for it?'

The camera was recording, but she stood beside it and he tried not to let his gaze linger over her high cheekbones or the long dark lashes that framed her beautiful eyes. He made himself ignore the burst of energy that gripped him whenever she spoke in that calm, silky voice, and the electricity that charged the air. That made fear trickle through him.

'Anyone can learn how to weigh the ingredients,' he said, forcing his thoughts back to his experiences of new recruits and the hours he'd spent as a child learning from Raymond, 'they can practise shaping and decorating a product. But some people learn faster than others. They have a special touch, they stand out from the rest.'

His voice trailed off as his gaze settled on hers and stuck there of its own volition. Her green eyes, rippled with grey, held him fast and the alcove, their private corner of the busy kitchens, became suddenly very still. The back of his neck prickled. He tried to extinguish it, but it percolated through him, a slow-burning yet unstoppable tide of need that he recognised.

He cleared his throat, he tried to clear his mind, but his thoughts were stuck on Lily.

Lily, his closest friend.

Lily, who was like a sister to him.

Always Lily.

Feeling concern for her, curiosity, needing to understand

her, enjoying her company, craving her company because it made him feel – feel . . . what exactly?

He wasn't sure, but one thing was for certain: it was wrong to feel like this. He was engaged to Corinne. He loved Corinne. And his feelings for Lily had always been fraternal, hadn't they?

Until he'd learned about Theo.

He hesitated a fraction of a second then continued rolling the oblongs of pastry to make *palmiers*. Learning about her lover had triggered something in him, a kind of rage, of . . . – he racked his brain, trying to identify the biting emotion – jealousy.

His brow furrowed as dismay followed the realisation. It couldn't be.

He loved Corinne. He was just getting mixed up – it must be the consequence of having been apart these last few weeks.

'We're meeting Corinne for dinner tonight,' he told Lily abruptly. 'I hope that's alright.'

She looked up in surprise, then flicked a switch on the camera. 'Are you sure?'

'Of course I'm sure.'

'I mean, I don't have to come with you. If you'd rather see her alone I'll be perfectly alright. I can do my own thing.'

'I'm not leaving you on your own,' he snapped. 'We're meeting Corinne at eight.'

'Oh. Okay.' She sounded a little bemused, no doubt by his brusque manner.

But he didn't know how to explain that he didn't like

what he was feeling. He lived a steady uncomplicated life, and these roiling eruptive emotions were not what he was used to.

'Ready to carry on?' he said, with a nod to the camera.

'Actually,' she said, 'It would be good to get a different angle. I'd really like to film over your shoulder.'

He tensed. 'What do you mean?'

She looked around, fetched a square stool and positioned it behind him. Then, holding on to his arm to steady herself, she climbed up and stood behind him looking down at his hands and the work surface.

'Perfect,' she said. 'This way viewers can see what you see as you work. Your perspective.'

Her breath was warm as it whispered against her neck, her left hand was still gripping his shoulder. He tried to dull his awareness of her body behind his, but fire filled his veins, and instinct was telling him to move away.

'You'll fall off and break your other arm,' he warned, not daring to turn his head in case she saw in his eyes the heat he was feeling.

'I won't.'

'You can't lift the camera.'

'I'll rest it on your shoulder. Do you mind?'

'It will make it difficult to work.'

'Then we'll do a series of stills. Let's try. Please. It's such a good angle.'

Her eyes were big and pleading. What choice did he have?

*

This had been such a bad idea, thought Lily. It was the perfect angle – it gave a bird's eye view of Olivier's hands as they rolled and stretched and smoothed the delicate pastry. But at what cost to her?

Pressed up against his large frame, she could feel his heartbeat, she could hear the steady whisper of his breathing, and it was causing curls of heat to unfurl deep within her, thickening her blood. He picked up a large chunky knife and began to slice the pastry into smaller blocks.

She wanted to ask questions: how did he cut the pastry so accurately, making identical rectangles each time? Why did he use so much sugar? And how did he manage to roll them into heart-shaped coils so quickly? But she didn't dare speak. Pushed up like this against his warm body, it was difficult enough just to keep breathing.

'*Merde!*' The knife fell and blood sprang up from his finger.

Lily jumped down and he grabbed a cloth and wrapped it around his injured finger. She put her camera down and said, 'Let me see.'

He looked away as she lifted the cloth. 'It's not too deep,' she said. 'Raise your hand in the air to slow the blood flow.'

To her amazement, he did as he was told without arguing.

'Sit down, Chicken,' she said gently, and guided him onto the stool. 'I'll get you a glass of water.'

She rushed over to the sink and searched for a glass.

All she could find was a small bowl, but that would do. 'You've gone pale. I didn't know you were so squeamish.'

'I'm not,' he said. 'Not normally.' He smiled but there was a strange look in his eyes as he followed her movements.

She handed him the bowl and he took a sip. 'Should I call the paramedics?' she joked.

'Don't be silly.'

'Or Corinne?'

The smile vanished from his lips. 'Not funny, Lil.'

His words cut her down. Clearly she'd said the wrong thing, but she had no idea what or why.

'How is the filming going?' asked Corinne.

The three of them were sitting in the little bistro near the hospital where Corinne worked. The small square tables were covered with pretty red tablecloths and old-fashioned lanterns which must be cosy in the winter, but looked superfluous in the stifling heat. Lily shifted uncomfortably in her chair. Olivier had insisted that she accompany them for dinner, but she felt like a wallflower.

'I've got some great footage,' she said. 'Olivier's good in front of the camera, and he talks passionately about baking. It all makes for fascinating material.'

Olivier didn't respond. Instead, he kept his gaze lowered and ran the pad of his thumb over the blue plaster that was wrapped around his finger. Lily's lips flattened. He was angry with her. He'd been hot and irritable anyway, then that accident with the knife had ruined a batch of pastry. That must be why he was glowering at his glass of wine.

'And are you enjoying it, Oli?' Corinne asked him. The blue of her eyes was accentuated by the turquoise and olive wood necklace he'd given her, Lily noticed.

'Yes,' he said, and fiddled absently with the salt shaker as he spoke. 'Actually, Lily's questions have made me think, and I've had a few insights as a result.'

Corinne's brows lifted queryingly.

'I've realised that what I've been missing in my work for the last few years is the hands-on baking itself. It's made me see that I've been spending too much time in the board room and not enough in the kitchen.'

'So what are you going to do?'

'I don't know yet. I need to think about it.'

The waiter arrived and brusquely took their orders, then they resumed their conversation.

'I have some good news,' said Corinne, looking at Olivier. 'My transfer has come through. There's a job for me in Marseille.'

'That's wonderful, said Olivier. 'When does it start?'

'In the autumn.'

'Fantastic,' he said, meeting her gaze, and Lily couldn't prevent the spike of jealousy as he smiled.

Yet she noticed that Corinne didn't look half as excited as Olivier. Perhaps she was nervous about leaving Paris. She had been chattering excitedly earlier about her new boss and it sounded like she and her hospital colleagues had a great social life.

'Any news on the house front?' Corinne asked Olivier. 'Did you say you've got some designs to show me?'

'Oh yes.' Olivier's expression brightened, and he reached for the document wallet he'd brought with him. 'I had some preliminary sketches drawn up. What do you think?'

He pulled out several sheets of paper and spread them across the table in front of her. Lily peered over Corinne's shoulder to take a closer look.

'It's to be built of stone rather than the modern breeze blocks and render which are fashionable now,' he explained. 'The stone is a pale sandy colour that will reflect the sun. And the house has old style wooden shutters and a chimney, a rustic style kitchen.'

'Not a modern kitchen?' asked Corinne.

He shook his head. 'I have modern kitchens with state-of-the-art equipment at work. I want my home to feel different. Relaxed. Same in the garden: lavender, oleander – plants which look natural and are suited to the climate.'

An uneasy silence settled around them. Lily shot a sideways glance at Corinne: she was staring at the drawings of the exterior.

'What do you think?' Olivier prompted.

Corinne glanced at Lily and swallowed. 'It – it looks just like Mamie's house,' she said finally.

Lily stilled.

'Does it?' He peered at the sketches.

So did Lily. Corinne was right: there were a lot of similarities.

'How?'

'The turret roof,' said Corinne, 'the farmhouse feel. I thought you'd want something more modern.'

'It's modern in some ways. Look, there's a large open plan living area downstairs. And I thought we could design it so our bedroom is at the front of the house with that fabulous view of the sea.'

Corinne said nothing, and Lily remembered how she'd said she was afraid of water. She sat rigid in her seat, not knowing where to look or what to say.

A deep frown cut through Olivier's brow. 'You don't like it, do you?'

Corinne chewed her lip. 'It's just . . .'

Lily looked up as another group of diners arrived. The bistro was filling up and the noise level was rising. But here in their corner quiet tension had settled around them like a chill in the air.

'Just?'

'I don't know. It's so far from what I was expecting. I just don't think it's . . . right. For me.'

'Oh.' Olivier looked so disappointed. 'What were you expecting?'

Corinne brightened. 'I'd love a spacious modern kitchen where the children can play while we prepare meals, lots of bedrooms, and a garden with a big square lawn, rather than–' She pointed to the plans, '–an orchard.'

'Olive grove,' he corrected. 'Okay. I'll talk to the architect and we'll draw up new plans.'

He folded up the sheet and put it away. Lily remembered how uncomfortable he'd looked when they'd visited the modern house that Corinne had liked. They seemed to have very different tastes.

Their food came, and as they began to eat Lily tried to change the subject, asking Corinne about her work in the hospital.

'I'm working with a fantastic team,' said Corinne. 'Some of our doctors are pioneering the most amazing new treatments.'

'Really?'

'Yes, it's very exciting.' She paused and glanced at Lily's scars. 'You know, they can do a lot to repair scarring nowadays? Medicine has really advanced in that area, especially here in France.'

Lily felt a sinking sensation at where the conversation was headed. 'Yes. I know.' She kindly but firmly met Corinne's gaze.

'I'm working with a surgeon who is at the forefront of research into this area. If you wanted to, I could introduce you.'

Olivier's head whipped up and his eyes narrowed. But Lily could see that Corinne meant well. 'That's very good of you, but I don't plan to have any more surgery.'

'He could help to reduce your scarring.'

'I've got used to them now. They're part of who I am.' Surgery was painful, and it would mean time off work, which was out of the question.

'The surgery he does has a ninety percent success rate–'

'Corinne!' Olivier gritted.

She stopped. Both she and Lily turned to look at him,

stunned by his fierce tone. His black eyes sparked with fury.

'Didn't you hear? Lily doesn't want more surgery.'

'I know, but I'm just trying–'

'You're insulting her. Implying that she needs medical intervention when Lily is beautiful as she is!'

Lily's brows lifted at his vehemence. Corinne looked mortified and Lily's heart went out to her. 'That's enough, Olivier. I'm not offended at all.'

He paused from glaring at Corinne to flash Lily a dark look. His words echoed through her head; *Lily is beautiful as she is!*

But they made no sense. She wasn't beautiful. Far from it.

Yet hadn't he told her she should tie her hair back? Her eyes narrowed with confusion. He was a good friend, but only a friend – so why was he so angry? Corinne's blue eyes were shadowed with anxiety, and Lily felt bad.

Olivier stood up. 'I think we should leave,' he told them. 'I'll take you home, Corinne.'

'No!' said Lily, horrified that she'd cause a rift between them. 'There's no need.'

Corinne turned to Lily. 'I'm so sorry. I never meant to say anything hurtful.'

'I know you didn't.' She turned to Olivier who was still standing. 'Olivier, you're totally overreacting and if you leave, I really will be insulted.'

His mouth flattened, and he reluctantly sat down again.

'My scars are not and should never be a taboo subject. But like I said, I'm not going to have surgery because they're part of me now.' She picked up her bag. 'I'll go. I need to call Mamie, and I'm sure you two would appreciate some time alone together.'

She should never have come here tonight. If she hadn't been there, he and Corinne wouldn't have argued. She felt utterly responsible. Could she have handled it differently? She was quite clear in her mind that she didn't want surgery. Her scars might make life uncomfortable sometimes, but she was determined that she shouldn't have to change the way she looked to be accepted. She refused to be moulded and sculpted to look how others thought she should look.

Then again, Olivier had overreacted, and she didn't understand why he'd been so angry. She could look after herself. Corinne wasn't the first person to have asked her questions or raised the subject of surgery.

She wished her arm would hurry up and heal so she could take off again. She hated to think that she'd been the cause of trouble between Olivier and Corinne. She might harbour feelings for him, but she would never wish to come between him and his fiancée.

Chapter Fourteen

'I was only trying to help,' Corinne said, when Lily had gone.

'By implying she needs surgery?'

'They can do so much nowadays to reduce scarring.'

'She doesn't want surgery. She spent the best part of a year recovering from her injuries. Of course she doesn't want any more operations.'

'A year?' Corinne said quietly.

'She's fine as she is. I'd have thought that you of all people would be able to see beyond the skin-deep surface.'

'Of course I do. Lily's a lovely person, kind and caring, and – I only wanted to help.'

He clocked her contrite look and suddenly the fury drained from him. He rubbed a hand over the rough stubble of his chin and sighed. 'I – I'm sorry.'

He'd overreacted, rushing to Lily's defence like an angry bulldog.

There was a short pause before she said softly, 'It's okay.'

The silence stretched a little too long. This was the first time they'd argued. And it had been his fault. Corinne was studying his expression, and he wondered what she saw because he couldn't explain why he'd reacted the way he had. It hadn't been rational; he'd just seen red.

'Lily and me, we go way back,' he said weakly. He dipped his gaze away, afraid of her calm scrutiny. 'She's like – like a little sister.'

'I know.'

A loud burst of laughter from another table made them both look up. The noise contrasted with the awkward silence which hovered between them both.

'Let's get out of here,' he said, pulling out his wallet, and signalling for the waiter. 'I'll walk you home.'

Outside, the temperature had dropped and the night air was a little fresher as they walked slowly back towards the hospital.

'She's tougher than you think, you know,' said Corinne. He looked up in surprise. 'She doesn't need – or want – looking after.'

How did Corinne know what Lily wanted? He felt another flare of anger, but this time he fought it down. He didn't want to argue.

'She doesn't have anyone, apart from Mamie,' he said, his voice gruff.

'Maybe that's how she wants to be,' Corinne said carefully. 'Maybe it's not because of her scars that she's alone.'

'It's not through choice, either! Her father died way too young!'

Her shoes tapped out a quick rhythm on the pavement, twice as fast as his long strides. A taxi raced past at breakneck speed, its exhaust spitting out dirty black smoke.

'What about her mother?'

'She was a waste of space. Lily left as soon as she could. She chose to board at school rather than live with her.'

'But she chooses to live a solitary life travelling,' Corinne said quietly. 'It's what she wants. She would have settled down and found somewhere to call home if that was what she wanted.'

It took a moment for him to absorb this. She was right. Lily chose to be alone, she was perfectly independent. So why did he feel the overwhelming need to draw her into his life and protect her from harm?

He raked a hand through his hair and tried to lay thoughts of Lily aside. He focused on Corinne and stopped, turned to face her. He said quietly, 'I suppose I find that hard to understand because it's so different from what we want, you and I.' She came into his arms and he inhaled the scent of her honey-coloured hair. But he felt a distance between them now, and the blame for that lay squarely on his shoulders; he'd caused it with his outburst.

'I'm sorry,' he repeated. 'I don't want us to argue.'

'It's okay. You and Lily are very close. Anyone can see that.'

No, he thought, they weren't. Lily didn't let anyone close. But there was something else gnawing at him, something Corinne had said. *She chooses to live a solitary life travelling, it's what she wants.*

Was it really what Lily wanted, or was there more to her wanderlust?

*

By the time Olivier got back to his place, it was late and the streets were quiet, the apartment block still. He closed the door quietly, expecting that Lily would be asleep in bed, but as he kicked off his shoes he noticed the doors to the terrace were open and the hushed sounds of the slumbering city drifted in. He went out and stood still for a moment, seeking her out amidst the night-blue shapes and shadows.

'I couldn't sleep,' she said quietly.

His head swivelled to the right and he realised she was sitting in one of the deckchairs he kept folded and never used.

'It was too hot inside.'

'It is hot,' he agreed, and picked up another deckchair and placed it beside hers. He sat down, carefully easing his large frame into the flimsy structure of wood and fabric.

Normally when he came out here, it was to lean against the balcony and look down over the city lights and humming streets. But the deckchair tipped him back so his gaze was directed up at the night sky. It was a beautiful night. The faintest breeze touched his face and ruffled the bamboo behind him. The moon shone and the stars glinted like sugar crystals strewn across the velvet sky.

'Perhaps it wasn't such a good idea to come to the city in the middle of a heatwave,' he said.

He heard Lily's head turn and felt her eyes searching for him in the dark.

'Did you make up with Corinne?' she asked.

'Yes.'

'So everything's okay?'

'It's fine.'

'Good. I was worried.'

He didn't reply. He didn't want to talk about it. He didn't like the person he'd become these last twenty-four hours. He especially didn't like that he'd hurt Corinne.

The distant call of a police siren spiralled through the night, and in one of the streets below a solitary moped scooted past.

'You can see the stars more clearly in St Pierre,' he said.

'Yes, but they're still amazing wherever you are. Even in London there's–' She gasped. 'Look! A shooting star!'

He heard the wonder in her voice, the excitement, and for some reason this made his heart leap with joy.

'I see it,' he smiled. He wanted her to be happy. He wanted it so much it was an ache in his chest, yet he couldn't understand why it mattered so much to him.

'How long have you been a secret stargazer, Skinny?'

'Forever. I used to watch the stars with Papa. He taught me all the constellations.'

'Really? Show me.'

'See those three there, almost in a line? That's Orion's belt. And that's Ursa Major . . .' She went on, pointing them out and listing their names.

'I'm impressed,' he said. 'I had no idea your father was so knowledgeable.' He paused, remembering Pascal and how tragically he'd died, far too young. 'You must miss him.'

She didn't answer, and he silently cursed himself. What

a stupid thing to say, Lacoste. Of course she missed him, she was an only child who'd lost her only significant parent.

'Every day,' she said quietly. 'And it's the little things. A song, the stars, a distant figure that looks a bit like him.'

In the darkness he reached for her hand and squeezed it. 'I understand.'

'You?' He heard from her voice that she was looking at him. 'Have you lost someone you loved?'

He swallowed and said quietly, 'I lost a baby.'

There was a beat of stunned silence. 'You mean – Corinne . . .?'

'No. Not Corinne.' He looked at the moon, remembering and reliving the crushing pain, the sensation of having been cleaved in two. 'My ex. Nathalie.'

A distant train rushed past in the night, the urgent clatter of metal on metal.

'What happened? Tell me.'

He inhaled deeply. 'I had been with her a couple of years. I thought I knew her . . .'

'Go on,' Lily whispered.

'She was pregnant – apparently. But I knew nothing about it until it was too late. She aborted it.' His baby. He managed to keep his voice low and steady but inside something cracked.

'Oh Oli . . .'

'If I'd known I would have offered to raise the child.'

'Alone?' She sounded shocked.

'Why not? Your father did.'

Her hand turned and now she held his. Her fingers

wrapped around his, small and slender yet with the tightest grip. Raw feelings swelled in him, but for once he didn't fight them down. And he was surprised by how good it felt to give voice to them, to release them into the night sky.

'Why didn't she tell you?' asked Lily. 'And why did she have an abortion? Maybe she had a good reason . . .'

How typical of Lily to believe the best in people and to search to understand, rather than to judge and condemn.

'She said that having a baby would kill her career prospects.' He gave a dry laugh. 'I was heartbroken when I found out what she'd done – for the child I'd lost. And devastated because I would have done anything for Nathalie. Anything.'

'You loved her?' Lily asked softly.

'I adored her. I couldn't imagine my life without her.' But it was all over in an instant. His heart had shattered the moment he discovered what she had done.

'Sounds like you had it pretty bad.'

'It was infatuation.' Perhaps if he hadn't loved her so much, her betrayal wouldn't have felled him the way it had. He'd been crushed. Inconsolable. And it had made him wary of opening up his heart again, of allowing himself to feel that kind of passion again.

Now his eyes had adjusted to the dark, he could see Lily watching him.

'But now you have Corinne. And you love her, don't you?' She looked up at the sky. 'Of course you do, you're getting married.'

'It's not the same kind of love. What we have is more mature. It's steady and reliable and enduring. I'm not the same man I was.'

'Of course. Once burned, twice shy,' she murmured.

'What does that mean?'

'It's an English expression. It means when you've been hurt it makes you more cautious.'

And yet, he ruminated, it was Lily, not him, who had been burned and bore the scars.

'I think I have all I need now.'

'Right.'

'Unless there's anything else you'd like to add. Any more recipes you want to demonstrate . . .'

'I think we've covered all the important ones,' he said.

'Well in that case, we can put all this away.' She began to dismantle the camera and the tripod, mentally checking that she hadn't forgotten anything.

He remained strangely quiet and still, watching while she put the camera back in its case. Normally he was quick to help out of concern for her injured arm. Today he was preoccupied. His thoughts on something else. Someone else.

'It will be good to get back and see Mamie.'

He nodded.

She frowned. He'd been distracted like this all morning. She'd asked already if there was something on his mind and he'd simply shaken his head. Was he annoyed with her? Last night, when they'd sat under the stars and talked, everything had seemed fine. In fact, hearing him speak about his ex, about losing his baby, had touched something in her. She'd heard the pain in his voice, she'd felt it through the darkness, and it had been the final piece of the jigsaw puzzle falling into place, explaining why he was so desperate to become a father. Because he'd already lost one chance. He'd lost a child.

And now she had a deeper understanding of the hurt he carried and the hopes he held for the future, it only confirmed what she already knew: that Corinne was everything he needed. Maternal. Dependable. Rooted.

'How about I treat you to lunch before we leave,' she suggested, 'as a way of saying thank you.'

He dismissed this with an impatient shrug. 'There's no need.'

'I'd like to,' she insisted. 'Unless you're in a hurry to get on the road.' She glanced at her watch. 'I suppose if we leave now we'll be back in St Pierre by nightfall.'

He looked away, as if there was something he was avoiding telling her, and warning bells rang immediately. Olivier didn't shy away from difficult conversations or uncomfortable truths.

'Actually,' he said, 'I'm not going back today.'

'Oh.' She bit her lip, annoyed with herself for presuming they'd make the return trip together. He had his own life, his own commitments. 'Okay. That's fine–'

'It will be simpler if you get the train back, because I need to stay a day or two longer.'

Why? The unspoken question hung in the air, as heavy as the shimmering midday heat on the street outside.

But he didn't say why. He didn't say anything at all. He could barely bring himself to look at her, and that was what hurt Lily the most.

He blamed her for his argument with Corinne, she decided. He'd said that it was fine between them, but why else would he be behaving like this now?

'I understand,' she said, forcing brightness into her voice. 'It's not a problem.'

It wasn't. She understood that he needed some time with Corinne. Lily had come between them, and now he was sending her home so he could put things right. She looked away so he wouldn't see the guilt and anxiety that knotted inside her. She made herself breathe, but her lungs seemed to be stuck tight.

'There's a train in an hour,' he said. 'Is that long enough for you to pack?'

She nodded. It was plenty of time.

'I'll bring all your equipment back with me in the car.'

'Thanks.'

The train scuttled away from Paris and towards the denim-blue skies and intense colours of the south. Lily tried hard to ignore the ache in her chest. She didn't miss Olivier.

This was exactly how she liked her life to be: travelling alone, her mind sifting through the scenes she'd shot. She had some great material, exclusive footage of him talking about his passion for baking, showing the miracles that his hands could work with nothing more than flour and water. When she was back in St Pierre she'd trawl through her archives and see what else she had from previous projects and work out if she could link it all together. She already had ideas for illustrating how bread was a basic food but could also be so much more.

It is an act of love.

She stilled, remembering the intensity in his eyes as Olivier had said that, and it sent a shiver down her spine, even now. At the time it had felt like he was speaking only to her, silently communicating a message for her to decipher. But that must have been her imagination playing tricks, because today he'd sent her away.

Which was fine. He'd let her film him so she could get on with her work and meet her deadline, and now that was over he was going to spend time in Paris, getting on with his life, perhaps seeing his fiancée. It was fine, it really was. She hoped that, whatever had been troubling him this morning, he managed to sort it out.

Chapter Fifteen

Olivier parked outside Mamie's green gates and cut the engine. He paused before getting out. It had been four days – longer than he'd planned to stay in Paris, but he'd needed the time to work things out in his head.

His head or his heart? He wasn't sure. But either way, he couldn't put this off any longer.

'Olivier!' said Lily, when he approached. 'You're back.'

She jumped up from the table where she'd been hunched over her laptop working. In the shadows of the pergola her eyes looked olive green and her hair glistened like molten chocolate as she self-consciously swept it forward over her left shoulder. He wanted to push it back, but he didn't. Nor did he kiss her in greeting, but kept his feet firmly planted, a safe distance away from her.

'I'm back.'

He laid her camera down on the table. 'I have the rest of your equipment in the boot of my car. I'll get it in a moment.'

'Thank you,' she said, and touched the camera case as if to reassure herself that it was alright. When she saw he hadn't moved a flicker of unease tugged at her brow. 'Do you – er – want a drink?'

'Yes. A glass of water would be good.' His forehead

prickled with heat, the drive had been long and quiet on his own with only his thoughts for company. He was grateful for a cold drink but, crucially, watching her step inside the kitchen and pour water from the fridge bought him a few more minutes until he delivered his news. He followed her in.

'Here you are.' She handed him the glass.

'Thanks. You're working?' he said, glancing at her laptop.

'Editing – yes. It's too hot to work upstairs. This heat-wave is becoming unbearable.'

'Yes. I was glad to get away from the city. At least here there's the sea breeze.'

She peered up at him curiously and he knew what she was thinking. They had never made small talk before: why start now?

'How is it going – the film, I mean?'

Her eyes lit as she smiled. 'Really well. I've got some great material.'

'Good.' He noted how animated she'd become talking about her work and reminded himself that that was why he'd taken her to Paris in the first place. Her goal was to make a film, then move on to the next project. And the next. Soon she'd leave St Pierre. As she always did.

'Thanks again for helping me out,' she said. 'I really appreciate it.'

He shrugged. 'It's nothing. What are friends for?' His words sounded hollow. He glanced at the door. 'Is Mamie around?'

'No. She's gone to the department store with Béa.'

'You didn't fancy it?'

She rolled her eyes. 'I hate clothes shopping. You know that.'

He nodded absently and gulped the water down.

'Why don't you take a seat?' She pointed at the chair he was gripping.

He ignored her.

'Corinne and I broke up,' he announced abruptly.

Her eyes widened. There was a stunned silence, and he watched as her expression flickered from shock to dismay to anxiety.

In the corner of the room the fridge began to hum. It was a languid, weary sound, as if the unrelenting heat had sapped it of its energy.

'Why?' she asked eventually. 'Not because of that argument at the restaurant–'

'Not because of that, no.'

He ignored the throbbing in his temples and glanced outside at the terrace shaded by the overhanging vine. While he'd been away the clusters of neat green grapes had hardly changed in colour or size. Yet in those few days so much had changed for him. Thanks to Lily, he'd gained a new perspective, had new insights into his own life. Her searching questions had made him think about his career and the direction it had taken. And by going back to the basics of handling dough and shaping pastry, he'd found himself again.

Yet, also thanks to Lily, his life was no longer the ordered calm he liked it to be. His pulse quickened uncomfortably. His plans were shot to pieces and something unpredictable, uncontrollable, had stepped in to take their place. This wasn't the direction he would have chosen to take, yet it seemed he didn't have any control over the matter. His heart had its own ideas.

'Then why?' asked Lily.

He blinked and looked back at her. How could he put it into words when he hardly understood it himself?

Because of our conversation beneath the stars, he wanted to say, but that wouldn't make any sense.

Because sitting there in the dark, looking up at the night sky, I told you things I've never spoken about to Corinne. Felt things I shouldn't feel . . .

He felt it now, a vibration deep within him, a gravitational pull, the need to be near her, with her, close. And the desperate hope that she might feel the same way.

'It wasn't working,' he said finally, and the painful conversation replayed itself in his mind:

'Corinne, I . . . ah—' He'd cleared his throat, wishing he could be anywhere else but here in her cramped, airless hospital accommodation, '—I don't think you should take that transfer.'

She'd blinked, a little distracted. 'The transfer? What do you mean?'

'With your job.' He'd taken a deep breath and reminded himself that although this was inevitably going to be painful, he couldn't contemplate the alternative: to hide from the truth. That would be cowardly and cruel, and Corinne deserved better. 'I think you should stay in Paris,' he finished softly.

Corinne had been silent. Her clear blue eyes watched

him cautiously, then clouded over with growing resignation. She knew what was coming.

With hindsight, it had been obvious. So why hadn't he seen it?

Because he hadn't wanted to.

He'd desperately wanted his relationship with Corinne to work, he'd believed that it was safe and solid and steady. Nothing like the turbulent storm which whipped up inside him when he thought of Lily.

'Corinne, my feelings have changed. I'm ashamed to say it, and I don't want it to be this way, but . . .' He swallowed and looked down at his lap. The explanation failed to come and his words were left suspended in the air.

Corinne had twisted the hem of her blue tunic, and said, 'To be honest, I've been having second thoughts myself.'

'You have?'

'Yes. About leaving Paris and . . . about us.'

He'd expected her to be angry – she had every right to be. But their relationship had never been like that.

'What's changed for you? Is it Lily?' she asked quietly. Without reproach.

His head lifted. 'Nothing's happened, I promise!'

She studied his gaze a moment before answering. 'I believe you. But you have feelings for her, don't you?'

He nodded. 'They don't make any sense, and I don't think she even feels the same way, but . . .' He sucked in air, hating himself, 'but I know I shouldn't feel this way. Not when I'm with you.'

She nodded. A sheen of tears stole across her eyes.

'Corinne,' he said, and his voice was hoarse, 'my heart isn't where it should be.'

And this scared him.

What he felt for Lily defied logic, it was wild, out of control. And he knew the feeling, he recognised the strength of it, he knew it was unstoppable.

Because this was exactly how he'd felt about Nathalie. His chest tightened, his skin broke into a sweat.

Corinne nodded again. 'When you said she was like a little sister to you, I took you at your word. But she isn't. Anyone can see it. She's so much more to you . . .'

'I don't know any more.' He dipped his head and despair made his shoulders sink because he was pushing away the best possible woman for him, his perfect match – and for what?

For Lily, who didn't love him and who had no intention of ever settling down. Madness.

'Corinne, I never wanted to hurt you . . .'

'I know. And it's okay. If I'm honest, I had doubts too. We get on well, but the spark isn't there, is it?'

He'd looked up, surprised. Then sighed. He hadn't wanted to see it, but it was true. 'I guess not. Corinne, I'm so sorry.'

'Don't be. Thank you for being honest with me. And I should be honest too . . .'

Now, in Mamie's kitchen the tap continued to drip quietly and regularly, like a beating heart. Outside, a cicada started up its rough, scratchy song.

'Oh Olivier, I'm so sorry,' said Lily, and he realised she was watching him anxiously. 'Is – is Corinne alright?'

He nodded. 'She's met someone else – a doctor at the hospital where she works . . .'

'*She* ended it?' Lily looked shocked.

He shook his head. 'We both agreed it was the right thing to do.'

Strange to think he'd believed Corinne was right for him when their relationship had been a dull, black and white film compared with the full technicolour he experienced with Lily. He saw that now – but he didn't say anything because it was obvious Lily didn't feel the same way. If he told her, he risked spoiling their friendship – their precious friendship – and he couldn't lose her again. He wouldn't give her another reason to run away from him and lock him out of her life a second time.

Besides, she was totally wrong for him.

Still, knowing that didn't stop him from watching her reaction, hoping for a flicker, a sign that perhaps he was wrong – perhaps she did feel something for him? Shock registered in her eyes, and sympathy too. But nothing more.

'I'm sorry,' she murmured. But didn't say anything else.

His stomach sank.

The last time he'd felt like this it had ended in heartbreak.

Lily and Mamie sat in the shade. Mamie was knitting a purple cashmere sweater for Olivier 'to keep him warm in the autumn', but her progress was slow and she stopped periodically to fan herself and take a sip of the iced water Lily had brought out.

Lily was reading *Lonely Planet* magazine, but even the stunning photography couldn't hold her attention, and her mind kept wandering. She was still astounded by the news that Olivier and Corinne's engagement was off.

'Was Olivier here this morning?' asked Mamie. Her gnarled fingers held the knitting needles loosely and clumsily, yet her stitches were as small and neat as they'd always been.

'Yes, he came over while you were out.'

He'd been so quiet. It was clear he was heartbroken over his break-up with Corinne, and Lily felt his unspoken pain.

'Did you work on the studio?'

Lily shook her head. 'It was too hot. We're going to get up early tomorrow and do it.'

Just another session or two and the paintings would all be sorted and ready for the exhibition. Then she wouldn't have any reason left to spend time with him. It would do her good to put some space between her and Olivier, because seeing his heartache hurt almost as much as if it were her own.

'Béa said that he and Corinne broke up,' said Mamie.

Lily looked up. 'Yes. He told me.'

Mamie tugged at the collar of her lilac kaftan, then picked up her knitting again. The sound of the knitting needles clicking was rhythmic and comforting. 'What else did he say?'

Lily pictured the bleak look in his eyes, and her chest squeezed painfully. 'Not much.'

'Well, better to end it now than after the wedding.'

'Yes. I suppose.'

'And he's withdrawn from buying that plot of land, too.'

'Has he?' Lily sighed and put her magazine down. 'It's so sad. He and Corinne were so good together.'

Sharp green eyes looked up at her. 'She was never his equal.'

Lily frowned. 'What do you mean?'

Corinne had been perfect for him: they'd shared the same dreams of settling down and having a family, and she'd been as beautiful as he was handsome. Perfect.

Mamie kept her lips pursed and her eyes on the purple wool while her fingers worked busily. 'She's a lovely girl, but she wouldn't say boo to a goose. Olivier's a strong character. He needs a strong woman to stand up to him.'

Lily sighed. Mamie was still trying to matchmake, and not in a subtle way. But her desire to see them together was nothing but an old lady's fantasy; it wasn't realistic. How to break this to her without dashing her gran's hopes?

'I know what you're implying, Mamie, but Oli and I could never be more than friends.' Mamie lifted a brow. 'We're too different. That's why we argue so much.'

'Pff! Nonsense. It's because you're so similar that you clash. Both pig-headed, both sure your way is the only way, and too stubborn to back down or meet in the middle.' She flashed Lily a smile that made her eyes gleam. 'You're perfect for each other!'

Lily couldn't help but laugh at such a ridiculous statement. Yet she was troubled by how much she wanted Mamie to be right. By the seed of hope which cracked open. A part of her – a secret, hidden part – wanted to whirl with joy and sing with hope that now he was single maybe, just maybe, he might see her differently.

But she'd seen how miserable he was. Silent, with that troubled look in his eyes. His engagement might be off, but his heart was still with Corinne.

'You know your grandfather and I grew up together?' Mamie peered at her from over the purple knitting.

'Did you?'

She nodded. 'Here, in St Pierre. We were in the same class at school, then childhood sweethearts. And although we didn't grow old together, I know I've been lucky: better to have had fifty years together, than none at all.'

Her needles clicked away matter-of-factly. Lily watched her grandmother and felt a surge of admiration. She was so accepting, so unfailingly optimistic – despite everything.

'You say you're lucky when you lost your husband *and* your son?' she said, remembering when her dad had died. Mamie had faced grief with such quiet dignity, and she'd always been there for Lily, no matter what she must undoubtedly have been suffering herself.

Mamie's eyes met hers. 'Losing them wasn't as hard as seeing you suffer. And I am lucky. Pain and loss are part of life. How could we appreciate the light if we never experienced darkness?'

'You're so wise, Mamie.' How was her gran so accepting?

'Pff. Not wise – just old.' Her eyes twinkled. 'And I have a lot to be thankful for. I have you, my precious Lily.' She put her knitting down and reached across to stroke Lily's face. Her fingers ran over the ridges of her scars as she said quietly, 'Promise me you won't let your suffering prevent you from seizing happiness.'

'Of course I won't. I live a full life, I embrace adventure and challenge and–'

'I'm not talking about your films, wonderful and important as they are.' She covered Lily's hand with her own. 'I mean in your personal life. Matters of the heart. You lost your papa, but love doesn't always have to end in pain. And even if it does, the price is worth paying.'

Lily felt tears prick the backs of her eyes. Her throat thickened. She shook her head, remembering the violent gash in her world that her father's death had made. Mamie was wrong; the price wasn't worth paying.

'Don't cry, my little Lily.'

A crooked finger wiped the tear from her cheek, and she felt ashamed. How was her gran so sanguine and stoic, when Lily was a quivering coward? Her heart swelled. 'I love you, Mamie,' she whispered hoarsely.

'Pff, I know you do.' Mamie smiled. 'And I'm so glad you came home this summer. So glad.' She gently cupped Lily's cheek and her eyes shone. 'Now. Instead of getting sentimental, why don't we think about getting supper ready? How about cheese and salad? I'm not very hungry, but you need to eat.'

Lily locked up the house that night, because Mamie

went to bed early. As she padded upstairs to her room, her phone buzzed. It was a message from Theo saying that he was going to be in London in the autumn. Would she like to meet?

Olivier's words haunted her: *You deserve better . . . You could have so much more.*

Her fingers hovered over the 'reply' button, but something had changed, and now she couldn't think of Theo as anything but a friend.

She went to bed and lay there, feeling restless, wondering if Olivier was regretting his break-up with Corinne. Was his heart aching for what he'd lost? Why did she – Lily – feel his pain as if it were her own? He was just a friend. Okay, a close friend who would always, no matter how many thousands of miles came between them, have a place in her heart. She turned over to switch off the light and her gaze fell on her passport with its dog-eared corners.

Her life and her career were encapsulated in those inky, stamp-worn pages. The village of St Pierre, beautiful as it might be with the peaceful olive grove and colourful harbour, was only a resting place where she briefly dropped anchor between assignments. She snapped off the light and tried to switch off her thoughts too. There was no point in getting attached or in laying down roots because she wouldn't be here for much longer.

'Is there anything more we need to do before the exhibition?' asked Olivier.

The gentle, milky light of early morning made his

skin glow as he looked around the studio. He still had the same flat-lipped, haunted expression that had been clouding his features ever since he'd returned from Paris.

'It's all in hand,' said Lily, as she straightened up from behind her camera, satisfied that she now had every painting on film. A permanent record of her grandmother's work. 'The agent will arrange for the paintings to be moved to the town hall and he'll take care of the display too. All we have to do is show up with Mamie on opening night.'

'Which is . . .?' he looked at his watch.

'Three weeks today.'

He raised a brow. 'I'm good with dates,' she said with a shrug.

But she knew he saw straight through her. The date was fixed in her mind because she'd be free to leave thereafter. Though of course, she had to finish her film first.

The eager chatter of sparrows drifted in through the open windows as she busied herself with unclipping the camera from the tripod. When she finished, she noticed that Olivier was watching her closely, a strange look in his eyes. Dark. Intent. Simmering.

She turned away and frowned. She was imagining things. He was still heartbroken for Corinne. He'd been pining for her all week. Even Béa had been watching him with concern. So that look Lily thought she'd just seen in his eyes must be her mind playing tricks, wishfully projecting her own desires and longing.

'Right, well I guess we've finished here, then,' he said.

She nodded. 'You're off the hook, Chicken. Free to go.'

It would be better for both of them to put some distance between them. He could use some time alone to lick his wounds and come to terms with his break-up, and she—

She could do with a break from watching him suffer. Though it would be a wrench not to be in his company, it would at least release her from the conflicting emotions that currently had her tied up in knots.

But Olivier didn't move.

And this time, when she looked up at him, she realised it hadn't been her imagination at all. He was watching her intently, his dark eyes two glinting pools of heat.

She swallowed, confused. Olivier had always treated her like a best buddy, teasing, mocking, joking around with her. This seriousness was new and unexpected. It threw her, it made her blood fizz.

What if . . .? a voice whispered in her head.

'Oli?' His name was a raw whisper.

His gaze was fixed on her mouth in a look of hunger and longing.

Hope unfurled in her, slowly at first, then in a sudden rush. She held her breath and her heart strained with emotions which had been unreciprocated for so long. He was only a few feet away, and she wanted to close the distance between them, but her feet didn't move.

Then he blinked, and his expression changed. The charge in the air dissipated, the spell was broken. He shook his head, like a man who'd been sleepwalking and had suddenly woken.

'Right,' he said. 'I'll go, then.'

Lily couldn't prevent the draining sensation of disappointment. 'Yes.'

'You don't need me any more.' His eyes were questioning.

'No.'

He made a show of looking at his watch, as if he had more pressing things to do. She tried to ignore the kick of hurt. He dropped a light kiss on both her cheeks. 'See you soon, Skinny.'

She nodded, and listened to his footsteps as he hurried away down the stairs. She didn't understand what had happened just then, but her response had been out of proportion, out of control. He'd only looked at her. Imagine how she'd feel if he touched her?

Her skin tingled. She had to stop this, she had to stop wishing, dreaming, hoping. He'd gone, and there was no reason for them to have any further interaction before the exhibition in a few weeks' time. Then she'd leave.

She lifted her chin and watched his dark-haired figure hurry across Mamie's garden and through the olive grove towards his parents' home.

She wouldn't miss him. She didn't need him. She would enjoy the few weeks she had left with Mamie, she'd finish her film, and then she'd set off on her next assignment. Looking forward, anticipating the next challenge – that was how she liked to live.

*

What had he hoped? Olivier asked himself, as he strode through the olive trees. That she'd look into his eyes and see what he was feeling and tell him she felt it too – this punch to the stomach of love and longing? Since when did he entertain such ridiculous flights of fancy? He was pragmatic, he was sensible, he prided himself on his ability to override emotion with rational thought.

That didn't happen with Lily. It seemed that the last few weeks he'd spent with her had rewired his brain. Now he couldn't be in the same room as her without being distracted. He was constantly on edge around her, his senses alert, his blood sparking at the sound of her voice and the fresh, soapy scent of her. And this wasn't a rebound thing. He saw now that these vivid breath-stealing feelings had been there all along, taking root, throwing up shoots and steadily unfurling, and now they refused to be ignored.

So why hadn't he told her how he felt just now in the studio? Surely, if one thing was guaranteed to kill dead his unwanted feelings it would be the look of horror on her face when she learned how he felt? And if she didn't react with horror, then perhaps he'd dare to hope . . .

No. If he told her, their friendship would be over.

Besides, what was he hoping for exactly? He knew Lily better than anyone. She was already counting down the days until she left St Pierre. He'd seen it in her eyes when they'd discussed the date of Mamie's retrospective.

He arrived, breathless, at his parents' house and paused to look back at the stone walls of the farmhouse and the terracotta-coloured turret. Let her be, he told himself, as he watched a dove poke its head out of the dovecote before taking flight. Keep your distance, Lacoste. It will be better for everyone.

The house was curiously peaceful when Lily woke. She listened, but couldn't hear the coffee machine's gentle clucking in the kitchen below, or the scrape of a wooden chair along the tiled floor, or the clatter of pipes as Mamie opened the tap.

She looked at the time: 8 a.m. Perhaps her gran had changed her mind and gone to the village after all, though last night she'd told Lily that she wasn't planning to.

Lily padded to the bathroom, rubbing the sleep from her eyes as she made her way down the dark corridor. Why was it so dark?

She stopped. Mamie's bedroom door was still shut.

'Mamie?' she called, pressing her ear to the oak door.

No answer. The only sound was the doves' energetic flutter of wings in the loft.

Her heart beat faster. She squeezed the door handle and turned it.

Mamie was in bed. Relief flooded through Lily, but it was immediately chased by anxiety. Was she ill? She couldn't remember her grandmother ever sleeping so late, not even when Lily had been a child. She tiptoed across the room. The shutters were closed but strips of light threaded through the slats and illuminated Mamie's peaceful expression, her lashes rested serenely on her cheeks.

It was only as she got closer that Lily noticed how pale she looked.

'Mamie?'

Frowning, she reached and touched one of the wrinkled hands which lay over the white sheet. It was cold.

Lily sucked in air. 'Mamie?' she cried, louder this time.

But her gran didn't move.

And then Lily knew: sleep had stolen her beloved grandmother.

Olivier was in the kitchen drinking coffee and checking through emails when the phone rang. He snatched it up, not wanting the sound to disturb his brothers, who were both still asleep.

'Oli–' He recognised Lily's voice instantly, 'it's Mamie! Come quick!'

He put his cup down, slopping coffee over the worktop, and he felt a hollowing in his stomach. 'What's happened?'

'She's not waking up! I've called an ambulance.'

'I'm coming.'

He ran barefoot to the farmhouse, hardly registering the rough grass of the orchard underfoot, nor even the gravel outside Mamie's kitchen. 'Lily?' he called, as he took the stairs two at a time. 'Where are you?'

'In here,' she called. Her words were high-pitched and strangled with fear. 'In her room.'

He ran in and saw Mamie's small body, serene and peaceful in her bed. Lily bent over her. He rushed across and felt for a pulse, put his cheek to Mamie's wrinkled face. Nothing. Her skin was dusty pale.

'I found her like this,' Lily said breathlessly. She looked up at him, her eyes wide, shining with fear. 'I – I think she's dead.'

He gathered her to him. 'Oh Lily,' he soothed, and had to shut his eyes to squeeze away the tears that threatened. He stroked her hair, he felt her breathing slow down and she pressed herself against his chest. 'It's okay. We'll get through this.'

The faint call of a siren travelled through the early morning air. 'That's the ambulance,' he said, and drew back to look at her. 'I'll go out to meet them, okay?'

She nodded bravely. 'I'll stay here.'

He glanced once more at Mamie before he left. But instinct told him there was nothing the paramedics would be able to do.

Chapter Sixteen

'I knew it would happen one day, I should have been prepared for this . . . but I didn't want to think about it.'

Lily curled her hands around the glass of water in front of her, and gazed absently at the stove, the dresser, her untouched plate of salad, trying to process what had happened. The sympathetic look on Béa's face told her that Lily might have deceived herself, but everyone else had seen it coming. Mamie had been weak and tired, and perhaps the heatwave had sapped the last of her energy. The village doctor had called by to see Lily and had assured her Mamie hadn't been hiding any medical problems. There would be an investigation, but it appeared she'd died in her sleep, most probably because her heart had stopped. A natural, peaceful death; her time had simply come.

Lily closed her eyes, squeezing back the pain. 'At least we had those last few weeks together,' she said, trying to draw consolation, but inside the fracture felt huge. Violent.

Mamie was gone.

Regret bulldozed through her that she hadn't had the chance to look after her gran for a change, and there was so much she hadn't told her or thanked her for. Lily had taken it for granted that there would be time for all that in the future – but time had run out.

'Yes,' said Béa. 'It meant the world to her to have you here.'

Lily let her head drop into the cup of her hands, aware of Olivier and his parents beside her. They were being so kind, helping in every way possible, but they were also watching her with that look in their eyes, that careful cautious sympathy that took her back in time to the fire and its aftermath. But she couldn't go there.

'Lily, are you sure you won't eat anything?' asked Béa, nodding at her plate.

'I'm not hungry.' She flashed her an apologetic look.

Béa placed her hand on her arm. 'Don't worry.'

Raymond began to clear the plates and his wife got up to help him. 'Oli is going to stay here tonight,' she told Lily as she finished. 'He'll sleep in the spare room – so you're not alone.'

Lily glanced at him and frowned. 'There's really no need.'

'I don't want you to be here on your own.'

'I'm used to being on my own.'

'You just lost your grandmother,' Béa said quietly.

'I'll be fine–'

'Yes,' she said kindly but firmly. 'Because Olivier will be here with you.'

Lily looked at Olivier. His expression didn't give anything away.

A little later, Béa and Raymond slipped away into the dark night, leaving them both. Lily watched as Olivier locked the kitchen doors after them. When he turned back she said quietly, 'You don't need to do this. I'm perfectly capable of looking after myself.'

His eyes locked her with hers. He shook his head and said, 'Sometimes, Lily Martin, you are the worst person at knowing what you need.' He added softly, 'I want to stay. I'm worried about you.'

'Why?'

'Because you're bottling it up and it's not good, Lil. It's okay to admit you miss her.'

Tears burned the backs of her eyes and she pressed her lips together angrily. 'Of course I miss her!' she said. 'I don't need to weep and sob to miss her!'

He looked surprised at her outburst and she bit her lip. 'I'm sorry. I didn't mean to snap.'

'It's okay,' he said softly, and drew her into his arms. Her cheek pressed against the warmth of his chest and his hands felt strong around her. She allowed herself to stay there a few seconds, then pulled away. 'It's been a long day,' she said, needing to put space between them. 'I'm going to bed.'

He nodded.

Before long the house was quiet and still. Lily lay in bed, wide awake. It was comforting to know he was in the next room, yet at the same time . . . it wasn't. She threw off the sheets, then opened the shutters to feel the cool night air on her skin. She looked up at the delicate sliver of moon and wondered if he was awake. If he was still missing Corinne.

Olivier was worried about her. But that was nothing new, he realised now. He'd worried, after she'd told him about the robbery in Colombia, about her going back there, he worried that she was alone, that she seemed to have given up on relationships, and he'd been torn up with jealousy when she'd talked about her lover in New York. He worried and he cared about her. He cared too much.

Which was why, when Béa had told him she would stay with Lily, he'd said no. He'd do it.

He wanted to be here, near her. He needed to be sure she was alright. It mattered to him more than anything. He'd hoped that his feelings would fade over time, that they'd return to simple, uncomplicated friendship. But they'd only deepened and intensified.

But his own feelings were not the issue right now. All that mattered was getting Lily through this. She needed him, and he would be there for her.

Despite the heat, the funeral was beautiful. Achingly so.

Lily threw the white lily that was handed to her onto Mamie's coffin, then stepped back as Béa, Raymond, Olivier and his brothers did the same. And Alain, who looked incredibly smart in a well-fitting suit, but the lines around his eyes betrayed how devastated he felt too.

So many friends from the village had turned up that there hadn't been room in the church and some had congregated outside for the service. Now the cemetery was crowded too. If Mamie could see this, she would have chuckled. To Lily it seemed fitting that her grandmother's life should be honoured in this way. She'd been a remarkable woman. Her paintings had been modern for their time and so had she. A strong and loving woman, she'd always be a role model for Lily.

And she missed her so much, yet she still hadn't cried. She sometimes wondered if she'd ever laugh or cry or feel anything again. It was as if there was a plaster cast around her emotions, but she knew it was protecting her, it was holding her chin up and keeping her spine straight so that when people came and touched her arm and gave her their condolences she was able to nod politely and thank them.

They went back to Mamie's farmhouse for the reception. Béa had arranged for caterers to provide nibbles, there was a display of beautiful cakes from the bakery, and the drinks flowed freely.

Lily did her best to circulate and speak to everyone she recognised, but the heat had intensified so the air was heavy and, as she began to sag with tiredness, she gravitated to Olivier's family. She found Béa, Raymond and Olivier sitting in the shade of the palm tree, talking quietly.

'Come and sit down,' said Béa. 'You must be exhausted.'

Lily sat and absently rubbed her right arm. Was it the heat or the emotion of the day that was making her bones ache?

'Have you eaten?' asked Olivier. 'You look very pale.'

'I'm fine,' she said. 'It's just so hot.'

'It is,' agreed Raymond. 'This heatwave is infernal.'

'They say there's a storm coming later,' said Olivier. 'I hope they're right.'

'We have some good news, Lily,' said Béa.

She forced a smile. 'What is it?'

'Raymond has decided to retire.' Béa's eyes gleamed with joy.

'Really?' said Lily, amazed. For years Béa had been urging him to retire, but he'd obstinately refused. His sense of identity seemed to be bound up in that village bakery. Lily wondered what had changed?

'Really,' he confirmed, and his arm crept around Béa's waist. 'Your grandmother's death has reminded me that life is to be lived, and it's a dangerous game to put off until tomorrow what I could do now.' He dropped a kiss on his wife's head and this unexpected show of tenderness made Lily's heart melt. She swallowed hard.

Life is to be lived. Which was why she needed to follow her dream, doing the work she found so rewarding and which could make a difference to other people.

'What will you do?' Olivier asked Raymond.

'I will spend time with my lovely wife,' said Raymond, and looked at Béa. Love shimmered in their eyes. Then he winked. 'And maybe I'll play *boules* more often.'

'What about the bakery?' asked Olivier. 'What will happen to it?'

'I could sell it. Or pass it on to you, if you want it . . .' Olivier's eyes lit up. He looked thrilled. 'I don't expect you do,' Raymond continued. 'It's small fry compared with your bakeries.'

'Actually, I'd be honoured to take it on,' said Olivier. 'I've been thinking it's time I scaled back and got back to the basics of working in the kitchen and getting my hands dirty. The management side of things bores me to distraction and it's made me lose sight of what I love: making bread, dealing with customers. The simple life.'

Raymond beamed. 'Then it shall be so.'

They clapped each other on the back. It was touching, and Lily sat back, feeling like an outsider, feeling like she didn't belong because her goals were so different. Olivier wanted more than anything to be anchored to this tiny village, whereas she – she was like the boats in Mamie's painting upstairs: bobbing restlessly on the waves, always ready and eager to sail away to a new destination.

That evening she and Olivier were sitting in the lounge as the wind rattled the shutters and the rain hammered down. They'd spent a couple of hours clearing up after all the guests had left, and it was good to sit down, to finally have some relief from the weeks of intense heat. But the ache in Lily's chest was stronger than ever. She missed Mamie's calm presence, her shrewd observations, her quiet humour and loving nature.

'When they said rain was coming I thought they meant a short shower,' she said.

A rush of cool air swept through the house. 'By the looks of it, it's going to be a full-blown storm. This rain is torrential and those clouds over there look even more menacing.'

'It's like the monsoon,' she said, her skin puckering with tiny goose bumps, her fingers twisting a strand of hair as she watched the clouds push closer, darkening the sky like bruises. 'I think we should close the shutters.'

'You're shivering,' he said when they'd closed them all.

He was still wearing black trousers and a white shirt, but he'd discarded his tie and his shirt sleeves were rolled back to his elbows.

She forced a smile. 'It's nice. I might finally get some sleep tonight.' But the smile faded from her lips as she thought of yet another wakeful night filled with bleak thoughts. Like when she'd driven along the pothole-riddled roads in remote Colombia, she wondered if she'd ever get through this in one piece. Without Mamie here, she felt so alone. Which was ridiculous. Alone was what she was used to. Yet today a black hole had opened around her. She shivered and tried to squeeze out of her mind the growing sense of panic.

'Here, wrap this around you. I'll make us a hot drink.' Olivier vanished into the kitchen, leaving her with the red and white quilt draped around her shoulders.

For the last week or so her days had been filled with preparations for the funeral. Now it was over, the reality that Mamie had gone ambushed her. She felt small and afraid. She hugged the quilt closer, still trembling as the rain whipped the shutters. Olivier returned, carrying two cups of hot chocolate and set them down on the wooden chest. He sat down beside her. He didn't touch her, yet she felt the heat of his body.

'How do you feel?' he asked.

'Tired. Sore feet.'

'That's not what I meant, Skinny.'

Lily looked at her gran's empty chair. 'I miss her. Even though I was so far away most of the time, I knew she was always here to come home to.'

He didn't say anything. When she looked at him, his eyes were gleaming. 'Why are you smiling?'

'Because you said *home*.'

Had she? She hadn't meant to. She never stayed in one place too long and, she realised now, she never let herself get attached because it was easier that way. She was careful to stay remote. Aloof. Detached. That way her heart was safe.

But tonight her heart was in pieces.

'I was scared this would happen,' she admitted quietly. 'Scared of spending too much time here, of getting close to Mamie, because deep down I knew this day would come.'

A gust of wind slammed against the side of the house, making the window shake. A loud crash outside made Lily jump.

'Probably one of the plant pots,' Olivier said calmly, 'or a roof tile.'

A flash of light burst through the slats of the shutters, and thunder followed a few seconds later. Her heart pounded.

'You okay?' asked Olivier.

'Fine.' She'd never admitted to feeling scared before. Not to Olivier. Especially not to Olivier.

'Here, drink this.' He handed her one of the cups of hot chocolate. She tried to hold it but her hand was unsteady. She took a quick sip and put it down again.

He frowned but didn't say anything. Another flash of lightning flooded the room, making the lights flicker, and a crack of thunder shook the lamp on the small table beside her.

'It – it's really close,' said Lily, her gaze darting anxiously from the shutters to the fireplace. They were perched on top of the hill. What if the lightning hit the farmhouse? The chimney top?

'It's only a storm,' said Olivier. 'It'll soon pass.'

She shuddered as the lights flashed again, more violently this time.

'You never used to mind storms,' he said carefully, and she realised he was watching her through narrowed eyes.

She shrugged. 'Lightning carries a huge risk of fire,' she said quietly.

'A risk, yes. But the odds of it striking are minuscule.'

She bit her lip. The silence stretched before she admitted, 'I've seen it happen. A wooden hut in Cambodia. It burst into flames and was practically incinerated in seconds.'

'Ah.' He took a moment to absorb this. 'But this house is made of stone, Lil. It's stood here for more than 200 years.'

'I know. The rational part of my brain understands that. But fear isn't rational. It comes from here.' She touched the palm of her hand to her heart.

Another bolt of lightning and this time the lights went out. Thunder juddered through the house, making everything shake and rattle in the dark. Lily gripped Olivier's hand.

'It's okay,' he said, and a strong arm came around her. 'The power's gone, that's all. Have you got a torch anywhere?'

'There's one in my room upstairs. I don't know if there are any elsewhere.'

He went to stand up. 'I'll go and–'

'No!' She shot to her feet and clung to his arm. 'Stay with me! . . . Please.'

He stilled. His arm came around her again, and she shook as he drew her against his chest. 'It doesn't matter. Your eyes will soon get used to the dark. Hey, don't cry. It's okay. Everything's okay.'

But it wasn't okay. It was insurmountable, it was bigger than her, this vicious terrible grief. 'I can't believe she's gone. I know I should have expected it but I wanted her to always be here.' The last few weeks with Mamie had been so special and she'd treasure the memories, the closeness they'd shared – but that closeness was what made the pain all the more crushing now. Lily wasn't sure how she'd ever face the world again now that everything she held dear had been torn away from her.

It was like losing her dad all over again. Her face burned, the disinfectant smell of the hospital came rushing back, and she could feel the pain. Something inside her broke open and spilled out. Olivier's arms wrapped around her and she let herself yield to his heat, his touch, his strength. Her defences dissolved, and she wept against his shoulder.

He soothed her, he shed tears too, he stroked her hair back from her face and told her, 'It will get better, Lil. You will get through this . . .'

'I'm going to miss her so much.'

'I know. We all are.'

You are strong, Mamie had told her when she was fifteen and she lay in hospital, her face so raw she couldn't speak. *You will get through this; it's what your father would have wanted, for you to grow from this. Not be defeated by it, but grow stronger.*

Yet now Lily doubted her own strength. She couldn't do this. Not again.

'Ah, the power's back on!' said Olivier, as the lights came back to life.

She blinked. His beautiful face was lit with golden light and his eyes creased as he smiled down at her. A rush of bright emotions flowed through her: relief that the darkness had gone, the warm love of age-old friendship, the bite of desire.

'Oli,' she whispered, and lifted her head to look at him. His eyes were dark, and shimmered in the syrupy light. She could lose herself in them, she thought, and pressed herself closer against him.

He registered the pressure of her hips against his with a sharp intake of breath. It made her stomach tighten. At Mamie's graveside this morning she'd believed she would never feel again, but now her veins were flowing and she felt more alive than ever. She reached up and their lips brushed tentatively. She pulled back, cautiously reading his reaction. This might be a momentary thing, an escape from real life, but she needed it right now.

The hunger in his eyes reassured her. He seemed to briefly do battle with himself, then gave in and bent his head. He kissed her, and this time it was fierce and urgent. She flattened her palm against his chest, needing to feel his beating heart, to explore him, wanting to tug at the buttons of his shirt. The blood pounded in her ears, so loud it drowned out the drumming of the rain.

When they paused for air, moments later, they were both breathless.

'Oli, I want you,' Lily whispered, astounded at herself, at this surreal situation they found themselves in. But then, nothing about the last few days had felt real.

He groaned against her mouth and kissed her again on the lips, jaw, neck. She sucked in air as he sighed her name, feverish with need, and her fingers moved to the top of his shirt. They tugged at the buttons, loosening them easily, revealing the dusting of dark hair on his chest. She pressed a kiss against his beating heart and he groaned.

God, she wanted this so much. She reached for his lips again. 'Stay with me tonight,' she whispered against his mouth.

She sensed a flicker of tension in him, a hesitation.

'Please, Oli. I don't want to be alone . . .'

Emotions warred in his dark eyes. Then his brow creased and his features twisted with the look of someone about to break bad news. She stilled.

'Lily, no,' he said gently.

Hope washed away instantly. She'd been here before. Why had she thought tonight would be any different?

Because she was desperate. Because she didn't want to be alone. Not tonight.

He must have seen her despair because he said, 'I'll stay, I'll be here for you – but I won't sleep with you. Not like this.'

The flash of pain was sharp and fierce. Hurt. Humiliation. Exactly like thirteen years ago. He'd had the same look in his eyes when he'd pushed her away, and since then they'd both changed so much. Her fingers drifted to her cheek. Now he only had more reasons to push her away.

She couldn't believe she'd done it again, inviting rejection a second time. Wouldn't she ever learn? Blinking hard, she turned away.

'Lily!' he said, and his hand caught her arm. She shook it off. 'Lily, listen to me–'

'There's no need. It's fine.'

'It's not fine, Lil. But this – it's not the right time . . .'

'Don't—' She held up her hand to fend off his words.

He didn't want her. That was what it boiled down to.

'I'm going to bed.' She tried to look at him, but found she couldn't meet his eye. She turned and ran up the stairs.

When she reached her bedroom, she shut the door behind her, pressed her palm against it, and bowed her head in despair. She vowed that this was the last time she'd make a fool of herself. She'd never expose her feelings for him again. Never.

She heard his footsteps approach. She thought she heard him pause in the hall and sigh. Then he moved away. Finally, the house became still.

Lily lay in bed, fists curled, and cursed herself over and over again. What had she expected? Yes, he'd broken up with Corinne, but that didn't mean he wanted her the way she wanted him.

Had always wanted him.

A tear pushed through, and she shook her head. She'd made a fool of herself, again. And this time she couldn't even explain why or what she'd hoped to achieve beyond temporary relief, because she and Olivier could never be a partnership.

It must be the stress of the funeral – her frayed emotions had driven her to behave impulsively, irrationally. She switched off the light and let the black of night throw its cloak around her.

Olivier lay fully dressed on the bed in the next room, furious with himself. He'd messed it up again. Hurt her again. Had he learned nothing since he was eighteen?

Yet he had done the right thing, he was certain of that, even if he'd said the wrong words. To sleep with her when she was at her most vulnerable? Only the worst kind of man would do that.

She'd looked so fragile tonight, so pale and exhausted from the effort of keeping her chin up and her back straight during the funeral and after as she'd shaken the hands of the hundreds of people who'd come to pay their respects. By the end of the afternoon her cheeks had been drawn, her shoulders sagging. No wonder she'd fallen into his arms. With any luck, she'd sleep tonight and tomorrow they would clear the air.

If she could sleep through this storm, he thought, remembering how she'd trembled in his arms. At least the lightning was gone now and the rain was easing off.

The unfamiliar sounds of the old farmhouse kept him alert: the drip of rain; the creak of old timbers as the wood adjusted to the sudden drop in temperature; a muffled sob.

He sat up, frowning, then got out of bed and crossed the room, his bare feet making no sound. He paused outside her door, and listened again. Her sobs were so quiet, they were almost impossible to hear, but they made his heart splinter.

She shouldn't be alone, not tonight. She needed someone to hold her. He might be *persona non grata* right now, but he couldn't bear to think of her alone.

He knocked quietly, then turned the door handle and went in.

'Lily?'

'What are you doing?' There was a rustle of sheets as she sat up.

In the grey of night, he could only see the outline of her form, but it was enough. He went and lay beside her.

'Don't cry,' he said as he drew her into his arms and she tensed. 'I'm sorry I upset you. Don't cry, Lil . . .'

The tension leaked from her and exhausted sobs wracked her slim figure. She might hate to admit it, but she needed someone to hold her. Everyone else saw an independent single woman, hardened by life and fiercely independent. But who could exist like that? Solitary. Isolated. He wanted to be at her side, supporting her, he wanted to cherish her and love her.

The realisation caught him off guard. He loved her.

Keeping the sheets between them like a barrier, he

kissed the top of her head and stroked her hair until her sobs quietened and sleep finally claimed her.

Olivier watched the shadows, relieved that she'd found peace, if only for a few hours, but sleep evaded him. His heart beat a heavy rhythm in his chest as he breathed in the scent of her hair and held her close. It felt as if he was balanced on a high wire, swaying in the air, about to fall, and he had an ominous sense of dread, an acute awareness of his own vulnerability. He didn't want to feel so much, to love so much again. He didn't want to need her like he'd needed Nathalie.

He swallowed, knowing he had to put the brakes on this storm he felt for Lily. They were wrong for each other. He wanted a lasting love like Béa and Raymond's, he needed to feel he had a home – in every sense of the word.

But loving Lily wouldn't bring him any of those.

He might want her and love her, but she couldn't give him what he needed.

Chapter Seventeen

Lily woke slowly, her mind hazily trying to refocus. She had the most beautiful, the warmest sensation of being in the right place – yet she was also conscious of an underlying, unbearable ache. She opened her eyes and stilled because her cheek was pressed against Olivier's chest.

Then it all came back to her. Mamie's funeral. Olivier comforting her, kissing her – pushing her away.

Closing her eyes, she sighed in despair at herself. She had to leave. Get away from this place. But there was the exhibition. She had to see it through, for Mamie's sake and for the village.

She tried to roll away, but Olivier had one arm draped around her and he was lying on top of the sheet, in effect pinning her down. She froze as she felt him stir. The change in his breathing confirmed he was awake, but she couldn't bring herself to look at him.

'Lily,' he said softly. Lovingly.

His voice had the deep purr of a man speaking to the love of his life. She wanted to laugh. That couldn't be further from the truth. She was more like the bane of his life, a thorn in his side.

'How are you feeling?' he asked, still in that early morning voice that vibrated right through her.

She remembered how he'd appeared in the darkness,

how he'd apologised and held her through the storm. She hadn't been able to stop the flow of tears, but it had felt so good when he'd wrapped his arms around her.

'Mortified,' she muttered quietly. Her cheeks glowed at the memory of last night. 'And – and I need the bathroom,' she said, trying to pull her arm free from beneath the covers, 'but I'm stuck.'

He chuckled softly. 'Sorry. Didn't mean to trap you. I thought we'd be safer if there was something coming between us.'

He rolled back, and she could feel his gaze on her but she didn't want to see the look in his eyes as she scuttled away to the other side of the bed.

I thought we'd be safer . . .? His words triggered butterfly wings of hope, but she instantly crushed that. There was so much coming between them, she thought heavily – a lifetime of it.

She hurried away to the bathroom, pausing a moment as she passed Mamie's bedroom and the bare mattress. I told you it could never work, she silently told her grandmother. I don't know why you always tried to push us together. It's just not going to happen.

When she finished in the shower and came out of the bathroom, the smell of coffee told her Olivier was downstairs in the kitchen. She dressed and went down.

'You must want to take a shower yourself and get back – get on with your day,' she said, wishing he'd leave.

His lips curved and he handed her a cup. 'You saying I smell?'

When she'd woken up to find him next to her in bed

he'd smelled of man, of him, and now he looked beautiful with his tanned bare feet and his jaw darkened by rough stubble that made him seem both dangerous and vulnerable at the same time. She wanted to cup his face with her hands and run her fingertips over his beard and–

She dropped her gaze and stared into her coffee because it was safer than looking at him.

He took a quick sip of his own and she could feel him watching her.

'I've got lots to do today,' she said briskly, 'so if you don't mind–'

'Lily.'

She ignored him and rattled on, looking at the table, the floor, anywhere but him. 'I'm fine, okay? Last night was just a blip, I was tired and emotional, but today I feel absolutely fine, and I want to get on with–'

'Lily!'

She looked up. His expression was fierce. 'I'm not going anywhere. We need to talk about last night.'

Fire flashed in her cheeks. She'd wanted to make love. He hadn't. How would talking about that help? It would only be mortifying for her. Her chest tightened just thinking about it. 'We really don't.'

'We do.'

'Why?'

'Because you deserve an explanation.' He breathed in, as if steeling himself. 'It took all my will power to keep my hands off you last night, Lil.'

She stared at him, and felt something give inside, like stitches unravelling.

But words were easy. His actions had spoken louder: he'd pushed her away. Just as she'd expected. Just as he'd done when they were teenagers.

'You had every right to say no. That's fine.'

'I didn't want to say no. That's the thing. I want you more than anything. But I care too much to take advantage of you when you were at your most vulnerable.'

She frowned, uncertain. Hope began to unfurl deep inside. *I want you more than anything?*

'You weren't in any fit state to make decisions about our relationship. You're grieving. This isn't the right time for us to–' he searched for the word, 'to start something. But that doesn't mean I don't want to.'

Lily stared at him. Despite her scars? Despite her being . . . her? The tomboy he always argued and fought with? The girl he thought of as a sister? Who was nothing like Corinne: not sweet or pretty or planning to stay still and start a family?

'What if it *is* the right time?' she said defiantly. Who did he think he was, making decisions for her? Only she was in a position to say how she felt.

He shook his head. 'It's not. You need time and space to think things through. I don't want us to do anything you might regret later.'

She drew her shoulders back. 'I'm not made of glass.'

'Last night you felt lost and afraid and lonely.'

'I didn't say that.'

'You didn't need to. I've never seen you cry before, Lil. Not in all the years I've known you.' He added quickly, 'And crying is nothing to be ashamed of, by the way.

That's normal. But you need time to work through your grief. To decide what you want.'

Perhaps he was right. Perhaps her emotions were still raw and she wasn't thinking as clearly as she normally would.

But she also knew she wouldn't change her mind. She wanted him. She'd always wanted him.

A woman's voice called out from the garden, footsteps approached, and Béa appeared in the doorway.

'Good morning,' she said, clutching a paper bag and looking anxiously at Lily. 'How are you feeling today?'

'I'm–' Lily stumbled. Her brain was like a wheel which had jammed and got stuck trying to understand Olivier's words. He was scowling – presumably because they'd been interrupted. 'I'm feeling much better, thanks,' she managed finally.

Béa studied her. 'You're still pale. Here, I brought you breakfast. You must eat, Lily.' She put a plate on the table and began to lay out croissants and *pains au chocolat*.

'Thank you,' said Lily, her gaze still fixed on Olivier.

He shifted impatiently from one foot to the other, but Béa didn't notice and took her time.

'Is there enough coffee for me?' she asked, then turned back to Lily. 'Come. Sit down. You know it's bad for the digestion to eat standing up.'

Lily smiled. 'That's what Mamie always says—' She realised her mistake and corrected herself, 'said.'

The smile was wiped from her face. And the inevitable fist of grief hit her square in the chest.

*

Olivier poured his mother a coffee, cursing under his breath when he accidentally splashed himself with the hot liquid. He grabbed a cloth and wiped his hand, watching in dismay as Lily crumpled with grief again and Béa pulled her into a hug.

'It will get better,' she soothed, shooting Olivier a look of concern over Lily's shoulder.

He put his mother's coffee down on the table, frustrated that Béa had interrupted their conversation, that she'd robbed him of the chance to find out how Lily felt. Had she wanted him last night because he was there when she needed comfort? Or did she have feelings for him the way he did for her?

But now he realised what a pointless question that would have been. Lily was a muddle of grief and tears, and it might be weeks, even months, before she got over losing Mamie. It would certainly be a long time before she could tell him how she felt about him. He had to be patient.

They prepared for the retrospective, delivering leaflets to shops and houses in the village, and overseeing the packing up and installation of the paintings in the town hall. Although Lily missed Mamie terribly, she did her best to hide it behind a front of efficient preparations and meetings about the upcoming exhibition.

'Are you hoping to raise money through the sale of the paintings?' asked the Mayor, who had kindly agreed to officially open the exhibition.

'They'll be sold at auction later,' said Lily, 'but that isn't the point of this exhibition.'

Olivier nodded. 'This is simply an opportunity for the village to see Simone's work. In fact, we could also include pieces of our own which Mamie gave us.' He looked questioningly at Lily and she nodded her approval.

That was a great idea. This way all Mamie's paintings, her life's work, would be exhibited together.

The Mayor nodded. 'It's a very kind gesture. Typical of your family. Of both families.' He looked from Lily to Olivier and back again, then smiled. 'I always knew you two would come good in the end.'

They looked at each other.

'What do you mean?' Lily asked.

'The mischief you used to get up to when you were together – you brought out the worst in each other, but also the best. Like this.' He waved his hand to indicate the leaflets they'd brought advertising the retrospective.

Lily and Olivier drove back to the farmhouse in silence. Since the morning after the funeral, they had avoided talking about that night. Lily could have raised it over the quiet meals the two of them shared, she supposed, or the evenings they spent sitting beside each other – though never too close – in Mamie's lounge. But she didn't want to spoil those moments of comfortable friendship. Everything between them had reverted almost to how it had been before – the gentle teasing, the shared jokes and memories. Almost.

She eyed him surreptitiously, wondering if she should raise it now. But what would she say? *When you said it wasn't the right time . . . when would be?* That smacked of desperation, of trying to nail him down to some fixed point in the future, and who would agree to that? People's feelings changed all the time, they were fickle, unreliable. She didn't want to twist his arm and force him to commit to something she knew would never last.

And yet.

She couldn't stop the ache she felt for him. Even through the haze of grief, her senses sharpened when he came near, her pulse quickened when she got up each morning to find him there in the kitchen, and she responded to the whisper of his lips against her cheeks as he greeted her each day. Sometimes his lips lingered on her cheek just a second longer than they needed to, and she closed her eyes and held her breath. Sometimes she caught him watching her with a dark look in his eyes. There was a tension between them.

I want you more than anything. His words played over and over in her head, making her wonder, triggering wishful fantasies. What was to stop them now Corinne was gone?

Their friendship.

The fact that they wanted opposite things from life.

That he was beautiful and she was scarred.

That she didn't do relationships and would soon be gone.

They were far more comfortable behaving like old buddies with their familiar rivalry and teasing, and she knew it was better if it stayed that way. Soon she'd be back at work, busy navigating the challenges of an unfamiliar landscape, getting to know her subjects, trying to understand their problems and unearth a new story. And the raw, heightened emotions she was feeling now would fade and become only a memory.

'I have a hospital appointment tomorrow,' she said, breaking the silence.

'What for?'

'To have this removed,' She held up her right arm, '– providing everything's healed, of course.'

'Already?'

'It's been six weeks.'

So much had happened in that space of time.

'Want me to drive you there?'

'There's no need. I can get the bus.'

His mouth became a flat line. 'I'll drive you, Skinny.'

Lily stood in front of her open wardrobe and surveyed its meagre contents. She needed – and wanted – to look smart for tonight's exhibition. It wasn't about what others would say or think, but because she didn't want to let Mamie down. Tonight was important. She wanted to look the part. She blew out a slow breath, trying to suppress the nerves, the tension, the gaping sense of sorrow that ballooned. Mamie might not be here, but Lily was determined that everything should be exactly as it would have been if things had gone to plan.

She ran her fingers over the rail of coat hangers one more time. She couldn't wear the satin trousers because she didn't have a matching top that was dressy enough, and the only skirt in the wardrobe was one she'd outgrown years ago. Obviously, none of her shorts and t-shirts and jeans were smart enough . . . Which left only the new dress which Mamie had bought for her the day Olivier had returned from Paris a few weeks ago.

Lily lifted it out and laid it on her bed. She hated dresses. They were restrictive and uncomfortable and liable to tearing, and this one was particularly fitted and smart, made from brown silk.

But she'd left it so late that now she really didn't have any other option.

'What are you doing?' asked Lily.

Olivier was in the kitchen, stirring and peering into the large orange stockpot which Mamie had always used to make stews. Beneath his white apron he was wearing smart navy trousers and a jacket, and a white shirt that looked pristine against his bronze skin. He didn't look up but even in profile he looked utterly gorgeous. She adjusted the neckline of her dress self-consciously and shifted her weight from one high-heeled shoe to the other.

'Preparing dinner,' he said, giving it one final stir before lowering the lid onto the pot.

Lily glanced up at the clock on the wall. 'But we need to go. The exhibition starts in thirty minutes.'

'I know.' He slid the pot into the oven and turned the dial to a low heat. 'This'll cook while we're out.'

He hung his apron over a chair and looked at her. His brows lifted and his eyes darkened in an expression she couldn't decipher.

'You didn't need to cook,' she said, to fill the silence more than anything. 'We could have bought a snack on the way home.'

His gaze remained fixed on her, grave and intent. 'I've made your favourite: *Daube de Boeuf* and potato *gratin*, followed by chocolate mousse.'

Something about the way he was looking at her made her still.

She hesitated, then asked, 'Why?'

'Because this is an important night. I thought we should mark it with a private celebration.'

Was that a glint in his eye? Or had she imagined it? 'Thanks.'

'Like the dress, by the way. I didn't know you owned one.'

She looked down at the coffee brown silk that hugged her torso and flared at the waist, swishing against her legs. It felt foreign and unfamiliar, yet surprisingly comfortable. And judging by the heat in Olivier's eyes, its figure-hugging shape was possibly flattering too.

'Mamie bought it for me, but – but . . .' She bit her lip and closed her eyes against the crowding emotions, '. . . she never saw me wear it.'

Olivier must have crossed the room because she felt his hands cup her face. 'Hey,' he said softly. 'It's okay. She's probably looking down right now, grinning because you're finally wearing it and you look beautiful.'

Her throat squeezed tight. 'Thank you.'

'You're welcome. Now, are you ready?' He picked up his car keys and went to leave.

She swallowed, but fear rushed at her, harsh, huge and overwhelming.

He reached the kitchen door and looked back over his shoulder. 'Lil?' he asked when he saw she hadn't moved.

'I don't know if I can do this,' she whispered.

He frowned. 'Do what?'

'Tonight – the exhibition.'

During her career she'd filmed in a notoriously dangerous mine which had threatened to collapse around her, she'd survived three weeks on a high plateau in sub-zero temperatures, she'd come face to face with a grizzly, she'd crossed zip wires and abseiled down sheer cliffs, but she'd never felt as small and as vulnerable as she did now.

Her legs wouldn't move. She was a fifteen-year-old girl again. Lost. Alone.

He crossed the room to stand in front of her. 'Course you can,' he said.

'This should have been Mamie's night, but she's not here, and there will be so many people . . .' It hadn't even started and tears were already biting at her eyes. It was a good job she was only wearing lipstick and blusher because any other make-up would have smudged or run.

His hands were warm as they closed around her shoulders and he looked into her eyes.

'You *can* do this, Lil.'

She shook her head, her throat so tight it was difficult to breathe.

He gently squeezed her shoulders. 'We'll do it together.'

She stilled and looked up at him, feeling those words wrap around her like a safety harness.

Together? She'd forgotten how hard this night might be for him, too.

'I'll be right beside you,' he promised.

His words vibrated through her, touching her core. She drew strength from them. 'Thank you,' she whispered.

'Look,' he grinned, and pulled something out of his jacket pocket. 'I've even got a handkerchief. Equipped for anything!'

She laughed as she used it to dab her eyes. 'A handkerchief? Who even uses those any more?'

He made a playful swipe for it. 'I'll take it back if that's your attitude!'

She smiled and kept hold of the soft cotton square. 'You won't want it back when I've finished with it.'

'That's better,' he said and brushed a finger over the upturned corner of her lip. The tenderness of his touch made her want to close her eyes and hold her breath. 'Ready now?'

She nodded. With him by her side, she felt strong enough to cope with anything.

The retrospective was a huge success. People were queueing through the corridors of the town hall to get in.

Lily looked stunning in her chocolate-coloured dress. Tall, slim, with that indefinable grace and elegance that was all Lily. All around the room heads turned to look at her, men's eyes lighting with interest. Olivier put his arm around her waist, trying to resist the urge to pull her tight against him, and instead gently steered her around the room so she had the chance to speak to everyone.

'I had no idea your grandmother was so talented,' said the hairdresser, Monsieur Canolle.

Lily smiled, absently rubbing the white skin of her arm where the bandage had been. 'She was very modest about her painting.'

'She could have sold these years ago and made a fortune.'

'Mamie wasn't interested in money,' said Olivier, though he was stating the obvious because everyone in the village had known Simone.

'She painted because she loved to paint,' said Lily.

'It's very good of you to have shared these with us.' Monsieur Canolle's eyes shone as he smiled.

'It's what Mamie wanted. She would be really touched to see so many people here.'

Despite Lily's dignified smile, Olivier felt her silent pain that her gran wasn't here tonight. He squeezed her hand and she shot him a grateful smile that made his heart catapult against his chest.

Christ, he thought. When had it come to this? That one tiny gesture from her was enough to rock him? He inhaled deeply to try and release the tension in his muscles, but his thoughts returned to the meal he'd prepared for them later and anticipation, anxiety, only wound themselves tighter around him.

He'd given Lily as much time as he could to work through her grief, but now the hourglass was running dry. She'd said she would stay for the exhibition but beyond that who knew? There was always the risk that she might fly off at any time, so while she was in his life he had to seize the moment. He had to lay his cards on the table and show her how he felt.

Monsieur Canolle moved on and Lily looked at her watch. 'It's ten o'clock,' she whispered. 'Do you think we need to stay much longer?'

'Not if you don't want to.'

'I – I'd quite like to slip out. While it's busy, no one will notice.'

He smiled. 'Your wish is my command. Back door?'

She grinned and nodded.

Outside in the cool evening air, Lily relaxed. 'It went well, didn't it?'

'It did,' he said. But as he drove them back to the farmhouse, he had to grip the steering wheel to try and quell the tremor in his hands.

She might not want this now. Her feelings for him might have changed. If they had, then it would confirm that he'd done the right thing on the night of Mamie's funeral. But he hoped he'd gauged this right. He hoped he hadn't imagined the sparks in her eyes when he greeted her each morning, the quickening of the pulse at the base of her throat when his hand made contact with hers.

He raked a hand through his hair, and wondered if he'd ever been so nervous before. The risks were high; their friendship mattered so much to him. But if it worked, it would be like fireworks, he was certain of it.

If it worked.

He pulled up outside the farmhouse, switched off the

engine, and everything went quiet. The starry sky reminded him of that night in Paris. The gate squeaked as he held it open for Lily, and their feet crunched on the gravel as they picked their way silently towards the house.

Inside, Lily disappeared upstairs to use the bathroom and while she was gone he laid the kitchen table. A candlelit setting would have been more atmospheric but it was out of the question so he went into the lounge and came back with a couple of small lamps. Perched on the dresser, they cast a more subtle glow than the bare light-bulb which hung from the kitchen ceiling. The beef stew was perfectly cooked, the bread was on the table, and the red wine was open. He loosened his tie and had just tossed it to one side when Lily reappeared.

She stopped in the doorway and stared at the table. At him.

'When you said you were making dinner,' she said, 'I wasn't expecting all this . . .'

'Sit down,' he smiled, and pulled a chair out for her.

He poured the wine and lifted the lid of the sturdy orange pot. The smell of the rich wine sauce rose in the air.

Lily closed her eyes and smiled. 'That smells so good.'

Her stomach gurgled in agreement and Olivier laughed.

'You've gone to a lot of trouble,' she said as he spooned stew into bowls.

'Not really. But I did want it to be special.'

'Why?'

Good question. He swallowed, thinking that he'd

cooked meals for many women before, but he'd never felt as unsure as he did now. Lily had always been a good friend; what if that was all she wanted to be?

And yet friendship wasn't enough for him any more. He needed – craved – more. He'd tried so hard to fight this ache for her, but it was futile.

'Because today was an important day,' he said, feeling a swell of admiration for how brave she'd been at the retrospective. Mamie would be proud of her. 'I hope you'll always remember it.'

He raised his glass and they drank a toast. As they ate, he tried to concentrate on his food, but all he wanted to do was drink in the sight of her sitting tall opposite him. Her hair was loose but draped back over her shoulders, revealing the slender lines of her face, those high cheekbones, and her beautiful eyes.

'This is delicious,' said Lily, pointing her fork at the meat on her plate. 'It tastes just like Mamie's *Daube*.'

'That's because it's Mamie's recipe.'

Her eyes widened. 'She gave you her recipe?'

He nodded.

'But she never gave her recipes to anyone!'

'She gave it to me.'

She stared at him, then smiled and said softly, 'You always were her favourite.'

'Now that simply isn't true. If you'd shown the slightest bit of interest in cooking, she would have given you the recipe too.'

She gave a small nod to concede that perhaps he was right.

'Can you cook at all, Skinny?'

'I can make a sandwich,' she smiled, 'and in sub-zero conditions I can heat a tin of soup. That's about the sum total of my cooking skills. So which other recipes did she give you?'

'Just this one. But she did give me a few tips too: the secret ingredients she liked to use, that kind of thing.'

Lily shook her head. 'You knew exactly how to charm her, didn't you?'

'It was never a competition, Lil.' His voice was low as he added, 'She would have laid down her life for you.'

She stopped eating and blinked hard. 'I know.'

The urge to wrap his arms around her and keep her safe rushed through him, fierce and unstoppable. He watched as she put a small forkful of meat in her mouth and chewed. He followed the line of her jaw, her throat, her chest. His muscles gripped. He wanted to kiss her. Not a quick brush of lips against her cheek, but slowly. Deeply. Passionately.

When they finished eating, relief coursed through him. Impatience too.

'Want any more?' he asked politely, though if she'd looked up, she would have seen that the look in his eyes was far from polite. He was wound tight with awareness. Anticipation.

She shook her head. 'It was delicious, thank you. I'll get the dishes.' She stood up and reached for his plate.

He pushed his chair back, and closed the space between them. 'No,' he commanded softly, and laid the plates back down on the table.

'But you've gone to a lot of trouble. The least I can do is clear up—'

'No,' he said firmly.

She blinked at him, and he wanted to lose himself in the depths of those sage-green eyes. Her hair had fallen forwards again, as it always did, and he smoothed the long strands back from her face. She stared at him and he saw the unspoken questions in her eyes, a flicker of uncertainty, a spark of hunger. It reassured him.

He inhaled deeply and touched her cheek. His gaze held hers. He dipped his head and brushed his mouth against hers. The contact was electric. Sizzling. He slipped his hand behind her head and his fingers settled in the hollow at the base of her neck. Her lips opened to him, and his pulse jumped. He tried to show restraint. He tried to hold back, probing, carefully tracking her response, aware of how much was at stake. He didn't want to push her if she wasn't comfortable with this. He didn't want to risk their precious friendship for the sake of a primitive release.

But every fibre of his being was coiled tight with hope that she wanted this too.

She sighed against him and satisfaction gripped him. He deepened the kiss, pressing her soft, slim body against the wall of his chest. And his hips. Christ, it took all his strength not to rush this.

They came up for air, both breathing raggedly, Lily's eyes dark and wide with wonder as she looked up at him. 'I thought–' she began, a frown pierced her brow. She swallowed and tried again. 'I thought you said that this wasn't the right time? That I was vulnerable.'

Two weeks had passed since the night of Mamie's funeral. Not long. And yet too long. There was only so long a man can wait, he thought wryly.

'Are you?' he asked.

'You said it, not me. I've never thought of myself in that way.'

He smiled and ran the pad of his thumb over her bottom lip, savouring the softness of it. 'No. You're strong. You're brave.'

He couldn't keep his eyes off her mouth, off her eyes, smoky with desire. 'But are you brave enough for this?' he asked, and bent his head and kissed her again.

This time he didn't hold back. This time he let her know how hungry he was for her, how desperately he needed this. Her. Lily. To be his. And he couldn't shake off the feeling that this was the perfection he'd been searching for all his life.

He felt her body relax and drew her closer. As their breathing became more urgent, his hands found the small of her back, the dip of her waist, and he savoured the feel of her, new and unfamiliar. She was almost as tall as him yet so slender, her skin smooth, the scars of her cheek and neck like creased satin beneath his touch.

He broke off, breathless. Her eyes were dark with desire, and this made his veins buzz.

'Let's go upstairs,' he whispered. Determined there should be no misunderstanding. That she should be in control.

That she should want this as much as he did.

Chapter Eighteen

Lily blinked, dizzied by his kiss, astounded by this whole evening and the meal – which she realised only now had been prepared with seduction in mind.

'But . . .' she faltered.

'But what, Lily? Why the disbelieving look?'

Did she need to say it? She was scarred; he was beautiful.

'You could have any woman you want,' she said quietly.

His fingers lifted to touch her face and she felt them slide over her scarred cheek. She looked up at him. 'You're the only woman I want.'

His mouth, his lips were mesmerising. She had to make herself focus on keeping eye contact because this was important. Her body might be leaning in to his with desire, but that was nothing but a physical impulse. She and Olivier shared so much more.

'When you're around, Lil, I feel things . . .' He pursed his lips, and seemed be struggling to find the words. 'It's been there all summer: the urge to spend every minute with you, to laugh and have fun together, to work together, to be together. I want you, Lil.'

The blood pounded in her ears as she processed this. *He wanted her.* Absently, she lifted a hand to her cheek. For years she'd believed that her scars had killed the hope of this ever happening.

'Your scars only add to your beauty,' he said, reading her mind.

And any doubt that lingered was swept away because Olivier only ever spoke the truth. He never hid behind lies.

Still she hesitated. 'But . . . I'm not the right woman for you.'

His chin went up. 'Don't you think I should be the judge of that?' he said.

Her heart was pumping so hard she felt dizzy. This was a huge step – one that had the potential to destroy their friendship – but the ache had been building steadily and persistently over such a long time. All the days and weeks they'd spent together, she'd been like a pot simmering on the stove. Now need exploded in her. He wanted her. He thought she was beautiful. Her fingers curled around his neck.

Why not give in to it? she asked herself as she looked into his dark eyes. They were both adults, they knew the score. It was only sex, not a lifetime commitment. Joy rose and span violently through her. How many times had she dreamed of this moment? Fantasised about it? And if Mamie's death had taught her anything, it was that she should live for the moment.

So, holding his gaze, she took his hand and led him up the stairs.

Their footsteps echoed on the wood and tapped out the seconds. It was only when they reached her room and she turned to face him that she realised she'd been holding her breath. He drew her to him and she kissed him again.

His hand brushed the curve of her breast, sliding over the silk fabric of her dress. She sucked in air. Their hips connected, friction and heat building. It was delicious. Frightening. Unbearable.

He paused. 'Dare you to take my shirt off,' he said, a wicked glint in his eye.

She smiled and unbuttoned it slowly, their gazes locked. She peeled away the white cotton, trying to still the quickening of her pulse as she ran her palms over the wall of his chest. How many times had she seen him without a shirt and longed to touch him like this? His hair felt rough beneath her fingers, his skin hot. His ribcage lifted as he sucked in air, and he briefly closed his eyes as if battling for self-control.

'Dare you to do the same,' she whispered.

His eyes were dark with intent as he carefully unzipped her dress and let it fall, a puddle of silk at her feet. The cool night air whispered against her bare skin, and the lace of her bra felt impossibly tight against the swell of her breasts. Conscious of the scars that ran from her cheek down to her shoulder and across, she watched him warily. But she needn't have worried: he drank in the sight of her with a look of awe.

With the tips of his fingers he stroked her mouth, her face, and his touch was impossibly tender. Captivating. He dropped kisses on her ear, chin, throat. His lips touched her skin slowly and lovingly, as if her scars simply didn't exist or didn't matter. Her head span. His muscles bunched beneath her fingers. She held on tight, and let the dizzying sensations overtake her. Her mind emptied as his hands explored the bare skin of her back, her waist, her breasts. She held her breath. Every part of her that he touched lit up, and he pressed her hips to his, making her body ache with need.

'Lily,' he said, and broke off. He rested his forehead against hers, breathing hard and smiling.

'What's wrong?' she asked. 'Why did you stop?' She didn't want him to stop. She wanted–

'Because we're not going to rush this,' he said, and his eyes were dark with promise. 'You deserve better. So much better. And, if it kills me, I'm going to make sure this is a night we remember. Always.'

She looked up into that face that she had known and adored since she was a girl, and her heart swelled so much and so fast she thought it might overflow.

They'd been so engrossed in each other last night that they'd forgotten to close the shutters, and now Olivier watched as the shy light of dawn trickled in and illuminated Lily's face. Her long lashes rested on the pillows of her cheeks, the silk river of her hair swept over her shoulder and down her back, and her breaths kept time with the slow, peaceful rhythm of sleep.

She looked delicate like this. A million miles away from the quietly defiant woman she presented to the world. His chest swelled with emotion. She might pretend to be brave and independent, but he knew her. The corner of his mouth lifted. He knew her intimately. And now he wondered, why had he ever feared his feelings for her?

What they'd shared last night had been profound, built on the special bond they'd always shared. It felt to him as sure and as permanent as the centuries-old trees in the olive grove. His muscles tightened and optimism rose in him like the sun over the horizon. The connection between them was so strong they couldn't ignore it any longer, and he was certain that this was the start of something more. Something lasting.

She frowned in her sleep and shifted restlessly. He drew her into the curve of his body and she settled again, her breathing became a soft, contented purr. He pressed a kiss to the top of her head, inhaling the familiar soapy scent that was uniquely hers, and it rushed at him – the urge to keep her safe and take care of her. She'd been alone so long. It was time she settled down with someone who would look out for her. Cherish her. Adore her.

He wanted to be that someone.

'No regrets?'

He was holding her close, his fingers woven into her hair, and she was savouring the sensations, still dazed and stunned because making love had never been like this before. Not with Theo, not with anyone. With Olivier it had been so intimate, urgent, meaningful. She hadn't known her body was capable of such pleasure. No man had ever made her feel so precious or desirable.

So beautiful.

Now, though, Olivier's question made her tense. 'Why would I regret it?'

Did he?

Her heart thudded and she steeled herself. Rejection was something she knew so well.

'Because we were friends before. Now we're lovers.' He rolled to lie on top of her, biceps bunching as he supported his own weight, and his gaze held hers. 'There's no going back.'

Her lips curved with relief, and pleasure vibrated through her at the thought. 'No regrets,' she confirmed. 'You?'

He chuckled, and the sound was deep and throaty. 'My only regret is that I didn't realise how I felt about you sooner. All that time I spent telling myself you were like a sister . . . I was blind to my own feelings.'

She smoothed his dark hair back from his eyes and smiled because she'd never thought of him as a brother, and she'd suppressed her attraction to him for so long, utterly convinced he would never feel the same way about her.

He lowered his head and his lips brushed hers. The sweetness of his kiss made her head spin, and she closed her eyes. It was enchanting, and for now she was happy to momentarily lose herself in it. She'd wanted him for so long that she was relieved they'd made love.

Yes, relieved. The heat, the tension between them had been unbearable, but now it had an outlet, it would inevitably die down to something more subdued, less all-consuming.

*

Lily watched as Mamie's paintings were lifted down from the walls of the town hall and carefully packed, ready to be shipped to the auction house. The exhibition was over and she fought the gritty sensation in the backs of her eyes as she said goodbye to yet another reminder of her gran.

The agent, Monsieur Masson, stood beside her, overseeing his men as they worked. He glanced at her. 'Are you sure you still want to sell them all? Given what's happened, it might be better to wait before making this decision. We could delay the sale if you need time.'

Her shoulders went back. Why was everyone treating her like she was made of glass? She was fine. She was a survivor.

'There's no need to delay anything. I have the paintings I want to keep,' she said, nodding at the brightly coloured fishing boats and the olive grove. 'You can go ahead with the sale.'

On the way home Olivier kept glancing at her with the same careful look as Monsieur Masson earlier.

'Everything alright?' he asked as his four by four made easy work of climbing the hill out of St Pierre's village centre.

'Fine. Why?'

'You seem a little emotional, that's all. It's to be expected, given all that's happened.'

She frowned, ignoring the burning in the backs of her eyes, and the jittery sensation in her chest. 'I'm fine.'

Back home, she escaped his scrutiny by disappearing upstairs. Her feet tapped along the landing and she hesitated a moment outside the closed door of the studio before continuing to her own room. There, she sat down at her laptop. She'd already begun editing the footage from Paris, but now her arm was feeling stronger, she could really get down to business. She'd make the film, she decided, send it off to the television company and enter it for the film prize.

Resolutely, she rolled her sleeves up and opened the file, feeling more in control now she had goals in mind again, feeling more like herself. All that talk about feeling emotional had been nonsense. What she needed was simply to get back to work. She had a film to make, and that was what she was going to do.

'What's this?' asked Lily, as she came into the lounge. She rubbed her eyes and rolled her shoulders, stiff after having spent the day hunched over her laptop working.

Olivier shot her a guarded look. 'One of your films,' he confessed, and was it her imagination or did he sound a little hoarse?

On his lap was the purple sweater Mamie had knitted for him. His fingers were curled around the cashmere wool.

Lily sat down beside him. On the screen a group of children in a South African slum were kicking a makeshift football made of rolled-up plastic bags.

'I thought you said that you've seen all my films before?'

'I have.'

'Then why are you watching this one again?'

'I watch it whenever I'm feeling down. It always cheers me up.'

She looked at his red-rimmed eyes, puzzled. 'You're feeling down?' she asked gently.

'I miss Mamie,' he confessed with a sad smile.

Grief splintered through her, and she looked away. She concentrated on forcing air into her lungs until she felt in control again.

It wasn't that she didn't miss Mamie. She just couldn't let herself dwell on it. She kept her thoughts focused on the future. The next scene she had to edit, the next email she'd send, the next commission she hoped to win.

'It's a beautiful film,' said Olivier. His gaze was fixed on the screen. 'So uplifting. It reminds me of all that's good in life.'

'They were very special children. They had no possessions, some of them didn't even have shoes, yet they were adorably happy.'

'That's what is so moving. Humbling too.' His eyes locked with hers. 'And it reminds me of our childhood; the games we played, the fun we had.'

He pulled her to him and she curled her legs under her, relaxing against the heat of his body. As the credits rolled, she realised her spirits had been lifted too. There was something special about sharing memories and moments like this with another person. Her life had always been about looking forward and anticipating the next adventure – yet right now the familiar felt good too.

*

Lily loved to watch him sleep. Daylight filtered in through the half-open shutters, lighting up the rugged line of his jaw, the darkness of his stubble, the unruly locks of black hair that fell over his eyes.

She sometimes found herself watching him in the kitchen too, when she was working at her laptop and he was preparing dinner. She was fascinated by the speed and skill with which he chopped food and by his look of concentration, she loved the way he hummed along to the radio, she was distracted by his masculinity. By her response to him.

Her thighs squeezed as she remembered how they'd made love last night. When he looked into her eyes it felt as if she was being plunged into a depthless ocean of emotion. The blood pounded in her ears, her breathing quickened. It was wild, it was blissful and it–

It scared her.

She didn't have a name for this dark, sweet emotion, but when he held her close and she looked into his eyes, it swamped her. Engulfed her. She'd gone into this believing that lust, like a candle, had a limited life and would burn itself out. But it hadn't. It was growing. Intensifying. Who knew where it might lead if she let it? Her heart tugged. Who knew what she might feel if she let herself?

She turned away from him and willed her pulse to slow a little. Beside her bed, beneath her watch and a small pile of coins, was her passport. She reached out and touched the creased burgundy cover. It was a reminder that this was not her life. She didn't do roots or standing still.

Behind her, he stirred, and strong arms slipped around her.

'*Bonjour,*' he murmured against her neck.

The effect of his kisses was instant, and heat stole through her, dissolving her strength. He rolled her back to him and as she looked into his eyes the ache in her chest was so powerful her breath caught.

She closed her eyes and tried to swallow down her fear. This was out of control. The last few days had been heady and surreal, but that couldn't last. Soon she would go back to normal life and the job she loved. She just had to stay focused on her goals.

'I was thinking we could take my boat out today, maybe take a picnic out to the cove,' said Olivier over breakfast. He nodded at her arm. 'If you don't feel up to swimming we can skip the diving and picnic on the beach.'

'That's a great idea! And I can swim. My arm's just a little weak.' She flexed and unflexed her hand before looking up at him. Her eyes narrowed. 'Why are you laughing?'

'Because with one arm weaker than the other you'll be swimming in circles.'

She thumped him playfully on the arm, but he grabbed her fist and pulled her to him, kissing her long and deep so that when he'd finished and she came up for air she was dizzy from it.

★

Lily broke through the water and savoured the sudden heat on her face, the dazzling sunlight. She pulled off her mask and snorkel and grinned at Olivier.

'Did you enjoy that?' he asked.

'Enjoy it? It was amazing!' They'd seen some great fish, but what she'd enjoyed most had been swimming and diving; the thrill, the exhilaration of being in the water and seeing that secret underwater world.

They reached the shallows and waded back in towards the shore, splashing as they ploughed through the clear water. She towelled herself dry and the salt and sand scratched her skin, but Lily didn't notice; her pulse was racing with adrenaline. Olivier stretched himself out on his towel and she did the same, leaning back on her elbows to enjoy the view. The cove was deserted today. Most of the tourists had left at the end of August, and this place was only accessible by boat which meant it was secluded at the best of times. The warm September sun bathed her skin. Since the heatwave had ended, the weather had been more temperate and today a gentle breeze ruffled her hair and cooled the air. Lily gazed around, admiring the jagged white cliffs and the sharp blue of the water.

'This place is perfect,' she said softly.

'It is. I used to love it when your dad took us diving,' Olivier told her.

She flinched a little at the mention of her dad. Until this summer she had avoided talking or thinking about him because it hurt too much. But spending time with Mamie and Olivier had helped her see beyond the pain of losing him. There were so many good memories for her to cherish. 'He took us on some exciting trips, didn't he?' she said.

'Yeah. Hiking, climbing, boat trips . . .'

'I think he would have been an adventurer, given the chance.'

'Really?'

She nodded. 'He never got the opportunity to travel because he had me to look after, and every penny he saved went on paying for trips home to see Mamie. But he loved to read about exotic places. He dreamed of climbing mountains and trekking through the jungle.'

'So that's who you take after,' said Olivier, as if it were a revelation.

'Yes. Well, it's not my mother. She couldn't be more different from me.'

Darcy Green loved nothing more than performing and being the centre of attention. Her music and her reputation had come before everything else – even her own daughter.

'Your dad took us on outdoor adventures whereas Raymond was always in the kitchen. Looking back, I learned different things from them both.'

'We were lucky kids.'

'Yeah. Although Raymond had to work long hours to establish the bakery.' He leaned back with his face to the sun, and the light bounced off his sunglasses. 'It will be easier for me. I want to be around for my kids. I want to be a hands-on dad, completely immersed in their lives.'

Despite the sun's heat, Lily felt a shiver of discomfort. 'You'll be a great father,' she said quietly.

'I hope so.'

She scooped up a pile of white sand and let it trickle through her fingers whilst darting him a quick glance. The thought of him having children with another woman punctured her chest. But, she told herself, she'd be gone by then. She'd be back on the road, absorbed in her work again.

'You hungry?' asked Olivier.

'Starving.'

'Time for lunch, then.'

He had filled an icebox with quiche and salads, cakes and fruit. He laid out all the food in the shade of a parasol and they tucked in hungrily.

'This is delicious,' Lily said, surveying the feast in front of her. She picked up a fat green olive and popped it in her mouth. A simple sandwich would have sufficed, but trust a master baker to provide a gourmet picnic.

When they'd finished eating he settled himself with his back to a large flat rock, and Lily rested her head in his lap. He threaded his fingers through her hair and her lids began to feel heavy. Hardly surprising given how little sleep she'd had the last few nights.

'I'm glad you came back this summer,' he said softly.

She opened her eyes and he was looking down at her, his black eyes earnest. Her lips curved. 'You mean you're glad I broke my arm?'

'Yes,' he said, looking down at her. 'I am. You wouldn't have stayed this long for any other reason, would you?'

'Probably not,' she conceded. Except perhaps if Mamie had been ill and had needed her.

'It gave us the chance to get to know each other again. To grow close again.'

'But I ruined your relationship with Corinne.' She still felt bad about that, and it worried her that he'd lost his perfect match – because of her.

'That wasn't love,' he said dismissively. 'Better we realised that before getting married rather than after.'

He sounded very sure. *That wasn't love.*

'You thought it was – at the time.'

'True. But with hindsight I see that the chemistry was never there, there was no passion. Whereas what I feel for you – it's on a different scale, it's out of control. There's no doubt in my mind that this is completely different.'

Though not love, surely? she wondered as the silence stretched between them.

No, of course it wasn't. He knew that.

But she didn't want there to be any misunderstanding. She sat up and twisted round to face him. 'Oli,' she said quietly, 'this isn't love, either. You know that, don't you?'

His brow furrowed and she stiffened at the steely edge that stole across his jaw. 'What is it, then?' he asked.

A butterfly flitted past. It hesitated over the remnants of their picnic, darting this way and that before moving on.

'I don't know . . . does it need a name?'

There was a long pause while he absorbed this. 'Don't tell me – have I been elevated to the same position as your lover in New York? Am I a "friend with benefits" now?' He spat the words, making it clear he was insulted. Hurt.

'No!'

Her connection with Olivier was nothing like her friendship with Theo. They could never be as casual, as detached. They went way back, and he meant so much more to her.

But love implied commitment, something long-term and lasting. Olivier wanted a wife, a family, a future. She'd be dishonest to let him believe she could give him those things.

'Then what is this, Lil?'

From high up on the white cliffs, a seagull called. Out at sea a small boat glided past the bay.

'Do we have to label it?' she said finally. 'Can't we just live in the moment and enjoy it?'

He didn't answer.

She licked her lips, feeling guilty. She didn't want to hurt him. But they'd gone into this with their eyes open. He knew who she was, he knew her better than anyone. That she would leave St Pierre had always been clear.

Still, an icy chill had settled over them, spoiling what had been an idyllic day. Tension rolled off him, even though he hadn't moved. She sat up, and felt his narrowed gaze on her, but she didn't know what to say or do to make things right.

The silence stretched, but in the end it was him who broke it with the quiet, yet certain words. 'But I love you, Lil.'

★

Olivier's heart slugged heavily in his chest. He was conscious of the risk of laying himself bare like this, but he had to say it. He couldn't hide the truth. And there was a part of him that suspected – hoped – that maybe she loved him too. How else could they be so close and share such a connection?

Yet if she'd loved him she wouldn't have paled at his words. She wouldn't be hugging her knees to her chest, her gaze darting nervously around, avoiding his.

'You thought you loved Corinne, but you were wrong.'

'That was different. I know you, Lil. I know you better than I know myself.'

She shook her head. Her features knotted in a pained expression. 'You think you love me but . . .'

'But?' He arched a brow, amused that she felt qualified to tell him how he felt.

'But it's friendship. A really strong special friendship, I admit.'

No, he thought. It was more than that. He opened his mouth to answer, but the glint of fear in her eyes stopped him. He stilled, sensing that if he pressed this further she might panic and flee.

So he kissed her instead. Perhaps it was cowardly, perhaps it was nothing more than a cheap distraction technique, but right now this passion they shared was the only part of their relationship that he could count on. He rolled her into the sand and kissed her salty lips, her neck, her shoulder, until she relaxed in his arms and became pliant again, breathless with desire. Then he drew back and watched her blink, trying to dispel the glaze of need in her eyes but not succeeding. Her breath came in short pants, her body was curved against his.

'You can call it what you like, my darling Lily, but friends don't do this . . .' And, in the shade of the parasol, pressed into the white sand of the little cove with its crystal blue water and tall sheltering cliffs, he made love to her. Gentle, possessive love, and when she gasped with pleasure he shuddered at the power of it.

Afterwards, when he rolled onto his back and gathered her to him and kissed the top of her head, he made a vow to himself. He wouldn't give in. He refused to believe that for her this was only physical. She needed time, but one day he would make her see that this was love.

Until that day came, he would be patient, and he'd do everything in his power to make her love him in return.

Chapter Nineteen

'How are you getting on?' asked Olivier from the doorway.

She looked up from her computer. It was late. Through her bedroom window she saw that the sun was dipping heavily in the dusky sky.

'Good, thanks,' she smiled, absently drawing her ponytail over her shoulder and smoothing her fingers through it. She'd almost finished editing her new film, *Bread*, and she was pleased with her work. She'd woven into it emotional story threads of need and hunger and love, and it was coming together well.

Now that it was almost done, she could begin to look forward and to plan the next project, though she wasn't sure what that would be because, unusually, she didn't have an assignment lined up. Her broken arm meant she'd disappeared off the radar a little, so she'd sent out a few feelers letting people know she was fit again and available for work.

Olivier crossed the room and laid his hands on her shoulders, dropped a kiss in the side of her neck. She shivered at the tenderness of it. 'Want some dinner?' he asked.

'Dinner would be great. I'm hungry.'

'Thought you might be. You lose track of time when you're working, don't you?'

She nodded. 'I get so absorbed in it.'

'Which is why you need me. To bring you back to real life. To feed you.' He nibbled at her ear, tickling her, making her giggle and duck away.

But at the same time his words disturbed her. She didn't want to need him.

You can call it what you like, my darling Lily, but friends don't do this . . .

Their conversation at the cove had been playing on her mind, eating away at her and keeping her awake at night. They wanted different things. His expectations didn't match hers.

But I love you, Lil.

And yet she couldn't help hugging the memory of those words close, as if they were precious treasure she had secreted away.

'Don't you need to get back to work, too,' she asked, 'now the holidays are over?'

Mid-September had come and gone and he hadn't mentioned anything about going back to work. He hadn't even made any day trips to Paris, and seemed to be managing his business by phone and email.

'I'm the boss,' he winked. 'I can do what I want.'

'Seriously, Oli.'

His smile faded. 'Seriously? I'm stepping back from my business. I've promoted a handful of my senior managers, and I'll hold interviews for a couple more. Then I plan to hand over the reins when I take over Papa's bakery in January.'

He was stepping back, whereas she was still striving to

make a name for herself and to be the best. He'd done all that. He'd made his name and was going back to his roots with the Lacoste *boulangerie* in the village. And Lily understood that that was where his heart lay, she really did.

What she didn't understand was how he could believe that he loved her when it was so clear the two of them could never be compatible.

Don't you need to get back to work?

Lily's words plagued him as he went back down to the kitchen and scattered a handful of olives over a bowl of *salade niçoise* while Lily finished her work. Truth was, he didn't dare go back to work. He was worried that if he left, she wouldn't be here when he returned. He hated the way she held back, keeping part of herself wrapped up and hidden away where no one could reach it.

He'd hoped she would love him in return.

He still hoped she would. What they shared was remarkable, it was rare. He ran a hand through his hair and sighed. He had to give her time.

But the question gnawed at him. What if she could never love him back? What if this was a temporary fling, nothing more? She'd begged him to sleep with her because she'd been distraught after Mamie's funeral. And when he'd seduced her, she'd succumbed to the physical attraction they shared. But she didn't do static or long-term, she was committed only to her career, and had always been upfront about that.

Restless, he went outside and watched the apricot light of the setting sun wash over the palm tree and the olive grove, lending the garden an exotic air of mystery and promise.

Everyone around here said they made the perfect couple; that they always had. His parents were thrilled for him, and Béa had confided in him that it had been Mamie's secret wish for him to marry Lily, too.

But Lily was exactly the wrong woman for him. She couldn't give him any of the things he needed: not the stability, not the family, not the love. Could he renounce his dream of settling down and having a family of his own?

He squeezed his eyes shut. The thought was too painful to dwell on.

Yet this love he felt for her was beyond his control. Despite his best efforts to fight it and contain it, it had mushroomed.

It might be easier to surrender himself to the harsh reality: he loved her. And there was nothing he could do about it.

'I think we should celebrate,' said Lily.

Olivier looked up from his laptop. She stood in the doorway of the kitchen, slightly dishevelled, but bright-eyed.

'I finished my film,' she explained, breathless with excitement.

'You sent it in?'

She nodded. 'Well before the deadline. And I entered it for the film prize, too.'

'Well done.' He crossed the room and drew her to him, pressing his lips to hers, sharing her delight, proud of her achievement. For weeks now she'd spent long hours working on this, getting it just right. Her focus and dedication were awe-inspiring. 'How do you want to celebrate?'

'Why don't we go out for dinner? By the harbour?'

He nodded. 'I know the perfect place.'

He took her to a Vietnamese restaurant, its entrance concealed in a little side street but with a first-floor terrace which overlooked the harbour.

'Wow,' said Lily, as they took their seats. 'What a view!'

She couldn't take her eyes off the boats and yachts bathed in gold from the streetlamps that encircled the marina, and their reflections that danced and swam in the water. The look in her eyes – of excitement and yearning – tugged at him.

He was pleased that she'd finished her film, but what did it mean for him? For them?

'You like Vietnamese food?' he asked, his gaze lingering on her lips. In the shadowed half-light they looked dark and full, seductive.

'Love it,' she smiled, turning back to face him. Her scars became clearer. There was a contradiction about her beauty: strength and vulnerability intertwined. Her scars marked her out as a survivor, but they were also a reminder of the cruel hand life had dealt her.

'Good. Some people find it too exotic for their taste.'

'Not me.'

'No, not you,' he said quietly, as the waiter poured champagne.

She thrived on the exotic, the unfamiliar. Whereas others found comfort in routine, she fled from it. Not even her love for Mamie had been enough to anchor her here, and it had taken a broken arm for her to stay in St Pierre all summer.

He knew her wanderlust was an essential part of her character and he admired her adventurous spirit, yet something about it niggled at the back of his mind, just beyond reach. What was it?

'Cheers!' she said, clinking her glass against his.

He smiled. 'To your film. May it be a runaway success.'

'A *prize-winning* success,' she corrected with a cheeky grin that lit her face.

He saw the hope and the hunger in her eyes, and it made his chest tighten. Of course he hoped she'd win the film prize, of course he wished success and recognition for her. But he was also afraid, he realised with a jolt. Afraid she'd leave again. Afraid she'd take his heart with her.

She flashed him a smile from beneath her lashes as she took a sip of champagne, and he had to remind himself to breathe. This was Lily, and if she'd taught him one thing when they were children with scabs on their knees and gaps in their teeth it was that fear could be conquered.

He might not fully understand what drove her to live the way she did, but he knew her. He knew her better than anyone.

'Can you imagine making films but not travelling so much?' he asked.

Her smile faded and he felt cruel for having caused it to do so.

'In all honesty? No, I can't. There's nothing like the feeling when you step off a plane and set foot in a place you've never seen before.'

'Is it only about seeing a new landscape? Meeting new people? Tell me about it, tell me what you love.'

Her eyes narrowed. 'Why?'

'Because I can't imagine it. I want to understand.'

He wanted to understand her. She was so closed up, burying herself in her work, enigmatic. She held back emotionally, as if their relationship was purely physical. Yet for him it was so much more. He remembered when she'd first arrived this summer, how she'd kept him at arm's length, as if he were an acquaintance and not someone special in her life. Well, now he was in her life, and he wasn't ready to sit back and allow her to shut him out. He had to break through that shell of hers and work out what or why she was hiding beneath it.

'Well,' she said, smiling, and taking on a dreamy look as she gazed out to sea and the black of night. 'It's like unwrapping a gift – you don't know what's going to be inside. I love the thrill of boarding a plane to a new place, of arriving in a culture that's alien to me, becoming immersed in it. And the challenge of getting to know the people I'm filming, uncovering their problems, but also what makes them happy, what's important to them. I love the colours of the world: how vibrant it is, how varied, and yet people are so fundamentally similar. We all need food, water, love, laughter. We're all basically the same.'

He nodded but he couldn't really imagine feeling that excitement. He just knew they were different: where he liked familiarity, she thrived on new discoveries. Where he valued constancy, she needed variety and adventure. His heart sank. It seemed they were incompatible.

And yet he stubbornly refused to accept this. They *felt* compatible. They could work this out if they tried, he was certain of it.

'But you've been home now – what, two months?'

Lily nodded.

'And how have you felt being here that long? Staying in one place?'

'That's not a fair question. I had no choice but to stay here because I broke my arm.'

'And you made a film. You filmed me.'

'Yes.'

He was talking quickly, raising his voice. 'You met your deadline, you entered the film prize.'

'I did. But–'

'So you did your job without getting on a plane or travelling far. You did it here, in France.'

She pressed her lips together and regarded him a moment before she said gently, 'But Oli, travelling and filming – it's what makes me happy.'

He looked around at the handful of diners in the restaurant and the port that was quietening down for the night. He didn't want to argue in public, he didn't want to pull her into his arms and kiss her so she was reminded of exactly how happy he could make her – because when she gasped his name and closed her eyes with pleasure he was pretty sure she was as happy as a woman could be.

Instead, he battled against his frustration and hurt, and he kept his voice steady as he asked, 'You're not happy now?'

She frowned and threw him a wary look. 'I am. You know I am. But it can't last. I'm all wrong for you. You want a house and roots. I don't.'

'We can work on that. Find a compromise.'

She shook her head. 'They're fundamental things. We can't change who we are.'

He was conscious that she was pushing him away again, exactly like she had done after the fire. 'I didn't have you down as the cold-hearted type, Skinny. When we were little I used to look at you and I knew what you were thinking. Now . . . you've changed.'

Her gaze held his. 'You've changed too. You were more adventurous before. This need to put down roots is new.'

She was right. Nathalie, and what she'd done had changed him. And, he supposed, learning that he was adopted had altered his perspective a little, too.

'When did it start, this wanderlust you have?'

She tipped her head to one side as she considered this. 'From when I first held a camera, I suppose. I made a film in school, but I knew it would only be better and more interesting if I filmed somewhere more exotic, unfamiliar.'

'Which was the first film you made abroad?'

'It was in Alaska, when I was at college. I won a scholarship and used it to fund the trip.'

'Must have been cold.' He glanced out over the port, enjoying the warm breeze as it brushed his arms and appreciating the beauty and charm of this small fishing village. Why would anyone want to leave this place?

'I loved it. I felt so . . . free.' Her slender fingers wrapped around the stem of her wine glass, absently stroking it.

His muscles strained with tension. 'Free?'

She nodded. 'In control. Like I'd got my life back on track for the first time since . . .'

'Since?'

The dreamy look was gone, and fear suddenly invaded her eyes. He saw flashes of sadness and heartbreak, and he felt them like they were his own. The silence stretched.

'Since the fire,' she said finally.

He frowned. Perhaps it was coincidence but that was also when she'd broken contact with him. Was her wanderlust connected in some way to the fire?

Their food arrived and they began to eat. Olivier didn't push the subject any more, but steered the conversation towards innocuous topics. They talked and laughed, and relief washed through him as she relaxed again and her eyes sparkled with joy.

When they'd finished eating, the waiter came over and they were quiet while he piled plates and bowls on one arm. Lily turned towards the port and Olivier saw that distant look creep into her eyes again. Her happiness was important to him. Even more important than his own, he realised.

So perhaps he should give up trying to understand

and explain her need to travel. Perhaps he should simply accept that she was his for now, but soon she would leave. And, no matter what the cost to him, he had to let her go, because to stop her would be like caging a wild bird.

A spark of excitement made Lily sit up in her chair. She checked the email again, and confirmed that she had read it correctly. A new project! A paid commission from a television company – bigger than the one which had taken her latest film – with filming scheduled to begin next week. Which only gave her a few days to prepare.

She bit her lip and glanced at the garden where Olivier had been trying to fix the sprinkler system, but he'd disappeared out of sight. Her excitement instantly drained as she faced the prospect of telling him. The job was on the other side of the world and she'd be gone several weeks. The cursor hesitated over the *reply* button. What should she do?

Outside, the sprinklers spat violently, then shuddered into life, showering the parched lawn with arcs of water. Moments later, Olivier appeared in the kitchen doorway.

'I fixed it!' he grinned.

She smiled. 'So I see. Well done.'

'I knew you'd be pleased. The question is, how long before you play your old trick of switching it on when I'm standing in the line of fire?'

She clicked the email shut and tried to formulate the words in her head. He'd be upset. She'd have to break it to him gently.

'How long . . . what?' she said.

A deep frown sliced through his brow. 'Are you okay?'

'Yes. Why?'

'You seem distracted.' He glanced at her laptop.

'I'm fine.'

Footsteps on the gravel outside made them both turn and she was grateful of the diversion when the postman, René, arrived.

'Morning! Just the one today,' he said, handing Lily a letter.

'Thanks,' she said, trying to ignore the lump in her throat as she read Mamie's name. At moments like this it was still difficult to believe her gran wasn't around any more.

René had taken his cap off and was helping himself to coffee from the cafetière. 'Ah, that's good,' he said, briefly closing his eyes with pleasure. Lily and Olivier shared a look of amusement as he made himself at home. 'I'm so thirsty!'

It was only when René turned around and saw Lily's smile that his expression changed to one of embarrassment. 'Sorry! I didn't think! Simone always told me to help myself . . .'

'It's fine,' said Lily. 'Please – sit down.'

'Thanks,' he said, looking relieved to take the weight off his feet, 'and I apologise again. I've been coming here so many years now that it's become habit.'

'Really. It's not a problem.'

Olivier sat down too.

The postman looked around the room before saying

to Lily, 'I heard this place is yours now. That Simone left it all to you.'

'The house, you mean?' The paintings too were part of her inheritance. She wouldn't need to worry about money again if they sold for the prices the agent had suggested.

'Yes. You're lucky. It's such a beautiful property – high up, with lots of space around it and Raymond's olive grove.'

'It is,' she agreed. She loved the sensual beauty of this place: the heady fragrance of pine trees and lavender, the explosions of colour from the red geraniums and fuchsia-coloured bougainvillea and rainbows of hollyhocks.

'Within walking distance of the village, too,' the postman added. 'So are you planning to settle down now?'

Lily stilled. She was conscious that both men were looking at her, awaiting her answer. 'Wh–what do you mean?'

He nodded at Olivier. 'Now that you two are together. Will this be your home?'

So it was common knowledge in the village that they were a couple now? She shouldn't have been surprised. Round here, word spread like wildfire.

She glanced at Olivier, thinking of the email she'd just received, and swallowed. If she took the job, she'd be leaving in a matter of days.

'I–I'm a filmmaker,' she told René tactfully. 'My job will always involve a lot of travelling.'

Olivier's dark gaze bored into her. 'But you're not

travelling now, and you're happy living here,' he said quietly. 'St Pierre is your home.'

The hopeful look in his eyes, the silent plea for her to confirm that this was true tugged at her. It would be so easy to agree.

'I'm not very good at small-town life,' she said automatically.

But even as she spoke the words, she found herself questioning them. Hadn't she begun to enjoy the routine here? Over the last few weeks and months, hadn't St Pierre grown to feel familiar and welcoming?

She remembered how frustrated she'd been at the beginning of the summer to be stuck here, how she'd resented village life and found it dull and restrictive. Yet, little by little, her outlook had changed. She appreciated how the locals, like René, had accepted her back into the fold as if she'd never been away, how they made her feel as if she belonged here in this small village with its narrow cobbled streets and lively harbour. As if it were her home. The sharp tang of fish and salt as the fishermen unloaded their hauls, the sound of the church bells, the sweet scent of the Lacoste bakery: she felt a deep affection for it all. So deep she could almost picture herself staying here. Settling.

Her skin prickled. But it was only a matter of time before she got itchy feet again. She couldn't stay still – not here, nor anywhere. She glanced at her laptop. And the next project was already beckoning.

'St Pierre will always have a special place in my heart,' she said finally, and fiddled with the hem of her shorts, twisting the frayed denim around her finger, aware of how evasive her words sounded. Weak. Non-committal.

Out of the corner of her eye she saw Olivier's shoulders droop, and she sensed his disappointment. How would he feel when she told him she was leaving? He wouldn't just be disappointed; he'd be devastated.

She lifted her chin and steeled herself. Like St Pierre, he would always have a special place in her heart too, but she couldn't give up her career for him. Filmmaking was her passion.

'Well, that's something. At least you have a place to call home,' said René, apparently unaware of the tension that filled the room. 'Somewhere to come back to when your work is done.'

'Yes,' said Lily, though she wasn't sure she'd be welcome here again. At least, not by Olivier. She closed her laptop.

Perhaps it would be easier for both of them if she simply severed her ties with this place once and for all.

'So, Lily,' said Béa, 'have you decided what you're going to do with Mamie's studio?'

They were seated around the Lacostes' table in the shade, enjoying a delicious lunch of baked salmon studded with black olives and herb-crusted *Tomates Provençales*. Since Olivier's brothers had left at the end of the summer, there were only the four of them for Sunday lunch.

Béa went on. 'Are you going to redecorate it to use as an office, or as another bedroom?'

'I don't know.' Her heart gripped. She hadn't even been into the empty studio because it reminded her so much of her gran. She broke off a piece of bread and wondered how best to say this. 'To be honest, I'm not sure what to do with the house.'

'The house?' Béa reached for the jug of water.

She nodded. 'I'm thinking perhaps I might sell it.'

Béa stilled, jug in hand, visibly caught out by this admission. Olivier and Raymond glanced at each other.

'Sell it?' Olivier asked her. The sun flickered through the leaves of the plane tree, casting shadows that accentuated his strong jaw and sculpted features.

'Yes.'

He shook his head in disbelief. 'Mamie left you the house so you would have a home. Not so you would sell it!'

'I–I'm trying to be practical. How can I keep it when I'm not going to be here most of the time? I don't want it to go to rack and ruin.' There was a long pause before she added, 'Mamie wouldn't have wanted that.'

'We'll help,' said Raymond. 'You're not alone, Lily. You know we'll help in any way we can.'

'Thanks,' said Lily.

But she *was* alone. She had been for a long time. It was what she was used to, and it was how she liked her life to be. No commitments, no ties. Just her and her camera.

'Why don't you wait a while before making such a big decision?' Béa said carefully, her brow creased. 'An irreversible decision.'

Lily nodded. 'I'll give it a few months but I don't think I'll change my mind.'

'What about the memories?' said Béa. 'What about–'

'I'll buy it,' Olivier cut in, his voice deep and rough.

Everyone stared at him. Lily blinked.

Anger made his black eyes glint and his jaw rigid as he met her gaze square on. 'I won't let you sell it to a stranger. I'll buy it and look after it the way Mamie would have wanted.'

'Are–are you sure?' asked Lily.

'Yes.' He snatched up his knife and fork and began to eat.

Lily waited, but he didn't say anything more.

'You're just going to sell it and leave?' said Olivier, as soon as they left his parents' house. He couldn't believe she hadn't mentioned it before. He couldn't believe she'd walk away from the place as if it meant nothing to her. Her grandmother's home.

'I don't know,' said Lily, her pumps crunching over the dried grass as they walked back to the farmhouse through the olive grove. 'Yes, I think so. Why not? It's only a house.'

'Only a house?' His hands curled into tight fists. 'When did you become so heartless?'

'Practical,' she corrected furiously. She stopped and turned to face him, her eyes silently imploring him to understand. 'Practical. I can't look after a house when I'm not here.'

He tried to ignore the sensation of having his chest cleaved in two. His tone softened. 'I hoped you would feel you had more reason to come back now that we – that we . . .'

'Oli, don't. Please. You know how much I need to work. It's who I am.'

'I disagree. It's who you think you need to be.'

'What does that mean?'

He wasn't sure, but he had a suspicion that her wanderlust wasn't only about the pursuit of new experiences. It was flight. It was fear. She was running away. He just needed to figure out what from.

'Oli, there's something else.'

'Something else?' The blood drained. He'd thought it couldn't get any worse, but he could tell from the look in her eyes that this was going to hurt. 'Tell me.'

She cleared her throat. 'I've had an offer of work. I'm leaving.'

He closed his eyes briefly. He'd known this was coming. It felt as inevitable as nightfall. 'Go on?'

'It's a bit last minute because another filmmaker had to drop out unexpectedly, and it's in Belize, filming a group of men who are in hiding – they've agreed to give me an inside view of what it's like to–'

'When?' he interrupted. Her lips snapped shut. 'You said it's last minute – when are you leaving?'

Lily swallowed. She shuffled her feet and looked left and right before she lifted her chin and finally met his gaze. 'Tomorrow.'

'T–tomorrow?' It was a punch to the stomach.

'Oli, I'm sorry. I tried to tell you, but–'

'But what?'

'I was afraid – of this. That you'd be upset. I didn't want you to be hurt.'

He shrugged, struggling to speak, and gave a weak laugh. 'You were right. I am hurt.'

Lily had hoped that, in the night, they might reach for each other and find some sort of reconciliation, if only a physical one.

But Olivier didn't come to bed. Instead, she heard the door of the spare room creak open, then quietly close and she hugged her knees to her chest because her bed felt cold and vast without him. She stared at the empty white sheet beside her where he should have been, and told herself the ache in her chest would disappear once she left. Things would go back to how they had been before this summer, life would return to normal, with work providing all the challenge and adventure and exhilaration she thrived on.

She told herself this, and as she lay awake, unable to sleep, she almost convinced herself.

Olivier rubbed his eyes as he came downstairs. His head was throbbing, he hadn't slept a wink last night. He'd been so angry.

Angry that she'd waited so late to tell him she was leaving.

Angry that she was leaving.

Angry and hurt. And he knew that while his emotions had been so alive and raw he would only make things worse and chase her away even sooner. So he'd told himself that a few hours away from her would do him good and might possibly iron out the confusion in his head.

It hadn't worked. He'd simply lain awake all night, missing her. Wanting her. Desperately hoping she'd change her mind.

He stopped in the kitchen doorway. But judging by what he saw now, she hadn't changed her mind at all.

'So you're going?' he said, his gaze sliding from the rucksack, packed and ready at her feet, to her anxious expression.

Even the citrusy glow of the morning sun didn't mask the grey pallor of her cheeks. 'I am.'

'You're walking away from this house, your home, and all its memories? From me?'

She looked around her at the flagstone floor, the stone walls, the wooden table, and her voice wasn't quite steady as she said, 'I have to.'

'You have to?' He shoved his hands deep into his pockets and blinked hard. It felt like someone had poured sand into his eyes, they were so gritty and sore. 'What about us?'

The flutter of wings outside made them both turn to look at the rusty green gate where a pair of slim grey doves were perched side by side. Their heads tilted this way and that as they observed the goings-on in the kitchen with grave, beady eyes.

Lily bit her lip, then said quietly; 'You know how much my career means to me. Would you stop me doing what I love?'

She looked so slender, her eyes too big for her face, and he thought again of a bird trapped in a cage, wings clipped. It made his chest constrict. 'Never. But you could do what you love and come home to me.'

She blinked hard and riffled through her bag, searching for something. She pulled out her passport and clutched it tight, that battered, dog-eared book that he knew was stuffed full of expired visas and airport stickers and stamps. Last night, in the depths of his despair, he'd thought about burning the damn thing. But of course he would never do such a thing.

'You're scared, Lily.'

Her head whipped up. Puzzled eyes frowned at him. 'What?'

'You're scared of standing still. But running away won't leave the pain behind. You've only just buried your grandmother. You need to grieve.'

'I have grieved!' she gritted, and her cheeks coloured with indignation, 'In my own way. Just because it's not your way . . .'

His heart clattered against his ribs. Emotions snapped at him, they warred and clashed – but getting angry wouldn't solve anything. So he settled for honesty instead.

'Don't go,' he said. It was a quiet, heartfelt plea.

Her expression softened, like butter in the sun. 'I have to.'

'I love you.'

She pressed her lips together, and her eyes shimmered. 'I'm not the right woman for you, Oli. I couldn't be the wife you're looking for, the mother of your children. I could never make you happy.'

'You do make me happy. And you'd make a fantastic mother.'

She gave a dry laugh. 'I hardly had the best role model.'

'You had Mamie. And your dad. They were the best role models, both of them. You know something, Skinny? I think that secretly you'd love to have a family and settle down. To have somewhere, someone to come home to.'

'Secretly?' She shook her head angrily, but her gaze slid away from his.

He nodded. 'But you say it's not for you,' he persisted, 'because you're too chicken to admit the truth.'

'The truth?' she said flatly. 'What truth?'

He crossed the room and stopped in front of her. Her chin went up and she placed her hands on her hips, but fear and desire danced in her eyes.

'That you're scared,' he said gently. 'Scared of becoming attached to anyone.'

'Oh really.'

'Yes. Really. You're scared of loving and losing like you lost your dad. And Mamie.'

Lily stared at him, and the blood drained from her face. Her dad's loving smile flashed before her eyes and the bite of grief snared her unexpectedly. She looked away, looked down at her feet, but couldn't focus because her vision was blurred.

Was he right?

No. He couldn't be.

His voice was rough with emotion. 'When you refused to see me in hospital thirteen years ago it felt like this. Like I'd lost not just a friend but a part of me.'

There was a pause.

'I'm sorry,' she said. Though it was lame. Though it was thirteen years too late.

'I've always regretted that I let you do that. That I didn't stand up to you and question you.' He dragged in air. 'I missed you, Lily. I could have helped you.'

Her spine stiffened. 'I managed. I didn't need your help.'

He smiled, as if she had just given herself away. 'You didn't need anyone, did you? Not even Mamie.'

She frowned. She didn't understand.

He lifted his hand and ran his fingertips over her left cheek with the gentlest touch. 'These scars are only the tip of the iceberg,' he said quietly. 'What happened that night will stay with you always, won't it?' He said it with such understanding that his words reached in and touched her core. They stirred a deep, dark pain that she'd never acknowledged.

Yet she couldn't prevent the rip of anger that tore through her. 'I lost my dad that night. Of course it will stay with me!'

He nodded, unruffled by her bitten out words. 'It's the fire that did it.'

'Did what?'

'Made you afraid to need anyone, to let anyone close.'

'W–what rubbish!'

She willed the taxi she'd called to hurry up and come, so this conversation would end, so things would go back to how they should have been. She'd prepared herself to say a painful but brief goodbye to Olivier. She hadn't expected this – this ambush of accusations and psychological analysis wrapped up in love.

'I'm right, aren't I?' he asked softly, and touched her arm.

She jerked it away. 'No! For once, you're not right, you don't know everything!'

And she was aware, even in her fury, that she was pushing him away just as she had done thirteen years ago in hospital when she'd refused his visits. Then, like now, she'd preferred to be alone than to be the object of his pity.

But he was undeterred. 'So tell me. What is it you're afraid of? Because when I hold you in my arms, when we make love, you feel something. I know you do.'

Lily looked up at him, remembering how it felt to be pressed up against the heat of his body, picturing the intensity in his eyes as he whispered her name, and she didn't know how to reply, because he was right. There were times, with him, when she felt so much that she thought her head – or her heart – would explode. It was overpowering, all-consuming. It was too much.

'I feel – I feel . . .' Her voice grated. She swallowed hard. 'It doesn't matter what I feel, because I'm leaving. I won't give up my freedom. Not for anyone.'

'So you do feel something?'

She couldn't answer that. She picked up her rucksack and turned away. 'I need to go, Oli. I have a plane to catch.'

She had only taken two steps towards the garden when his quiet words made her freeze.

'Dare you to stay.'

Her feet wouldn't move. She was rooted to the spot, there on the terrace. 'W–what?'

'Dare you to stay, Lil, and face whatever it is you're running away from. Face it with me.'

'You're not making any sense.'

He moved past her and stopped, barring her way and blocking out the sun with his solid frame and his dark eyes that were creased with love. 'I don't believe that it's only your job that keeps you on the move, I don't believe that it's only your love of travelling and filmmaking . . .' He paused for breath. 'I believe you're also running away.'

Her pulse hammered. Running away? She shook her head.

He went on, 'From your past, from the fire, from being alone.' He cupped her face. 'But you don't need to be alone, Lily. I love you.'

She pressed her lips together, battling the emotions that strained to escape. Hard as this was, and much as it pained her to hurt him, she had to leave. 'You're wrong. I'm not running away. I love my job.'

'You do, and you're so talented, your passion for it is what makes you the best. But do you really love it more than everything and everyone else?'

She stilled, suddenly thinking of her mother. Her cold, ambitious mother for whom relationships ranked so low in her priorities, and success and fame were the only things which mattered.

I'm not like her, she told herself. *I'm not like her.* Tears slid down her cheeks. She blamed the lack of sleep, the emotion of the last few weeks because she never cried. Never.

'I'm sorry, Oli. I didn't want to hurt you but I was honest with you from the start.' She clutched her passport and tried to hold in the emotions that were choking her.

'Dare you to love me,' he said quietly.

She blinked, caught off guard by the sudden swift winding sensation. It knocked the air out of her and made her legs shake.

'Dare you to love me the way I love you, Skinny. No holds barred.'

Her heart folded. Silence stretched. Cars streamed past on the main road, and one pulled up outside the rusty green gate. Lily glanced over her shoulder. She could tell from the rough diesel sound that it was her taxi.

She turned back to Olivier. 'I – I told you. I don't do relationships. I don't do . . . love. Oli, I'm sorry, but I can't be the woman you want me to be.'

Chapter Twenty

She had done it a thousand times before: showed her passport to the airport officials, walked through the barriers, boarded a plane. Yet as the aircraft accelerated on the runway and lifted into the air, Lily didn't get the familiar curl of excitement in her belly, nor the fizz in her blood that she was used to. This assignment had the potential to be eye-opening, she assured herself. An inside take on British criminals living in exile, it would generate interest for all sorts of reasons . . .

It was no use. She couldn't muster her usual energy or enthusiasm. Her heart felt heavy, and she watched the land below shrink and fade as the plane climbed higher.

Why did it feel like she'd left a part of herself behind? There was nothing for her now in St Pierre. Mamie was gone. Her chest squeezed painfully and she swallowed. And Olivier . . . She didn't do relationships. He knew that. She knew that.

A flight attendant offered her a drink, but Lily shook her head politely and turned back to the stark blue sky and blinding sunlight. This was simply the result of taking a long vacation, she told herself, of being away from work for almost three months. Give it a few days, a couple of weeks of filming, and she'd be back in the saddle, engrossed in her work again. Because that was what defined her. Lily Martin, filmmaker.

One by one, Olivier yanked open drawers and threw clothes onto the bed. Trousers, shorts, t-shirts: they landed in a muddled heap beside his small suitcase.

His brother Claude cast him a wary look and began to fold them. 'When I came home for the weekend, I expected to have some downtime, not to get embroiled in your love life.'

'Feel free to leave. I don't need your help packing.'

Claude raised a brow. 'That's debatable.'

Olivier closed the wardrobe. Claude finished folding the last t-shirt and laid it on top of one of the three neat piles he'd made. 'Thanks, bro,' Olivier said quietly.

'So you're really going, then?'

'I'm going.'

'Do you even have a passport?' joked Claude.

Olivier picked up the nearest object – a recipe book beside his bed – and threw it at him. 'You're not funny.'

He sighed and placed the piles of clothes into the case. 'Course I have one. I just don't like to use it.'

Claude watched him. 'But for Lily you will?'

The dilemma had tormented Olivier for weeks now: did he give up on his dream of having a family, or give up on Lily? He'd battled with it, torn both ways, unable to find a satisfactory answer.

Yet now she was gone, the solution was clear as day. He chose Lily. Always.

And since he couldn't switch off these feelings he had for her, it had become evident that he must go to her.

He would never know what it was like to hear a voice that sounded like his, to see his eyes or his smile reflected in his child's face. But he'd have Lily. The woman he loved more than anything. She would make her films and he would be there, by her side, supporting her in whichever capacity he could.

'For Lily I will,' he confirmed.

For Lily, he'd do anything.

Lily hadn't told Olivier that the men she was going to film were gangsters. She hadn't wanted to worry him. Besides, who was to say that they wouldn't be fair and open-minded people? Perhaps even reformed by their experience and regretful of their pasts now they were living in this isolated village, a long drive from the nearest city and a day's trek or donkey ride up into the remote mountains.

Unfortunately, they lived up to the stereotypes expected of them: they were thugs. They swore and drank heavily, they didn't have much respect for women, and kept making disparaging comments about Lily's sensible trousers. Apparently, they would have preferred her to wear short skirts. If Olivier were here he'd be furious, he'd be stepping in to defend her and protect her—

Lily didn't allow herself to follow that line of thought. Instead, she ignored their sexist comments and patiently kept on filming, kept on asking questions.

She was determined to unearth these men's human side. She'd seen the odd flicker of it, tiny clues: like when one had brought a cup of tea for his mate because he was feeling down; and another carried a photo in his wallet of the woman he hoped to go back to when he'd earned enough money. She was interviewing the group leader, Gary, when suddenly she made the breakthrough she'd been hoping for.

Gary was a hard man, a proud career criminal. His arms were decorated with tattoos and the piercings in his eyebrow glinted as he spoke. But when he mentioned his father his expression changed. The unexpected gentleness in his eyes made Lily's breath snag. She knew before it even unfolded that this piece of film would have impact for its surprising emotion. While he talked she was planning in her mind how to juxtapose it with another piece where, furious with one of his men, he'd grabbed him by the scruff of the neck and pushed him up against a wall. If the others hadn't dragged him off, Lily wasn't sure the other guy would have lived to tell the tale.

Now, though, his voice was quiet as he said, 'I wasn't there when he died.' His face creased with sorrow. Regret. Guilt. 'I had gone out to get something – can't even remember what it was. And when I came back he was gone.'

Behind the camera, Lily held her breath. Experience had long since taught her never to interrupt at moments like this. Let the pause happen. Give the person time and space to carry on speaking if they chose to.

Gary looked down at his hands and sucked in air.

A moment later he lifted his head and looked straight at Lily. His grey eyes shone like sharp metal. 'He died alone. And I'll never forgive myself for that,' he said.

His words sounded raw and she could see how he'd carried the pain with him since, unable to leave it behind. Perhaps it had shaped him and contributed to the hard shell he wore like armour. Of course it had.

Lily felt a snap deep inside her.

She'd lost her dad and her world had collapsed. But once her injuries had healed, she hadn't let herself shrivel up or hide away, she'd refused to be a victim. A strong, successful filmmaker; that was how she regarded herself.

But inside, what had happened?

What happened that night will stay with you always, won't it? You're running away . . . From your past, from the fire, from being alone.

She'd pushed Olivier away, she went to live with her mother, then boarded at school when Mamie would have welcomed her with open arms. Lily had seen this as being independent, but had she been afraid? Was Olivier right? Had she been running scared?

'What's going on? Are you alright?' Gary jumped up and Lily realised the camera was shaking. He lifted it out of her hands and his red eyes widened when he saw the tears streaming down her cheeks. 'What did I say?'

She'd spent the last fifteen years globetrotting rather than spending any length of time with Mamie. Or Olivier. Too afraid to let anyone close again in case she lost them.

Well, she'd lost Mamie. And, despite the distance she'd tried to keep, Lily had still felt the pain.

Gary was rummaging in his pockets. 'Here – take this.' He handed her a grey handkerchief, and scratched his head and shot her concerned glances.

Lily thanked him, and smiled through her tears because this big hardened criminal, this burly man was completely flummoxed by a woman crying.

Back in her room, she replayed the footage she'd recorded left-handed when her arm was in plaster. The pictures swam in and out of focus as the camera jerked around clumsily, but Lily was riveted. In her mind she was back there, in Mamie's garden, looking up at the farmhouse, the dovecote, walking through the olive grove. She could smell the dry earth, feel the sun's heat on her shoulders, she could hear the doves' soft calls and the cicadas' chant. It *was* her home, she knew that now.

She'd told herself she felt trapped by small-town life, but now she missed it. Walking down to the village, friendly exchanges with people who knew her by name and had done since she was a child, people who cared about her and would look out for her. She missed Béa and Raymond, Claude and Mathieu who were like family.

But most of all, she missed Olivier.

She missed the quiet moments when they sat down to share a meal, or curled up in front of the television.

She missed his arms around her at night, and the loving look in his eyes that made her feel strong, made her feel brave.

Was she afraid? Yes, she conceded finally. That was why she hadn't spent too much time with Mamie – because she'd loved her, and in Lily's mind love left you open to loss and terrible pain. She hung her head, devastated by this realisation. All this time she'd believed she was brave and adventurous, when in fact she was the biggest coward of them all, running from love whenever it appeared on her horizon.

Running away from Olivier, breaking his heart.

She began to frantically throw things into her rucksack. She had to go home. She needed to see him and tell him how she felt – before it was too late. Perhaps it was already too late; she wouldn't blame him if he pushed her away again, for the final time. She yanked the rucksack shut, dragged it over to the door, and scooped up her passport and money. She had no plan beyond going to the airport and getting the next flight out of there. She bent to pick up the heavy rucksack.

'Let me help you with that.'

She froze. That voice. Deep, familiar, with a hint of wry humour. It couldn't be . . .

It was. Olivier was indeed there, standing in the doorway, a small suitcase at his side. She straightened and blinked, thinking she must have conjured him up, but when she opened her eyes he was still there, watching her gravely.

'It's you,' she murmured. 'You're here.'

'I'm here.' He shook his head. 'Though you wouldn't believe how difficult it was to get to this godforsaken place. It's taken me three days. Three days! Why couldn't you pick somewhere more civilised to make a film? And near an airport so I don't have to take the death ride that passes for a taxi service, or travel by mule!'

'You travelled by mule?' Her lips twitched.

'Yes! It took almost a whole day, riding on the back of a damn donkey. It wasn't comfortable, I can tell you.'

She smiled. 'Why?'

'Why wasn't it comfortable? I'd have thought that would be obvious. Though the poor mule probably fared worse.'

'Why are you here?'

He looked into her eyes. 'You know why. Because you are.'

The blood pounded in her ears.

'You mean more to me than anything else,' he went on. 'Even having a family of my own. I don't need children to feel I belong. I have the best parents anyone could wish for, two brothers who are great. The only other person I need in my life is you. I can't live without you, Lil. You are . . .' He hesitated, searching for the word, and his deep brown eyes locked with hers, 'you are my world. And if you won't – can't – stay with me in St Pierre, then I'll have to come with you.'

'No,' she whispered hoarsely, and glanced at the rucksack by her feet. 'There's no need . . .'

He looked stricken. 'You don't want me here?' he asked flatly.

Her heart squeezed. *Dare you to love me the way I love you, Skinny. No holds barred.*

'I do want you here. Because I love you, Olivier. I've loved you for a long time. I was just too chicken to admit it, even to myself. But there was no need for you to come here because I was on my way home. To you.'

She showed him the passport she was clutching in her hand, and understanding brightened his features, lit up his dark eyes and made them gleam with happiness.

He bent his head, and the brush of his lips quickly became a feverish kiss.

'But what about your job? Your career?'

'We'll work something out. Find a middle way. Perhaps in the past I was afraid to leave room for anything other than work in my life. Now – my priorities have changed. Now I realise how much I need you. How much I love you.'

He grinned, and bubbles of joy burst up inside her.

'You love me?' he smiled.

She nodded. 'Even when you were out of bounds and I knew I shouldn't, I couldn't stop my feelings.' She added, 'And I think maybe Mamie knew all along.'

'That doesn't surprise me. There was no one sharper than Mamie.'

'I think she'd be very happy if we got married . . .'

He stilled, and scoured her face as if he couldn't quite believe what he'd heard. 'Really?'

'Really. Just a quiet wedding, in the olive grove,' she suggested tentatively.

His eyes creased as he smiled and nodded, apparently lost for words.

'Oli, I want to spend the rest of my life with you.'

He swallowed. He kissed her fiercely. Lovingly. And when he drew back, he told her, 'I'm game if you are.'

Epilogue

Applause filled the hall as Lily's name was announced. She looked at Olivier, sitting beside her, and he grinned.

'I'm so proud of you,' he whispered in her ear, and she blinked hard as she got up.

Shots from her film, *Bread*, played on the enormous screen as she made her way up to the stage and collected the award. Lily smiled and looked around the rows of faces, but there was only one that stood out for her. His dark eyes gleamed as he grinned proudly back at her. Her best friend. Lover. Husband.

When she returned to her seat, her heart was still hammering furiously.

'How does it feel?' asked Olivier. 'Dream come true?'

She smiled and he looked away as the next award was announced. Lily stared at the trophy in her hand. It was a dream come true, and she'd hoped for this for so long – yet success didn't feel how she'd expected it to.

Her fingers touched the base of her stomach. She was pleased her film had won the prize, she was excited for the recognition it would bring her and hopefully the opportunities ahead, but tonight felt nothing like the euphoria she'd experienced when she'd learned she was pregnant, and then, at the scan, when she and Olivier had seen their baby and heard its healthy heartbeat.

They'd already begun to make changes and they'd have to make more when the baby arrived, but that was alright: now she was pregnant, Lily was choosier about the assignments she took on. She didn't want to travel too far just now, and healthcare was important because she was responsible for another life as well as her own.

But she was still making films – because Olivier had been right: her films were about people and their stories. And interesting people could be found on every continent.

She closed her eyes, clutched her trophy, and thought of Mamie and of her dad and knew how thrilled they would be.

When she opened them again, Olivier was looking at her, and she felt a rush of love. And gratitude. They were so blessed.

Acknowledgements

For reasons too complicated to go into here, my books haven't been published in the order they were written and this was actually the second I wrote after *A Forget-Me-Not Summer*. I found 'second book syndrome' a challenge and I'm hugely grateful to Jacqui Cooper, without whom this novel would never have been finished. Thank you for your support and friendship – and the occasional stern talking-to.

Thanks to Kimberley Atkins and Amy Batley whose editorial feedback is invaluable. And Megan Carroll. You're all a delight to work with.

To Jane Dodds, for your advice on art, filmmaking and photography. And our fabulous chats.

To Mum, with love and thanks for checking the French.

And finally, to Grandmère who adored books and loved me in a way I didn't deserve, but that love stays with me.

Discover more from Sophie Claire . . .